Resolution

Huck Finn's Greatest Adventure

By

Andrew Joyce

Resolution
Huck Finn's Greatest Adventure

eBook ISBN: 978-0-692-66263-2
Softcover ISBN: 978-0-692-67090-3

Published by William Birch & Assoc.

This one's for

Emily

A tip of my hat and thanks go to:

Jay Tuttle
for help with the research

Pamela Beckford
for her help with proofreading

Don Myers
for help with keeping me sane

Danny
for being a good doggie
(sometimes)

Jere Swain
for being a royal pain in the butt

Chris Graham
for being a good guy

The Guys and Gals at the Tiki Hut
for keeping me fed during lean times

&

Emily Gmitter
for her editing prowess

Author's Note:

The story you are about to read incorporates the true account leading up to and immediately following the largest gold strike in the annals of human history before the outside world knew of it.

Prologue

They were five days hunting the killer, and now they had him trapped. He was above them, up on Ghost Butte. There was no way down the other side, it being a sheer cliff. Along the way they had lost men. Of the eight that had started out, four were still alive—four were dead.

After five days in the saddle, they were ready—more than ready—for the action to play out. However, that would have to wait until the morrow. Twilight had come and it would soon be full dark. To go up after him now would be just plumb loco. It could mean sure death for any one of the four remaining posse members.

The marshal's name was Tom Sawyer. He had broken his leg the previous day when thrown from his horse. Consequently he turned the duties of leading the posse over to his best friend, Huck Finn. The other two members of the posse were Molly Lee McMasters and Mister Morton. No one had ever heard Morton referred to as anything other than "Mister" Morton.

They had very little food left. Some hardtack, some beans, some coffee—just enough for one meal. There would be no waiting out the killer. This would have to end tomorrow.

Huck made sure Tom was comfortably on the ground and leaning against a boulder before giving orders to get a fire going and to throw on the grub. Morton collected the firewood, and Molly prepared their scant repast.

After eating, Tom and Huck conferred and decided that a lookout would have to be posted to ensure the killer did not sneak by them in the night.

Tom offered to take the first watch, but Huck asserted his new authority, "No, you ain't much good with that leg of yours."

"I don't see with my legs. God gave me two good eyes, and they're working just fine. If that sonavabitch tries to get by us, I can get a shot off and that should wake up the camp. Even you, Huck," said Tom with a slight smile.

"Alright, take the first watch. I'll relieve you in three hours and then, Morton, you relieve me."

Morton was by the fire, the light of which reflected on his pinched face. "Why don't we go up there and take him now? Just be done with it."

Throwing the dregs of his coffee onto the dirt, Huck answered him. "You're free to go up if you're in such an all-fired hurry. But you ain't gonna be able to see your hand afore your face because you've been staring into our fire. I don't see any light up there, so I'll lay you odds his eyes are well adjusted to the dark by now. He'll pick you off before you can get anywhere near him."

That silenced Morton for the moment. Then Molly threw in with her two cents.

"I can take a watch. It's been a long haul and we all could use as much sleep as possible. So why don't we each take two hours?"

"Tom put me in charge, Molly, and I don't cotton to no mutiny. You'll do as I say. I want you to stay near Tom in case he needs something or we get rushed in the night. He ain't moving as fast as he used to. I don't want to worry about him, and I sure as hell don't want to worry about you."

Huck felt sure he was gonna have some more words spoken at him, but Molly just shrugged, and Morton went off to lay out his bedroll. Tom Sawyer smiled.

The stars were bright against the dark vault of the heavens. And even though Molly was dog-tired, she found it hard to fall off to sleep. She lay on her blanket looking at the silhouette of the ridge line against the Milky Way and thought of things past.

She pondered on how she had come to be at that particular place, at that particular moment, at that specific time in her life. Why, at fifty-three years old, was she lying on the hard ground, about to have a shootout with a murderer?

Those thoughts prompted her to think back on her life.

She had first met Huck Finn when she was a naïve and innocent girl of eighteen, living on her family's farm in Virginia. Huck had come into her life at the beginning of the Civil War. He and his friend Tom were deserting the Southern Cause. The day after their arrival at her farm, three Yankee soldiers showed up and one of them tried to rape her. Huck had quickly put an end to that by shooting the Yankee right through the heart.

Molly, being the young and impressionable girl that she was, fell in love with the handsome Huck Finn and wanted to go with him when he continued on to Missouri. Huck had other ideas. He was twenty-four years old and not quite ready to settle down. When Molly discovered that he'd left without her, she set out to find him. She never did. Instead, she found a life that begot one harrowing adventure after another.

It had been a tough life until, at twenty-five years of age, she married. Less than a year later, she found herself a widow with an eleven-year-old stepdaughter to rear. Through hard work and perseverance, she built her Montana cattle ranch into the largest in the state.

Then, five weeks ago, while enjoying a cup of tea, she read an article written with the byline of "Huck Finn" in an old copy of The New York Herald. *There can be only one Huck Finn*, she thought. So she boarded a train and set out to confront the man who had left the eighteen-year-old Molly Lee behind all those many years ago.

She found him and gave him a slap right across his face, as she had promised herself she would do. Then she asked him why he lit out from the farm without her. Huck had a good answer: "Honorable men do not steal young girls away from their home no matter how much they want to be stolen." Then he redeemed himself by adding, "I must admit, there have been many times over the years I have regretted that decision."

Prior to Molly showing up, Huck had decided to quit his newspaper job and go out west to visit his old friend Tom, whom he had not seen in twenty-two years. Once Molly was in the picture, one thing led to another, and now here they were in Colorado chasing a murderer.

One

The continual clack, clack, clack of the wheels soothed his spirit as the train moved ever closer to Redemption. Huck Finn was a year shy of sixty and he had calmed down a mite from his younger days when he was a lawman. He was sitting next to a woman he met down in Virginia about a thousand years ago. Her name was Molly and she was a looker. *And* he could attest to the fact that she packed quite a wallop.

The train pulled into Redemption right on time. Huck had sent Tom a telegram telling him about Molly and when they would be arriving. He stepped off the train and turned to help Molly off, but before he could turn back around Tom was there slapping him on the back.

"Huck, you old so-and-so! It's good to see you."

Tom hadn't changed much in twenty-two years. A little gray at the temples and a few lines around his eyes, but his smile was the same as ever.

"Howdy, Tom, it's mighty good to see you. And you too, Mary."

Mary Simms, Tom's lady friend, stood next to him. Huck knew her from before. She owned the town's only hotel as well as the adjacent restaurant.

"Tom, you remember Molly from back down in Virginia?"

"I sure do. Hello, Molly. This here is Mary Simms."

The women smiled at each other and shook hands. Tom picked up Molly's grip and they all started off for the hotel. The women strolled ahead of the men, deep into a conversation of their own.

As they walked, Tom filled Huck in on the latest happenings in and around Redemption.

"You recall Bob McNally? He was the sheriff for the county."

"Sure I do. He had that spread just east of town."

"Yep. Well, he died last month, and the town fathers asked me to fill in until an election can be held. I reminded them that when they asked me twenty years ago to be sheriff, I declined because I didn't want to spend my days in the saddle going from one end of this big county to another."

"I remember. You wrote me about it."

"Well, this time I accepted, figuring it'll only be for a few months. So now I'm marshal *and* sheriff."

"Are congratulations in order?"

"Nope. Just wanted you to know in case I get called out on business. I had planned on spending most of my time with you in The Silver Dollar Saloon talking over old times. And Mary wants us to take you and Molly out for a picnic down by the river. A lot of trees have grown up along its banks since you were here last, and it's rather nice. Mary drags me out there every so often."

At the hotel, Mary asked if Huck and Molly would prefer separate rooms.

Molly answered for the both of them.

"That's very kind of you, Missus Simms, but seeing as how we're not paying guests, we wouldn't dream of taking advantage of your hospitality by taking up a second room that a paying guest could occupy."

With that out of the way, Tom took them upstairs to their room so they could settle in.

"Ya'all make yourselves comfortable, and we'll meet up in the dining room a little later for supper, say around seven o'clock."

As Tom neared the door, he turned and said, "It really *is* good to see you, Huck. And you too, Molly." Then he was gone.

When they were alone, Molly went and turned the key, making sure the door was locked.

"We've got us a couple of hours to kill. Whatcha think we oughta do, Huck?"

"Why is it that I kinda figure you already have a definite something in mind?"

"Probably because you also have the same definite something in mind."

"Probably."

They undressed and enjoyed each other's company as the afternoon sun slanted in through a small gap in the white lace curtains.

The next three days were good days. Mary and Molly got to know one another while Tom and Huck swapped lies over at The Silver Dollar Saloon. Tom would walk them around town, pointing out new buildings and telling them how Redemption had grown since Huck left.

Huck would run into men he had known and, of course, being Huck, he had to invite them over to The Dollar for a drink so he could properly catch up on the latest gossip.

Late in the evenings when they were alone in their room, Huck would undress Molly, taking his time, kissing her shoulders as the dress fell from her body. With her chemise off, he would teasingly kiss her belly as he slowly unbuttoned her pantalettes, sending chills up and down her spine.

Back when Huck was Redemption's marshal, he liked to sit outside his office and watch the world pass by, or at least that part of the world known as Redemption, Colorado. On the morning of his fourth day back in town, he was sitting in his old spot with his feet up on the rail, enjoying the warmth of the morning sun. Tom had some minor business to attend to and then he and Huck were going to meet up. Molly and Mary were having coffee in the hotel restaurant.

Huck was just thinking about going across the street to The Dollar to do his waiting there, with a glass of beer for company, when he saw a solitary rider coming towards him. The man sat a bay mare; he was clean-shaven and looked to be about thirty years old.

Pulling up in front of Huck, he asked, "Howdy, can you direct me to the livery stable?"

"Down the street, to your left; you can't miss it. There's a big blue-and-white sign outside. You'll see it."

"Thanks, mister."

On second thought, Huck decided against going across the street, at least for the time being. *Tom should be showing up soon.*

He was enjoying the peaceful morning when the shots rang out. Coming towards him was the man who had ridden into town a short while before, riding hell-bent for leather, bullets whizzing past his head. Huck leapt to one side, hoping he wouldn't catch a stray one.

After the stranger galloped past, Huck looked in the direction from which he had come. A man with a gun in his hand stood in the middle of the street, waving his arms all about. He was yelling something, but he was too far away for Huck to make out what it was. About then, people started coming out of the stores along the street. He started in the direction of the commotion. Along the way, he met Tom.

"What happened, Tom?"

"I don't know, but let's find out."

The man at the center of all the attention was named Morton. He was surrounded by town folk who were all talking at once. Tom and Huck pushed their way through the crowd and, upon reaching Morton, Tom ordered everyone to stop their yammering and quiet down. When the noise dropped to a murmur, he asked Morton to explain why he was shooting off his gun in the middle of the street.

"The man that just rode out of here—the one I was shooting at—he killed Julie June!"

Tom's mouth tightened slightly and his eyes narrowed to slits. There had not been a killing in Redemption since he and Huck had it out with Cantry, twenty-two years ago.

"Where is she?"

"Out back of the livery stable."

"I need you to go with my friend here. I'll see to Julie June, then I'll come over, and you can tell me what happened.

"Huck, you take him to The Dollar and pour some whiskey into him. I'll be there presently." Tom then scanned the faces of the crowd until he found the man he wanted. "Sam, you go and get Doc Martin. The rest of you folks go about your business. This is no concern of yours."

While they sat in The Silver Dollar waiting for Tom, Morton absently spoke a few words as he fiddled with an empty whiskey glass.

"Julie June and I were to be married. I came into town to set a firm date for our wedding. When I didn't find her at the eating house, I inquired as to her whereabouts. One of the women who worked with her told me she had gone out the back towards the barn. I went looking for her. But instead of finding my sweet Julie June, I found a man kneeling over her motionless body, removing her engagement ring.

"Seeing her like that froze me in my tracks, but when my wits returned, I yelled for him to unhand her. He jumped to his feet and took off running. I drew my gun and fired, but missed. I kept firing at the son-of-a-bitch until my gun was empty."

The first Molly heard that there was any trouble was when Huck came back to the hotel and told her he was heading out with a posse to track down a killer.

"You're going to do *what*?"

"I'm going to help Tom."

"And what . . . please tell me . . . am I supposed to do while you're off gallivanting around the countryside? Stay here and bake some goddamn cookies?"

"Come on, Molly, only five men volunteered for the posse. He'll need my help."

"Listen, *Mister* Huck Finn. I know you're going, but what I'm trying to tell you is that *I'm* going too. You being so old and feeble, and seeing as how you haven't ridden a horse in years, you might fall off and then who would tend to you if I wasn't around?"

Huck said nothing in response; he only nodded. He knew he didn't stand a chance. Then he said, "We leave in an hour. I'll tell the man at the livery to saddle you a horse. And since you're coming along, I better go and get me a bottle of whiskey because sometimes it's hard enough to put up with you when I'm sober." He smiled as he said that and his eyes crinkled in a smile of their own. As he left, he kissed Molly full on the mouth and smacked her behind.

Seven men and one woman rode out after the killer. Tom led the way with Molly and Huck riding beside him. Huck didn't know any of the men they rode with—they all had come to Redemption after his time—but Tom filled him in on who they were.

Ian McGregor, an immigrant from the old country, spoke with a noticeable Scottish accent. He was a big man, not tall, but well-muscled, with hair the color of a fiery sunset. His ranch bordered Morton's.

Billy Dowd was a skinny youth of twenty years. He worked for McGregor as a wrangler.

Len Dawson and Dick Jones were partners in a spread just north of town. Dawson was a man of fifty with a full head of gray hair and a pleasant personality. His partner was the exact opposite. Jones was as bald as a billiard ball except for some brown fringe. He was about forty and had the disposition of a rattlesnake with a toothache. They came along because both of them had entertained hopes of maybe marrying Julie June. But that was before Morton entered the picture.

And, of course, there was Morton. He looked to be in his late forties and wore his black hair cut short. He was dressed like a dude; he wore a creased black suit, a clean white shirt, and a black tie. The set of his mouth was that of a man who had just bitten into a lemon, but that might have been because of what had just happened to his intended.

Huck asked Tom about Morton and Julie June.

"Morton moved here first, about three years back. He bought old man Edwards' ranch. Like most people from the east, he's kind of standoffish. He hardly ever came into town; he would send his help in for supplies and what not. But one day when he himself came in to purchase provisions, he stopped in at Abigail Murphy's eatery. That's when he first laid eyes on Miss Julie June Watts. After that, he came to town every day.

"Julie June stepped off the train eight months ago. According to legend, she was headed to California. For some unknown reason, she took to Redemption and asked the depot master to retrieve her bags. The west-bound departed a few minutes later minus one passenger. She was a comely girl, with long auburn hair that she wore loose. I'd say she was about twenty-five. The most striking thing about her was her eyes. They were a light green . . . the color of a cactus.

"She secured lodging at Missus Butterfield's rooming house, and employment at Abigail's. After she had been working there for a short while, something funny happened. The restaurant's business doubled. Men were coming in for a second meal only an hour after finishing their first. The cowpunchers from the surrounding ranches somehow found the time to make the ride into town and eat supper at Abigail's on weeknights. On Sundays, there was a line of men waiting to get in. All of them with their hair slicked back and smelling of *eau de cologne*.

"I reckon mere cowpokes aren't much competition against a rich man like Morton because it wasn't long before he announced their betrothal. The womenfolk were pleased as punch at the news. They had been talking among themselves and decided that Julie June would either have to get married or they were going to have to run her out of town.

"There's only one thing, though. I don't know much about the fairer sex, but I do know when a woman is given an engagement ring with a diamond big enough to choke a horse, she shows it off at the drop of a hat, even if she has to drop the hat herself. However, Julie June never showed the ring around unless she was asked to. I think I was the only one in town to find that a bit queer, but I kept my thoughts to myself."

Two

At first, the other members of the posse didn't cotton to having a woman along. They grumbled and mumbled amongst themselves just loud enough to let their feelings be known. Molly was about to open her mouth and say something, but Huck smiled at her, shook his head, and winked. Molly rolled her eyes, but said nothing.

Tracking the killer was easy; he had left a trail that even a blind man could follow. Tom pointed out that his horse's right front shoe had a nick in it. There was no mistaking his tracks. The posse made eighteen miles that first day before having to stop because of darkness.

About mid-morning the following day, as they were coming around a dogleg in the trail, a shot rang out. The next thing they knew, McGregor lay dead on the ground. He had taken a bullet right through the middle of his forehead. They all dove for cover and waited for the next shot. When it became evident there would be no more, they left the safety of their cover. Billy ran to McGregor's body and cradled it in his arms.

For Molly—who had once embraced a man in a similar fashion as he slowly died—it was a heartbreaking sight to behold.

Tom gave the boy a few minutes, then said, 'I'm sorry, son, but we've got to be moving on. You take him back to town. We'll get the man that did this. I promise you that."

Billy looked up at Tom and said, "We'll pick Mister McGregor up on the way back. He's beyond any help now. He treated me like a son. In fact, he's the only man that ever did treat me decent. I'll be going on with you. I've got me a man to kill."

Tom nodded and told the boy to bring McGregor's horse along. "No use leaving her for a saddle tramp to make off with." They laid the body behind a large boulder and the posse resumed their hunt for the murderer.

They didn't catch up to him right off like they thought they would. His tracks were not in a straight line; he was crisscrossing north to south like he was drunk or confused. Finally, at about noon, they figured out what was going on. By then they had picked up Indian signs. Clearly, the killer was trying to keep out of their way.

Two hours before sundown, they ran into the trouble the murderer was trying to avoid. The Indians spotted the posse from a bluff and came a-whoopin' and a-hollerin' down on them. Luckily, they had passed an outcrop of rock about a mile back and they made for it, pronto. They all got there in one piece and now had the high ground with plenty of boulders for cover, but the Indians had them pinned down.

Once they caught their breath, Huck called out to Tom. "It's 1896, for God's sake! I thought the Indian problem was over and done with for good."

"Sometimes the younger ones get a mite rambunctious. Life is hard on the reservation, and they think if they can live like their fathers and grandfathers did, life will be good again. They just don't realize those days are over."

They fought the Indians off until dark. Then things simmered down some. The Indian campfires could be seen in the distance, but that didn't matter. They knew scouts would be nearby, so there'd be no making a run for it under the cover of darkness.

They made a fire figuring, "What the hell?" Their location wasn't exactly a secret. Billy had first watch. Dawson was talking with his partner, Jones, as he prepared to fry up some salt pork. Tom and Huck had their heads together, speaking quietly. And Morton was off by himself, sipping whiskey from a bottle. Molly, feeling a little left out of things, joined Tom and Huck.

"Alright boys, what are we going to do? We don't have much food or water. We can't make a stand here for too long."

Tom responded: "We don't aim to just sit here, Molly. Tomorrow at gray light, I'm gonna run up a white flag and parley with them. See what we can work out."

Eventually, the posse bedded down for a fitful night's sleep.

When the purple clouds to the east turned pink around the edges and the last of the stars had faded away, Tom asked Billy to bring him McGregor's horse. "I won't be needing the saddle, but keep the bit in her mouth." A minute later, Billy was back.

With a nod to Huck, Tom mounted his horse and, trailing McGregor's, he rode down to the Indians.

An hour later, he returned, still trailing McGregor's horse. Molly stoked the fire to heat up the coffee from the previous night. After Tom had a cup in hand, Morton spoke up, "If they refused your offer, what took you so long down there?"

"You just don't go up to an Indian and say, 'Here's a horse; I want to trade it for my life.' No, first you gotta smoke his sacred pipe. Then you break bread with him. Well, maybe not bread, more like dried deer meat. And when he feels like moving things along, *then* you can start dickering for your life."

The camp was quiet after that. They all thought they were headed for the last roundup. Morton was busy writing out his last will and testament. Dawson and Jones sat by the fire, drinking coffee and speaking quietly between themselves. Billy was still on lookout. He sat staring towards the Indian camp. At length, he shouted, "They're a-comin'!"

Everyone got in position. Tom and Morton were the only ones with rifles. The rest had only their six-shooters, so they would have to wait until the Indians were pretty damn close before they could open fire. There must have been thirty braves yelling their fool heads off, charging right for the outcrop. Bullets and arrows flying every which way.

A moment later, Dawson cried out, "They've killed my partner!" He jumped up and started for Jones, but before he made two steps, an arrow entered his back. Then he was spun around by a bullet cutting into his left side. He died reaching out for his partner.

Just when one and all thought they had breathed their last, the fight was over. At least for a spell. Six Indians lay dead out on the prairie. Up behind the outcrop, two of the posse—Dawson and Jones—had cashed in their chips.

A short while later, three Indians left their camp, their horses pulling pony drags. They were coming out to pick up their dead.

Morton cursed under his breath and raised his rifle. He sighted the closest brave, but before he could squeeze the trigger, Tom grabbed the barrel of his gun and pointed it skyward. "*I'll* be tellin' you when to shoot at unarmed men. They mourn their dead same as us." Then he smiled to himself and softly said, "Damn!" Without another word, Tom mounted his horse and rode off toward the Indians.

When he was out of earshot, Morton said, "Well, of all the nerve!"

Tom rode past the Indians putting their dead on the drags, his Colt in its holster. They paid him no mind.

Morton said to no one in particular, "That's the last we're ever going to see of him."

Huck quickly turned in his direction and with contempt dripping from every word, he said, "Don't you count on it, *mister.*"

After what seemed like a lifetime, Billy shouted, "Here he comes!" And sure enough, there was Tom riding slowly back in the direction of the outcrop. He rode in, but did not dismount. Instead, he asked that the three dead men's horses be brought to him. While he waited for Billy to get them, Tom sat astride his horse as Morton peppered him with questions, but he said nothing.

When Billy returned, Tom held out his hands for the reins, turned to Huck and Molly, smiled, and then rode out. Four Indians met him halfway. He handed over the reins to one of them and spoke a few words. After that, Tom turned his horse and spurred him back to where his posse anxiously awaited his return. When he rode in, he told everyone to mount up; they had to move out—fast. "I just traded for our lives. I'll tell ya'all about it down the trail, but right now we have to ride. I believe the Indians to be honorable, but there were a few hotheads wanting to finish us off. It's best we put some miles between us and them while we can."

Billy asked about Dawson and Jones. "Ain't we gonna bury 'em?"

"I'm sorry, son, but we have to make tracks. They're past carin' if they're above ground or not." No one argued the point. Dawson and Jones were left lying where they were, partners in death as they had been in life.

As they rode, Tom explained what had happened.

"After I grabbed Morton's rifle and told him that Indians mourn their dead just like we do, an idea came to me. It was kind of a bluff, but I figured it was the only chance we had. We had killed six of their braves and unless the Indians were crazy, they wouldn't throw away any more lives than they had to for a few horses. So I thought of a way for them to save face. I tripled the original offer. To sweeten the pot, I told them we had plenty of ammunition, food, and water to hold out for a long time. With the cover we had, many more braves would die before they got anywhere near to us or our horses. So they accepted the deal."

Tom then became quiet. So did the rest of his posse— each of them contemplating their close escape from Death.

Morton was the first to break the silence by grumbling, "He's probably halfway to California by now; we'll never

20

catch up to him." It was obvious he wanted to go back to Redemption, but was ashamed to come right out and say so. He was ignored until he came out with, "If we're going to continue on, maybe I should go back for more supplies."

Tom and Huck looked at each other and Huck nodded. Tom then turned to Molly, and she nodded too. They knew what Tom was silently asking. He needed to know if they wanted to go on. When he had their answer, he turned to Morton and said, "'*If* we're going to continue?' You listen here, Morton. Three men have died chasing that man up ahead. We're going to get him if we have to pursue him to the gates of hell. If you want to go back, you go. But if it was my woman he killed, I'd stay out until I got him."

Tom must have shamed Morton because he looked embarrassed and said, "I'm not talking about going back. I was just thinking we'd be needing more supplies."

"Don't you worry about that. We'll have him by tonight. He must be a stranger in these parts. He's headed straight for Ghost Butte, and there's no way over it. There's a sheer rock face on the far side. We'll have him bottled up. If you have any more suggestions, keep them to yourself."

No more was heard from Morton after that.

They followed the killer's tracks to the Green River where they disappeared into the cold, fast-moving water. In the distance, Ghost Butte could be seen through the haze.

Tom splashed in first, followed by Molly and Huck, Morton behind them. Billy brought up the rear. They were having a tough time of it. For every foot they made forward, they lost four floating downstream.

Huck was three quarters across when Tom rode out of the water and up the steep bank. Huck was using Tom as a marker, trying to get his horse to swim toward him when Tom did the dangdest thing. He took off like a bolt of lightning, galloping west along the bank of the river.

Huck came out of the water and waited for Molly. When her horse had a firm footing, he told her to stay where she was and he lit out after Tom. Of course, Molly being Molly, she did not listen. She spurred her horse and stayed right behind Huck as he raced west, following the river. A few minutes later, they came upon Tom. He was on the ground holding his right leg. Huck pulled up, slipped his horse, and went over to his friend.

"What in tarnation are you doing?" he asked.

"We got no time for talk! Billy's in trouble. You didn't see it, but he slipped his horse and the river took them both downstream. I was trying to catch up when my horse threw me. I think my leg's broken. Now move your ass, I'll be fine."

By then Molly was standing next to Huck. He told her to stay with Tom. He knew that this time she would do as she was told.

Huck remounted and took off. He didn't have far to go. He soon came upon Billy hung up on a boulder in midstream, his head cocked at a funny angle. His neck looked to be broken—there was no sign of his horse. Normally he would have left him where he was. Huck was not much on burying people. He figured once you're dead, you don't give a fig's leaf about what happens to your body. But Billy was young and so passionate about avenging his boss' death that Huck couldn't leave him

22

there. He secured a rope to a close-by cottonwood, tied it about his person, and swam out to float the body back to the shore. He would bury him later.

While Huck was busy with Billy, Molly was checking Tom's leg. It was broken alright, and she could see that he was in a great deal of pain. She was trying to make him comfortable when Morton rode up.

"What's going on? Where's Finn?"

Tom started to say something, but Molly put her hand to his mouth. "Tom, you take it easy. Until Huck gets back, I'll handle things." He lay his head down and said, "Have at it, Molly."

To Morton, she said, "His leg is broken, and we need to make a splint. Find two cottonwood branches of the right length and bring them here." He was still on his horse, so she had to look up to him, and she didn't like it. "Why don't you get off your goddamn horse and do like I said?"

Morton stayed where he was and informed Molly that he did not take orders from women.

She winked at Tom so Morton couldn't see and stood up. "Mister Morton, are you going to cut me those two branches I asked for or not?"

Morton looked at Tom, then he looked up at the sky, and finally he looked back towards Molly. "Why can't you do it? I'll look after the marshal."

"I *could* do it. But then, what good are *you*? I have had about all I can stand of your bellyaching." She drew her Colt Navy and pointed it directly at the center of his face, just about nose level. "If you aren't down from that horse by the time I cock this here gun, then I reckon I'll have to cut the branches myself *and* look after the marshal because I'm gonna ventilate your head."

Needless to say, he slipped his horse and made tracks for a nearby grove of cottonwoods.

Turning to Tom, she said, "I'm just not partial to that man."

Tom was grinning from ear to ear. "Molly, I'm the law. I can't have you talking to one of Redemption's leading citizens like that." Then he laughed out loud. That must have cost him because he grimaced in pain and laid his head back down.

A few minutes later, Huck rode up. Nearby, doing a little grazing, was Morton's horse.

"Where's Morton?" he asked.

"He volunteered to cut some splints for Tom's leg," Molly answered.

Tom asked about Billy.

"He didn't make it."

"Damn!" was all that Tom said. Molly said nothing aloud, but she was remembering how she always thought Billy's innocent smile was the best part of him.

Morton soon came back carrying two trimmed branches. Each about two feet long. He had a sour look on his face, more so than usual. Huck looked inquiringly at Molly, but she only shrugged and continued with her preparations to set Tom's leg.

Huck got the bottle of whiskey out of his saddle bag and handed it to Tom. "Here, put a good dent in this. You're gonna need it."

They got Tom taken care of; then it was time for a pow-wow. Huck asked if they should go on.

"I'll be okay," said Tom. "We're within spitting distance of the killer, so we can't stop now. But, Huck, I need you to take over as leader of the posse . . . or what's left of it."

Morton wanted to turn around and go back to Redemption, but this time he did not have the option of leaving. His gun would soon be needed.

They buried Billy and rode due west into the setting sun as it kissed the rim of Ghost Butte.

Three

The posse arrived at Ghost Butte just at sunset; they made camp and ate what little food they had left. It had been a long trail that led them to the killer, and they were worn out. There was no way they could take him in the dark, so they bedded down for the night, leaving Tom to take the first watch.

Later that night, when Huck's watch was over, he went to Morton and prodded him awake with the toe of his boot. Then he walked over to where Molly lay sleeping. Looking down at her, he experienced a strange feeling in his chest. It was a nice feeling, but totally alien to him. He sighed and went to his own bedroll. It would be gray light in a few short hours; it was time to get a little sleep. Soon, he would have to go up the Butte and kill a man.

The black night slowly gave way to a little gray in the east. There were no clouds. One solitary, lonely star hung low in the eastern sky. Molly was the first to awaken. She looked over to a sleeping Huck; she would let him be for a few more minutes. Morton was slouched next to a boulder with his rifle cradled in his arms—sound asleep.

Damn!

She threw off her blanket and went to check on Tom. He was just blinking his eyes open. "Good morning, Molly."

"Good morning, Tom. Morton's asleep. What should I do?"

"Damn!"

26

"That's what I said."

Tom smiled. "Let's hope the killer didn't slip by. No use worrying Huck about it until we know. Besides, we're gonna need Morton's gun. I'm afraid Huck might be a little rough on him if he knew he shirked his duty. Go wake the bastard and tell him to wake Huck. Then please come back over here. I'm gonna need a little help getting situated."

Molly shook the sleeping man's shoulder until he opened his eyes. He looked around as though he had no idea where he was.

"Get up, you good-for-nothing. You better hope the killer's still up there."

Morton opened his mouth to say something, but Molly cut him off. "Save it. Go wake up Huck. It's time to get this done."

A truculent Morton prodded Huck awake with the barrel end of his rifle and said "Seeing as how you're running things, let's get up there and kill the son-of-a-bitch. It's light enough now."

It took Huck half a tick to remember where he was. He was wondering why he wasn't in his bed back in Redemption with Molly lying next to him. *Why am I being accosted by this son-of-a-bitch?* When the fog of sleep dissipated sufficiently for him to recall where he was and why, he turned to see Molly helping Tom as he limped over to a large boulder. Ignoring Morton, he bid his friends a cheery good morning.

Tom was the first to respond. "Mornin'. Sorry there's no coffee, but now that we don't have to fight Indians and follow tracks all the way to hell and back, we can wrap this up and be sitting in Mary's restaurant in less than two days, sipping all the coffee we could hope for."

Molly chimed in with a question for Huck. "So, how do you want to play it?"

"First, I'm going behind that rock over there to relieve myself, and then I'll give him one chance to surrender. If he takes it, then that's it. If he doesn't, Morton and I will go up after him."

Morton didn't seem to like that plan. "We shouldn't give that bastard a chance. I say we go up there and kill him without hesitation."

Huck looked him in the eye and said, "Do you mind if I take a pee before I have to listen to your shit?"

Huck returned, buttoning up his pants. "You ready, Tom?"

"Yup."

"Molly?"

"As I'll ever be."

"Morton?"

Morton said nothing.

Huck took a few steps forward, cupped his hands around his mouth and yelled, "You up there, can you hear me?"

After a momentary pause, an answer: "I hear you just fine."

"You got one chance, and then we're comin' up. Do you want to surrender peaceful-like or do you want to die here? It makes no difference to us."

None of them expected an answer right away. They figured he'd have to think on it for a spell. Either way he was a dead man. But he fooled them, and in a clear, loud voice they heard, "I've been thinking all night. I shouldn't have run in the first place, and killing that man on the trail was an accident. I want to explain things. I'm coming down."

"Just make sure your hands are empty and out where we can see 'em."

They waited about two minutes and then saw the killer walking down the path with both hands reaching for some sky. He was not wearing a gun. As he struggled to keep his balance, a shot rang out, and a bullet ricocheted off the boulder next to him. Huck turned to see Morton sighting for another shot. He moved fast and slammed the stock of Tom's Winchester into Morton's stomach. Morton bent over, dropped his rifle, and fell to the ground. Turning to Molly, Huck said, "Take his guns." Then to Morton, "I gave that man my word. I know you feel strongly about what was done to your intended, but I'm running things. If you do anything like that again, I'll put a bullet in your leg. And if you keep annoying me, I'll gladly put one between your eyes."

The killer hadn't even flinched when the bullet hit the boulder. He just kept on walking until he was standing in front of Huck. Morton was still on the ground hugging his stomach. Tom was off to the side, propped up on a rock, Molly standing next to him.

The killer asked if he could put his hands down, and Huck told him to do so. "My name is Mike Killeen; I hail from Roanoke, Virginia. I came to your town to see my girl; she'd sent me a letter asking me to come. It's kind of a long story, but right now all I want to know is why that man started shooting at me back in town." Killeen was pointing to Morton.

Huck obliged him with an answer. "Because you killed his girl."

"I did not kill Julie June. I was in love with her. All I know is that she was dead when I walked into the barn, and that man was kneeling over her. It looked like he was taking a ring off her finger. When I came in, he ran, and I went to Julie June. A minute later he was back, firing at me."

Morton got to his feet and hollered, "Don't listen to a thing that murdering son-of-a-bitch says!" That had the opposite effect of what he had intended. Now, for sure, everyone wanted to hear what Killeen had to say.

Huck looked at Molly and said, "If Morton says one more word, put a bullet into his right leg." Turning to Killeen, he said, "Alright, let's hear your story."

"Well, Julie June and I planned on getting married, but I wanted a stake to get started. My uncle owned a ship that was going out to the Far East to trade. He offered me the position of first mate with ten percent of the profits.

"However, we never did make it to the East. The ship went down during a storm in the Indian Ocean. We lost our sails; there was no controlling her and she started to break up. My uncle gave the order to abandon ship. He, the captain, and I were to be the last ones off, but as we were lowering our dingy, a wave washed over the gunwale and knocked me into the sea. That was the last I ever saw of my uncle, the ship, or my shipmates. I don't know how I stayed afloat in that maelstrom, but I did. Finally, after what seemed like hours, the seas calmed, and a hatch cover floated by. I grabbed onto it and it kept me afloat until I was picked up by a Russian whaler a day later.

"It was almost a year before we docked in their home port of Nevelsk and another four months for me to make my way back to Virginia. It turned out all but two of the crew drowned that night. Those two were picked up by a ship headed for New York and were back in the States within two months. When they arrived, they reported the rest of us as dead.

"When I returned home, Julie June's mother told me that after more than a year of mourning, her daughter thought it best to start a new life someplace other than Virginia. There were too many memories of me in Roanoke, so she headed out for California.

"Anyway, her mother wrote to her that my reported death had been in error and that I was back. Shortly thereafter, through her mother, I received a letter telling me that she had made a horrible mistake. She had become engaged to an older man, but she did not love him. She was only looking for security. She asked me to come to her in Redemption, and then together we could start a new life in California.

"You saw me ride into your town, mister, and we spoke a few words. I asked for the livery stable because Julie June wrote that her place of employment was next to it. When I went into the restaurant, she was busy, but she told me she was going to meet the man she was engaged to in a few minutes and give him back his ring. She asked that I meet her out back, in the barn, in half an hour. The rest you know. As I've said, that man took a ring from her and then started shooting at me. For all I know, he killed her. Back in town, I didn't stop to think. All I knew was that bullets were buzzing my ears, so I ran."

Huck was quiet. He rubbed the stubble on his chin in a thoughtful way, and then he said to Killeen, "You got that letter she sent you?"

"Yes, it's here in my vest pocket."

"You better let me see it."

As Killeen reached into his pocket to retrieve the letter, Morton took a lunge for his six-shooter, which Molly was holding; she had no trouble side-stepping him. Huck walked over and without saying a word, backhanded him, knocking him to the ground. He walked back to Killeen and accepted the letter from his outstretched hand. Killeen did not move a muscle as Huck read the missive. Morton stayed on the ground rubbing his face where Huck's hand had made contact. Molly came up and stood next to Huck. Tom still leaned against the boulder.

When he had finished reading, Huck folded the letter and handed it back to Killeen. "Alright, I got just one question for you. If you're so innocent, why did you shoot McGregor back there on the trail?"

Killeen swallowed hard and, in a hesitant voice said, "My horse was played out; I'd been shot at; my girl had been murdered, and I just wasn't thinking right. My intention was not to kill anyone, only to scare you. I shot past *you*, but right as I squeezed the trigger, that man came around the dogleg. I never wanted to kill nobody."

"You say you saw Morton removing a ring from the woman's finger. He says *you* took it. I want both of you to empty your pockets—now!"

Killeen started to comply, but Morton jumped to his feet and screamed, "Are you going to believe this . . . this . . . murderer over me?"

At first, Huck said nothing. Then he pulled his six-shooter from its holster and pointed it at Morton, saying, "If your pockets ain't empty by the time I spit, you're a dead man."

Needless to say, Morton started to go through his pockets, but he was slow at it. Huck told Molly to collect what Killeen had while he watched Morton.

Molly put down the guns she was holding; that was a mistake. That, and drawing Huck's attention away from Morton by asking what she should to do with the contents from Killeen's pockets. Huck turned to answer, and Morton made a dive for his six-shooter lying on the ground. Before anyone could react, he got a bullet into Killeen. Huck was fast. He slapped leather—his gun bucked and coughed lead—and Morton was a dying man.

Almost before Morton hit the ground, Huck was over him, going through his pockets. He stood up holding Julie June's engagement ring.

Molly was kneeling beside Killeen. Huck came over and knelt down on one knee. "You should not have run off, son. If you hadn't, five good men, including you, would be alive now. Eleven, if you count the Indians."

Killeen, who was shot bad, smiled up at Huck, "I'm sorry I killed your man, but I'm glad that son-of-a-bitch killed me. As I was running from you, I slowly realized that I didn't want to live without Julie June." Then, with a deep sigh and a smile, Killeen went off to meet up with his beloved Julie June.

Morton was still alive, lying on the ground crying out for help. After closing Killeen's eyes, Huck went to him. "You're gonna die. Is there anything you'd like to get off your chest to maybe save your soul?"

"I'm an important man. I own the largest ranch in the county; you can't let me die!"

Huck said nothing; he just waited. Finally, Morton, in a weak voice, said, "I didn't mean to kill her. I lost my head when she said she wanted to break off our engagement to marry another man, that she didn't love me—that she had never loved me. I would have been the laughing stock of the county. You understand, don't you?"

Huck shook his head and walked away without saying another word. Molly stayed with Morton until he died. She believed even a man as evil as he was shouldn't have to die alone.

As the sun cleared the horizon in the east, the posse— what was left of it—rode out to meet a new day.

Four

Back in Redemption, the doctor reset Tom's leg properly. Sitting comfortably in his rocker on the front porch of the hotel, Tom asked Huck if he'd take over as marshal while his leg mended.

"I have an itch that needs to be scratched, so I'll soon be moseying on. I'm sure you can find plenty of men to fit the bill as your deputy. You should have a full-time deputy anyway, you're no spring chicken."

"Haven't had need of one in over ten years. Things were quiet in this town until you showed up," Tom said with a chuckle. "But you're right; I've got my pick of at least five men that would love to pin a star on their vest. I just thought you might want to get back in the saddle, so to speak, after all the excitement."

"Funny you should say that because I am hankering for a little adventure. But I don't think I'll find it here in Redemption collecting taxes and arresting Saturday-night drunks. Now if you'll excuse me, I reckon I'll get myself a beer over at The Dollar. You want me to bring you a bottle?"

"No thanks. I think I'll take a short nap here in this chair and work up an appetite for dinner."

Molly was standing by the window in their hotel room, staring down onto the main street of Redemption. She had things on her mind.

The events of the last few days had gotten her thinking about the men she had killed over the years. *How many were there? Five? Six? No, seven.* All but one of the killings had been in self-defense. That other one was for revenge, pure and simple. But he had it coming. He led a militia in an effort to kill a band of Indians made up mostly of women and children. If it had not been for Molly's quick action, he would have succeeded. At the time, she thought revenge was worth killing for, but now she was not so sure. When they were out on the trail, she had pointed her gun at Morton and told him she'd kill him if he didn't get the splints for Tom's leg. But that had been a bluff. If he had called it, she would have holstered her gun and cut the splints herself.

She hadn't always minded killing if she thought a man needed it. She had had a hard life and in some ways it had made her a hard woman. Besides being raped, kidnapped and put in prison, she had lost the only two men besides Huck that she had ever loved. John Stone died in a fire trying to save a child, and Jeff was killed in a stampede just months after they were married.

What got her thinking that way was a book she had recently read about a religion practiced in India. It seems those fellas believe that people live a whole bunch of lives. Not just one, like Christians are taught. It's one life after another. They call it *reincarnation.* At first she didn't put much stock in it. She didn't fancy coming back as a cow or horse. But as she kept reading, she learned that people never come back as animals; they always come back as people according to those who claim to be in the know. In their belief, there is no heaven or hell. There's only making things right. They call it karma and that's what was worrying Molly. The book said that karma ties two people together when one does something bad to the other. *I've killed men. Does that mean I'm going to have to come back and make things right with the men I've killed?*

36

She was deep in thought when the door opened and Huck walked in.

"You ready for something to eat?"

"Hello, Huck."

"Come on. Mary's got some thick steaks downstairs with our names on 'em."

"That's nice, but can we talk first?"

The smile faded from Huck's face and he sighed. "It's been my earthly experience that when a woman wants to talk to you, it means you're in deep trouble."

"It's nothing like that. I was just wondering what we're going to do now. I overheard you tell Tom that you'd be leaving soon. You plan on going back to the ranch with me?"

I knew it! I am in trouble. Huck closed the door and went over to Molly. She was standing by the window, looking down onto the street as though it was the most interesting street in all the world.

He came up behind her, wrapped his arms around her waist, and whispered in her ear. "I've been meaning to talk to you about that. Why not go down to the dining room? It's empty, and we can have a nice long talk. Besides, I'm so hungry I could eat a horse."

Molly turned around and gave him a look that said, *Men!*

Huck gave her a look right back that said, *Women!*

They held each other's gaze for a few seconds and then broke out laughing.

"Alright, Huck. You go down and secure us a table while I freshen up. And you might want to go across the street and get us a couple of bottles of beer."

"Yes, ma'am! Is there anything else you would like?"

"Yes, give me a kiss and get outta here. I've got lady things to attend to."

He kissed her long and hard and then left to do as he was told.

As she looked in the mirror, fixing her hair, she thought to herself, *Goddamn him! I'm going downstairs, and he'll tell me he wants to go off and play cowboy or sheriff somewhere. He'll pat me on the head and tell me that I should be a good girl and go back to the ranch and wait for him. Well, he's got a big surprise coming because I'm not going to put up one single word of protest. Goddamn him, I am not going to cry!*

The dining room was empty except for Huck sitting over in the far corner. When he saw Molly, he stood up and, with a lopsided grin plastered on his face, he called out, "Molly, over here!"

She smiled to herself. *Like I didn't notice the big galoot.*

When they were seated, Molly facing Huck and a blank wall, and him facing Molly and the rest of the room—a holdover from his lawman days—Huck reached out to her with an opened bottle of beer, but then quickly pulled it back.

"I'm sorry. Let me get you a glass. The waitress won't be here for a few minutes; the restaurant doesn't open for supper until five. I'll be right back."

He disappeared into the kitchen and returned holding two glasses and wearing his grin. He was trying too hard. But Molly was going to let him play it out his way. It might be fun to watch him squirm as he tried to come up with the right words to send her on her way.

As he poured the beers, Molly innocuously asked, "What should we drink to?"

"Let's drink to friendship and finding one another after all these years."

Huck Finn may have many rough edges, but he can be smooth and charming when he wants to be. "Okay, Huck, let's drink to friendship." *You son-of-a-bitch!*

After they lowered their glasses, Huck got down to business. "You wanted to talk to me about something?" he asked as though butter wouldn't melt in his mouth.

She was not going to make it easy for him. "I asked you a question upstairs. I asked if you were going back to the ranch with me."

He looked down at his beer, played with the glass, started to take a sip but then put the glass back down and said, "Molly, I don't rightly know how to say what I want to say. But I'll try my best."

"You do that. But first, let me fortify myself for what you're gonna say," she said somewhat sarcastically. And as she drank her beer, she looked at him from over the rim of the glass. *He's nervous. Good!*

After downing the last of her beer, Molly patted her lips with a napkin and said, "Alright. Let's have it, Mister Finn."

"It's just this, Molly. As you know, I've been holed up in New York nigh on to twenty-three years. I got used to that kind of life and didn't miss the old days at all. Then we came out here, and right away we're in the middle of an adventure. I'm sorry that people died, but the whole thing got my juices flowing again. I don't want to go back to your ranch, at least not right away; and I sure as hell don't want to go back to New York."

It was his turn to finish his beer. She said not a word.

When Huck saw that she wasn't going to say anything, he continued. "What I want to ask you . . . I mean what I want to say . . . I mean . . ."

Here it comes.

"Hell, Molly! What I'm trying to say is, would you mind not going back to the ranch right away and, instead, come with me to Alaska?"

It took a moment for her to comprehend what he had just said. She had been ready to be sent home with a pat on her rear end. But here he was asking her to go to Alaska with him. *Alaska of all places!* She needed another beer, or perhaps a whiskey. All she could think to say at the moment was, "Alaska?"

Huck smiled and said, "Why don't we eat over at The Dollar? We can have some whiskey while they're fixing our dinner, and I'll tell you all about it."

"Sounds good to me; lead on."

In The Silver Dollar Saloon, Huck put his elbows on the table, leaned forward, and looking into Molly's beautiful green eyes, he said. "Yes, Molly, Alaska. It's wide open. When I worked for the *Herald*, we had a man up there sending down dispatches about life on the last frontier.

"When I read them, I'll have to admit I got a mite wistful. I never thought seriously about going, but then you came into my life, and I started thinking that maybe, just maybe, I could talk you into making the trek with me. I know it'll be rough for a woman, but I'll be with you every step of the way . . . I'll take care of you."

At first, Molly didn't say anything. She sipped her whiskey and toyed with her glass in between sips. At length, she said, "Let's eat and you can tell me about Alaska."

They had steaks with all the trimmings, and he told her what little he knew of Alaska. As the barkeep was taking away the plates, Huck finished up with, "So there you have it. I'm not quite sure what will be waiting for us when we get there, but that's why I want to go; to experience new things, new sensations, in a new land. I want to go to where there isn't another person for hundreds of miles. Although I wouldn't mind having *you* within a hundred miles, preferably right next to me."

Molly smiled and said, "Alright, you've talked me into it. Now let's go back to our room. I want to talk *you* into a little something."

"I don't think it'll take that much persuasion, but let's make our way over there and find out," was Huck's eager response.

Five

As she lay in their bed, listening to her sleeping lover's easy breathing, she witnessed the night gradually give way to the morning light. She had been pondering the dilemma of how to tell her daughter that she would not be getting back to the ranch anytime soon.

Last night when they returned to the room, Huck had taken his bottle of whiskey from the bureau and brought it over to the bed. They had no glasses, so they passed the bottle between them as they talked about the great adventure awaiting them up in Alaska.

Molly had caught Huck's enthusiasm. She found herself wanting to go as badly as he did. At length, they had nothing else to speculate about. Their knowledge of Alaska was limited; they would truly be going into the unknown. It was about that time the bottle had run dry. So having used up their words and their liquor, they had turned their attentions to one another.

Now, along with a slight hangover, Molly was having second thoughts. Huck didn't want to go up there for only a few months. He wanted to spend the winter, and that meant it would be almost a year until she could get back to the ranch. *Do I really want to do this?*

Huck turned over and saw Molly lying next to him, looking as pretty as ever. She was a woman to be proud of; she was the woman that got the blood flowing through his old carcass. She was the woman he wanted by his side as he set out for what he figured would be his last adventure. But right now, he simply wanted *her*.

"Good morning, Molly. Whatcha thinking about?"

"The kids . . . back home . . . Alaska. What are *you* thinking about?"

"Come over here and, I'll show you."

Afterward, with her head against Huck's chest and her body still entangled with his, Molly felt totally weightless with pleasure. She wanted the moment to last forever, but she could sense Huck was becoming restless. It was time to get on with the day. Molly dressed and went down the hall to the convenience while Huck fumbled with his clothes. He was dressed and ready to go when she returned. Holding hands, they went downstairs to rustle up some breakfast.

They spied Tom sitting by himself over by the window, sipping on a cup of hot coffee. They walked over to his table and, once seated, Huck asked how the leg was doing.

"Not bad. Doc says I should be walking around just fine in a month or so."

"That's good, Tom. As long as you're on the mend, I reckon we'll be heading out."

"So you have an itch and gotta scratch it? Mind me asking where you're going to be doing your scratching?"

"Molly and me are figuring on going up to Alaska to see what the country's like."

"Whew, that's some trek. Have you told the folks back in Montana yet, Molly?"

"To be honest, I don't quite know how to break it to them. Maybe I'll wait until we're in San Francisco and then send a wire."

Tom sat with them while they ate their breakfast and talked about how the West had changed in the thirty-some-odd years since he had first arrived. Tom was happy with the changes. He said the railroad expansion had made life so much better in so many ways.

Molly agreed, "It used to be if the store-keeper had to order something for us, we'd have to wait months for it to arrive. Now we have it in a week or less. It's amazing!"

"I was back East when the railroads came, but I have to admit—moving from town to town sitting in a railroad car sure beats the hell out of going from town to town sitting in a saddle," was Huck's astute contribution to the conversation.

Once they had the talk and the food out of the way, Molly and Huck made sure Tom was comfortable in his rocker on the hotel porch. Then Huck said, "We'll be leaving tomorrow, and Molly and I want to say good-bye to you and Mary in a proper way. You'll be our guests for dinner over at The Dollar tonight. That is, if you can hobble over there on those crutches of yours."

"I can get around just fine, and a dinner out will be nice for Mary. She doesn't get to do that very often. Not with running the hotel and taking care of me. What time?"

"I was thinking around six o'clock. If Mary's good with that, we'll meet up in the lobby and then all go over together. If later suits her better, you can tell me about it when we get back from the train depot. We're going there now to get our tickets."

44

On the way, Huck told Molly that he had to wire his bank in New York to send him money. "I reckon I'll have them wire it in care of Wells Fargo in San Francisco. I don't rightly know how much it's gonna take, but I figure $5,000.00 oughta do it."

Of course, Molly had something to say about that.

"Look, Huck, we're partners and we're gonna split everything down the middle, fifty-fifty. And besides, I'm a bit better-heeled than you are. You wire for $2,500.00 and I'll do the same. And I don't want to hear no back talk!"

Huck shook his head and, under the circumstances, said the only thing he could say, "Yes ma'am."

Because Molly had to have her stepdaughter, Betty, send the money, she bit the bullet and informed her about their intended jaunt to Alaska.

They got their telegrams off, secured the tickets, and then took a long leisurely walk around Redemption. Huck was thinking it would probably be the last time he would see the old town, which got him to thinking that, in all probability, he might never see Tom Sawyer again once he was on the train. He shook off that thought because no matter the distance in miles or the distance in time, Tom would always be a part of him. Either as that freckled-faced kid who constantly talked him into things that ended up getting them both into trouble, or as the man who twenty-two years ago had backed him in his life-and-death struggle against Cantry and his gang of killers.

It was a festive party that took place later that night over at The Silver Dollar. Earlier in the afternoon, Molly had procured a table cloth and instructed the bartender to have it and a vase of flowers on the table when they arrived. The four of them went through two bottles of champagne and half a bottle of the house's best whiskey. Huck even got up and danced—once with Mary and twice with Molly.

Their train was scheduled to leave at 9:00 the following morning. Mary had to be up at the crack of dawn to open the restaurant, and Tom had to sit in his rocker all day watching the street traffic, so they called it an early night.

In the lobby of the hotel, the sojourners said goodnight to their hosts and promised they would not leave without saying good-bye. They kept their promise and were on the train as it pulled out of Redemption at exactly 9:02 the next morning.

Molly had enjoyed meeting Huck's friends; they were nice people and she hoped to see them again someday. Mary and she had promised to write each other because men weren't much good at that sort of thing. Molly said that, if possible, she'd send a letter from Alaska to let them know that they had made it there in one piece.

The journey to San Francisco took three days and two train changes. Huck pointed out that when he and Tom had gone to San Francisco back in '61, before the railroad, it had taken them a month to cover the same amount of miles.

They checked in at the Fairmont, reckoning they might as well stay at the best hotel in town, seeing as how the living accommodations for the next eight months or so were going to be a little on the rough side.

The next day, they set out to make arrangements for their journey to Alaska. It turned out they would have to book passage on two boats. The first, *The City of Pueblo*, would take them to Victoria in British Columbia where they would catch *The Queen* to Juneau.

They purchased the tickets and went down to the Wells Fargo building on Market Street to pick up their money. Molly's came with a lengthy telegram. Betty was a little disappointed that Molly wasn't coming right back, but she knew how Molly felt about Huck, so she wished her well and said that everyone back home sent their love. Molly was glad that Huck had been busy with the clerk when she read the message because she became a little emotional and had to fight back a few tears. She didn't want him to see her like that before they had even left the city.

They had decided to do a little prospecting while in Alaska. Not that they were looking for riches, they just wanted to try their hand at it. Huck said there had been a few small strikes over the years, and he supposed where there was smoke there might be fire. "Even if we don't strike pay dirt, it'll be an interesting endeavor," he surmised.

It turned out that *The City* was sailing in two days, so for a day and a half, they ran around the city buying their outfit: Shovels, pick axes, a Yukon stove, a tent, and things of that sort. The supplies were a tenth of the cost of what they would have had to pay in Alaska. They also bought warm clothes, but Huck wanted to wait until they got to Alaska to buy the furs and such they'd need to survive an Alaskan winter. "They'll have what we need up there. And it will be a better quality than anything we can get here."

A day later, they were passing through the Golden Gate, heading north. North to Alaska. They spent the first twelve hours in their cabin, alternating between making love, drinking whiskey, eating, and sleeping—in that order.

When they finally emerged onto the deck and into the sunlight, they enjoyed the rolling sea, the salt air, and the view of the California and Oregon coasts as the ship made its way north.

At Victoria, they transferred to the *Queen* and three days later, at two o'clock in the afternoon, they were standing on the wharf in Juneau.

"Well, what now?" asked Molly.

"We get the lay of the land, and the best way to do that is in a saloon. Let's go and see what the town's *old ladies* have to say." By *old ladies*, Huck meant men who hung out in saloons and gossiped their days away.

They found a place to store their outfit and made their way down Stewart Street. At Third Avenue they came to a place called *The Moose* and, to put a fine point on it, there was a large rack of antlers nailed above the entrance. An eighteen-pointer!

Once inside, they ambled to the bar where the barkeep asked Huck to name their poison. With drinks in hand, they surveyed the room. Off to the right stood a gent with garters on his sleeves, dealing to a few men standing at the faro table; across the room, six men sat at a table playing poker. At the bar, to their left, three men were intently studying the amber liquid within their glasses.

Huck looked at Molly and hoisted his glass, "To gold!"

That got the attention of two of their companions at the bar who momentarily looked towards Huck when they heard the word *gold*, but then went back to contemplating their glasses. The third man paid them no mind at all. Huck winked at Molly and downed his whiskey.

After the barkeep refilled his glass, Huck told him to leave the bottle, flicked a ten-dollar gold piece onto the bar, and told him to keep the change.

The barkeep smiled a thousand-watt smile and said, "Yes sir! You need anything else, you just let me know," and retreated from whence he came.

Huck turned to the man closest to him and said, "My woman and I just got into town, and we'd be honored if you'd let us buy you a drink."

The man smiled and said, "That would be right neighborly of ya."

Huck extended the offer to the other two men. The one who showed no interest at the word *gold* said nothing. He placed a coin on the bar and left. The other man accepted Huck's offer of libation and said, "Don't pay no never mind to Charley; he just ain't sociable." The speaker's named was Ed Mulroney. The other man went by Lon Tapper.

Huck suggested they secure a table so they could spread out and relax. The two men thought that a capital idea. By the time they had emptied half the bottle, they were all fast friends. The locals were telling tall tales of the north; they had both been in Alaska for many years and had travelled throughout the territory. They had originally come seeking gold, but somewhere along the way the dream had died. Now they were happy to cadge free drinks in *The Moose* and the other bars that lined Stewart Street.

Eventually Huck steered the conversation onto the topic he was most interested in. "Molly and I came up here to see if we could find a little gold for ourselves. Any advice you gents could give us in that regard would be mighty appreciated."

Mulroney held his empty glass in his hand and looked from it to the bottle a few times before Huck caught on. "Help yourself, Ed, and pour one for Lon."

With the niceties out of the way, Mulroney looked to Tapper and shook his head. Then he said, "You folks seem like nice people. The best advice me and Lon can give you is to go back from where you came. This here is a hard country and winter will be coming along soon. You *chekekos* don't know what you'll be up against. This ain't no place for a woman in the winter. Ain't that right, Lon?"

"If you say so, Ed, but I think we oughta let 'em make their own mistakes . . . like we did. Who knows? Maybe they'll get lucky."

Molly butted into the conversation to ask what *chekekos* meant.

"It's a Kaska Indian word. It means newcomers," answered Mulroney. Then after a moment's thought, he smiled and said, "I think you're right, Lon. I mean about letting them make their own mistakes." To Huck, he said, "What do you want to know?"

"Where would you fellas go if *you* were seeking gold?"

"To the Bank of San Francisco," answered Mulroney. He then slapped his knee and said, "I'm only funnin' with ya."

After taking a long swallow of whiskey and wiping his mouth with the back of his hand, he continued, "Well," he said, taking his time and drawing out the word. "There was a strike back in '78 by a man named Holt. Then, in '85, someone hit pay dirt on the Stewart River. In '93, a couple of half-breeds made out pretty good up by Circle City at a place called Birch Creek. But the gold's played out. There ain't nothing to speak of in that neck of the woods no more."

Huck and Molly looked to one another, and then Huck asked his new friends where those places were located.

"They're up the Yukon River. But I'm a-tellin' ya, there ain't no more gold!"

Huck drained what was left in the bottle into Lon and Ed's glasses. Then he said, "If a man was dumb enough—or crazy enough—to go traipsing into that land, how would he get there?" Both men shook their heads, and Lon Tapper said, "The easiest pass to traverse into Yukon country is White Pass. Go to Skagway; from there, anyone can point you in the right direction."

Huck laid a half eagle gold piece on the table and told Tapper and Mulroney to get themselves another bottle on him and Molly. They left the two men a whole lot happier than when they had first met them an hour earlier.

Six

Outside on the street, Molly asked Huck if he was figuring on them going to Skagway. "Hell yes! Not only are we going to Skagway, we're going up the Yukon River. And if we're lucky, maybe we'll find a little excitement along the way."

The next few days went by fast. Huck and Molly completed their outfit, buying two rifles and enough ammunition to start a small war. They bought flour, bacon and beans; dried fruit and three sacks of potatoes—to ward off scurvy. They also picked up a few tins of tobacco for Huck. They found a man with a small, steam-driven boat that could hardly accommodate them, let alone their outfit, but he got them *and* their outfit the eighty-six miles to Skagway in under twenty-four hours.

Skagway was a revelation. Never had there been a town as lawless and corrupt as the town of Skagway in 1896. The unofficial mayor was one Soapy Smith. Molly liked him immediately, but Huck had a feeling. "A con man's stock-in-trade is to make you like him so that he can get close enough to steal the gold fillings out of your mouth. And then he'd have you thanking him for doing so. It goes without saying that we're going to give Mister Soapy Smith a wide berth."

The gold strikes they had been told about had taken place five hundred miles to the north along the Yukon River. The word *Yukon* is a Chilkoot Indian word meaning *Great River*. The locals informed the travelers that there were no trails going north; the river was the only way to get to where they wanted to go. They'd have to first make their way to Lake Bennett—thirty-five miles to the north—and the only way to do that was by going over White Pass. Once at the lake, they would have to build themselves a boat or a raft to make the five-hundred-mile journey into the Yukon Territory. Molly wanted to know how they were going to carry an outfit of five or six hundred pounds across White Pass and up to Lake Bennett.

"Back at the store, I spoke with a nice gent who filled me in on a few things," declared Huck. "We can hire Indians to carry our outfit to the lake. We have maybe two months before the river freezes, so I reckon we better get a move on."

That evening, they were in their room tying up their outfit into manageable lots when Huck said, "It's gonna be a long hike tomorrow, so I think we should go downstairs for a drink or two. Anyway, we're gonna need a couple of bottles to get us through the winter."

With a smile, Molly said, "Did I hear that right? Did you say 'a couple of bottles to get us through the winter'? The way you drink, a couple of bottles won't get us through the pass!" Huck gently patted her fanny and said, "Aren't you the funny one."

They were billeted in Soapy Smith's Dead Horse Saloon & Hotel because it was the only room they could find for rent. It was either that or set up their tent on the outskirts of town. Downstairs, they acquired a bottle and two glasses from the bar and sat down at a table. The next day's trek was on their minds, so there wasn't much talk between them. After a few minutes of silence, Huck excused himself to use the convenience and asked Molly where it could be found.

"Out back. It's impressive, a four-holer."

"Thanks. I'll be right back."

When Soapy Smith, who had been standing at the bar, saw Huck leave, he walked over to Molly and, flashing a snake-smile, said hello. Molly nodded, but said nothing. Then Soapy leaned into her and whispered something that prompted her to slap his face. Huck had just returned and, witnessed the slap. When Soapy saw Huck, he hightailed it out the front door.

Huck came over and asked Molly what was happening.

"Nothing. Mister Smith was just demonstrating to me that you were right about him."

Huck's jaw tightened, and he looked at the front door. "Be right back," was all he said.

Molly grabbed the sleeve of his coat and stopped him. "Promise me you won't kill him. He's not worth it. Besides, it might delay our departure. He seems to have many friends hereabouts, and they may not take kindly to you killing him."

"Don't worry, I'm not heeled."

Huck found Smith across the street, standing outside the Elkhorn Saloon and Dance Hall. He was speaking with two gentlemen and when Huck asked if he might speak with him alone about a matter of importance, Smith looked like he wanted to bolt. But Huck had a firm grip on his arm. He steered Smith to an adjacent alleyway, gripped him by the throat, and said, "The lady that you just accosted is my friend. If you ever bother her again, I will kill you. If you see her walking down the street, you cross to the other side.

If you see *me* walking down the street, you better run. Do you understand?"

Smith was shaking pretty badly about then and didn't answer right away, so Huck gripped deeper into the flesh of his throat. "Maybe I'll just kill you now. It'll save me the trouble of having to do it later."

Smith quickly found his voice. He gasped in a whisper, "No! Please! If I see her coming, I'll run the other way. You won't have no trouble from me."

"*I* don't mind trouble from you, but *she* better not have any. Got it?"

"Yes . . . yes sir."

"Good. Now get outta my sight while you're still vertical."

Huck went back to Molly; she asked no questions. They had a few more drinks and Huck bought his bottles of whiskey, deciding that, if two were good, three would be even better. With his arm around Molly, they walked up the stairs as the piano player played *You've Been a Good Old Wagon But You Done Broke Down.*

"Did you request that in my honor whilst I was out?" asked Huck.

"If the shoe fits . . ." answered Molly.

They got going before daylight and went looking for Indians to haul their outfit. After an hour of asking around, they came across a Tutchone Indian by the name of Kaska Pete. He told them he could round up some of his relations to help get them to where they wanted to go, but first he needed to see their outfit.

Up in their room, he poked into the bundles and hefted a few. Finally he said, "Twenty cents a pound and twenty cents a mile each man. We need six more men. How you pay, in gold or paper?"

"Paper."

Pete shook Huck's hand and said, "It will take three . . . maybe four days, depending on how the woman holds up."

Molly looked around the room for something to throw at Kaska Pete. She found what she was looking for in the form of a rolled-up newspaper lying on the bed. As she reached for it, Huck gently took hold of her wrist and said, "Not now. Up at the pass you can let fly a few snowballs in his direction if you still feel the need to."

Pete did not know what they were talking about, but he did know one thing: All white people were crazy. "I be back in one hour. We leave then."

Huck and Molly headed out following seven Indians due north. It was a brisk walk and they made miles. Just before sunset on the second day, Pete halted the march. "White Pass up ahead. Dangerous going. We go over in full daylight." That night Molly and Huck spent most of their time swatting mosquitoes. Although the mosquitoes didn't seem to bother the Indians.

The next morning at the pass, which was more a series of sizable hills, they encountered large boulders that had to be circumnavigated very carefully or a person could slip into one of the many mud pits that lined the trail. Sharp rocks tore into their boots. But those things were mild compared to the place in the trail, known as Devil's Hill, where-of a two-foot-wide path with a five hundred foot drop-off had to be crossed over. Before starting out, Pete informed his charges that the pass had claimed its fair share of men, horses, and mules.

"What, no women?" asked Molly.

They hugged the rock wall on their left and took small steps on the slippery slate rock. Huck made the mistake—once—of looking down into the yawning, cavernous mouth of the gorge below. His stomach did a backflip. He hugged the wall harder and glanced at Molly up in front of him. She was sashaying and swinging her rifle about, looking for all the world like she was out for a walk in the park! Once she glimpsed back and smiled, which upset Huck. "Don't look at me! Keep your eyes in front of you!" he all but shouted.

When they were once again on more or less level ground, Huck walked next to Molly for a minute before saying, "I'm sorry I yelled at you back there. It's just heights and I don't get along very well."

She patted Huck's cheek with her right hand. "My poor baby. Who would have ever thought the famous lawman, Huck Finn, would be afraid of a walk up a small hill?"

Huck knew then and with a certainty that he was never going to hear the end of it.

They next encountered Porcupine Hill, which wasn't so bad. Then came Summit Hill; it was Devil's Hill all over again. Huck took a deep breath and told himself not to look down this time.

They made Lake Bennett by mid-afternoon of the fourth day. Huck paid off the Indians and thanked them for their work. After they were gone, the isolation, the immensity, and the stark loneliness of the country settled down around them.

The first order of business was to set up the tent and collect firewood because it would soon be dark. Molly gathered the wood while Huck fought valiantly to get the tent erected. When they completed their respective tasks, Huck rummaged around for one of his bottles while Molly spread out a blanket down at the water's edge. There was a good, strong breeze off the lake that would keep the mosquitoes at bay.

Sitting in the waning sunlight, they shared the whiskey and marveled at the beauty of the country that surrounded them and at how lucky they were to be there. What made it even better for them was the fact that there was no one else around. After her second pull from the bottle, Molly wanted to get the cooking going while it was still light out. She fried up some bacon and potatoes; Huck took charge of the bottle and stirred the beans.

Afterwards, all Huck wanted to do was lie on the blanket, look at the stars, and smoke his pipe. But the wind had died down, so self-preservation compelled him and Molly to beat a quick retreat into their tent. When the opening flap had been tied up tight, Huck said to Molly, "Compared to these damn mosquitoes, White Pass wasn't so bad after all."

• • • • •

Two months earlier and four hundred miles to the north from where Huck would one day battle his nemeses, the mosquitoes . . .

He could not see to the far side of the river. It appeared as wide as an ocean . . . a gray mist hung just above the water's surface. Nevertheless, he gave it little consideration. Yes, it was strange; however, he had somewhere he had to be and could not delay.

There was only one problem. He could not remember where he was going or whom he was to meet once he arrived. He slowed his walk to ponder those things. Again, his attention was drawn to the river when the water started to boil fiercely and great plumes of steam arose into the air. As he observed this strange phenomenon, two salmon leaped from the water.

The salmon did not immediately fall back into the river as any self-respecting fish would do. Instead, they hung in mid-air, their tails swishing back and forth. There was something about them—something different besides the fact that they were hovering over the water; that, he took in stride. *Don't all fish, at one time or another, float about out of the water?*

At first he couldn't fathom what was bothering him concerning the fish. Then he saw it! Their scales were made of gold and their eyes were of gold nuggets. "This is peculiar," he said aloud.

George Washington Carmack awoke with a start.

That was one bizarre dream, he thought as he climbed out of his bed. George believed in visions. He believed dreams foretold the future. He would have to decipher the message behind the dream. Maybe his brother-in-law could discern its meaning. Indians knew more about that sort of thing than white men.

Seven

George Carmack had come up to Alaska in '85. He had been there once before back in '82 when he served as a US Marine aboard the *USS Wachusetts*. On that tour of duty, he had fallen in love with the country and its wide-open spaces.

He and the Marine Corps soon went their separate ways after his ship docked in California. Actually, he deserted when not given leave to visit his sick sister. Once his sister had recovered from her illness, George returned to Alaska as a civilian.

From Juneau, he went over the Chilkoot Pass and down to Lake Bennett where he built himself a boat on its shore. He was determined to get to the solitude of the Interior as soon as possible. Once the boat was finished, George loaded his substantial outfit onto it and shoved off for the Forty Mile Region, four hundred and fifty miles to the north—straight down the Yukon River.

This looks like a nice isolated place, thought George as he passed the confluence of the Yukon and Fortymile Rivers. Hence, he set his boat onto the western bank of the Yukon.

A month later, he had half of his log cabin completed. That was the easy part. The logs were in place six feet high. It was going to be a chore to finish her off, even with the block and tackle he had brought along.

It was getting on to noon. George stopped work and sat by his campfire, the embers still aglow. He blew on them and added kindling. He didn't need much of a fire. The bacon in the pan was already cooked, having been left over from breakfast. He wanted to melt the grease that had congealed on the bottom of the pan so that he would have something to dip his hardtack into.

George Washington Carmack was a happy man. At this rate, he would complete his cabin well before first snow, even though what was left to do would be a lot harder than any of the work that had gone before. He had plenty of ammunition for hunting, and sacks of dry fruit to ward off scurvy. His liquor supply could have been a bit more copious, but he also had a sack of potatoes that would make up a good sour mash. He planned on making himself a still and had brought along a small amount of copper tubing for that very purpose.

A woman would be good, but one cannot have everything, he thought as he dragged his bread through the sumptuous bacon grease.

Upon finishing his repast, George heard a rustling behind him. Thinking it a deer, he grabbed his rifle and turned to receive the shock of his life. Three Indians stood not thirty feet away. He had thought there was not another human soul within a hundred miles. He recovered quickly and smiled as he laid the gun against a tree stump.

With his right hand raised in the universal sign of peace, George intoned, "Welcome to my camp. Do you speak English?"

The tallest of the Indians stepped forward.

"Ay, I speak your tongue. I am Keish. I am Tagish. The whites call me Skookum Jim."

"My name is George Carmack. Who are your friends?"

61

Pointing to the younger-looking of the two, Keish replied, "My brother's son, Káa Goox. White men call him Tagish Charlie. The other is husband to one of my sisters. He is called Ch'iyone Ligedet'e, Two Wolf in your tongue."

Even though George had come to the Far North to be left alone, it was good to have company after a month's isolation. He invited them to sit and offered food and tobacco. The food, they politely declined. The tobacco, they readily accepted.

George had not met many Indians in his day, but he knew they did not jump immediately into a conversation. So he took out his pipe and filled it; he was in no haste to get back to work. Three hundred miles south of the Arctic Circle, George sat with his new friends in front of his half-finished log cabin, smoking his pipe, enjoying the sunshine, and saying not a word.

At length, Keish said, "We seen ye when ye first come, but left ye alone. But now that ye are ready to be lifting logs high up, we help."

George had been dreading the next phase of his endeavor and eagerly accepted the offer of assistance. "That's mighty friendly of you folks. Your help will be greatly appreciated."

"It is good. Come tonight to our village; we are a small band—sixty-seven including the children. Ye will eat with us. On the morrow, we build lodge."

"Where is your village?"

"North. Follow river. Come as sun dips below mountains in west. Now we go."

The whole time there, the other two Indians had not spoken. George shook hands with all three men before they left.

That night, the Tagish Indians put on quite a feast for their guest. George sat at the main fire with Keish seated next to him. In the reflected firelight, he beheld the smiling Indian faces as they spoke among themselves. He could not understand what was being said, for they spoke in their own language, but he could see that all were having a good time.

A few of the women were going from fire to fire, serving food to the children. Other women served the men at the big fire. George's eyes followed one girl in particular. She was pretty, almost beautiful. George asked Keish her name.

"Shaaw Tláa. My sister."

"Is she the sister who is married to Two Wolf?"

"Shaaw Tláa's husband and child died of winter sickness."

It took a while, but presently George understood that Shaaw Tláa's husband and daughter had died of influenza.

While chewing on a piece of roasted deer meat, George said softly, and more to himself than to anyone else, "She looks like a Kate to me."

He slept in the village that night, and the next morning he, Keish, and six other men headed down river to his camp where they put in a full day's work. They got more done before the sun went behind the western mountains than George would have accomplished in a week had he worked alone. The Indians were hard workers, and the cabin was completed shortly thereafter.

There were no windows, the door was hinged by two wide leather straps, and the floor was trodden dirt. But it was home and George was still a happy man. There was just one thing a little off. It was going to be a cold, bitter winter; the warmth of a woman lying in his bed would help alleviate the boredom of those long arctic nights. *Winter is still a few months off, but no use waiting until the last minute.*

George had not spoken to Shaaw Tláa since that first night, and then it had been only a few words. However, he had spoken about her to Keish many times over the last few weeks. He washed up in the river and put on his best clothes. They were not Sunday-go-to-meeting duds, but there were no holes in the britches . . . or the shirt either, for that matter.

On the way to the Indian village, he rehearsed what he would say to Keish. Their father was dead, so it fell to Keish, the oldest son, to make the decisions for his unmarried sisters. Once married, their husbands would take care of them and make their decisions for them.

Keish knew why his friend had come that day. *White men are peculiar when seeking a wife. An Indian will buy the maiden he wants . . . if he can afford her father's price.*

George looked uncomfortable, but Keish had decided not to make it easy for the white man. He would first have some fun with him. "Tis good to see ye, my friend. Why are ye not back at yer cabin?"

"I came up here to ask you something."

"Ay?"

"Damn you, Keish! You sure as hell ain't making this simple for me. You *know* why I'm here. So what do you say?"

Keish laughed a good, vociferous laugh. "Many signs have ye made, my friend, with yer talk of her. And those signs have not gone unnoticed. I have spoken with Shaaw Tláa. She is of a mind that ye will make a good husband. Go to our house and tell her to gather her belongings. Tell her that she is no longer of this village and take her back to yer lodge. Welcome to the Crow Clan."

It was that easy. *White men sure have a lot to learn from the Indians,* thought George as he made his way to Shaaw Tláa.

On the way back to his land, George told Shaaw Tláa that from then on she would be known as Kate Carmack. Shaaw Tláa, now Kate, had no objections.

That is how George Washington Carmack became the brother-in-law of Keish, also known as Skookum Jim Mason. They soon went into business together, hunting, trapping, fishing, and then selling their bounty to white men or trading with Indians of other tribes. In this manner, they kept busy for most of the year. Of course, in the dead of winter, one ventured out only if one needed food.

The next year, white men came and built the town of Forty Mile. At first it was only a trading post with a few log cabins, but when gold was discovered on Fortymile River, the population swelled to almost one thousand souls.

On occasion, George would try his hand at prospecting. Sometimes he found a little color, but that was about all.

However, when he went into the town of Forty Mile, he'd tell everyone he met, "This time I hit pay dirt!" Because of his exaggerations of finding gold, he came to be known as "Lyin' George." *That*, he did not mind so much, but it irked him to be called Squaw Man. He had had more than a few fights in the saloons of Forty Mile concerning that topic.

Eight

It has been eleven years since George Carmack took Kate for his wife. He now speaks the Tagish language as though born to it. He is a well-respected member of the Crow Clan of the Tagish Nation.

The morning after his strange dream, he washed up in the river, ate the large breakfast Kate had prepared for him, and then made his way to Skookum Jim's house. It was high time they checked their trap line. George collected Jim and together they set off to the northwest. As they walked, George broached the subject of his dream.

"I had the craziest dream last night. I'm sure it means something, I just don't know what."

"We go many miles. As we walk, tell me."

George relayed the dream. He told of the two salmon covered in gold, having gold nuggets for eyes, and floating in mid-air. When he had finished his recitation, he asked, "So, what do you think, Jim?"

"I know naught. I will ponder on it for a spell."

There was no more talk between the men until they reached their trap line. Then it was all business. As they walked the line, they found each trap empty.

"The French and the English have wiped out our small game," said George.

"It well may be," agreed Jim.

There wasn't much more to add to that, so, in silence, the two men collected their traps. If nothing else, they could sell them to a sucker in town. After the traps were bundled for easy carrying, Jim suggested they take a breather before heading back. "I got hooch. We sit down by creek, have drink, and we talk of yer dream."

"Sounds good to me, Jim."

They sat cross-legged on the ground and stared at the slow-moving water of the creek. After the bottle had been twice passed between them, Jim spoke. "Long I thought on yer dream. But first tell what *ye* think it foretells."

George took a minute to respond, like he was marshalling his thoughts. At length, he said, "It can mean only one thing. I'm to become a full-time salmon fisherman. The rivers are full of the fish this time of year and, as you know, we can sell all that we catch to white men."

"Ay, those be my thoughts. Ye be mighty catcher of fish."

"And seeing as how we're partners, it looks like you're going into the fishing business with me, Jim."

"We start on the morrow. We need Charlie. He is young, he can empty the traps for us. After all, we are chiefs; he will do the hard work."

George laughed and said, "One more swig and then let's go."

Two days later, George Carmack, Skookum Jim Mason, and Tagish Charlie were fishing for salmon, but the partners were not having much luck. They were thirty-eight miles south of Forty Mile, down at a small river that flowed into the Yukon. Its Indian name: Tr'ondëk, which was later Anglicized to Klondike.

"It took us seven hours of hard paddling up the Yukon to get here and another hour going up this damn river. And for what? We haven't caught enough fish for our own dinner, let alone enough to sell." To say the least, George W. Carmack, at that moment, was a discouraged and unhappy man.

As usual, Jim had sage advice for his friend.

"It be a long way from the big water. The salmon come. They just be late this year."

"Good for them, but I'm going back to camp. You let me know when those damn fish get here."

Being the junior partner, Tagish Charlie said nothing.

Two days later, at 11:08 in the morning, Jim and George were having basically the same conversation when Charlie interrupted them.

"Look up river! Boat poling this way."

They shielded their eyes against the bright sun and looked to see a tall, thin man working a pole into the muddy bottom of the river. One did not usually run into other men in that wild country. The three partners waited expectantly until the boat pulled up on the shore. Robert Henderson had floated down the Klondike from Gold Bottom Creek, as he called it, and he had news of some import to convey.

"Howdy, George." He did not address the Indians.

"Howdy, Bob. What brings you to this neck of the woods?"

"I've been up to Gold Bottom Creek and I found me a little color. Going up to Forty Mile to trade for coffee and other things I'll be needing. I think there might be a lot more yellow sand lying about in that creek. You're welcome to give it a try if you'd like. But leave them siwashes behind. I don't want no damn Indians anywhere around my claim."

"I'm glad that you hit a little pay dirt, but I'm a fisherman now, so I don't reckon I'll make it up there anytime soon. And I wish you wouldn't call my kinfolk siwashes. I don't think they like it any more than a Negro likes being called a nigger."

"As far as I'm concerned, they're all niggers. Well, I got to be shoving off. I want to make Forty Mile before full dark."

"Okay. See you around."

No one spoke until Henderson was out of earshot. Then Skookum Jim said, "Henderson still not like-um Indians. Indians still not like-um him!"

An hour later, the salmon arrived and filled their traps. They emptied from the traps as much fish as their canoe could hold. After drying them over a smoking fire, they started back to Forty Mile.

For the next two weeks, George, Jim, and Charlie made the trek down to the Klondike River and fished for salmon, always returning with a canoe heavily laden with freshly dried fish.

Before they left on their next foray, Kate had something to say. "You men go away for two, three days at a time, leave me here alone. When you go this time, I go with you."

"Then we'll need two canoes." George Carmack had an easy-going personality and did not like to argue.

On the way down, George and Jim were in the lead canoe and Kate and Charlie followed closely behind in a canoe of their own. Just to have something to say, Jim observed, "Mayhap we make enough to last through the winter."

George nodded and said, "This will probably be our last fishing trip. You noticed how the salmon have kinda thinned out?"

"We have-um two canoes; we fill 'em both. We get back, we go into town, stay drunk for days."

"You got a deal."

Fishing was sparse on the Klondike that day. There were very few fish in the traps, leading George to propose, "Why not go visit Henderson up on Gold Bottom? We can see for ourselves if his poke has grown in size since we last saw him."

The others were not thrilled with the idea. "Me no like him," said Jim.

Kate added her two cents. "He bad man."

Tagish Charlie, as was his custom, said nothing.

In the end, George prevailed. They packed up their gear and headed east on the Klondike. At that time of year, Gold

Bottom Creek was a little too shallow to handle a boat of any size. So they pulled their canoes onto the sand at the mouth of the creek and walked the mile or so to Henderson's camp.

Upon seeing the foursome headed his way, Robert Henderson's mouth tightened into a serious frown. "I told you I didn't want no damn siwashes anywhere near my claim. Now, if you would be so kind as to take your Indian friends and depart, I'd be most appreciative."

George laughed and said, "Sure, Bob. We're just passing through and thought we'd say howdy. Say, did you find any more color?"

"None of your damn business. Now git!"

On the way back to the canoes, Kate observed that it was not very nice of Henderson to act that way.

"It's just his manner. His bark is worse than his bite," said George.

"I bite *him* if he comes near me!" exclaimed Jim.

"Okay, okay," cried George. "I was wrong, but as long as we're here, why not do a little panning ourselves? You never know."

"We first eat." Jim scowled as he added, "We find own creek to work. Not want to be near that man."

They got into their canoes and headed back west until they came to Rabbit Creek. It was deep enough to handle the canoes . . . barely. They paddled up-creek for two miles and set up a small camp.

After a meal of salmon and fried potatoes, Jim offered to do the washing up. He splashed into the cold water to about ankle deep. There he squatted, grabbed a handful of sand, and started rubbing it onto the greasy frying pan.

Jim wasn't thinking of anything in particular. He was satiated, satisfied, and speculative. Life was good. *What more could a man want? A full stomach, good friends, and enough whiskey to last until we get back to Forty Mile is all a man should want for.*

He looked about as he scoured the cast iron pan. George was smoking his pipe. Kate was doing the clean-up, and Charlie appeared to be napping. A glint of light caught his eye; the sun was reflecting off something on the bottom of the creek. Absently, he reached down and picked up the object. Immediately upon seeing what he held, he dropped the pan and splashed to the shore.

"George! George! Look what I find!"

It was a gold nugget as big as Jim's thumb, and Jim was a mighty big man.

Gold nuggets are rather scarce. Sure, anyone can find color on the bottom of a stream. But gold nuggets are found only where there is an abundance of gold, and seldom were the nuggets as big as the one Jim held.

After seeing the find for themselves, the other three splashed into the creek with Jim right behind. Within minutes, their hands were filled with gold!

After an hour of "prospecting," the four had a pyramid of gold nuggets six inches high and six inches wide at the base. It took their breath away.

They celebrated by finishing off the whiskey they had brought with them. Even Kate, who hardly ever consumed spirits, took a turn drinking from the bottle. Then it was time to get down to business.

"You made the find, Jim. So I reckon the claim is yours," declared George.

"It may well be, but we are partners. We file claim together."

For the first time that day, Tagish Charlie spoke. "White men not honor claim filed by Indian. George should file claim."

"It be true! You file claim, George, and we will all be rich," imposed Jim.

Nine

Two months later, and four hundred miles to the south, on the shore of Lake Bennett . . .

In the morning, Huck and Molly got started building their raft. The first order of business was to find a location in which to construct it. They needed a place with a slight incline towards the lake; the felled logs would have to be rolled down to the water's edge. Molly found the perfect spot two hundred yards to the north, on the lake's eastern shoreline.

With a cross-cut saw over his left shoulder and an axe in his right hand, Huck went looking for a tree of the right height and girth that was not too far from the lake. Finding just what he wanted, he got down to work. An hour later, the wind picked up and shortly thereafter the rain came . . . and the rain stayed.

Days, they toiled to the roar of thunder and in the blinding rain . . . every day, all day long, for a week. It was a cold rain; the water poured from their hats and into their eyes making the work with an axe even more dangerous than it already was.

Nights, they were tired, wet, and cold. They didn't even think of cooking anything. And even if they had, they couldn't make a fire because there was not a stick of dry wood to be had for love nor money. They had been living off raw bacon, dried fruit, evaporated potatoes, and dried beef since the rain started. All they wanted to do at the end of each day was crawl into the tent and fall asleep.

Mid-afternoon on the seventh day, the deluge ceased—the sun came out and the sky turned blue, dotted with cottony white clouds. The next day, they finished the raft and were ready to lever it into the water.

She was a fine craft. Huck had told Molly that he and Tom had made more than a few rafts during their days on the Mississippi, so he knew what he was doing. "The raft Jim and I floated on downriver the time we met up with the King and the Duke had been constructed by *yours truly*, and it had nothing over the vision of beauty I now behold," so said Huck Finn.

She was twenty feet long and almost as wide. They had fashioned a small tipi frame about three quarters of the length from the "bow" and covered it with an oil cloth. Things they did not want to get wet would go inside. The rest of the outfit would be lashed securely to the "deck." They rigged up a mast just forward of the tipi; the sail was a blanket and it would get them out of the lake. Then the current of the river would move them along from there. At the rear, Huck had fashioned a swing arm for steering.

Once they had her floating, Huck said, "She's first-rate and she oughta have a name that befits her. What do you say to the *Molly Lee*?"

"I won't argue with you. Are you going to christen her with one of your whiskey bottles?"

"Maybe I will. But I'll have to wait until I have use of an empty one."

They laughed and walked back to camp. They would start for the Yukon in the morning at first light.

The next day, as the sun was trying to make its way over the horizon, and as Huck and Molly ate their breakfast, Huck took a piece of paper from his shirt pocket and unfolded it.

"Come around here," he said to Molly, "and sit by me."

When she was by his side, she looked down at what he was holding and saw a hand-drawn map. "Whatcha got there, Huck?"

"It's a map of the Yukon Country. I had a geezer draw it for me that last night in Skagway while you were sleeping. And don't you look at me like that, missy. I couldn't sleep, so I went down to the saloon. I was thirsty."

Molly smiled and said nothing.

"Now see here, this is where we're at," Huck said, pointing to a mark on the paper. "When we leave the lake, we'll be on the Yukon River . . . this line here. It will take us northwest and get us near those previous strikes we were told about. This other line is the Fortymile River, and that spot there where the two rivers meet is the town of Forty Mile. It's the only civilization we're gonna be seeing for a while. And it's where we'll have to go for supplies and to file our claim . . . if we hit pay-dirt. Or so I was informed."

"See the two X's marked along the river? Those are the two main rapids we'll have to traverse. The old-timer who drew me the map said if the first one didn't kill us, the second one would be sure to do the job. The first rapids go through a place called Miles Canyon. The second place is called White Horse Rapids."

Seeing the look on Molly's face, Huck had to ask, "What's the matter? The rapids got you worried?"

"No, it's not that. I was just wondering if maybe the old-timer was pulling your leg. Maybe they're not so bad."

Huck was thoughtful for a moment. "I don't know how rough they'll be, but I did ask if anyone had ever made it through, and he said, 'Sure, but more didn't than did.' So I figure if others can do it without being smashed up and drowned, then we can too. Now let's get her loaded and get going."

With Molly on board, Huck pushed the raft out into the lake and climbed on. They had made a crude paddle and now, with Huck working the swing arm, Molly paddling for all she was worth, and the sail doing its part, they made their way north to the Yukon River. Once on the Yukon, they flowed north at a leisurely rate of five miles an hour.

Six days after leaving Lake Bennett, they heard rushing water ahead. The sound was so fierce that they made for the shore, left the raft tied to a tree, and walked along the river until they came to Miles Canyon. They were astonished at what they saw. The river funneled into a narrow gorge. Its precipitous walls appeared to touch the sky. Most notably there was no shore upon which to land if things went wrong. The rapids were the devil incarnate; no raft could make that passage.

"Huck, I sure don't look forward to packing our outfit the rest of the way, but I can't see how we can get through in one piece."

Huck didn't say anything right away. He stood looking at the raging water like he was studying it . . . which made Molly a little nervous. Finally he turned and said, "Let's make camp and give this some thought."

"What's there to think about? If we go into that canyon, we'll be smashed into one of those rock walls."

"Just the same, Molly, let's make camp."

Molly shrugged and started for the raft. She had taken only a few steps when she noticed that Huck was not following her. He was still looking at the river as though mesmerized. She left him where he was and set up camp herself. When she had finished and Huck still hadn't appeared, she went looking for him. He wasn't where she had left him, so she started to shout his name, but then realized she was being foolish. He couldn't hear her over the water's roar. Shrugging her shoulders, she went back to camp and built a fire. The coffee was just about ready when Huck walked up.

"Where you been? I couldn't find you."

"I went up to the rim of the canyon so I could get a good look-see at the whole shebang. And I'll tell you something, Molly. I think we *can* make it.

"Hey, that coffee smells mighty good, how about a cup?"

After pouring him a cup, Molly asked Huck to explain himself.

"I watched the flow of the river. It will be a stiff gallop and, of course, we'll have to stay dead center, but I think we can do it by using the swing arm as a rudder."

"What about the portage trail?"

"We *could* portage our supplies in lots, but the raft will still have to negotiate the rapids no matter what. It will save us a lot of hiking if we keep everything together. But you can wait for me on the other side while I bring the raft through."

Molly slowly shook her head and said, "Huck Finn, if you ain't the livin' end-all. But you're my man and I'll be proud to go down those rapids with you, even though I don't think we have a chance in hell."

Huck smiled and kissed Molly. "We should probably eat something. If we're gonna drown, I don't want to do it on an empty stomach."

After they had eaten, Huck went out to find an appropriate sapling to use as a fending-off pole. He found what he wanted, cut it down, and cleaned off its small branches. It measured nine feet long and four inches thick at the base, three at the top. Huck would do the steering because it would take a lot of strength to hold the swing arm while fighting the rapids. Molly would be ready and waiting with the pole if needed. They still had a few hours of daylight left, so they decided to go for broke before they regained their sanity and scrapped the whole thing.

With Molly on the raft, Huck walked it out until he was waist deep. Saying a silent prayer, he pushed off and climbed on board. The current took them downriver at an easy pace for a while, but when their speed picked up, Huck steered right for the middle of the funnel. As they neared it, the raft started rocking to and forth. Then they hit the mouth of the gorge and it got dark real quick. The sun was too low in the sky to shed light over the high cliffs. In twilight, they entered Miles Canyon.

Molly was standing, but within seconds she was sitting on her backside—thrown there by the turbulence of the river. She tried to stand up, but could not gain purchase, so she stayed down on her knees, one hand embracing the pole and the other gripping the rope used to lash the logs together. They were now thoroughly drenched, and there was no use in trying to converse with each other; the fury of the maelstrom precluded all conversation.

Just then they fell into a valley of water and it looked like they would go straight down to the bottom of the river, but they rebounded and the raft flew into the air. Molly, if she had not had a firm grip, would have been lost for sure. When they were again up on an even keel, the raft was turned sideways. Huck worked the swing arm in a futile attempt to get them straightened out, but they hit another valley and the resultant mayhem spun them in a half circle. Now they were heading at an alarming rate of speed for the south rock face—backwards!

There was nothing Huck could do. But Molly wanted to go down fighting. Somehow she had managed to hold on to the pole through the tempest. She ran to the back where Huck stood, took a stance with her feet wide apart and watched the wall of rock rush right at them. At the last possible moment, when they were less than three feet from destruction, Molly extended the pole and pushed off. The pole broke in half, but her effort was enough to get the raft caught in another current that pulled them back to the middle of the river.

By then, they were pointed in the right direction and in calm waters. Molly had a big smile on her face. Huck steered them to the bank, jumped off and, pushed the raft onto the shore, wedging it into the sand.

They looked like two drowned rats, but they were alive. Molly started to get off the raft, but Huck told her to wait a minute. He went to the tipi and retrieved one of his bottles.

"I don't know about you, partner, but I sure could use a drink."

Shaking the water from her hair, Molly replied, "You and me both, Huck!"

That night, rather than make camp, they stayed on the raft and slept the sleep of the just.

Ten

Wanting to get the rapids behind them, they took off early the next morning and passed through the relatively calm Squaw Rapids without incident. Then, shortly before noon, they came to White Horse and decided to keep going—no studying the lay of the land, no overthinking the prospects for success. They'd either sleep in their tent that night—or on the bottom of the Yukon. Either way, they had to put White Horse behind them.

It's called White Horse for a reason. The rapids also funneled like Miles Canyon, but instead of rock walls, there were large boulders along the bottom that stuck up out of the river, some of them as high as ten feet into the air. They pushed the water to the center, agitating it into a white froth. That's the mane of the horse. If they were to navigate White Horse Rapids, they would have to ride its mane or be smashed against the rocks on either side.

They entered White Horse on an even keel, both of them holding onto the swing arm. Right away things started to go awry. Within seconds of hitting the mane, the raft turned sideways and headed for a massive boulder. They bounced off with only minor damage. By then, they had come to the realization that there would be no controlling her until they were on the other side of the torrents. They still held on to the swing arm, but only to keep from being pitched into the water. A swirling whirlpool drew them to an area between two groups of enormous boulders. They circled once, they circled twice; on the third go-round, somehow, together, they managed to steer out of it and back onto the mane where the river took a hard right. A few seconds later, the raft plunged nine feet straight down and then rebounded twelve feet into the air. They were at the mercy of the river and Huck thought that this might be it for him and Molly. He leaned over and kissed her cheek. "I'm sorry I brought you here," he shouted over the water's roar.

Molly gripped his arm—her face a pale white—and shook her head, wordlessly telling him she was happy to be with him no matter what.

By the grace of God, they hit no more boulders. And three minutes and forty-eight seconds after entering White Horse Rapids—an eternity—they were out of its clutches and gently floating down the Yukon.

They lessened their grip on the swing-arm and hugged each other. Huck swept the wet, matted hair out of Molly's eyes and cupped her face in his hands. He did not kiss her. He did not say anything. There was nothing to be said. Instead, he looked into her green eyes for a long minute. Molly nodded, then buried her face in his neck and hugged him as tight as her depleted strength would allow. They both were very happy to be alive.

Thirty or so miles later, they entered Lake Lebarge and passed through without running into any of the foul weather the lake region was known for. Perhaps the allotment of rain for that area had been used up the previous week.

Still four hundred miles to go.

The scenery along the river was majestic: tree-covered banks on both sides, low hills behind the trees rolled gently outward, toward snowcapped mountains off in the distance. There were numerous sandbars. The raft went aground at least four times a day. The many islands that inhabited the river were easier to circumvent. There were places where the river ran faster, cutting into the soil of the tall banks and carrying it away downriver, coloring the water a muddy-brown. Trees toppled in and became a hazard to be avoided. In an effort to escape the mosquitoes, they stayed on the river as much as possible, taking turns sleeping and steering the raft.

Just before dark, nineteen days after White Horse, they came to a bend in the river that revealed the town of Forty Mile. And just in time. The temperature had dropped almost thirty degrees since they had left Lake Bennett. It was getting mighty cold out.

They jumped off waist-deep into icy brown water and pushed the raft onto the sand, making sure she was secure. They retrieved a change of clothing and went up the steep incline, headed for town.

Forty Mile was a fair-sized burg. There were numerous buildings, mostly log cabins, but not many people about.

The first establishment they came to was the Red Dog Saloon, and without hesitation, they went inside. Huck ordered a bottle of rye from the barkeep and asked for the use of a room where they could change out of their wet clothes.

"Privy's way out back," was the barkeep's belligerent answer.

Huck looked hard at the man for a moment and it looked like there might be a little trouble until Molly touched his arm. He smiled, and instead of doing what he was about to do a moment before, he said through clenched teeth, "Thanks, friend." Then to Molly, he suggested she get into some dry clothes. "I'll wait here. I want to sample this here rye first."

By the time Molly returned, Huck had put a good dent in the bottle and was in a considerably better frame of mind. She told him that the privy was his anytime he wanted it, but Huck was happy imbibing his whiskey. "I'm dry enough. Standing here next to the stove has done the job." Adding, as he hoisted his glass in a salute, "Well, Molly, the first leg of our adventure is over."

Adventure was all well and good, but at that moment, the only thing Molly could think about was food.

"That's real nice, Huck. But how about we go in for a little adventure concerning two thick steaks?"

"Sure, Molly. Anything you want."

Getting the barkeep's attention, he asked for two steaks with all the fixin's.

"All we got are caribou steaks."

"A steak is a steak, my good man."

The bartender nodded and plodded off to his kitchen.

Huck was not in the mood to eat by the time the steaks were placed on the table—he was too busy drinking. As Molly tore into hers, Huck looked about the room and observed that the clientele was rather sparse. The place was downright empty. The gaming tables were shut down and besides Molly and him, there were only three other patrons scattered about the room. He mentioned this curiosity to Molly. "It's dark out; you'd think some of the people in this one-horse town would be flocking in for the gay nightlife."

Just then the door flew open and an old-timer walked into the room, bringing a sweep of cold air in with him. To no one in particular, he declared, "It's gonna snow tonight, I can feel it in my bones. Getting mighty chilly out there." After his grand pronouncement, the old-timer shuffled to the bar and ordered a whiskey.

The barkeep, while continuing to run a rag around the glass he was wiping, gave out with words instead of whiskey. "You know the boss said no more credit until your bill's paid. Sorry, White Water."

Huck overheard the exchange and winked at Molly before calling out, "Hey, White Water, join us for a drink?"

At the mention of his name, the man turned and squinted in their direction. "You speaking to me, stranger?"

"I sure am—if your name's White Water."

The man walked over to the table and stuck out his hand. "I don't reckon I know you, but the name's William Cage. I'm called White Water Bill because I was the first white man to go through Miles Canyon *and* the White Horse. Leastwise the first man to make it through in one piece."

Huck introduced himself and shook the man's hand. Indicating Molly, he said, "This here is Molly Lee McMasters. We've just come down the Yukon and did the rapids ourselves."

White Water looked impressed, but made no comment. Instead, he secured a glass from the frowning barman and took a seat at the table. Once his glass had been filled, he made an observation with reference to the barkeep. "That fella is the most unpleasant man I know. I do believe he has a permanent toothache."

They talked around things for a while until Huck asked where all the town folk were. White Water threw back his head and let out with a prodigious laugh. When the laughing had subsided a bit, he said, "Ain't you heard?"

"Heard what?"

"About the supposed find out on Rabbit Creek! That's why the town's empty. All them suckers are out chasing gold. When George Carmack come in with a nugget as big as his thumb and filed a claim, this town was as hot as a whorehouse on nickel night." He paused for a moment while he helped himself to a good healthy shot of Huck's whiskey. Then he continued, "George Carmack is also known as 'Lyin' George.' I put no stock in anything he says. But the rest of the fools believed him. Hell, the owner of this saloon owns a sawmill. He dismantled it and hauled the whole shebang down to where the Tr'ondëk meets the Yukon. Says he's gonna build himself a whole new town. He plans on selling lots and getting rich. You had to pass the place on your way here. It's up river, about thirty-five . . . forty miles."

"Yeah, we saw activity on the eastern side back around there. But it looked like a sandbar or a marsh with only a few tents on it. We wanted to make Forty Mile before dark, so we passed it by," said Huck.

White Water shook his head in dismay. "That's it." As an afterthought, he added, "The folly of some men!"

Huck looked at Molly, "What do you think? Do you wanna backtrack and see what's going on down there?"

She responded with a smile and a wink. "I've followed you this far. Might as well go the whole hog. But if you take me someplace that I'm not happy about, believe me, I'll let you know right fast."

"Mind me asking you folks what it is you're looking for? Is it gold? Because if it is, you'd be better off going on up to Circle City," suggested White Water as he helped himself to his hosts' whiskey.

Huck thought he better pour himself and Molly a shot before White Water emptied the bottle. Having done so, he addressed the man's query. "We don't rightly know what we're after. This is a new land, and that's what pulled us up here. If we can be at the start of a new town, then that might be interesting. We thought we might do a little panning for gold, but that's not why we ventured two thousand miles. Anyway, you can't do much panning when the creeks are frozen over."

White Water nodded his head and agreed with Huck that any panning for gold would have to wait until spring. He then emptied the bottle into his glass, swallowed the contents, and let out with a deep sigh; he stood up on wobbly legs and said, "That was mighty fine whiskey. I do thank you folks for the company and the drinks. Now if you'll excuse me, I have to make it to my digs ere it starts to snow."

Molly said that it had been an honor to meet him, and Huck shook his hand. Then they were alone at the table with an empty bottle of whiskey between them. Molly smiled at Huck and said, "I thought that *you* could put it away. That little man must have a hollow leg."

The bartender had overheard Molly and without being asked, joined the conversation. "He's here every night cadging drinks. I should have thrown him out when he first came in."

That really got Huck's hackles up. "Let me ask you something. What is it that makes you so ornery? It was our whiskey and we enjoyed his company. But you, on the other hand . . . you're wearin' a mite thin on me, mister."

The man behind the bar put down the newspaper he had been reading, and looked right at Huck for a few ticks. Finally he smiled, reached for an unopened bottle and a glass, and walked around the bar.

"Mind if I buy you and your lady a drink?"

"We don't mind at all. Sit down. The name's Huck Finn and this is Molly Lee McMasters."

"Glad to meet ya. I'm Martin O'Conner. And I must apologize for my manner this evening." Holding up the bottle, he said, "This is the best in the house." He then proceeded to fill the three glasses. Hefting his glass, he toasted Molly and Huck. "Here's to whatever it is you're looking for."

The three of them clinked glasses and leaned back in their chairs, sipping their whiskey. At length, O'Conner cleared his throat and started in with an explanation. "I'm not really a bad sort. Hell, I used to slip White Water a drink every now and then when he couldn't afford the tariff. But then I got caught doing so and was warned that I'd lose my job if I did it again. What's got me angry is the fact that everyone is down on Rabbit Creek striking it rich while I rot up here."

Having gotten out what he wanted to say, he downed his whiskey and refilled his glass.

Molly wanted to know: "How come you're not down there getting yours?"

"I ain't got an outfit and I can't afford one. If I went, I'd be scratching at the frozen earth with my bare hands."

Huck interjected with: "According to White Water, the whole thing is a rigamarole anyway."

"No, it's not. I've seen Carmack's nuggets. He brought his poke in here before he even filed his claim. He couldn't wait to flaunt those things around."

By then the last of the few patrons had departed. Molly and Huck sat at the table and drank very good whiskey with a very amiable Martin O'Conner in a very empty saloon. When the subject came up about where Huck and Molly were going to sleep that night, Huck said, "Reckon we'll pitch the tent and get the stove going. At least if it snows, there won't be no damn mosquitoes."

O'Conner had another idea. "There's a room upstairs. It's the boss', but he won't be using it tonight. He's down at his new town, he won't mind. And there's a small stove in there."

Molly, thinking how nice it would be to sleep in a bed once again, was the first to speak. "Thank you, Mister O'Conner. That is very nice of you. Huck and I would be happy to take you up on your generous offer. Wouldn't we, Huck?"

Huck was busy filling his glass and was thinking on something, so he heard only part of what O'Conner had said and just the last part of Molly's statement. He knew from the tone of her voice that he too would have to be for whatever it was she was asking—or else. So he said the only thing a sane man could say, "Sure, Molly. We sure would."

Molly knew he didn't know what he was agreeing to, but patted his arm and smiled at him just the same.

When Huck had his glass in hand and had swallowed a fair amount of whiskey, he asked about the new town. He was kind of intrigued with the concept. It opened up a whole new world of possibilities.

"So . . . tell me, Martin. What's the deal with the town? When we passed by, there were only a few tents on the sandbar and one half-completed building."

"Well, it's a bit more than a sandbar. Mister Ladue got him 160 acres from the Canadian government and it's his just as long as he develops it. His plan is to make money any way he can. He'll sell business lots to the men who will flock in when word of the strike gets out. Then he'll sell them lumber from his sawmill to build their places of business. Their workers will buy liquor from him. When the miners come in from the creeks with their pokes full, they'll find games of chance in his saloon and they'll be drinking his liquor while they play. And the men who run those games will pay a hefty price to have a gaming concession in his place. As soon as he has his saloon built, he's gonna dismantle this place and bring the furnishings down to his town. The lumber, he'll sell. No doubt he'll get a damn good price for it." All those words gave O'Conner a bit of a thirst. It was a damn good thing he had a half-filled bottle of good hooch in front of him.

Huck wasn't thinking about drinking; he was thinking about what he had just heard. Maybe this is what he was looking for. He and Molly would definitely have to go and have a look into Ladue's new town. *There just might be something in that neck of the woods that will interest an ex-lawman and a cattle baroness.*

Molly was just about to say something to bring Huck out of his reverie when the front door crashed open and a large man filled the doorway. He wore the kind of fur skins that Indians wore at that time of year. His beard was long and dark with a few strands of gray throughout. He had the hood of his parka up covering his head, but his long braided hair was outside, falling over his shoulders.

Molly, Huck, and O'Conner turned at the same time and looked toward the apparition. But only O'Conner said anything.

"Well, if it ain't ol' George Carmack hisself!"

Eleven

The big man stomped his boots to shake off the snow and removed his parka, placing it over the back of a nearby chair.

"Howdy, Martin. It just started to snow and it's getting a mite cold out there. Got anything to warm the insides of a weary wanderer?"

"Sure. Come on over, I want you to meet some nice folks."

Carmack walked over, nodded to Huck, and smiled at Molly. When he was seated at the table, O'Conner did the honors.

"George, this here is Huck Finn and his lady friend, Molly . . . Molly . . . I'm sorry, ma'am, but I've forgotten your last name."

Molly stuck out her hand to Carmack and said, "You just call me Molly. And this big fella sitting next to me, you just call him Huck. We're pleased to meet you."

"The pleasure's all mine, ma'am. Now, Martin, you think I can get that drink you offered a while back?"

"You're gonna need a glass, but I'll get it for you, seeing as how you're all settled in and such."

When Carmack's glass had been filled, O'Conner made sure everyone else's glass was in the same shape. There was no talk while Carmack warmed up by getting a few belts in him. When his white cheeks started to turn a little pinkish, they knew he was on his way to thawing out. That's when Molly broached a question.

"We've been hearing a lot about you, Mister Carmack. Is it true that you have found the Bonanza Gold?"

In way of an answer, Carmack reached inside his coat and pulled out a leather pouch—a rather large leather pouch. He delicately untied the strings and then, with a dazzling smile that would have given the midnight sun a run for its money, George Carmack emptied the contents onto the table.

Now, Huck and Molly were well-off, each in their own way. They had no desire for further riches. They had enough to last them for the rest of their lives . . . and then some. However, the sight of those nuggets in the dim light, lying on an old and scarred wooden table, took their collective breath away. For Carmack had tossed down a pound of pure gold onto the table, all of it in large, outsized nuggets. It was a sight very few men had ever seen—and even fewer women.

Carmack noticed the impression his little show had made on his new acquaintances and smiled even more broadly, if that were possible. "You know, Miss Molly, I like how you called it the Bonanza Gold. I think I'll rename Rabbit Creek, Bonanza Creek. It sounds a bit more dignified."

O'Conner sat with his mouth agape. When he found the wherewithal to close his mouth, he said, "George, those are a lot bigger than the ones you brought in last time."

"I picked them outta the creek when I got back to the claim. I know they're impressive. That's why I haul them around . . . for the fun of it. But when I go back, the real fun begins. We gotta dig down to bedrock to hit pay dirt. It's gonna be a long winter."

"Who's watching your claim?" asked Molly.

"My partners are looking after things. I needed some tools; we're building us a cabin at the creek. That reminds me, Martin. Joe asked me to tell you he'd be up here in two or three days to dismantle the saloon. He says you're to have everything packed up and ready to go."

"Can't be soon enough for me," said Martin O'Conner. "Things around here are deader than Kelsey's nuts. If it wasn't for Huck and Molly showing up tonight, I would have gone crazy. It's bad enough missing out on the strike of a lifetime, but to stand around all day wiping glasses and *not* selling any liquor is a little more than I can stand."

Carmack poured himself another shot and looked thoughtful for a moment. Then he slammed his hand down on the table, startling the other three members of the conclave. "I got it! It's been bothering me since I first sat down. That name . . . Huck Finn . . . I know you! We've never met, but I know all about you. Hell, you were my hero when I was a boy."

Huck sighed and his eyes flicked to Molly. He was asking for help. But none would be forthcoming from that quarter. Molly wanted to see how Huck would play it. So, with an impish, woman's smile, she innocently asked Carmack to explain himself.

"When I was a boy, I tended sheep. It was a lonely business, out by myself all day long. To pass the time, I read a lot. I'd read anything I could get my hands on. But where we lived, there weren't that many books. However, I had a friend whose father bought those dime novels that were popular at the time. And when they were through with 'em, they'd give 'em to me. How I loved those stories! There was Kit Carson, Wild Bill Hickok, and Bill Cody, but my favorite was Huck Finn. Those other fellas was alright, but Mister Finn was the toughest of 'em all."

Molly looked over to Huck. He might have been blushing, but it was hard to tell through the beard he had grown since coming to Alaska.

Carmack, after quenching his thirst, went on. "Tell me, Mister Finn, was it really thirty men you bested when you went after the Cantry Gang?"

Huck threw a quick look to Molly that said, *Thanks a lot.* To Carmack he said, "Those stories were highly exaggerated. First of all, Cantry did not have a gang. He was a rancher. He did have a few hired guns, but I had a lot of help in keeping him in line."

"I'd say you kept him in line. You killed him and all his gunslingers too!"

There was no use in even trying. Every time this sort of thing came up, Huck liked to think of Ned Buntline—the man who wrote those books—as roasting in hell. In an effort to change the subject, Huck asked Carmack what he was going to do now that the creeks were freezing up. "I don't reckon you'll be plucking too many nuggets out of your creek for a while."

"You're right about that, Mister Finn."

"Please, call me Huck."

"Alright, Huck. Are you familiar with placer mining?"

"Can't rightly say that I am."

"It just means that we scratch the surface for gold. We dig down to bedrock, that's where we hit pay dirt. Gold's heavy, it sinks through the dirt until it hits bedrock and then it can't go any farther."

"How deep to the bedrock?"

"Anywhere from ten to twenty feet if you're lucky. Some places, maybe a little deeper."

"Okay, last question. How do you dig when the earth is frozen solid?"

"A good question and one most *chekekos* don't usually ask. We burn a fire throughout the night. Come morning, we move the embers out of the way and dig. We dig until we hit frozen ground and then we build another fire. As we dig, we are constantly looking for gold in the dirt. If we find any, then we start to "drift." By that I mean we dig horizontally. Every shovelful is put into a bucket and emptied onto one of two piles. One is the muck pile. That's the dirt we've taken out before we found traces of gold and started drifting. The other is the pay dirt pile, dirt we've taken out while drifting. We do this all winter long—it's called the "winter dump." Once the creeks are flowing again, we make our sluice boxes and sift out the gold from the winter dump. Until spring comes around, you never know if you are a rich man or if you wasted an entire winter at back-breaking labor for a few ounces of gold."

Carmack finished his whiskey and collected his nuggets. He tossed a medium-sized nugget to O'Conner and said, "That's for you. I'll be sleeping by the stove tonight. But I'd like something to eat before I turn in."

"Thanks. Just let me know when you're ready and I'll rustle ya up something."

Carmack turned to Huck and Molly. "I'd be pleased, if you're ever down my way, if you would stop in at my claim. My wife would enjoy some female company and I can show you how placer mining works."

Huck filled everyone's glass. "Funny you should mention that. Molly and me were planning on heading down that way tomorrow."

"How are you getting there?" asked Carmack.

"We got a raft," answered Huck.

"It would be easier going against the river in a canoe. I've got one at my cabin not doing anyone any good. It's yours if you want it. Why not come with me tomorrow? We'll get the canoe and what I need, then we can be on our way down to Dawson City."

"Dawson City?" inquired O'Conner.

"Reckon I didn't mention it, but Ladue has named his town Dawson City. It's named for that Canadian surveyor that came through here a while back. We all reckon he's trying to get in good with the Canadian government. You know how they feel about Americans coming in here and taking over."

Molly had to ask, "You mean he's from the States? Ladue sounds French Canadian."

Carmack laughed, "Ol' Joe Ladue is from New York and he's more American than William Jennings Bryan himself!"

It was getting late, the bottle was getting low; it was time to bed down.

Huck and Molly went upstairs after retrieving a few items from the raft. O'Conner went into the kitchen to prepare a caribou steak for Carmack. And as for George Washington Carmack, he sat in an empty saloon in the soon-to-be ghost town of Forty Mile and sipped good whiskey, thinking on how he would spend his first million dollars.

They got an early start the next morning. The raft was left where it was and the three of them—Carmack, Huck, and Molly—used Carmack's canoe to get to his cabin. They retrieved the canoe and Carmack's tools and were back at Forty Mile while the late autumn sun was still trying to get a foothold in the sky.

Carmack took some of Huck and Molly's outfit in his canoe and they shoved off for Joe Ladue's new town. It was hard paddling up river, but they were making about three miles every hour. At that rate, they would get to Dawson sometime after midnight.

After four hours, Carmack paddled over to the western bank. Huck and Molly followed. When the canoes were secured on the shore, Carmack said, "I figure we oughta rest here for a spell and eat something. I've got a pail of deer stew that O'Conner packed for me. We can heat it, eat it, and be on our way in an hour. You can't fight the river on an empty stomach."

Huck and Molly readily agreed. They were using muscles they hadn't used for a while; an hour's break was just what they needed. Molly walked to the tree line looking for an appropriate bush or tree to shield her while she emptied her bladder. Huck went the other way in search of firewood. Carmack unpacked the stew and eating utensils.

They had a fire going in no time and were making small talk while waiting for the stew to heat up when an Indian boy of about ten ran out of the woods. When he saw the three white people, he froze in his tracks. He was starting to turn to run back from whence he came when Carmack called out in the Tagish language. "Wait, Little Bear, it's me—Carmack." Then he said to his companions, "I know that boy. He's usually not so shy around white people."

When the boy heard Carmack, he turned back around, but did not approach. So George went to him and spoke a few words. Presently, he took the boy by the hand and walked him over to the fire.

"This is Little Bear," he said in way of an introduction. "He speaks no English. But he has a story I think you should hear. He tells me that two white men killed his father and his uncle just a little while ago. They would have killed him too, but he ran away."

Molly stood and went to the boy. At first, he shied away from her and tried to run, but Carmack had a firm grip on his hand. Carmack said something to the boy and he calmed down enough to allow Molly to put her arm around him. A moment later, Little Bear had his head buried in Molly's bosom, crying like the little boy that he was. Molly made soothing noises and rocked him to herself.

Carmack looked at Huck and said, "I knew his father, Big Eagle; he was a friend of mine. I think he and his brother were killed because of gold. I had given him a handful of nuggets for helping me cut down the trees to build my new cabin on the claim. He must have shown them to the wrong white men."

Huck's jaw tightened. "We're going out after them, right?"

"I wasn't going to ask, but I could use the help."

"What about the boy?"

"He'll show us where it happened and then we'll pick up their trail."

Huck and Carmack went to the canoes and retrieved their guns. Carmack owned a Greenfield Double-Barrel. Huck got his Colt .45 and Molly's Navy .36, their two Winchesters, and a sack of ammunition.

Huck didn't have to say or explain anything to Molly. He held out her Colt, she gave Little Bear a final hug, stood up and took the .36 from Huck and strapped it on. When she had her long gun in hand, she said, "I thought I came to be against killing, but sometimes some men need to die. Let's go and get them sons-of-bitches."

Twelve

Carmack led the way, guided by Little Bear. Shortly thereafter, they came upon a clearing where lay two corpses. Molly stayed with the boy while Huck and Carmack inspected the bodies. "It's them," said Carmack.

"Alright," asked Huck, "how do we do this? We can't take the boy with us, and someone should attend to the bodies before the animals get to 'em."

"Seeing as how you're the lawman, I thought you'd take charge."

"Ex-lawman."

"Excuse me?"

"I'm an ex-lawman," explained Huck. "Where's the boy's village, George?"

"About two miles to the north."

"Send him to tell his people what happened here and for them to come and take care of the bodies. Also, tell him that we are going to handle things. When the men who did this are dead, you'll bring word. Are you good with that?"

"Right as rain."

"And ask him what the men looked like."

After a few words with Little Bear, Carmack shook his head. "He says things happened too fast. When his father knew there was going to be trouble, he told Little Bear to run. He only got a glimpse of the men as he ran away, but says that it doesn't matter because all white men look alike to him."

"Okay, send him on his way and let's get going."

When Little Bear had left for his village, Huck, Molly, and Carmack started out after their prey. The murderers' trace headed in a mostly southerly direction, but then abruptly turned east. "They're heading for the river," observed Carmack. At the shoreline they came across the Indians' canoe. They also found boot prints and indentations in the sand that indicated a boat had recently been pushed off the sand and into the river.

"This complicates things," said Huck, "not knowing what they look like and all."

"I can identify the poke holding the nuggets, that's simple enough. I burned a "C" into the leather. When I see that poke, we'll have our men. The problem is, which way did they go—north or south?"

"If you had money to spend, which way would you go?" asked Huck.

"I'd head south. Forty Mile and Circle City are practically ghost towns. Everyone is down in Dawson."

"That's my thinking also," agreed Huck. "You reckon so too, Molly?"

"I reckon we should get to our canoes and get a move on. I want to catch up to those bastards while they still have the gold. It's Little Bear's and I aim to make sure he gets it back."

They got into Dawson City a little after 3:00 a.m. There were a few boats tied up at the new wharf, but there was no way of telling if one of them belonged to the men they were after. They were cold and tired, and they could have used a little something to eat, but they had a job to do first.

Huck took charge. "You know the town, George. Any saloons open this time of night?"

"There's only one saloon in the whole town, and that's Ladue's up on Front Street. Until he gets his new one built, he's operating out of a tent . . . and it's always open."

"Lead the way. Molly and I will follow."

In the early morning darkness, with a fine white mist hanging in the cold air, the three shadowy figures walked north along Front Street, passing only the occasional lost soul.

"Not much of a town," observed Molly.

"You just wait until word of my strike gets to the Outside. This town will rival even San Francisco. Hell, Frisco was a small, jerkwater town until the rush of '49," said Carmack with exuberant civic pride.

At the end of the street, they came to a large tent with wooden sides. It sat next to a half-completed wooden building. "This is Ladue's place. You've probably already guessed that from the noise," declared Carmack.

Huck made sure his Colt was loaded and loose in its holster; Molly did the same. Carmack checked that both barrels of his Greenfield held shells. Then they pushed their way through the flap that constituted the saloon's front door.

It was bright and warm inside, at least compared to the outside. It was most definitely a makeshift saloon, but it

105

had all the essentials of a drinking establishment. The bar was a long plank sitting on two pickle barrels. The back bar was made up of four upturned cracker barrels with an array of different whiskeys sitting upon them.

There were even a few games of chance. To the right, a man shook a pair of dice in his left hand and implored an unseen entity by the name of Little Joe to "Bring home the bacon!" before he made his roll onto a green-felt cloth. At a table close by, men asked to be "hit" in a serious game of blackjack. There was a roulette outfit and a poker layout on the other side of the room. Business was brisk, given the time of night. There were men seated at every table and seven men at the bar. All told, there were about twenty men in the place, not counting the bartender. There were no women present.

Carmack nodded toward the bar and said, "That's Ladue back there. Why don't we get a drink to take the chill off and do a little reconnoitering at the same time?"

"I want to get something straight among the three of us. I used to do this for a living. You two are amateurs. I don't want to have to worry about either one of you. If they're in here, I'll handle it. All I want from you two is to watch my back." Huck paused, and looked sternly from one to the other. "Do you understand?"

Carmack answered right away. "Sure, Huck. But let me ask you something. Are you going to try to take them alive?"

"I don't reckon Ladue has built himself a jail yet?"

"No, I don't reckon he has."

"And I don't think the Canadian government has gotten around to appointing a judge for this jurisdiction?"

"Hardly."

"Then, I'm going to kill them without hesitation if they even think of going for their guns."

"Whatever you say, Huck."

Huck eyed Molly for a full ten seconds before saying. "I ain't heard from you yet."

"I'll slap leather only if you're in trouble. But let's get this party started. I'm tired, cold, and hungry."

At the bar, Carmack introduced his friends to Ladue. After the drinks had been poured, Huck said, "We're looking for two men who would have come in together, about an hour or so back."

Ladue thought for a moment. "I don't keep a real close watch on the front door, but those two gents sitting at that table over in the far corner might fit your bill." The men he had indicated were young, in their early twenties. One was wearing a bowler hat; the other was bare-headed. They both looked like they had seen better days.

Huck hefted his glass. When it was empty, he held it out for a refill and asked, "I see they have a bottle on their table. Did they pay for it in gold?"

"Most men pay in gold. That's why I have this scale sitting on the bar."

Huck nodded. "I'm paying with paper. That all right?"

"Sure, as long as it's American paper."

"I'll settle up after I've talked to those two men. George, Molly, you stay here."

Huck walked over to the table with his drink in his left hand. "Howdy, gents. Kinda cold outside; mind if I sit here while I warm up my insides?"

Bowler Hat said, "Won't your friends over at the bar get lonely for you?"

"Them? I don't think so. They don't like to gamble. I'm trying to get up a poker game. You boys interested?"

Bowler Hat spoke again. "The only thing we're interested in is being left to ourselves."

"You don't leave much chicken on the bone, do you? You just say what you feel? Well, nothing wrong with that. I was only trying to be friendly. No offense." Huck made a motion like he was going to turn and go back to the bar. But instead, he dropped his glass onto the dirt floor, pulled his Colt, and pointed it at the two men. Molly appeared a second later, gun in hand.

Huck didn't think it was the time in get into an in-depth discussion with Molly about her, maybe for once, doing what she was told to do. Instead, he sighed deeply and shook his head. Then he addressed the two men. "This is what we're gonna do. You're gonna show me your pokes. And me and my lady friend here are gonna keep our guns on you while you do it. You boys okay with that?"

The whole place had quieted down. Everyone taking in what was going on at the table in the corner. By then, Carmack had ambled up, him and his shotgun, which for the time being was pointed at the floor.

"Is this a hold-up?" the one without a hat asked.

Huck sighed. "I don't want no talk from you. I want to see your poke . . . and your partner's. If they ain't out on the table in about five seconds, I'm gonna have this very nice lady who's standing next to me shoot you both. Then, just for the fun of it, the man with the large shotgun will blow both your heads off. He's got a barrel for each of ya."

Ladue had come around from behind the bar and was about to say something when Carmack cut him off. "Stay out of this, Joe. If we're wrong, we'll apologize and buy everyone a drink. But for now, we need you to go back and tend to your own business."

Ladue was about to interject that what went on in his bar *was* his business, but after seeing the look on Huck's face, he hesitated for only a moment before going back behind his bar.

Bowler Hat looked into Huck's eyes and saw Death staring back at him. So he shrugged and said, "Why not?" He reached into his coat pocket and threw a poke onto the table. Huck's eyes darted to Carmack. Carmack shook his head.

"Now it's your turn," Huck said to the other one.

"I'll be goddamned if I'll let you waltz in here and shove us around like this. You go to hell!"

Huck cocked his gun. Carmack raised his shotgun and pointed it dead at No Hat. Molly's gun was already cocked. Something in their eyes told No Hat he was a dead man unless he produced a poke—and very quickly. He pulled it out of his shirt pocket and tossed it onto the table next to his partner's. There was a large "C" burnt into the leather.

It was then that Bowler Hat went for his gun. Molly's gun coughed lead first. Followed by Huck's. Between them, they put a total of seven bullets into the two men. Carmack did not fire his Greenfield.

When the smoked cleared, Huck turned to the room and said, "They were murdering sons-of-bitches. Did they have any friends in here? If so, let's have it out now." No one said a word, so Huck called out to Ladue, "Set 'em up. Drinks are on me." There was a cheer and a rush to the bar.

Molly picked up the two pokes and handed them to Carmack, saying, "Please get these to Little Bear." Carmack accepted them with a nod. Huck looked at Molly and shook his head. "Do you think you can do just *one* thing that I ask of you?"

"Sure, Huck. Whatcha want?"

"Get us a bottle while I drag these two outside. We'll take over their table."

"I was just about to. *And* I'll clean up the blood from the table. How's that?"

"That's just great," said Huck while still shaking his head. "And George, would you please go and explain things to Ladue?"

Molly got a bottle and wiped down the table with a wet rag. Huck got rid of the bodies while George Carmack smoothed things over with Joe Ladue.

Sitting around the table, sipping their whiskey, the talk turned to what Huck and Molly were going to do next. "It's gonna be hard to top the first impression you made in this town," offered Carmack.

Huck had only one really important question he needed answered. "Do you think we can get anything to eat in this place?"

"I'll see what I can rustle up for ya. Be right back," said Carmack.

When they were alone, Huck started to chastise Molly for getting involved in the shooting, but then changed his mind. Instead, he leaned over and gave her a kiss—*smack*—right on the mouth.

Carmack returned with Ladue in tow. "Joe has sent someone to his place to get you some bacon and beans. That was all he could rustle up on short order. While we're waiting, he was wondering if he could buy us a drink and sit down for a while."

Huck shrugged. "It's his place and I seldom refuse a free shot of whiskey. How about you, Molly?"

"A man who offers to share his food with me, when I'm as hungry as I am now, can sit at my table anytime."

They drank Ladue's liquor until the bacon and beans were brought in, arriving with a loaf of freshly baked bread. "This bread is good," said Molly. "Who makes it for you?"

"I have a cook. When my saloon's finished, he'll be running the kitchen."

They made more small talk until Ladue broached the subject he had come to talk about. "That was pretty impressive how you handled those two men. George told me what they did, and I agree that they had it coming. I don't reckon there's much that scares you, Mister Finn."

"You call me Huck and I'll call you Joe. Okay?"

"Okay."

"Now, first of all, Joe, you saw the whole thing. I wasn't alone. Miss Molly here got more bullets into them than I did—I think. And George was right next to me with his Greenfield. It was three against two. Not much bravery involved with those odds."

When their plates were empty, Huck leaned back in his chair and pulled out his pipe. As he tapped down the tobacco, Ladue asked him if he'd like to be the town sheriff. "I used to read about you in those dime novels. I'm sure not everything was one hundred percent true. But even if only half of it was, then you're the man to keep the peace while I get my town up and running."

Huck looked at Molly and smiled. She smiled back with a smile that said, *Not now.* Huck nodded and turned to Ladue.

"If you don't mind, can we talk about it later? Molly and I are kinda tired, and the only thing we want to do at the moment is find a place to get some sleep."

Ladue stood up. "Come with me. I've got a room behind my new saloon that you can sleep in. It even has a stove. We're starting on the second floor tomorrow, or I should say today, but I'll tell my men to work quietly."

Huck wanted to know what Carmack was going to do.

"My claim is twelve miles up the Klondike. I'm heading back there now. Come out and I'll show you around. When you come to a fork in the river, bear left. That's Rabbit Creek, I mean Bonanza Creek. I'm two miles up."

After he had finished the liquor in his glass, he said in way of parting, "I'll put the portion of your outfit that's in my canoe into yours. Hope to see you soon. Goodnight Huck. Goodnight, Molly. Goodnight, Joe." Then George Carmack pushed through the flap, letting in a blast of cold air as he went out.

Huck knocked the tobacco in his pipe out onto the table and drained his glass. "You ready, Molly?"

"I've been ready."

Huck asked Ladue what was going to happen to the two bodies lying outside. "You just gonna let them freeze for the winter? I sure as hell don't want to be tripping over them as long as we're in town."

Ladue set Huck's mind at ease. "As soon as it's light out, I'll make sure they get buried. We have to start a town cemetery sooner or later. Now is as good a time as any."

The room had no furnishings, but, as promised, it did have a stove. While waiting for things to get warm, Huck went to the canoe and got their bedrolls and Molly laid them out on the floor. When they were reposed, Molly kissed Huck on the cheek, turned her back to him, and fell off to sleep in a matter of seconds. Huck followed her lead shortly thereafter.

Thirteen

"DAMN! I DROPPED THE HAMMER. I'LL HAVE TO GO DOWNSTAIRS AND GET IT. PLACE THAT BOARD OVER YONDER, I'LL NAIL HER DOWN AS SOON AS I GET BACK." Ladue might have asked his workers to tread quietly, but they either didn't hear him or they ignored the directive.

Huck opened his eyes to see Molly lying next to him wearing a bemused look. "What is all that noise?" she wanted to know.

"Sounds to me kinda like someone's building a second story onto a saloon," was Huck's conjecture. Molly leaned in and kissed him. "I can always count on you to tell me the obvious, but how about being useful in a different way? That stove needs to be lit before I'll get up off this nice hard floor."

Huck sighed heavily to indicate she was demanding of him a difficult task. But he threw off the blanket, made a dash for the stove, and fumbled around for a moment. "Okay, she's going. Are you gonna stay in that nice warm bed, such as it is, all day long?"

"How old are you, Huck?"

"What are you talking about?"

"My point is that you're old enough to know a woman needs some time alone in the morning. Why don't you get my pack out of the canoe? Then rustle up some water so that I can wash my face. If you were so gallant as to do all that for me, I'd love you forever."

"That's nice. And after I do all that, do you mind if I get a cup of coffee?"

Molly threw his boots at him—one at a time. "Now get about your business, mister. After you've brought me my things . . . and the water . . . you can have your coffee." Huck put on his boots and went out to do Molly's bidding.

A short while later, with her morning ablutions out of the way, Molly met up with Huck in Ladue's saloon. "How did I know that I would find you here?" Molly cynically asked as she sat down.

"Most likely because it's the only saloon in town," was Huck's helpful reply.

"Most likely, but can a lady get a cup of coffee in this place?"

"Most likely . . . *if* she asked a tall, good-lookin' hombre sitting in her vicinity to get it for her."

"If there was a tall, good-lookin' hombre sitting in my vicinity, I'd ask him. But seein' as how there's none around at the moment, how about *you* getting me one, Huck?"

"My pleasure, Molly."

They held the repartee and conversation to a minimum until Molly had finished her first cup. At the start of her second, she wanted to know what the plan was for the day.

"Ladue's not around, but he left word that we're to have anything we want. He must really be hankering for me to take on the sheriff's job. Anyway, I've ordered us some breakfast. Bacon sandwiches made with that bread you liked."

"No eggs?"

"No eggs."

"Once you've fed me, what then?"

"I thought we'd go up the Klondike and visit with George; see what all the excitement's about."

They off-loaded their outfit and stored it in the room they had occupied the previous night. Just as they were shoving off, Joe Ladue walked up.

"Morning, folks. Going up the Klondike?"

"Thought we might visit with George," informed Huck.

"Good idea. Freeze-up is late getting here this year, but it's coming. By the by, have you given any thought to my proposition?"

"I'm thinking on it. We'll talk when we get back."

"You know where to find me," said Ladue as he turned in the direction of his saloon.

They came to the fork that Carmack had mentioned. However, they could not traverse the creek because it was frozen solid. "Reckon creeks freeze up afore rivers do," observed Huck with a bit of disappointment in his voice.

Molly smiled and said, "A two-mile hike is just what the doctor ordered. It's a nice day and a little walk won't hurt you none."

Ten and a half claims made up a mile. They passed twenty claims on the way to Carmack's and at each, men were furiously digging into the ground or building fires to

116

melt the gravel and dirt so that they *could* dig furiously into the ground.

"Looks like a lot of work," observed Huck.

"Don't you worry, Huck. Neither one of us is going to get into one of those holes. I don't know what we're going to be doing all winter long, but it certainly ain't gonna be something like that!" said Molly with authority.

As they rounded a small bend in the creek, they came face to face with a plank of wood nailed to a tree. In letters six inches tall, it read: ***Discovery #1***.

"Ahoy!" came the greeting from a little up-creek. They looked to see George Carmack walking their way, carrying an empty bucket in each hand and wearing a broad smile. "Glad you could make it. Come with me."

"What's that sign mean?" asked Huck.

"That's the name of my claim."

A moment later they were standing over Discovery #1's number one (and only) shaft; a windlass lay across its opening. George knelt down and attached the buckets to a hook and lowered away. "Heads up, Jim."

George explained. "Jim's down there. We take turns with the digging."

Molly went over and looked down the shaft. "How deep is it and why all the smoke?"

"We're down ten feet. The smoke is from the fires, it has nowhere to go. We can only melt a foot or so at a time, so there's always a fire when we're not digging."

"What about cave-ins?" Huck wanted to know.

"That's the only good thing about digging in frozen earth. The sides don't cave in."

George was busy. It was his job to haul up and empty the buckets once they were filled by Skookum Jim. Huck said that he and Molly were going to get out of his way and take a little walk up the creek. "Maybe we'll do a little explorin'."

"We'll be noonin' in a couple of hours; come back and we'll put on the feedbag. My wife is out visiting relatives, so you'll have to catch up with her at another time."

Huck and Molly waved good-bye, but George did not see them do so; he was vigorously hauling on the rope holding two buckets of muck. Pay dirt would come later.

They passed claim after claim, the miners all engaged in the same strenuous activity that occupied George Carmack and Keish, who was also known as Skookum Jim Mason.

Molly observed that, during the summertime, it must be a beautiful country. The last of the colorful flowers that carpet the hillsides in summer were just giving up the ghost to make way for the winter snow that would soon cover the landscape. "I can imagine what this place must look like when all the flowers are in full bloom."

Huck only grunted. It was hard walking along the creek. Where the surface ground was not completely frozen, they had to make their way through a thick layer of muck, sometimes as much as a foot in depth, though it didn't seem to faze Molly.

118

After twenty minutes of walking and slipping on stones, twenty minutes of pulling their boots out of the muck, and twenty minutes of Huck complaining every step of the way, the creek narrowed. Molly noticed a small hill on the other side. "Let's go over yonder and get a glimpse at the countryside," she lightly suggested. "And look at those bushes. There's a blueberry bush, and over yonder is a *huckleberry* bush with berries still on it! Let's pick some." Molly was in a playful frame of mind.

All Huck wanted to do was to find a tree to sit under, or a boulder to sit on, pull out his pipe, and contemplate the nature of life. But he knew he was not going to be allowed that pleasure, so he made a deal with Molly. "Don't point out any more huckleberry bushes to me, and I'll help you across the ice *and* climb your damn mountain." She saw the slight incline as a hill, but Huck saw it as a mountain.

Once the "summit" had been scaled, they saw a country of small hills and small creeks. It looked as though only Bonanza Creek was being worked. The others were sparse on population. A camp could be seen here and there, but for the most part, all the activity in the area lay on Carmack's creek.

Huck took Molly by the hand and tried to turn her around in anticipation of going back from whence they came. However, Molly was fixated on something in the distance. "Look at that solitary camp over yonder. I wonder what that man's story is."

"Me too," replied Huck in a fashion that conveyed he was anything *but* interested. "Are you ready to go?"

"Huck, have you no romance in your soul? I think we should go down to him. Perhaps he's lonely."

"I've got plenty of romance in my soul. What I'm lacking is grub in my stomach."

"Come on. We'll be back by the time George and Jim are ready to eat."

Molly did not wait for Huck to respond. She was halfway down the hill before he could catch up with her.

Walking up to the camp, they noticed something different. There was no frantic activity like at the other camps. What they beheld was a man sitting on a tree stump, calmly smoking a pipe, looking like he hadn't a care in the world.

Huck took the initiative. "Howdy. Mind if we sit for a spell? Things look mighty peaceful around here."

The man jumped up and said, "I sure don't mind. You're mighty welcome."

Molly picked out a nearby fallen log to sit on and Huck joined her. The man held out his hand to Huck. "The name's Jass Holloway. Glad to meet ya'all."

Huck shook his hand and introduced Molly and himself, then took out his pipe and filled it. When he had a good burn going, he asked, "Is this a claim or are you merely out camping?"

"It's a claim alright. In fact, I just made a deal to sell it. Got $6,000.00! Not bad for three months' work."

Molly jumped in with a question of her own. "I don't see a shaft or where you've done any placer mining. Why would anyone buy your claim when they could have their own to the north or south of here?"

Jass took a pull on his pipe and thought a long moment before answering. "I wouldn't want this to get around. Leastwise not until I've deeded over my claim. But you look like nice folks and the dust for the payment will be here in a few days, so I reckon there ain't no harm in telling you. The work was in the getting here and finding this place. I didn't come across it right off. All the claims on Rabbit Creek were taken. I thought for sure that I had lost out. But before I turned for home, I took a walk down this creek. You're sitting on Eldorado Creek. I named her and I reckon it's appropriate because I found her."

Molly leaned forward a mite, but Huck didn't seem interested one way or another.

"If a geezer was to claim next to me," Jass continued, "he might, or he might not, hit the motherlode. But there ain't no speculation on this five hundred feet of creek. Let me show you somethin'." He stood up, went into his tent for a minute, and came back holding two cans that had once contained sliced peaches.

"Look here at these nuggets. This part of the creek is just lousy with 'em. I walked the stream in both directions, a mile each way, and saw nothing like what's on this section!"

The cans held more than nuggets; they contained lump-gold. Some of it as big as a hen's egg. That got Huck's attention.

"You just found that on the creek bottom?"

"Yep."

"No mining for you?"

"I did a little skim digging. Just scratched the surface, but every shovelful was pay dirt. My pans were averaging forty dollars or more! And if you'll recollect, back in California, panning out a dollar was something to hoot and holler about."

Molly did not recollect anything about California, but she did want to know if his claim was so rich, then why was he selling out.

"Well, ma'am. That's simple. I've got all I need and I ain't been touched by the gold fever. When I heard tell about the strike, I knew if I could get here soon enough, I could get mine and get out fast. I only wanted enough to get me and my family back to the States and have enough left over for a stake. Now I've got it. This here—what's in the can—is worth a mite over $6,000.00, and with what I'm getting' for my claim, I'll be going back a rich man!"

"Where's your family?"

"We've got us a cabin up in Tanana Country; about four hundred miles northwest of here, as the crow flies. It's six hundred miles by trail. My missus and my boy are there holding down the fort. She's with child and I have to get back in sufficient time for the baby. My son is ten years old. He's big for his age, and he's taking care of his mother until I get back. But still, he's only a boy. I have to be there!"

Molly made no judgment, but she didn't think it wise to leave a woman alone when she was in that condition. Anything was liable to happen. Jass must have sensed her disapproval because he ventured, "In a couple of weeks, when the Yukon freezes, I'm heading back. I bought me a dog team and a good freight sled. I'll be back in plenty of time for the birth."

Things then became quiet. Huck refilled his pipe, Molly stretched and yawned. Jass got a faraway look in his eyes and—for him—all time stopped. He was back in his cabin. It was two-and-a-half months previous. Mid-September. He had just come inside and his wife wanted to know who he had been talking to. Their cabin was out of the way and sometimes they could go a long spell without seeing another soul.

"Who was that, Jass?"

"That was Beeson. He's on his way to the creek. Says he's gonna float down to the Yukon and then head south."

"You didn't invite him to stay over for dinner?"

"I sure enough did. But he's in an all fired-up hurry to get down to Forty Mile. Says word is going around that there's been the strike of a lifetime in that neck of the woods."

"Where's Jack?"

"He's doing a few miles with Beeson. You know how he likes Beeson's stories. I told him to be back here within the hour, so he can't go far."

"Dinner will be ready by the time he's back. Why don't you leave the firewood for later. Go and wash up. You can have a

pipe and converse with me while I peel the potatoes."

"My thoughts exactly. And a dram wouldn't hurt . . . I mean, cutting that firewood has sure worked up a mighty thirst within me."

His wife good-naturedly swiped at him with the cloth she was holding. "Now be gone with you, Mister Holloway. Go and wash up and leave your woman to her duties."

When Jass returned, he sat at the table and poured himself a short whiskey. After his pipe had been packed and lit, he sat back in his chair and reflected. "You know, Mae, if that strike is on the level and I can get there ahead of the stampeders, that could be our grubstake for getting back to the States and buying that apple orchard we're always talking about."

Mae said nothing. She was thinking. Yes, she desperately wanted to get back to the States. And yes, the only way that was going to happen was if they came into an unexpected windfall. Like maybe finding a gold mine. But there were other considerations. She was with child and she was afraid. The birth of their son, Jack, had been difficult. He had been turned to the side. If the doctor had not been there, she and the child may have died. The doctor had called Jass in and showed him how to overcome the problem if it ever happened again and there was no doctor around.

The baby would come sometime in February. Jass had to be there. He could not be off seeking a gold mine. And she was not feeling well enough to make the arduous trek down to Forty Mile.

Jass dropped the subject after he cottoned to the fact that Mae was not going to contribute to the conversation.

That night, while they lay in bed, it was Mae who broached the subject. "You know, if you were to get there early enough, you could stake a claim and then sell it. You could be back here before the baby is due to arrive. After the birth, when the thaw comes, we could catch the paddle wheeler to St. Michael and then a steamer down to Oregon."

Over the next two weeks, a plan was hatched and things taken care of. Jass chopped firewood as he never had before. Mae and Jack would need a three-month supply. When not chopping wood, he was out hunting. He could not leave his family without meat enough to last them while he was gone.

The plan entailed Jass getting to the area of the strike and filing a claim on a promising bit of real estate. Collect as

125

much gold as he could without doing any
mining. Then, when he had something to
show, sell the claim and get back home for
the birth of his son or daughter. In the
spring, the family Holloway would head
south and become apple farmers in the
State of Oregon.

With a start, Jass was brought back to the present. "What was that, ma'am? I'm sorry, I must have been daydreaming."

"I said, 'good-bye'; it was a pleasure meeting you, Mister Holloway. And we, Huck and me, wish you all the best."

"Thank you, ma'am."

"Come on, Huck. Let's see what George is serving for dinner."

Fourteen

As it turned out, George was not serving anything for dinner. He was down in the shaft shoveling away like there was no tomorrow. Skookum Jim introduced himself, but he too was busy with his one-man bucket brigade. Huck leaned over the hole and shouted down to George, "Molly and me gotta be moving on. We'll see you the next time you're in town."

The reply sounded more like a grunt to Molly's ears. However, Huck discerned from the bottom of the shaft, "You're on." They bid Jim a fare-thee-well and headed for their canoe. Once on the Klondike, Molly asked Huck if he was going to take the sheriff's job.

"I reckon so. Ladue tells me there are about two hundred people in and around Dawson. Most of them, by far, are men and most of them are out on the creeks. He supposes that the number will swell to a thousand by the end of winter. And after word gets to the Outside, the town will house 20,000 people or even more. He envisions saloons, whorehouses, hotels, and all sorts of businesses catering to the miners. He even sees an opera house in Dawson's future!"

Molly was in the front of the canoe. She stopped paddling to turn around and face Huck. And with a bit of sarcasm in her voice, she said, "An opera house? Imagine that."

"Don't you worry. We'll be gone long before then."

Huck went on: "Ladue said he'd give me two lots that we can build on or sell. We can camp in that room of his behind his new saloon for as long as we want with no rent, and any fines that I levy will go directly into my pocket."

"So there's no salary?"

"Not if you put it that way."

"Any thoughts of what *I* should be doing this winter? Maybe I could open the town's first whorehouse on one of those lots Ladue's giving you. And another thing. What if you have to lock someone up? This new town of his sure as hell has no jail, so are you planning on locking up the miscreants in our room?"

"Actually, I was planning on fining everyone for their crimes, short of murder that is." Then with a touch of mischief in his voice, Huck teased, "But if there were any women around, I'd go in with you on that whorehouse instead of taking the sheriff's job."

Molly jutted her jaw into the air and let out with a loud "Humph!"

After that, they made their way in silence . . . the only sound, the splash of the paddles as they came in contact with the frigid waters of the Klondike River.

Approaching Dawson's town wharf, Molly confessed, "I was only funnin' with you about being sheriff. The job will keep us warm and fed this winter, but you're gonna have a deputy if you want one or not. And she carries a Colt Navy .36."

Huck knew better than to argue the point.

Ladue and Huck hammered out the fine points of their agreement with a little assistance from Molly. She insisted that Ladue find her a bed from somewhere, and she wanted it understood that they would do their eating and drinking in his saloon . . . gratis. The bed was no problem. Ladue was going up to Forty Mile to dismantle and bring his old saloon down to Dawson—lock, stock, and barrel. Molly would have her choice of one of three beds. Ladue had no problem with meals three times a day for the two of them. However, he demurred about supplying unlimited whiskey. "Do you know what I have to pay to have that stuff hauled in here?"

In the end, it was agreed that Molly and Huck could drink Ladue's whiskey without paying the freight from 7:00 p.m. to 10 p.m. seven nights a week. But they were not allowed to "buy" drinks for others during that time period.

When they were back in their room, Molly laughed and said, "Your reputation as a drinking man must have preceded you, Mister Finn. Did you see the look on his face when you demanded unlimited whiskey twenty-four hours a day?"

"I only did that as a bargaining ploy."

"Sure you did, Huck."

Four days later, Molly had her bed and their life fell into somewhat of a routine. Huck had no authority outside of Dawson. If there was trouble on the creeks, the miners took care of it themselves, usually in a miners' court. Those courts could be quite harsh. Sometimes a man was hanged for the slightest transgression. But that was not Huck's concern. He spent the majority of his time in Ladue's new saloon. It was warm and there was always at least a poker game in progress that he could sit in on.

For the most part, there was little trouble. The few times a man got out of line, the name "Huck Finn" seemed to settle things down right quick. Huck had yet to levy a fine, but he made up for the lack of revenue by doing the majority of his drinking in Ladue's saloon between seven and ten—every night.

Molly had her work to do also. She figured her first job was to look out after Huck, but after seeing how he handled things on the rare occasions he found himself in a tight spot, she cast about for a secondary interest.

She sought out the few women in the vicinity and formed a sort of women's club. It had no walls or meeting place, but the members knew that if they needed help or support for something that men just wouldn't, or couldn't, understand, then their sisters would be there to lend a helping hand.

It looked like they were all set. They were going to make it through a Yukon winter in relative comfort and be in on the ground floor as a town—no, a city—grew out of the wilderness.

Then it happened.

It was just after 11:00 a.m. on a cold Tuesday morning. It hadn't snowed yet, but things looked to be headed in that direction. The door to Ladue's newly built saloon burst open and four men placed a squirming bundle, wrapped in a blanket, on the roulette table, after removing the wheel.

"Someone send for Doc! He's at Claim #9 South up on the Bonanza. Tell him to bring his tools!" one of the men yelled. The rest of the occupants of the room got up from their tables or left the bar to crowd around the roulette table.

Huck was back in the kitchen discussing the options for his and Molly's noon meal when the commotion commenced. "I better see what's going on. The moose steaks with potatoes will do us fine. See you in about an hour."

Exiting the kitchen, Huck asked the throng of men what was going on. They had been crowded around the roulette table, but as Huck approached, they took a step or two back—clearing a path for the sheriff. Huck walked up and looked down into the eyes of a frightened Jass Holloway.

Jass was obviously in great pain. His teeth were clenched and his eyes silently begged for help. Huck yelled over his shoulder for someone to get a bottle of whiskey and bring it to him quickly. When he had it in hand, he lifted Jass' head just enough so that he would not choke. "Don't talk. Just get some of this in ya. Drink as much as you can." As he held the bottle to Jass' lips, he again asked—to the crowd in general—"Tell me what happened."

From across the table, a man spoke up. "If you'd move the blanket away from his legs, you'd see what happened. He was helping me and my partners cut trees for our cabin. He was through the tree, just inches to go, and he took a step back to be out of the way when it fell. But it didn't fall. It should have, but it didn't. That damn tree just stood there! So Jass went up and gave it a shove. That did the trick. But when it hit the ground, it took a bounce and, because of the incline, it slammed into Jass' right leg, smashing it all to hell."

Huck placed the bottle in the suffering man's hand and said, "You take charge of this." When Jass had a firm grip, Huck lifted the blanket. It was hard to see the degree of damage. The pants were soaked in blood that was already crusting and turning brown. Huck had heard the call to send for Doc. He wasn't sure if the man was a real doctor or a veterinarian or what. *Whatever he is, he'll probably know more about what to do than me*, thought Huck Finn while he pondered whether he should cut away the pant leg or not.

Before he could make a decision, Molly was there at his side. "I just heard about it. How is he?"

"Ask him yourself. I'm gonna expose the damage so we'll know what we're dealing with. I have to get a knife from the kitchen. You handle Jass."

Huck took two steps, but then stopped. He turned back around and made a declaration. "You men there. I want you to go back to what you were doing. For those of you who don't know me, I'm the law in this town. The men who brought him in, you stay close by, the rest of you keep clear of that table." He didn't wait to see if his directives were obeyed; they usually were.

Molly mopped the wounded man's brow and spoke softly, "How did you get yourself into such a fix?"

"I had time to wait for the river to freeze up, so I volunteered to help them cut trees for their cabin."

"Whose cabin?"

"The men who bought my claim. They're the ones who carried me into town. They're hail-fellows." After the exertion of doing all that talking, Jass laid his head back and tried not to cry out from the pain.

Huck walked up carrying a large knife, the kind used for cutting moose steaks. He looked at Molly and nodded.

To Jass he said, "I want you to put a real dent in that bottle, and that's the law talking. Now, I'm gonna be as gentle as I can, but I've gotta put a slice up your pant leg."

He waited while Jass took a few swigs. Then he said, "Molly, be ready to hold him if you have to. Jass, you lay back and look up at the ceiling." Huck gingerly took the hem of the right pants leg and slipped the knife beneath it. Slowly, ever so slowly, he cut up to the knee. Then, he exhaled deeply. Starting at about three inches below the knee, the leg was thoroughly destroyed. The bones had been pulverized.

Molly gasped and involuntarily turned her head. That got Jass interested. He was trying to look down at his damaged leg when Huck said, "I told you to keep hitting that bottle. I'll attend to what's going on down here."

Thankfully, before Huck had to do anything else, the door opened and three men entered. Joe Ladue, Martin O'Conner, and a stranger whom Huck did not know.

They approached the table and, without acknowledging Huck or Molly, they assessed the situation. After a moment, Ladue looked at Huck and said, "This is Doc. Why not leave him with his patient? Come over to the bar and I'll buy you a drink. You too, Molly."

Molly said that she was staying with Jass. Then the man known as Doc spoke for the first time, "That will be fine. Always a pleasure to have a pretty nurse help out. You talk to him and keep his mind occupied while I do my examination. The rest of you clear out. I don't want anyone within ten feet of this table. Now scat!"

At the bar, Ladue was filled in on how it happened and who the wounded man was.

A few minutes later, Doc came over. "How 'bout a drink, Ladue? I've got my work cut out for me. This ain't gonna be pretty."

"Sure, Doc. Here's the bottle, help yourself. I'll get you a glass."

When Doc had gotten outside of a few ounces of whiskey, Ladue introduced Huck. "This here is Huck Finn. He's my sheriff."

"I've heard of you, Mister Finn. Normally, I'd say it was an extreme pleasure to meet you, but under the circumstances . . ." Doc's voice trailed off as he looked over at Jass Holloway lying on the roulette table.

Huck wanted to know, "What's the deal, Doc?"

"The deal, my friend, is that I'm gonna have to cut off that man's leg . . . and without any chloroform."

"Do you have to do it on my roulette table?" asked Ladue.

Doc gave him a long, hard stare.

At length, Ladue—looking kind of uncomfortable—said, "Okay, Doc. It's just that it's the only roulette table for six hundred miles. I'm sorry. Just tell me what you need."

"What I'm gonna need is another table, one that has been scrubbed clean. And I mean *really* clean. Get someone on that right away. Then I'll tell you what else you have to do."

Ladue turned to Martin O'Conner. "Take care of it."

"And when it's clean, clear out a place by the front window and put it there. I'm gonna need all the light I can get," instructed Doc.

Huck asked if there was anything that he could do. "Yes, Mister Finn, the bag containing my instruments, such as they are, is over by the door. Get it and take it to the kitchen. Have the cook boil some water and when it's got a good boil on, put the contents of the bag into the water."

On the way to get the bag, Huck stopped at the table and told Molly and Jass what Doc was planning on doing.

Molly looked stricken, but Jass seemed to take the news in stride. "Things could be worse. My only concern right now is for my wife and my son. What's to become of them when I don't show up?"

Huck looked at Molly and stared into her exquisite green eyes for a tick or two. In that fraction of a moment, she knew what Huck was asking and she nodded her agreement. When he had her answer, Huck said to Jass, "Don't you worry. We'll see that you get there before the birth. Won't we, Molly?"

"Damn right we will. Now, Jass, finish off that bottle and hopefully it'll knock you out. Doc's gotta go to work on your leg."

Fifteen

While they waited for the table to be cleaned and the instruments sterilized, Huck spoke with Doc over at the bar. Molly had not left Jass' side since she first entered the saloon.

"Have you ever cut off a man's leg?"

Doc didn't look at Huck; his gaze was fixated on the small mirror behind the bar. Eventually, he turned his head and said, "More than I care to recollect."

That seemed to satisfy Huck. He did not want a horse doctor cutting away on Jass. He once had to cut off a man's lower arm due to gangrene, and it was not a pleasant experience for either one of them. But Huck was ready to do what he had to do—if it turned out Doc wasn't up to the job.

Presently, O'Conner walked up and told Doc that a table had been scrubbed clean and was over by the window just like he wanted. "I need you to do a few more chores," Doc informed O'Conner. "First, clear the room. Tell everyone they can come back later when I'm done. Then get me five lanterns and place them on a table next to the operating table. Also, put that mirror from behind the bar on the same table. Set it up so that it's reflecting the light from the lanterns onto my operating table. I'm gonna need a whole lotta light. You understand?"

"Sure, Doc."

"Okay, get going."

"About time for one more drink," Doc said aloud, but to no one in particular.

"You sure about this?" Huck wanted to know.

Doc poured himself a shot and downed it. "Put your mind at ease. I don't practice anymore, but I've still got the skill. And besides, I don't see no other volunteers."

Huck nodded and said, "What do you want me to do?"

"Find a fire poker or something similar and stick it in the kitchen stove, right in the middle of the fire. I'm gonna use it to cauterize the stub. Then we'll move the boy to the operating table. And you stick around, I'm gonna need you to hold him down while I saw off his leg. You might want to find a stick or something he can bite into. It seems to help."

The last to be ushered out of the room were the four men who had brought Jass into town. As they were leaving, they filed by the table. A tall man with yellow hair spoke for all of them. "We're real sorry this happened, Jass. We truly are."

Jass could only nod at that point, but he did it with a tight smile. Shaking their heads at the unfathomable nature of life, they sadly, one by one, exited the saloon.

It was time to go to work. Doc fished his bone saw from the boiling water. Jass bit down on a wooden spoon Huck had procured. Molly and Huck were at the head of the table. Molly spoke soothingly to Jass while Huck stood ready to hold him down if he started to thrash about. Doc said, "Think of home, boy," and started to cut. When he had gone through the bone, he tied the arteries off with cotton threads and, using the red-hot poker, he cauterized the wounds. The end and edges of the bone were scraped smooth, so that they would not work back through the skin, which Doc pulled across and sewed closed, leaving a drainage hole. As it turned out, Huck was not needed. Jass had mercifully passed out five seconds into the procedure.

Jass woke up staring at a wooden ceiling. He was disorientated, very thirsty, and his right leg was on fire. He was lying on a bed, a soft bed. The first he had been in since leaving Mae and Jack three months ago. Without meaning to, he spoke aloud. "Where am I?"

"You're in Dawson City, behind Ladue's saloon."

Jass turned his head in the direction from whence the voice had come and beheld a smiling Molly Lee McMasters.

"I'm glad that you are with us once again. You've slept for a whole day. But I reckon you needed the rest. Can I get you something?"

"Some water, please."

Jass struggled to sit up. He got as far as propped up on one elbow when a glass of water appeared in front of his face. "Here, take this. And don't struggle so. You're gonna be laid up for a while, so you might as well get used to it."

"Thank you, Molly." He drank heavily and emptied the glass. "That was good. But now I have a few questions, if you don't mind."

Molly fluffed up the pillows and relieved him of the glass. "Lay back down and I'll fill you in."

Jass started to lean back, but then stopped. He reached down to scratch an itch on his right foot before realizing it

138

wasn't there. Noticing the perplexed look on his face, Molly asked, "Are you all right?"

"Things are just going to take a little getting used to. I could have sworn that I had an itch on a foot that's not there anymore."

Molly didn't understand, but she didn't let it get in the way of what she had to say. Clearing her throat, she jumped right in explaining the facts to Jass.

"You lost your right leg from the knee down, but I reckon you know that. One of the men who bought your claim brought in your belongings. Most importantly, your gold. Your tent and outfit are outside. Your gold is in Ladue's safe. We weighed it out, it comes to $12,835.50. You're in my room, Huck's and mine. And you're gonna stay here until we set out for your homestead. That's enough information for now. Huck will be back in a short while. I'm going into the kitchen to scare you up some food. Lay back and rest. I know you have a lot to think on, so get started because when Huck gets here, he'll try to do the thinking for all three of us. It's just his way."

Molly smiled and patted Jass' shoulder. Then she was gone and Jass was left alone with his thoughts.

Goddamn! Goddamn it all to hell! How could I have let this happen? How could I have been so damn stupid? I should have taken my gold and sat on my ass until the freeze-up. I had *to be helpful. Goddamn it all to hell!* He fell back and cried until he ran out of tears. Then he cried some more. Eventually, he was completely cried out. That was the turning point. He had had his emotional breakdown. But now he would have to fight to get back to Jack and Mae. From this moment on, he would be steel. He would not break or bend. He would be there in time for his unborn child. *I swear to God, I'll be there!*

Huck walked in carrying a set of crutches. "I was just over at the sawmill and had one of Ladue's men turn these out. Ain't they a beaut? They're made of pine. So, how are you feeling?"

Jass was sitting up, with his back to the wall. He reached out for the crutches, but Huck placed them near the bed instead of handing them over. "They'll be here when you need them. Doc said you're not to move around anymore than you need to for a day of so."

Molly walked in carrying a tray. "I've got a bowl of moose stew and a big cup of coffee for you. Oh, hi Huck. I didn't know you were back."

"I'm back. I don't reckon there's enough stew to go around?"

"Yours is in the kitchen. Why don't you go and keep the cook entertained while you eat, and afterwards come back here. By then, Jass will have finished eating and the three of us can have a nice little talk."

Huck looked at Jass and started to say something, but then figured the boy wasn't in the mood for one his wise-acre remarks. Instead, he shrugged and left for a bowl of moose stew and maybe a little banter with the cook.

After eating, and as he was leaving the kitchen to go back to their room, Huck saw Jass emerging from the outhouse using the crutches. "How they working?"

"Just fine, Huck. I'm thinking of doing a little dancing in the saloon tonight."

"Well, please don't mention it to Molly because then she'll want me to take her dancing."

They laughed and Huck held the door open for Jass to go inside.

Once Jass was comfortably back on the bed, and Molly and Huck were seated at the small table Ladue had donated, they got down to business. Huck started things off. "Doc said he'd come by in a day or so to check on your leg. He wants you to rest for now. You've lost a lot of blood and it will take a little time for you to get your strength back, which should fit into our plans perfectly."

Molly took it from there. "The freeze-up should be in about two weeks. According to the old-timers, it's late this year. They say that will make the end of winter just that much colder, but that's no concern to us. When the river does freeze, hopefully you'll be strong enough to start out for home. But we have loads of preparations to make between now and then."

Jass was confused and it showed on his face. Molly and Huck looked at each other and Molly nodded for Huck to do the explaining. "This is gonna be thirsty work. Would you mind going into the saloon and getting us a bottle, Molly? I'm sure Jass could use some for medicinal purposes."

"I'm sure that he could, but what is *your* excuse, Mister Finn?"

"The same. It's chilly in here. I just want to ward off that cold I feel comin' on."

With faux exasperation and a heavy sigh, Molly stood and left to perform her errand of mercy. When she had gone, Huck got serious. "Let's take things one at a time. First of all, there ain't no way in hell you're gonna get six hundred miles in the dead of winter hobbling about on one leg. Molly and I promised you we'd get you home in time for the birth of your child. And we aim to do just that."

Jass started to say something, but Huck cut him off. "Just listen to me first. I've got it all doped out and if you interject anything, you might confuse me. You can have your say and ask your questions when I'm done. Savvy?"

"Sure, Huck, go on."

"Alrighty. You told us you had a dog team that you were going to use to get to the Interior. Well, I've asked around town and haven't found them. So where are they?"

Molly walked in just then carrying a bottle and three glasses. "It's kinda convenient living in a saloon," she commented. After the whiskey had been poured and everyone had a glass in hand, Huck again asked Jass where the dogs were.

"They're up on Rabbit Creek with an old sourdough by the name of Wes Adams. I bought the dogs and sled from him and he was keeping them for me until I sold my claim. His claim is a little north of Carmack's. About four miles up-creek."

Huck took a sip of whiskey and nodded to himself. It was good whiskey. "For the record, Rabbit Creek is now known as Bonanza Creek, not that it makes any difference. Okay . . . I'll go up and get your dogs. I only hope you know something about dog sledding 'cause I sure as hell don't."

Molly patted his hand and said, "I'm sure you're a fast learner. At least I hope you are." Huck downed his whiskey and gave Molly's hand a squeeze.

Jass thought it about high time that he said something. "Listen, folks. I'm overwhelmed. I will not pretend that if I'm ever gonna get back home, I'm not gonna need a lot of help. I don't even know you people. Why would you set out in the dead of winter on a six hundred mile journey, lugging a one-legged man you don't even know? The temperature will drop to seventy below before we get to where we're going. Hell, a warm day will be when it goes all the way up to forty below! Why are you doing this?"

Huck simply said, "Because we said we would."

Molly offered another reason. "Because this big galoot sitting next to me came up here looking for adventure. And God help me, so did I. If it makes you feel any better, Jass, we'd probably pay you to do this. You're the reason we came to Alaska, though we didn't know it at the time. I hope that answers your question as to why. Now let's concentrate on the how."

Jass hadn't touched his whiskey. He now downed it in one gulp and said, "If you two aren't the beat-all! It sure was my lucky day when you wandered into my camp." Huck looked a little embarrassed and Molly blushed a mite.

Besides learning how to run a dog team, Huck had to settle things with Ladue. "I'm sorry, Joe, but I'm gonna have to back out of our deal. Molly and me will be taking that boy back home in a couple of weeks. I'll gladly pay you for the use of the room. He's occupying it. We have our tent set up in back, but it's still on your property. Just tell me the freight."

143

Joe Ladue laughed, "Of course your tent is on my property. This whole goddamn town is on my property!" Then he became earnest. "What kind of man do you think I am? I'm not charging him, and I'm not charging you—for a damn thing. You folks eat and drink in here as much as you like. What you're doing is a wonderful thing. And if you need anything at all for the journey, you just let ol' Joe Ladue know and he'll supply it."

With that out of the way, Huck went up the Bonanza to retrieve the dogs. There were nine of them, all Siberian Huskies. He had to be shown how to put them in harness, which ones were the wheel dogs, and which ones were the swing dogs. He was introduced to the lead dog whose name was Bright. "I named him that 'cause I never seen a smarter dog," said Adams with pride in his voice. "He's six years old and he'll get you to where you wanna go if you'll follow his lead. By that I mean, if he stops on the ice and doesn't want to go any farther, then you better see what's spookin' him. Don't try to force him to go on. And just remember this: Out there, without your dogs, you're dead. It's that simple."

"What do I feed them?"

"Dried salmon. Feed them at the end of trail each day. Anything else you want to know, Holloway can tell you. He's a fair musher. At least he knows his stuff."

When the dogs had been harnessed to the sled, Huck walked in front of them on the trail to Dawson. Bright stayed right on his heels and, of course, so did the other dogs . . . they had no choice. But even when not in harness, they would always follow their lead dog.

Sixteen

Doc came by as promised. He liked the way the wound was healing and said that all things being equal, meaning that if the wound did not get infected and continued to heal as it was, then he saw no reason for Jass not making the trek. As he was walking out, he said, "In a few months' time you'll be able to handle a peg leg. You'll be stompin' around all over the place. Get yourself a nice mahogany one. Termites leave 'em alone." Having given his perspicacious advice, Doc took leave of his patient for the final time.

As they awaited freeze-up, Huck, Molly, and Jass made ready their outfit. Huck had the added task of learning how to mush a team of dogs. The days were relatively warm. The thermometer hovered around minus five or ten below zero. Taking advantage of the weather, Jass would sit outside with Huck as he attended to the dogs. It was at these times that Jass would tutor Huck in the ways of dog sledding.

"Make friends with your dogs, especially the leader. I hear that Bright has a good reputation in these parts. Put your trust in him." Jass took a pull on his pipe and thought for a moment. "I'll tell you what. Why not harness 'em up and we'll go for a jaunt along the trail that leads down to the Stewart River. There's enough snow for the runners and, along the way, I'll give you a few pointers."

Huck harnessed the dogs and, helped Jass into the sled; then he said *the* word for the first—but not the last—time, "Mush!" And off they went.

When they came to a rough patch, Jass explained about *pedaling*. "Hold on to the handlebars and run, keeping pace with the dogs. You'll do a lot more pedaling than you think. Every once in a while when things are smooth and the dogs have a good gait, you can stand on the runners. But when the snow has been sanded down to a hard crust by the wind and the dogs are having a rough time gaining traction, you'll be pedaling or running alongside the sled until the ice gives way to snow again. It could be for miles."

A few hours later, they were back in Dawson, huddled around the stove with Molly. "How is Huck with the dogs?" she asked.

"He's a natural. He has a feel for mushing that I can't explain. You should have seen Bright taking commands from him. It was like they'd been together for years. You would never know Huck was a newcomer."

Huck looked a little embarrassed, but then he said, "Let's get down to brass tacks. How many salmon will we need for the dogs? I'm gonna have to go and scare it up, and I don't want to wait until the last minute."

Jass did a quick calculation in his head and said, "We have six hundred miles to cover. If we're lucky, we can make fifteen or more miles a day. Add a few days for mishaps and we should make it in about forty to fifty days. We'll need at least one salmon a day, per dog; one and a half if we can't find any meat to supplement their diet. Beaver is good for that. We have nine dogs, so I'd get four hundred fish for the trek and a hundred to hold us over until we leave. There's a geezer five miles downriver that has that many and more. He sells to all the mushers. Get some of my gold and get us five hundred fish."

146

Huck stood to put on his parka. "Both you and Adams have told me that the dogs come first. I'll go now while I can still maneuver the canoe through the ice and before the geezer sells out. Don't worry about the gold. Molly and me have more greenbacks in our pockets than we know what to do with. You'll be needing that gold for your orchard." Jass started to protest, but Huck ignored him and walked out the door. A minute later he was back, asking what side of the river he could find the geezer on. "The west side," Jass informed him.

Jass had been propped up on the bed, but with Huck gone, there was an empty chair, so he hopped over to it without using the crutches. Once seated, he said to Molly, "There are a few things we can take care of while he's gone."

"Such as?"

"Such as your boots . . . and Huck's. They're fine for this neck of the woods, but out on the trail, in the snow, you'll be wanting moccasins. Two pair—for when one gets wet. If you can get me some beaver pelts, I can fix you and Huck up. I made my moccasins and they're a lot warmer than leather boots. I can tell you that."

"Alright, I'll ask Ladue where I can find some beaver fur. You stay put until I get back. You've moved around enough for one day. We don't want that leg opening up."

Huck harnessed the dogs every day and took them out for a run. While he was gone, Molly and Jass prepared the outfit. They bundled up the tent and stove, though Jass said most of the time they would be sleeping outdoors with an open fire. But those things would be nice to have along in

147

case they couldn't travel for a day or so because of a blizzard.

One morning, while Huck was out with the dogs, Jass remarked as he looked over the outfit, "It's a good thing we have a large sled, Molly. There's a lot to haul. Besides all this," he said pointing to their supplies, "that sled will have to carry you and me."

"Have you ever mushed six hundred miles?" asked Molly.

"No. But I did do close to three hundred once, a few years back. I ran into no trouble then. We should be fine. When we get to Circle City, that's where we'll head into the Interior."

It was now mid-December. The temperature, on most days, stood at a brisk twenty-five below. There were ice jams on the river; the freeze-up was only days away. Huck, Molly, and Jass were sitting around a table in Ladue's (that was now the official name of the saloon) talking about the forthcoming trek.

"Right up there with the dogs in importance are matches," offered Jass. "To be safe, we should have three hundred. We'll each carry a supply of one hundred wrapped in oil paper." Molly wanted to know why the matches would be split among the three of them.

"If one person held all the matches and if he—or she— got wet, then that would be the end of our fire-making ability," Jass explained.

The river was almost there. Between the large chunks of ice, the mush-ice barely flowed, and that too was hardening fast. In the end, the Yukon surrendered to the inevitable and stopped its movement. A few people from Dawson tentatively made their way out onto the river. The man in the lead carried a long stick that he used to test the thickness of the ice.

In two or three days, the ice would be thick enough to support a sled and dog team.

As the last items were being added to the outfit, Molly remarked to Huck, "Did you forget something? I don't see any whiskey."

"Nope. We've got a job to do. They'll be plenty of time for drinking once we deliver Jass to his family. He tells me he's got a bottle of some good stuff up at his cabin. Knowing that, I figure I'll have just that much more incentive to get him there and get him there fast," answered a smiling Huck Finn.

There was one small hitch in their plans. Once they had the sled loaded, leaving room for Molly and Jass, there was no space for the tent and stove. Food for themselves and the dogs were the only necessities. Everything else was unimportant, so those two items were jettisoned.

On a cold and clear December morning, a few days before Christmas, 1896, a loaded freight sled carrying a one-legged man and a beautiful, middle-aged woman with dazzling green eyes, mushed by an ex-frontier marshal, left Dawson City for a six hundred-mile run into the interior of Alaska in the depths of a Yukon winter.

They made two miles before they were stopped.

Up ahead, energetically waving his arms stood a fur-clad individual. Huck halted the dogs twenty feet from the apparition and waited for the man's approach. He had the hood of his parka pulled up, but his face was exposed. It was George Carmack!

"Leaving town without even sayin' good-bye to an old friend?"

"We were hoping to," said Huck in a deadpan voice, but with a big smile on his face.

Molly threw off the fur that had been protecting her from the elements and got out of the sled. "Don't you listen to him, George. We should have come up and seen you before we left. It was just with the preparations and all . . ."

"Molly's right," said Huck as he reached out to shake Carmack's mitten-covered hand. "We should have."

After the men shook hands, Molly gave George a tight hug. As she let go, Carmack said, "Little Bear has a new rifle. I bought it for him with the gold we got back from the killers. That's what his father was going to use it for. He told me it was about time that Little Bear went hunting with the men. He cut those trees for me to buy a gun for his son, and I made damn sure the kid got one. Just wanted you to know, Molly."

"Thank you, George."

"That's about it. God speed on your journey. And if you ever find yourselves in California, down around Salinas way, look me up. I'll be the gent with the largest ranch. As soon as I get my homestake, that's where I'm headed."

Turning to go, George bent over and whispered in Jass' ear, "You're in good hands. I've known those two for only a short while, but I know they're people to ride the river with. You'll get to where you're going with them breaking trail for you."

Huck and George shook hands one more time as Molly climbed back into the sled and covered up. Huck took hold of the handlebars, nodded to George, and for the second time that day shouted, "Mush!"

The dogs had been sitting in the snow, content in their furry warmth, but when they heard the command, their ears pricked forward and they got to their feet. Bright gave a look over his shoulder at Huck to verify the command. Huck clicked his tongue twice, and the teamed moved off.

They were a mile to the north when Huck looked back. There stood a lone figure; a small, dark, and insignificant silhouette against the vast whiteness. There stood George Washington Carmack, the man who started it all. Because of George's desire to do a little panning before laying up for the winter with his wife and a bottle of the good stuff, the Yukon and the Alaska Territories—with a combined land mass of almost 1,000,000 square miles—would never again be the same. Not to mention the 100,000 men (and the few women) who would flock there in the twelve months ahead.

Jass had suggested they stay on the trail that ran along the east side of the river for as long as they could. Travelling on ice had its own set of difficulties. From overflows, drum ice, and black holes, to sand-spits and stalagmites of ice formed by ice jams. They would have to traverse many rivers and lakes in the days ahead, but it would be prudent to put off riding the ice for the longest possible time.

At the ruins of Fort Reliance, they stopped for an hour to rest the dogs and eat a little of the moose stew Ladue had packed for them. After building their fire, and while they waited for the stew to heat up, Huck inspected the old buildings of the fort. *Looks like this might have been a going concern at one time.*

Jass hobbled up next to Huck and expounded on the fort's history. "Yep, this was a trading post for fur trappers. It's been here in one form or another since '33. But it was abandoned in '86 when gold was found up on Birch Creek. All the trappers quit trapping and went looking for gold. The Fortymile River gets its name because it's forty miles from here. Well, it's actually forty-six."

They mushed for six and a half hours that first day. The sun had not deigned to make an appearance until ten in morning and called it a day around four in the afternoon, so their time on the trail was short. That was all right for day one, but thereafter, half their time mushing would have to be done in the long twilight hours or in darkness if they were to cover miles.

They set up their first camp seventeen miles below the abandoned town of Forty Mile. The first order of business was to attend to the dogs. They had decided that Huck would look after them—from the harnessing in the mornings to unharnessing and feeding at night. If their paws needed looking after, it was Huck who would take care of it. Huck and the team had to bond. A strong bond had developed between Huck and Bright in the two weeks they mushed together prior to leaving Dawson. Now, during these first days on the trail, Huck would strive to gain the unconditional trust of the other dogs.

While Huck tended to his business, Molly collected firewood and got a fire going. Jass, who could get around fairly well despite the crutches, cut the spruce boughs Molly and Huck would sleep on. He would sleep in the sled.

After the dogs had been fed, Blackie, one of the wheel dogs, pointed his snout skyward and let out with a long, satisfied howl. Then his partner, Red, the other wheel dog, joined in. Within seconds, all the dogs were howling at the gray sky. "That's their *thank-you* howl," said Jass. "They're thanking you for feeding them, Huck. I've never known dogs to do it in town, but for some reason, out here on the trail, they'll thank you every night. Must be something to do with having done a full day's work and the satisfaction it brings. Even dogs feel it."

Huck and Molly sat comfortably on spruce boughs covered with wolf fur, but, Jass, because of his leg, sat on one of the boxes that held the salmon. "Not a bad day's run," he observed. "If things keep up this way, we'll have this trek behind us in no time at all."

"I checked the dogs' paws after I fed them and they were all in good shape," Huck informed his companions.

"For the most part, snow will not do anything close to the damage that running on ice will do to their paws. That's one of the reasons we'll stay off the ice as much as possible," said Jass.

Molly prepared their meal while the three of them talked of the day's run and what to expect the next day. After eating, Huck went to cut pine boughs for the dogs to sleep on. Jass tried to help Molly with the clean-up, but the lack of a leg hindered his efforts somewhat.

"You sit and have your pipe," commanded Molly. "I can handle this."

Huck returned after making sure the dogs were bedded down and content. He crouched by the fire, pulled out his pipe and when he had her going, leaned back on his heels and looked over to where Molly sat. She sure looked pretty in the light of the fire. Afraid of saying something stupid, he suggested they turn in. He helped Jass to the sled and got him situated. Then he moved his bedding closer to Molly and lay down beside her. She put her right arm across his chest and nestled closer. Her feel, the softness of her skin, and the warmth of her body were almost intoxicating. Huck fought against it. He fought hard, but not long. Then he said what had been on his mind for a while. "Molly Lee, if you don't watch out, I just might fall in love with you."

Seventeen

Huck awoke to the sound of a crackling fire and the strong smell of coffee. He looked over and saw Jass sitting on his box, tossing twigs onto the fire. Without turning away from his endeavors, he said, "Good morning, Huck. Thought I'd get things started. Coffee will be ready in a minute. Why not wake Molly up and, as soon as we get outside of some coffee and a little bacon, we can hit the trail."

Came a sound from Huck's right: "Molly's awake."

Huck turned to see a yawning and stretching Molly Lee McMasters. "Morning, boys."

"Morning, Molly," said Jass. "Come and get a cup of hot coffee."

"I'd love some!"

Over breakfast, Jass suggested they cross the river and travel the west trail when they set out. "We're gonna have to do it sooner or later, so might as well get over there. The track will take us into Forty Mile where we can catch our breath and rest the dogs before moving on."

After breakfast, Huck harnessed the dogs while Molly and Jass made ready the sled. Then Jass got in, leaving room for Molly. Huck took her hand in anticipation of helping her into the sled, but she stayed were she was. "I think I'll ride the runners with you for a while. Lying down in the sled for hours yesterday put a kink in my backside."

Huck shrugged, "There's a hell of a lot more pedaling and running than riding, but I'd enjoy the company."

Hence, with Molly standing on the runners and Huck behind her, holding onto the handlebars, he clucked his tongue to get Bright's attention, then yelled, "Mush!" and they were off.

They crossed the ice without incident and started on the trace to Forty Mile. The dogs were making good time, about five miles an hour, which was plenty. There was no need to wear them out; it was going to be a long haul.

After an hour of trail time, Jass yelled to Huck to hold up for a moment. Even before the sled came to a full stop, Jass was pointing to the northern sky. "Have you noticed that?" he asked, turning his gaze toward the black snow clouds that were quickly coming their way.

"I've seen 'em," replied Huck. "Don't reckon there's much we can do about it, but go on."

"You're right about that. Just wanted you to know that we're gonna get hit and hit hard. Trust in your dogs. If you're blinded by the snow, your lead dog can smell where other dogs have trailed and follow the scent, even when it's buried under several feet of snow."

Molly patted Huck's hand to let him know that she was game and not to worry about her. And just to make sure his mind was on the trail and the dogs and not on her, she said, "That's nothing. You should see a Montana snow storm. I've ridden the fence line in snow as deep as you are tall. Nothing to it!"

"That's nice, but for now, you get in the sled and under the furs with Jass. I got me some mushing to do and you'll just be in the way back here." It wasn't that. Huck wanted Molly as warm as possible when the storm hit, and Molly knew it, so, for once, she did not give him a hard time. Instead, she did as she was told.

As soon as she was in the sled, Molly looked back at Huck. With a lopsided grin, he said, "You should have seen *me* in New York City when a storm hit. I waited it out in Clancy's Saloon with a bottle of JR's Imported Scotch Whiskey for company. Nothing to it!" Without further comment, he clucked at Bright and they moved off. A short while later, the storm hit.

One moment Huck could see a good mile down the trail and the next he couldn't see past his wheel dogs. He prayed they would hit Forty Mile before the snow got too deep for the dogs. If that happened, he would have to put on his snowshoes and break trail for them by trampling down the snow, one step at a time. That would be a long, slow process.

They got lucky and pulled into Forty Mile an hour later, before the trail became impassable, but with the blizzard still raging. The dogs pulled up in front of a building Huck hadn't even seen because of the intensity of the storm. The windows had been removed, so it wouldn't afford much more protection from the wind and snow than being outside. Telling Molly to stay put, he went in search of shelter. A moment later, he was back. "There's an intact cabin over yonder. You can't see it through the blizzard, but it's there. I'll turn the dogs and get them to pull the sled up by the front door. You two get inside and get things warmed up; there's a stove and a little firewood. I'll see to the dogs."

Molly helped Jass into the sparsely furnished cabin. There wasn't much; two bunks against the far wall, a stove off to the left, a whip-sawed pine table with four stools around it, and a meager pile of firewood. Jass settled onto one of the stools as Molly went to work building a fire.

Outside, Huck ran into trouble unharnessing the dogs. The wind was blowing snow into his eyes as he fumbled with the traces. By the time the last dog had been uncoupled, his fingers were close to being frozen. He had intended to feed the dogs and then go inside, but instead, he put his mittens back on, grabbed a box of fish, and kicked open the door to the cabin. "In here, you mangy curs," he shouted over the howling wind.

Even though the dogs would have been comfortable curled up in the snow, they were not stupid. Following Bright, they rushed past Huck and invaded the cabin. Huck came in and tossed the box to the floor. "It's too damn cold out there for man or beast. We'll feed them in here; their body heat might help warm this place up a mite."

Jass thought he—being the more experienced musher in the room—should point out that the dogs could stand it a lot colder than it was now. "Hell, Huck. Did you see the spirit thermometer outside the door? It's only thirty below. Wait until it edges down to fifty or sixty below."

"Maybe so, Jass, but I couldn't see what I was doing out there. That's some storm!"

Molly knew better. If Huck had to, he would have stayed out until he had things done. He brought the dogs in because he had a soft spot for animals.

Huck walked over to the stove and rubbed his hands together, enjoying the warmth. "Why don't we get organized? Jass, you feed the dogs. Molly, you bring in the grub from the sled and get some food going. I'll go out and scout up firewood. And afore you say it, Molly, I'll say it for you. *'You're acting like the captain of a ship, Mister Finn!'* And you're right, I am. But it's only because my rear is near froze off and I can't loosen up until I'm sure I won't have to go out into that storm again." He put on his mittens, smiled at Molly, and walked out the door, letting in flurries of snow as he did so.

Bending into the wind, he made his way to the shack with no windows. There was no door either, so he walked right in and looked around. The place had been stripped bare. Only the walls remained. Huck shrugged and kicked at the bottom of the closest wall. He kicked and kicked until he thought he'd break his foot. *At least I'm keeping warm*, he thought. At length he had kicked a hole large enough for him to get a hand into. He grabbed the board and pulled. He was expecting a fight, but that section of the wall came off with no trouble at all. He ended up with a board two feet wide and seven feet long. *Three more of these should do it.*

As soon as he had his four boards, he dragged them— two at a time—over to the cabin and laid them just outside the door. Retrieving an axe from the sled, he brought it in with him. Molly had gotten the coffee going, and just the smell of it warmed his insides. After he had stomped the snow off his body, he made a beeline for the stove, careful not to step on any of the sleeping dogs. Jass had fed them and now they were resting from the rigors of the trail. Molly was at the stove frying up bacon and pan biscuits. "What's the axe for? Gonna chop up the furniture for firewood?"

"Don't you worry about that. Firewood's my job. Yours is to pour me a cup of that sweet smellin' coffee."

159

"It's ready. Can you pour a cup for yourself and Jass? I'm a little busy at the moment."

Huck leaned the axe against the wall, poured the coffee, and handed a cup to Jass. On his way to take a seat at the table, he patted Molly on her backside and whispered in her ear, "You're a good girl, Molly Lee."

"Sorry to tell you this, Huck, but covered in layers of flannel and wearin' these marmot skin britches, the patting don't have the same effect. But I liked the words."

Huck crinkled his eyes with a smile and went over to the table.

"Well, Jass, looks like we're gonna lose a day because of the storm."

"Can't be helped. Are we okay with the firewood? You weren't gone long."

"Fine. I got it stacked right outside. Figure when we need some, I'll do the choppin' in here."

"Wish I could help out."

"Don't fret. Your knowledge of mushing is more than enough. And I wouldn't know where to go in this country if you weren't guiding the way. Each one of us—you, me, and Molly—will all pull our fair share of freight in the days to come."

Huck got out his pipe and loaded it. "Hope the tobacco holds out," he said in passing.

"We should be hitting a few trading posts along the way. I'll buy you all the tobacco you want," said Jass.

"Mighty nice of you," responded Huck.

Thenceforth the cabin became quiet . . . the only sounds the crackling of the fire and the crying of the wind. There would be no more covering trail until the storm abated. For the rest of the day—and a day beyond that—the wind blustered, the snow fell. The storm raged on.

Early on the second morning, Molly awoke to silence, Huck lying next to her in the bunk. She shook him awake. "Listen," she whispered.

He raised himself up on one elbow and cocked his head. "I don't hear anything."

"Precisely. It's over. We can make trail again."

"Before we do anything, I'm stoking the fire. Let's warm up some and then I'll wake up Jass."

"Too late. Jass is already awake," said Jass from the other bunk.

With the stove going great guns and the coffee almost ready, Huck opened the door to see what the outside world looked like. He beheld a sea of white—three feet deep with drifts twice as high; the sled, buried, nothing showing but the handlebars, abandoned ghost buildings striving to reassert their supremacy over the landscape but failing—a sea of white silence that stretched to the ends of the earth.

Jass hobbled up on his crutches. "Looks like we'll have to take to the ice. We'll never get anywhere if you have to break trail for the dogs. Maybe in a day or so, mushers going down to Dawson will have trampled the snow enough for us to make trail. But until then, we stay on the ice."

From the stove, Molly yelled over her shoulder, "Close that damn door! You're letting all the cold in. But before you do, let the dogs out."

Huck kicked at the snow before the door and clucked for Bright. When all the dogs were out frolicking and floundering, Huck walked outside. Jass stepped out, but hung back by the door. The snow was too deep for him to maneuver through on crutches. Huck went over to the sled and started to dig it out from under the snow with his mittened hands.

Jass watched Huck for a moment and then inquired, "Whatcha up to?"

"Reckon I'll get my snowshoes and trample the snow between here and the river. I'd like to get a move on as soon as we have something to eat. How about going in and telling Molly to fix us some beans and bacon? That'll stick to our ribs."

"Sure, Huck, but is there anything I can do to help you out here? I know I'm pretty useless with only one leg and all, but I still want to pull my weight."

Huck figured it was a matter of self-respect with Jass, so he gave him a job to do.

"The harnesses and traces are right where I dropped them in front of the sled. Can you find 'em, dig 'em out, and get 'em ready? I know it'll be hard while you're holding on to those crutches, but it'll be a big help." Huck didn't know if Jass believed him about how big a help it would be, but the smile on his face told Huck that he had done the right thing. With snowshoes firmly laced on, he started his march to the river . . . with nine dogs in hot pursuit.

After their breakfast, they were sitting at the table sipping the last of their coffee, trying to build up resolve to hit the trail, when there was a knock at the door. They looked at each other in amazement. Forty Mile was supposed to be deserted!

Molly reacted first. "Come in," she said.

With an accompanying blast of cold air, in walked White Water Bill.

"Didn't know any folks was around. I was fit to burst when I saw the smoke from your chimney." White Water paused in his exuberance when he noticed that he was talking to his old friends, Huck and Molly. "Man alive, if it ain't Mister Finn and his lady friend!"

"Hello, White Water," said Molly. "I'd like you to meet our friend Mister Holloway."

When White Water noticed the missing leg, he walked up to Jass, stuck out his hand, and said, "Don't bother getting up. The name's William Cage, but you can call me White Water Bill. Everybody does."

With the niceties out of the way, they all sat down at the table. Huck spoke first. "We can explain why we're here, but what about you? Why aren't you down at the Klondike making your claim?"

"I was going down two days ago, but then the storm hit. I reckon ol' George did strike it rich after all. I expected everyone to come flooding back real fast when they found out he was only exaggerating again. But after almost three months, and then Ladue hauling his saloon away, well, even a Doubting Thomas like me has to bow to the obvious. So I'll harness up my sled dogs and go down to Dawson tomorrow."

"Tomorrow? Why not today?" asked Molly.

"Because I'm a-gonna spend the day here, in Forty Mile, with friends."

Huck spoke up, "Sorry, White Water, but we're pulling out in a few minutes."

White Water Bill did not look crestfallen at the news. Instead, he reached under his parka and pulled out an unopened bottle of Three Star whiskey. *"MERRY CHRISTMAS!"*

"I'll be damned! It *is* Christmas." said Huck.

"I had completely forgotten," exclaimed Molly.

Jass, contemplating his three companions, said, "Next to my family, I can't think of anyone I'd rather spend Christmas Day with. Pull the cork, Mister White Water. I want to offer a toast to Molly and Huck."

Huck somberly asked Jass if he were certain. "We can make miles before dark. I know you need to get back."

"If we could be to my cabin by day's end, then I'd say let's leave now. However, we have a month to go, so this one day won't matter. Besides, Huck, I overheard you tell Molly you did not bring along any hooch because you were committed to getting me home. Well, it's Christmas, goddamn it, and I insist we drink some Christmas cheer with our good friend White Water. It's damn cold out there. I believe a little whiskey is just what the doctor ordered."

As White Water pulled the cork out of the bottle, he dryly commented, "I've seen colder."

Eighteen

The next morning, four hours before the sun was scheduled to make its appearance, they were mushing for the Tanana Country on the wind-swept snow of the Yukon River. Circle City was three hundred and eighty miles away.

Molly preferred riding the runners and pedaling to sitting in the sled; it helped keep her warm. Jass had no choice but to ride the sled, and at forty below that presented a problem. Even though protected from the relentless cold with his parka and three layers of wolf fur, movement was essential in forcing blood to his extremities. Huck would halt the dogs every two hours so Jass could get out, grip onto the handlebars, and stomp up and down on his one foot until he felt the blood prickling his toes. Then he would thrash his arms about and beat his hands on his chest until his fingers started to sting.

They made their fifteen miles for the day and pulled up at Old Man Rock—situated on the western side of the river. They went about the work of setting up camp and, in no time, the dogs had been fed, the camp-fire was warming up the last of the moose stew, and boughs had been cut for bedding.

After eating, while elongated streams of green-violet and blue-white northern lights playfully danced overhead, the three travelers huddled close to their fire. Jass, thinking he would turn the conversation to the local terrain, asked a question. "You see this rock we're sitting under?"

Huck looked up at the massive blackness that blotted out a segment of the night sky and said, "Can't miss it."

"It's called Old Man Rock and, as you can see by its black outline against the stars, it towers over us at about two hundred and fifty feet.

"Now, if you remember, back when we pulled off the ice, there was a larger rock on the other side of the river. Do you recollect?"

His audience nodded in unison.

"I'd say that one was about three hundred feet in height. What do you think?" asked Jass.

Huck and Molly agreed.

"Well, that's called Old Woman Rock and there's an interesting story regarding these two monoliths. I heard the tale from an old Indian when I first hit this part of the country."

Huck fumbled beneath the fur he was wrapped in and came out with his tobacco pouch. After loading his pipe, he held the pouch out to Jass.

"No thanks. I'm still good. There's a trading post five days from here, we can stock up there with a few ounces."

Exasperated with the delay, Molly appealed to Jass, "Will you please go on about the rocks? I'm sure Huck can smoke and listen at the same time."

Huck tilted his head upwards and blew out some smoke. He took a moment to appreciate the stunning show being staged overhead by the aurora borealis and then declaimed, "I reckon I can do that. It might be a little taxing, but if I lose the thread of the story due to my pipe smoking, I'm sure Molly will fill me in on what I've missed."

She gave him a good-natured nudge in the ribs with her elbow and implored Jass to continue.

"Sure, Molly, I'd be happy to.

"It seems that in the remote past, there lived a man who had the great misfortune of being saddled with a wife who scolded him insistently. He lived that way for a long, long time without complaint, hoping that someday the woman would run down like an unwound watch. But as time went on, her scolding only increased. At last, he could take it no longer and sought the help of the local shaman. The priest, being able to see into the future, comforted him and sent him on his way with assurances that soon all would be well.

"Shortly thereafter, the man left the village to hunt food for himself and his wife. His luck was bad and he came back empty-handed. He was disillusioned and tired. And he was in no mood to listen to his wife's latest harangue. All the scolding he had endured over the years came to a boil within him on that night. He gathered up all his strength and gave his wife one swift and vicious kick to her rear end, booting her over the river. Upon landing, she turned into the large rock you saw earlier. It was the priest's magic that turned her into a memorial and a warning to all future wives. And the man was so astonished at what he had done, he turned into this rock we now sit beneath."

Huck said to Molly, "Let that be a lesson to you."

Molly demurely smiled at Huck. "If any part of you touches *my* backside, it better be your hand!" Turning to Jass, she implored, "Now, how about telling us a little something about yourself and your family."

Jass looked down to where his leg should have been and thought for a moment. "There ain't that much to tell. I reckon that you know most of it; leastwise the important part. We came up here in '86, to Juneau, hoping to get a new start; a year later Jack was born. I took whatever employment I could find, that's how I learned to mush. I delivered freight for the Treadwell Mine, and mail for the government, along with the many other jobs I've held.

"We could have gone back down to the states then, but there wasn't really much to go back to. I'd still be doing the same kind of menial work there as I was doing here. I wanted to hold on for just a little while longer and see if something didn't present itself, and Mae went along with me.

"When gold was found on the Stewart River, I wanted to stampede down there with everyone else, but Mae thought the boy was a little too young for that sort of thing. Then in '93 when they found gold on Birch Creek, Mae and I decided to go for broke. We spent all the money we had saved and bought an outfit and transportation on a paddle wheeler headed up the Yukon. All the good claims were already taken by the time we got off at Circle City. Anyway, the gold started to play out shortly thereafter. We *had* gone for broke. There was no money left to get back to Juneau. So I found a place to build a cabin and did whatever I could to feed my family, from trapping to working other men's mines to stoking fires on paddle wheelers during their summer runs. I even built log cabins for the wealthier miners. That was hard work, but good money.

"For the past three years, Mae's and my dream has been to scrape together enough to get back to the states. That's all; we just wanted to go home. And now that we have the means to do so—and then some—I'm going to build for her the prettiest little house that you ever did see. It will be in our apple orchard located along a section of the Oregon coast. I can picture it in my mind. For years, I've been thinking about that house.

"It cost me a leg, but I don't mind. In all the time we've been up here, not one word of complaint have I heard from Mae. And you can believe me, she's had plenty to complain about. She has worked like a dog keeping our home together and raising Jack. She let me chase after my dream and now it's her turn to have her dream come true.

"When I get that mahogany leg, I'll be the same man I've always been. And as far as I'm concerned, it was a fair trade—half a leg for the fulfillment of my sweet Mae's wish."

He stared into the fire for a minute, then raised his head and declared, "If the baby is a girl, her name will be Molly, and if a boy, Huck!"

Huck stood to go check on the dogs, but first he said, "If you name that kid Huck, I'll drag you all the way back to this very spot and let you make your own way home. I ain't doing this so you can saddle a poor baby with a name like Huckleberry." Having had his say, he started for the dogs, but just before the darkness swallowed him, he glanced back at the two figures silhouetted against the firelight and winked.

Molly had hoped for a little more information from Jass, like maybe how he and Mae had met—things a woman cares about. However, she did not press the issue.

For the next few days, they made their miles before stopping for the night. They had decided to stick to the river because the trail was still too deep with snow. "It's

170

strange that we haven't passed any stampeders or mushers going south," remarked Jass.

"Maybe it's too goddamn cold for them to be out," observed Huck.

"When gold's involved, nothing—not freezing cold, not even hellfire and brimstone—will halt a stampede from getting underway. But maybe everyone got down to Dawson before the freeze-up."

At night, Huck would repair the harnesses that needed mending and looked after the dogs. Sometimes he would massage their muscles if the day's run had been particularly grueling. Jass was in charge of bough cutting, and Molly did the cooking. One evening, Huck shot two beavers and made a stew for the dogs.

Five days after leaving Forty Mile, Huck noticed a dark shape in the never-ending whiteness along the banks of the Yukon. It was on the western side; he could tell it wasn't a boulder, it was red in color. Being a curious type, Huck headed the dogs in that direction. As they neared the bank, Huck could see that what had caught his attention was the figure of a man wearing a red flannel coat, sitting on a snow bank. He was hunched over and hugging himself as though trying to keep warm. Huck halted the dogs and ran over to him with Molly right behind.

He looked alive, but barely. Shortly, Jass was standing at Huck's side and he said, "This is strange. He has no pack and I don't see any dogs or a sled around. Why would a man be out in this weather wearing only a flannel coat?"

"Do you think he's alive?" asked Molly.

"The only way to find out is to try to bend his arm. Frozen flesh won't bend," offered Jass.

Huck gave it a try. The man was dead.

"What are we going to do about him?" asked Molly.

"Ain't much we can do," said Huck.

"We're about a day or so away from Jack McQuesten's trading post. Jack might know who he is. He's gotta be from someplace close by," advised Jass. "Anyway, McQuesten can send someone out to recover the body."

"Good idea," said Huck. "Now let's get going. I'm low on tobacco and it'll be good to sit around a nice warm stove."

Late the next day—over to the west—they spotted white smoke rising from the chimney of McQuesten's trading post. As they neared the log cabin, Huck pulled up the dogs and asked Jass a question.

"How well do you know this McQuesten fella?"

"Jack? Everybody knows Jack. Why do you ask?"

"The hairs on the back of my neck just did their little dance. It don't happen often, but when it does, I've learned to pay attention."

"Well, you don't have to worry about Jack. He's known as Golden Rule McQuesten. He'd give you the shirt off his back . . . if you needed a shirt."

"Just the same, I think it might be prudent to stack the deck a little in our favor." Turning to Molly, he said, "You get your Colt out of the kit, but leave the holster be. Slip the gun under your parka, into your belt."

Jass smiled at Huck with forbearance and said, "You'll see."

"Just playin' it safe," was Huck's comeback.

With Molly heeled and back on the runners, Huck clucked twice at Bright and they made the short run to McQuesten's.

Everything looked all right. Jass got out of the sled and led the way. Inside was warm and welcoming. Huck entered last and closed the door behind him. It was a small room that held two tables and a stove. There was a counter at one end, separating the shelves that held the trade goods from the rest of the room. There were three men scattered about. Two sat at one of the tables playing a card game. The third stood with his elbows leaning on the counter, reading an old newspaper. None of them were Jack McQuesten.

"Howdy," said Jass. "Where's Jack?"

The man standing at the counter straightened up and said, "Welcome, strangers. Come on in and git yourselves warm."

Again Jass asked the whereabouts of Jack McQuesten.

"He sold out just before freeze-up and took the last paddle wheeler going down river. Said he had had enough of arctic winters. My name is Frank Knight. Those two gents at the table are Al Vance and Curtis Loew. They be my partners."

Huck nodded to the three men and made his way over to the stove. Molly and Jass followed. They removed their mittens and rubbed their hands together in an effort to get the blood flowing. Huck turned around and faced the room to let his backside bake for a while. "Reckon we could get a shot of whiskey and something to eat?"

"That's our trade. Got a good caribou stew this week. And the first drink is always on the house. We figure it's a good way to build up business."

"Don't reckon you get much competition out around here," said Huck.

Knight laughed, reached under the counter, and came out with a full bottle of Three Star. "Nothing but the best for our guests." The other two men had not yet said a word.

Huck informed his hosts that he had to attend to the dogs before he had anything to drink. Jass said he was going out back to use the outhouse. Molly said nothing. She stood by the stove and took things in. She had come to one conclusion, though. In the short time she had been at the trading post, she knew that she did not like the looks of its proprietors.

Pointing the bottle toward Molly, Knight asked Huck if the lady would like a drink. "She'll drink when we do." He gave Molly a look before going out. Silently telling her to keep her wits about her. Something was not right.

Once Huck and Jass were outside, Molly expected at least one of the three men to say something rude, but none of them did. Vance and Loew continued with their card game, ignoring her. Knight went back to leaning on the counter, his newspaper forgotten. After a minute or so, he asked Molly where they hailed from and where they were headed.

"We just came up from Dawson and we're headed into the Interior."

"Must be hard, travelin' with a man with only one leg."

"Not at all, mister." Molly was being polite, but was volunteering nothing.

That seemed to be enough information for Knight. He asked nothing else and walked into the back room. Things then became uncomfortably quiet.

Outside, Huck unharnessed the dogs and fed them. After their thank-you howl, they settled down and curled up in the snow, their bushy tails covering their feet and noses.

Huck had decided to do a little reconnoitering before going back inside. He walked around to the back and ran into Jass as he was exiting the outhouse. "What do you think, Jass?"

"I don't know. Jack loved this country. I can't see him packing it in and leaving for the States, but I suppose anything's possible."

"Look at that kennel over there. It has to be holding at least thirty dogs. Did you ever know McQuesten to keep that many dogs?"

"Not that I recollect. But Jack's not here. The new owners could be dog fanciers for all we know."

"Are they also sled fanciers? There's five sleds sitting next to the kennel. Give me a minute. I want to do a fast walk around."

"Sure, Huck. I'll wait out front and if Knight or one of them others comes out, I'll say you're using the convenience."

"Good fella. And if one of 'em *does* stick his nose out, make like you're getting something from the sled so it doesn't look like you're keeping watch. There may be nothing to any of this, but it's best we don't show our hand until we have to."

Jass shuffled through the snow on his crutches, and Huck went towards the tree line. He had glimpsed a mysterious snow-covered mound right at the edge of the trees. From where he stood, it looked to be four feet high and about six feet long. When he got close, he saw a human hand—about knee high—sticking out from the pile. He brushed away a little of the snow and found six bodies, stacked three high, in two piles, covered with an old piece of canvas. He did not see any bullet holes in the few seconds he took to examine the two bodies on top.

Huck came around to the front of the cabin to see Jass leaning against the sled's handlebars. "I think I found McQuesten," he informed his friend.

"What?"

"Unless I miss my guess, he's out back, lying under a few of his ex-customers—dead. And so are they. They're stacked like firewood. What's more, I think I know how that man we found yesterday ended up frozen on the trail. I bet you he made a run for it and they let him go, knowing he wouldn't last long the way he was dressed. We're gonna have to play this close to the vest, so when we go in, you follow my lead."

"Should we get the guns?"

"No. If we went in heeled and loaded for bear, they might get the drop on us. Molly has her gun. That should be enough for when the ball goes up."

Jass pulled himself erect and stood up on his pine crutches. "Let's get this done. I'm getting hungry."

Huck smiled, "I think you've been hanging around Molly a tad too long."

They walked into the cabin and were met by three guns staring them in the face—two Colt revolvers and a double-barrel. Huck looked over to Molly. She smiled and shrugged back at him.

Nineteen

"Come on in, boys. We've been waiting for you," invited Frank Knight.

Molly was seated at a table close to the stove. She didn't seem to be any the worse for wear, so Huck thought he'd let things ride for the moment. He waited until Jass was seated and then ambled over to the stove. "You mind telling me what this is all about?"

Knight smiled, showing a missing front tooth. "I seen you out the back window, inspecting our handiwork. So I reckon you already know what's going on."

Huck shrugged. "What now?"

Knight looked over to his partner, Vance, and said, "He wants to know what comes next. Why don't you show him?" Vance lowered the shotgun he was holding and placed it on the nearby table.

"Al is going to check you and One-Leg for firearms. We want to keep this friendly. If you started shooting at us, then we'd be obliged to shoot back and, before you knowed it, someone might get hurt. And keep in mind that me and Mister Loew will have you covered the whole time."

Vance went to Huck first and had him pull up his parka. When he found no gun, he turned his attention to Jass. After he had been satisfied that Jass was not armed, he went back, picked up his shotgun and pointed it in Huck's general direction.

"Now that we got that out of the way, I'm gonna sit down . . . if you don't mind," announced Huck.

"Sure, make yourself comfortable," said Knight. "We got us some things to work out."

Huck pulled out his tobacco and started to fill his pipe, but stopped and addressed Knight. "Seeing as how you're doing all the talking for your side, I reckon I'll have to ask you."

"Ask me what?"

"I'm getting low on tobacco. You got any you can sell me?"

"I don't reckon so. It's a long time to spring. We'll be needing what we have for ourselves."

Huck shrugged like it was not important and continued to fill his pipe. When he had her going, he blew out some smoke and looked at Molly. "You alright?"

"Never better."

"That's my girl. And you, Jass. How about you?"

"The same as Molly."

"Good. Now let's get down to business. You, Mister Knight. What's the play?"

"Well, ain't you folks the cool ones. Having guns pointed at you don't seem to bother you none."

"It ain't the first time we've had guns pointed at us," said Huck. "But before we get down to business, shouldn't you check the lady for a gun? She might be heeled."

"I don't think so. If you gents ain't carrying, she ain't."

Huck's ploy had worked. He wanted Knight and his partners to keep their attention *and* their guns on him. Jass had one leg and Molly was only a woman, what could they do? If Knight had checked her for a gun, Huck would have come up with a different plan than the one already half-formed in his head.

Vance and Loew pulled out chairs and sat down, but they still kept their guns pointed across the room—mostly at Huck. Knight laid down his Colt, pulled out the Three Star, and set up six glasses. "Can't spare no tobacco, but ol' Jack McQuesten left us with enough liquor for the winter. Why don't you folks join us in a drink while we decide what we're gonna do with you?"

Huck whispered to Molly and Jass. "Don't drink anything unless they do."

He was overheard by Knight. "So you figured out how we did away with McQuesten and them other geezers. Sure, we put a powder in their liquor when they weren't lookin' and when they fell off to sleep, we'd drag them outside where they would freeze to death. It's not that bad of a way to go. But you folks don't have to worry on that account."

He finished pouring the liquor and brought two glasses over to his partners, then placed a glass of the amber liquid before each of his "guests" and went back to the counter. "Drink up. You saw me pour all six glasses out of the same bottle. You don't think I'd ruin a good bottle of whiskey, do ya? Maybe ordinary tonsil varnish, but not Three Star! Here, we'll drink ours first." He picked up his glass and said, "Here's to better times," and downed his drink. Vance sipped at his; Loew downed his and complained, "Frank, this ain't getting us nowhere. What's with this cat-and-mouse game? We know what we gotta do."

"Curtis . . . we was so bored before these nice folks showed up, we was ready to murder each other just for something to do. Spring is three months away; we have time to figure things out. And what about the lady? You want to do away with her? Like I said, spring is a long way off."

Jass was about to say something, but Huck shook his head and Jass eased back in his chair. Huck picked up his glass and downed its contents in one swallow. "Not bad. Jass . . . Molly, you oughta try it. It's not every day you get whiskey this good. It sure warms your insides."

Molly and Jass emptied their glasses as Huck had done.

Knight smiled and said, "That's the spirit!" He then went over and refilled their glasses, dawdling in front of Molly. "You ain't no spring chicken, but you're still a looker."

Molly batted her eyelashes in an exaggerated fashion and shyly smiled. "Why, thank you, Mister Knight. That's the nicest compliment I've gotten in a coon's age."

Knight removed his hat and bowed from the waist. "My pleasure, ma'am."

When Knight was back at the counter, Huck thought it was time to move things along. He was getting hungry and he would not be able to eat until things were settled. So he spoke out. "I've got the basics, but just for some conversation, you mind telling me what you gents have been up to? I'm sure me and my companions would be most interested in hearing all about it."

Huck could not have set things up any better. Knight had himself an audience, and he was just dying to play to that audience. He slowly refilled his glass and then pointed the bottle in the direction of his partners, but they both shook their heads. They weren't enjoying themselves half as much as Mister Knight. He stood in front of the counter as though it were a stage and started his performance with a flourish.

"Me, Al, and Curtis partnered up a while back to do a little placer mining. We got us a claim a little north of here and worked it all summer, but all we came up with was sore backs and a pile of muck. We heard about the strike down on Rabbit Creek, so we packed it in and started south. We got as far as this here spot and decided we didn't want to moil the winter away. That's when Curtis came up with the bright idea of going into the trading post business. And seeing as how Mister McQuesten already had a going concern, we bought him out . . . so to speak."

At that point, Loew stood up, empty glass in hand, and went over to the counter. "You talk too much, Frank. But maybe you're right. This sure beats the hell outta cheating Al at five-card. Gimme a drink. All your talkin' has made me thirsty." He filled his glass and took the bottle back to the table.

Knight reached under the counter and came up with two bottles. One, he took over to Huck. "Here, this will save walking back and forth." From the other, he poured himself a stiff one.

Huck filled their glasses and, while doing so, winked at Molly. It was not a flirtatious wink. Huck was telling her to be ready for the play when it came. She was the only one of them with a gun.

Back on his stage, Knight continued. "Where was I? Right. So we did away with McQuesten and thought we'd sell out his stock and pocket the money. Then, when the thaw came around, we'd get outta this godforsaken country. There was only one problem. Nobody was coming by. We had only two customers that first week and they came in more to get warm than anything else. After that, we figured we'd just kill the geezers, rob them of their pokes, and be done with it. As a bonus, maybe we could sell their outfits and dogs. But everyone was heading south and their pokes was kinda light. We went through five of 'em, of which, I believe, you have made their acquaintance, mister. By the way, *what* is your name?" The question was addressed to Huck.

"It's Finn."

"Glad to meet you, Mister Finn. And how about your companions?" Knight asked as he leered at Molly.

"This here is Molly, and the one-legged fella is Jass."

"Pleased to meet you, Molly."

Molly nodded to Knight and said. "Won't you please go on? I'm finding your story ever so interesting."

Knight grinned from ear to ear. "My pleasure, ma'am. But there ain't that much more to tell. When you showed up, we was gonna let you be. Buy you all a drink and send you on your way. I figured seeing as how you're coming up from the south, you can't be carrying much dust. The strike was just made and there hasn't been time enough for any serious mining. And we sure as hell don't want no more dogs. We can't feed the ones we have. Probably end up having to shoot most of 'em."

Molly took a small sip of whiskey and asked, "So what changed your mind about us?"

"It was your friend, Mister Finn there. He had to go and poke his big nose into something that was none of his concern."

Molly sighed, "He does that a lot."

Huck was anxious to get the ball rolling, but he wanted to know one more thing. "We ran into a man about twenty miles down trail. He didn't have much to say because he was frozen solid. Could it be that you knew him?"

"You must be talking about Jake Early. Was he wearin' a red flannel coat?"

"Yup."

"The poor man made a run for it after he refused a drink, and Al had to draw his gun. But it was too cold to go chasing after him. We figured he wouldn't get far 'cause we had his parka and kit. Twenty miles, you say? Reckon he had a bit more in him than we thought. It's a good thing he was beyond talkin' when you came across him."

"Yeah, just great."

Huck, tiring of the conversation, picked up the bottle and filled his and Molly's glasses. Jass' was still full. "Alright, Mister Knight, how do you plan on doing it? Take us out back and shoot us? Or have us drink something that will make us sleep?"

"I must say you are taking this like a gentleman. No crying or begging for mercy?"

"Would I get any?"

"Any what?"

"Mercy."

"Most likely not."

"Didn't think so. But seeing as how I was the one that went snooping around, how about letting my friends go? There ain't no law in these parts. No constables will come after you."

"That's enough!" shouted Loew. "Nobody goes. I say we shoot the geezers now and keep the woman for later. Whatcha think, Frank . . . Al?"

Al sipped his whiskey, and nodded his agreement while keeping his Colt pointed at Huck.

Frank had had his fun. "You're right. The woman we definitely keep. Sorry gents, but would you mind standing up? We're gonna go outside. We don't want no blood on the floor or Miss Molly would have the unpleasant task of cleaning it up."

Jass stood up, but Huck stayed where he was. "Maybe we can make a deal. You were wrong about us not having much gold. We got thirty-five pounds of nuggets on the sled."

Immediately upon hearing that news, Vance and Loew laid their guns on the table and ran out the door without even putting on their parkas. Knight picked up his Colt and waited.

The door burst open and the two came in carrying the skins that held the gold. They went to Knight and poured the contents of one of the skins onto the pine surface of the counter. That distracted Knight. The three of them were mesmerized by the deep-yellow brilliance reflected in the dim light of the slush-lamp.

Huck looked at Molly and nodded.

She stood with such force that she knocked her chair backwards and it started to fall. She had her gun out and in her hand before the chair hit the floor. The scraping noise of the chair as Molly stood turned the men's attention from the gold to the table. It was the last act of their lives. Molly had a bullet into each one of them before they knew they were dead.

Jass couldn't believe it. He took the bottle of Three Star, tilted it to his mouth and drank a goodly portion. Then he sat down and wiped his brow. In spite of the cold, he had been sweating. Huck went to Molly and gently touched her cheek with the back of his hand. "Good girl," was all he said.

Molly was delighted that Huck and Jass weren't laying out back, bleeding their life's blood onto the snow. She was very glad of that indeed, but still she thought of that strange concept called karma. Would she have to meet up with those three bastards in a future life and tell them she was sorry for killing them?

Huck went right to work. He dragged the bodies out into the snow. He didn't waste time bringing them around back. He left them right out front so they could be seen. Then he came inside and went to the kitchen and started a fire in the stove. While he waited for it to get going, he went to the outer room and sat down with Jass and Molly.

"That was a close one," he noted.

Jass could only shake his head in silence. Molly stared straight ahead and said nothing.

Huck asked, "Are you alright, Molly?"

"I'm alright. It's just that a while back I told myself I wasn't going to kill no more. That those days were behind me. And here I am, shooting away like I always did. I know it had to be done, and the same with those jaspers down in Dawson, but it don't make me feel any better. And worse than that, I'm forgetting my proper English," she said with a small, sad smile.

Huck squeezed her hand. "You have a drink while I rustle up some food. You don't have to eat if you don't fancy to, but it will be here if you want it. Jass, look after her for me."

Jass could tell that Molly was in an introspective frame of mind and he let her be. Though, at one point, he did say, "I want to thank you for saving my bacon. I thought I'd never see Mae or Jack again. The whole time that man was talking about taking us out back and shooting us, I was thinking about the baby and wondering if it would be a boy or a girl."

A short while later, Huck came out of the kitchen carrying a tray that he placed in front of Molly. "Look what I found. Tea! I don't know how McQuesten got 'em, but he had china cups back there. So you can have a decent cup of tea. That little bowl has sugar in it. And I found this can of milk. It wasn't even opened. There's two more back there.

187

We'll take them with us and you can have some on the trail."

Molly looked up at Huck and smiled. *He's being so nice because he knows I'm upset.* "Thank you, Huck. A cup of tea is just what I need."

Huck beamed and said, "The water will be ready in a minute. There's one of them china cups for you too, Jass, in case you want some tea." Then he hurried back into the kitchen to attend to his culinary chores.

Huck had also found two cans of mock turtle soup. They had that before a main course of sourdough bread, and what was left of the caribou stew. They finished off the feast with the remains of an apple pie. One of the sons-of-bitches had been a pretty good cook.

After eating, Huck went out to check on the dogs. They were content in their beds of snow. He felt bad about the dogs in the kennel. He figured they probably hadn't been fed in a while, so he went back there to see what he could do concerning the situation.

Next to the kennel stood a small shed. The starlight reflecting off the snow gave him enough light to see what was inside. As he had thought, it was filled with sled harnesses and boxes and bags of dried salmon. He threw forty salmon into the enclosure. The dogs would fight over them, but hopefully each dog would get at least one. In the morning he would open all the boxes and bags and spread the salmon around. Then he would open the door to the kennel and let the dogs have at it. His purpose was two-fold: Huck couldn't leave the dogs locked up; he had to give them a fighting chance at survival. And he wanted to keep them busy while he mushed *his* dogs down trail. He didn't want any of the kennel dogs following behind.

They slept that night on the pine floor of the cabin, close to the stove. It was the warmest sleep they'd had since leaving Dawson. In the morning, Huck harnessed his dogs and took care of the kennel dogs while Molly wrote a note explaining the three dead bodies in the front yard and where to find the murdered men out back. She left it on the counter, held down by Knight's half-empty bottle of Three Star. Jass found the tobacco tin and filled his and Huck's pouches to overflowing.

They hit the trail early.

The date: 1 January, 1897.

Twenty

It was a crisp and dry day; the temperature still lingered at forty below, but at least it wasn't getting any colder. The wind was blowing in from the north at a good rate as they glided along the ice north of McQuesten's.

Huck noticed that the trail on the western bank of the Yukon had been beaten down enough to allow the dogs easy passage over the snow. Grabbing the gee-pole, he commanded. "Arrah!" Bright turned left, obeying the order. As the other dogs followed, Huck leaned on the sled's left runner, lifting the right runner from the ice ever so slightly. He had to be careful not to apply too much pressure or the sled could capsize. It was team work between man and canine, as all mushing is. When they came upon the trail, Huck repeated the maneuver, but in reverse, "Oluk!" he shouted. Bright responded to this command by leading the dogs in a turn to the right.

Huck labored on. The frost from his breath formed a fine, white crystalline deposit on his beard and eyebrows.

The next leg of their journey would take them to Central City, three hundred miles away. According to Jass, it was not completely deserted as Forty Mile had been. However, of the one thousand residents that were calling it home when the news of Carmack's strike reached that far north, fully ninety percent had stampeded south.

It started to snow before they made many miles. It was a Yukon snow, light and feathery. Molly stood on the runners, in front of Huck, as they sped through the swirling snowfall. Huck would jerk the sled this way and that when they came to a bend in the trail. The creak of the birch-wood runners was quite audible as the sled made the corners. Jass seemed warm and content wrapped in his furs. The dogs were straining in their harnesses; they were real "trail eaters." On straight runs, Molly would sometimes run alongside the dogs, which would prod them to run even faster, as though they thought it a contest to determine the fleetest between the species.

The sled was the only thing moving. Except for the commands Huck issued to Bright, there was no sound. While mushing, the silence was not so evident, but when they stopped to let Jass get his blood flowing, the silence descended and enveloped them. The country became bigger; they became smaller—insignificant beings in an enormous universe.

The trail was good, the snow light. Every day for five days straight, they made their fifteen miles and then some. On the morning of the sixth day after leaving McQuesten's, they came to a snow drift in the trail that they could not get around. Huck halted the dogs and climbed the hard-packed drift to see what lay ahead, then came down and conferred with Jass. "Reckon we'll have to go back out onto the ice for a spell. It looks like the trail is blocked for miles."

"Okay, but I've been noticing the ice. This is a rough patch of river, it will have humps and bumps in it. Let Bright have his head; the dogs will have to crisscross back and forth to protect their paws."

"Alrighty then. Let's get a move on."

Huck got the dogs onto the river ice and pointed them north. A short while later, they were headed northwest, then northeast, then due west! Huck was beginning to think they would not make Circle City until spring. At least not at that rate.

As Jass had said, the ride was a bumpy one. There was one rather large hump that Bright decided, for reasons of his own, to go over rather than around. When they passed over it, the resulting thud as the sled again made contact with the ice caused Molly to lose her grip on the handlebars and slip off. In astonishment, Huck looked back to see her sprawled on the ice, smiling.

He yelled *"Whoa."* When the sled came to a rest, he walked back and helped Molly to her feet. Once he determined she had not been hurt, he asked, "You reckon you can hang on for a while?" He couldn't help but add, "Between you falling off and the dogs crisscrossing this damn river, we'll never make Circle City."

"Don't you worry about *me*, Mister Finn. You just watch out for those bumps in the road."

Huck went to pat her on the rear, but she side-stepped him, saying, "Now . . . none of that. If you're in such a big hurry to get to Circle City, then come on." Huck shrugged and followed her back to the sled.

They had been on the ice six hours when it started to get colder. The temperature was inching down past fifty. The wind had stopped, but the snow continued to fall. After a while it had gotten deep enough to smooth out the ice so the dogs could head in a straight northerly direction, more or less. Though occasionally they would veer left or right to avoid a precipitous rise in the ice.

Then, without warning, the dogs splashed through water—water that should not have been there. Huck yelled, "What the hell?" The ensuing spray startled Molly and she involuntarily raised her hands to cover her face. As soon as she let go of the handlebars, she slipped off the runners.

She rolled twice and came to rest face-down in three inches of freezing water. Even before she had stopped rolling, Huck was off the sled and splashing through the ankle-deep water to get to her. He pulled her to her feet and carried her back to the sled. Jass was up on his one knee, facing the back. "Put her in here, I'll strip off her clothes and wrap her in the furs. You get us to shore and build a fire, fast!"

Molly was shivering and shaking. Her teeth were clattering so much she couldn't talk. Jass pulled off her parka and slipped off her moccasins. Before going further, he said, "I'm sorry, Molly, but I gotta do this." He tore off her wet clothes and wrapped her in the wolf furs.

By then they were at the bank, but still on the ice. The incline was too steep for the dogs to ascend. Jass already had the axe in hand and held it out to Huck. "You get a fire going. I'll take care of Molly."

Huck grabbed the axe and ran up the bank and over the rim. Jass pulled Molly to him and held her close in an effort to share his body heat. "Don't worry, Molly. Huck will have a nice big fire going in a few minutes. Until then you just think warm thoughts." Molly couldn't talk; she nodded and tried to smile, but she could not stop shaking long enough to get the muscles around her mouth to work.

Huck went to the tree line at the high water mark. There he found dead, dry wood that had drifted in with the current. He picked up only twigs and small sticks. These he laid in a pile under a large spruce. Then he brought the axe to bear on the lower, green branches of the tree; these he positioned on the snow. He placed a few scraps of birch bark on them, then added the twigs. He was in such a hurry to get the fire going that he fumbled in his pockets looking for his matches. He couldn't find them and he was growing increasingly agitated. *If I don't get this fire going, Molly's gonna die. But I'm no help to her like this. Take a deep breath and calm down. Then find the damn matches!*

On his second try, he located the matches and got the birch bark burning. The twigs soon caught fire, making it safe to add larger pieces of driftwood. When he was sure the fire would not go out, he ran back to the sled.

He picked Molly up in his arms and started up the incline. Over his shoulder, he shouted to Jass, "I don't know how you're gonna get up there. Let me take care of Molly, then I'll come back for you."

"Don't worry about me. Get Molly warm. And keep her hands and feet away from the fire. Rub them with snow until she can feel the prickling, then she can move them closer to the heat. I'll bring her clothes."

While carrying Molly up the bank, he smiled at her and said, "As soon as you're warmed up and got some hot coffee in you, I'm gonna put you over my knee and give you the spanking that you so richly deserve for scaring me half to death like this."

As soon as they got to the fire, Huck removed his parka and slipped it over Molly. He took one of the furs, laid it on the snow, and placed her on it; he had her sitting sideways from the fire. Then he knelt down and rubbed her feet with snow. Molly was still shivering, but she managed a smile, and her eyes glowed with love as Huck worked on her feet.

When the feeling came back, he reached for her hands, but she said, "I'm getting warmed up. I can do this. Maybe you should run back to the sled and get Jass and some clothes for me. And you'll need your other moccasins. Your feet got wet too. You'll lose some toes if you don't attend them right quick."

Huck gave a deep and happy sigh. With Molly giving orders again, he knew she would make it. Just then, Jass stumbled up on one crutch, carrying a kit. "I've got Molly's clothes in here, the coffee pot, and some coffee. I've also brought your moccasins."

Huck looked at him in amazement. "How the hell did you get up that bank?"

"It weren't easy. But enough of that. Molly, you get dressed. Huck, you get out of those wet moccasins and start with the snow rubbing. I'll get the coffee going. As soon as you two are in one piece again, the dogs will have to be looked after."

Once Molly was fully dressed, and Huck could feel his feet again, they sat around the fire with Jass and drank hot coffee. After one cup, Huck said he was going down to look after the dogs. But before he left, he asked Jass what they had run into out there on the ice.

"That was an overflow. It's when pressure builds up on a thin portion of ice and the water bursts through. It then seeps along the ice, under the snow, and it can be quite dangerous for the dogs. The water gets between their toes and freezes fast. The ice can then cut them up pretty bad. Overflows don't usually affect mushers too much. Usually, just wet feet is the only concern." Then looking towards

Molly, he said with grin, "But then again, most mushers don't fall off their sleds."

Molly laughed. "You got me there."

Huck said, "I think from now on, she'll do most of her riding *in* the sled."

"You think so, Mister Finn?" was Molly's sardonic retort.

"I gotta look after the dogs. I'll leave it to you, Jass, to try to talk some sense into that woman of mine." With a farewell wink to Molly, Huck headed for the river.

The dogs were lying in the snow, licking the ice out from between their toes. Huck checked every dog's paws and where the ice was too deep for the dog to dig it out, he put the paw to his mouth and attacked the ice with his own teeth. After the dogs were taken care of, he took them out of their traces and fed them. He waited for their thank-you howl, then grabbed Molly's ice-encrusted clothes and her parka, some food, and a few things to cook with. He went back up the incline to camp and along the way, he decided there would be no more traveling for that day.

With Molly's parka and clothes suspended over the fire and their moccasins on sticks close to the heat, Huck burned some bacon and made watery flapjacks as a flabbergasted Molly and Jass looked on.

"Didn't know you were such a cook," commented Molly.

"There's always dried salmon if you'd prefer," rejoined a complacent Huck Finn.

Huck's cooking didn't turn out as bad as they thought it would. They ate it all and afterward complimented him on his epicurean prowess.

Sitting next to Molly with his pipe glowing, Huck observed, "I reckon we've knocked off close to one hundred of those three hundred miles to Circle City. Figure we'll be there in two weeks. You reckon so, Jass?"

"I reckon so, Huck. But we're gonna have to break trail for the dogs soon and that will slow us up some. Their paws can't handle the ice much longer. How were they just now?"

"Their paws? A little tore up, but not too bad. As you said, the covering of snow helped."

Molly snuggled into Huck. He put his arm around her and drew her in even closer. Despite getting dry, and being warmed by the fire, she was still cold inside. Huck's inviting body next to hers was just what she needed.

After a while, it started to snow again . . . a light snow. Huck unhitched himself from Molly and stood up. "Gonna cut some boughs to sleep on and get some blankets from the sled."

Molly offered: "I can get the blankets."

Huck looked her in the eye. "If you move one inch from that fire, you'll get that spanking I've been promising. You hear me?"

"Yes, *sir!*"

On his way out of camp, he felt Molly's parka; it was dry. He took it down and tossed it to her. She was swimming in his, hers would keep her warmer. They traded and as she went to put hers on, she reached into the inside pocket she had sewn into the fur lining and brought out her supply of matches. They were ruined from the water. The oil paper was brittle and crumbled in her hands.

Jass saw the look of dismay on her face. "Oil paper's good for keeping things dry, but ain't much good when it gets this cold, it gets brittle. And I reckon I don't have to tell you what water does to sulfur matches. Don't worry; between Huck and me, we still have plenty of 'em."

Molly gave a rueful smile and tossed the mess onto the fire.

Before he did anything, Huck checked on the dogs. They couldn't have been happier curled up in their slight depressions in the snow, looking cozy and snug. He went to Bright, knelt down and scratched him behind his ear. "How ya doin', old boy?" Bright's tail wagged once or twice in answer. Satisfied all was well on that front, Huck grabbed the blankets and went to do his cutting.

With his tasks complete, he returned to camp and set up their beds. What was left of the coffee, he poured into three cups and passed around two of them, keeping one for himself. "We should bed down and get an early start in the morning."

There were no objections.

Jass, situated on his boughs, shrouded himself from head to foot with a blanket to keep the snow off him. Molly was already on their bed, waiting for Huck. He lay down beside her and threw the blanket over them, covering their heads.

The sojourners shivered under their blankets and wolf furs as they anticipated sleep and contemplated on what the morrow would bring. The wind had died; the temperature stood at fifty-four below zero, the light snowfall continued throughout the night, slowly covering the recumbent forms until the only indication that they existed at all were three slight mounds of snow in a silent, vast whiteness.

Twenty-One

It had stopped snowing by the time twilight crept over the mountain. In gloaming's grayness, one of the prominences of snow moved slightly. Without warning, as a volcano, it erupted and the man sat upright, throwing off his blanket of snowfall.

The fire had gone out hours ago. Huck dug the snow from on top of its remains and laid fresh kindling on the dead ashes. Shaking from the cold, it took him three tries to strike a match and get it to flame. When successful, he held it to a fragment of birch bark, then held that to the tinder until it took hold of the flame and made it its own. After adding a few pieces of larger driftwood, he filled the coffee pot with a hunk of ice he had brought up from the river the night before and hung it over the fire. He shook Jass awake to get him going and went over to Molly. He knelt down, leaned over her sleeping form and softly kissed her. She opened her eyes, smiled, and said, "I've been waiting for that."

"So, you've been playing opossum on me?"

"Just wanting my good morning kiss, that's all."

"Seeing as how you're back to your old spry self, you can do the breakfast. I'll go down to the sled and get something for you to work with. Would you care for anything in particular?"

"A roasted chicken and green beans sounds wonderful."

"I'll see what I can dig up. But you might have to settle for bacon and hardtack."

The dogs were, as always, doing just fine. Either running the trail or lying about, it was all the same to them. Huck took a few minutes saying hello and spent an extra moment interacting with Bright.

Back at camp, as he sipped the last of his coffee, Huck asked Jass if he thought they should try the trail again. "After what happened yesterday, I'm a mite skittish about being on the ice."

"I'm with you, Huck. But first I want to tell you and Molly something."

"Sure, Jass. What is it?"

"I probably should have mentioned it earlier, but I was waiting to see how cold it got. It's just this. When the temperature hits this low, you have to be careful about exerting yourself. The cold air will surely scorch your lungs if you breathe it in too deeply. Molly can't be running alongside the sled no more and you have to slow up on your pedaling. I've seen men pay no heed to that advice and a short while later they start in with the coughing; six months after that, they're dead.

"We even have to take it easy on the dogs. They can hold out better than us, but still, we have to be careful of their running."

"You hear that, Molly? You're riding in the sled. If I have to break trail for the dogs, you can walk with me or ride the runners, if you want. But no more running around like you was a kid again."

"Are you saying I'm old, Mister Finn?"

"I'm saying you're just right . . . as long as you do as I say."

They kept close to the western bank; overflows were less likely near the shore. Three miles to the north, the trail became passable and Huck maneuvered the dogs and sled onto it.

They hadn't made many miles before the snow was back. At first, the feathery lightness was of no concern. However, as the hours and miles receded, the snow slowly buried the trail. The dogs were straining to make mere feet through snow that extended up to their necks. It was slow going.

At length, Huck cried, *"Whoa,"* and got out his snowshoes. As he was lacing them up, Molly sat down next to him with *her* snowshoes in hand. "Two can break trail faster than one. Besides, I need to move around some."

"You'll get no argument from me."

Jass' job was to ride the sled and, if need be, mush the dogs. With only one leg, it would be hard to balance on the runner, but Jass said he was up to the task. Then he added, "Besides, I'm as tired of riding in the sled as Molly is, if not more so."

The trail was about five feet across—wide enough for the sled, but not quite wide enough to accommodate two *chekekos* wearing snowshoes for essentially the first time.

With his snowshoes laced on, Huck stood and spoke to Molly. "Alright, this is how it's done. First, take a step, then raise your other foot perpendicular to the first step. Every other step is to the side. That way, you'll trample more snow than if you just marched straight on. Watch me."

With the snow up past his knees, Huck took a step with his left foot. Next, he raised his right snowshoe and turned it so that it was at a ninety degree angle from his body. He tottered for a moment, but kept his balance. When he went to lower the shoe, he fell over face first.

Molly laughed so hard she tumbled backwards into the snow, softly landing on her backside, her snowshoes pointing to the sky. Jass couldn't help it. With his two companions splayed out and almost buried in three feet of snow, he started to laugh, causing him to lose his precarious perch on the runner. Now all three of them were lying in the snow, two of them laughing. Even the dogs joined in on the merriment. They were smiling and bouncing about in their traces, enjoying the show the humans were staging for their enjoyment.

Huck got to his feet first and shook his head. "That's a nice how-do-you-do! I reckon the old-timer who told me about that particular maneuver neglected to mention the aspect of raising my snowshoes high enough to clear the snow." Then he joined in the laughter and went to Molly. After he had her standing, he assisted Jass with getting back on the runner. "Okay, we'll just walk like we're supposed to. Molly, stay near me. With my skill at snowshoeing, I may need your constant assistance."

After the fun, they plodded on, lucky to cover a mile every hour. The snow continued to fall, the temperature remained at fifty-five below, and there was absolutely no wind. At that point, frostbite was not a big concern. However, when the sun rose high enough to ride the top of the mountains for a short while before slipping back below the horizon, they stopped to build a fire. More to warm themselves than to cook anything, but they had some beans and a little bacon to keep the fire of life burning within.

His leg gave out after a while and Jass had to get back into the sled. But that was all right. There was no need to mush. The dogs had been dutifully following behind Huck and Molly since they started out, though they did not like the slow pace. They had been bred to run.

After eight miles, they stopped for the night. While setting up camp, Huck took the canvas holding one of the kits together and stretched it from a low-lying branch at a forty-five degree angle, anchoring it in the snow. He would build their fire under it, so the heat could reflect back onto them, and not rise into the trees and be lost. It was getting colder by the day.

Before turning in, Huck and Jass discussed the feasibility of going back onto the ice. "If the trail doesn't clear up in the next few miles, I'm afraid your baby will be old enough for school by the time you see him," Huck explained.

"I know," acknowledged Jass. "I been thinking along those lines too. Overflows are rare, so if we keep an eye out, and nobody falls off the sled—sorry, Molly—then the worst that can happen is wet feet. You'll have to stop to dry out and attend to the dogs, but the time we save by traveling on the ice will more than make up for delays of that sort. And the dogs' paws should be alright with the layer of snow we have now."

With business out of the way, they lay down on their boughs of spruce to rest, perchance to sleep, for on the morrow they would take to the ice once again.

In the morning, as Huck was harnessing the dogs to the gang-line, Bright broke away and ran down trail, plunging through the snow at a fast clip. "What the hell! Get back here, Bright! Now!"

Bright continued on as though he had not heard his master. Whatever he was up to, he sure was being single-minded about it. Huck sighed and looked to Jass. Jass shrugged, he had nothing to offer.

Huck threw his hands into the air and shook his head from side to side in an exaggerated manner, then started out after the miscreant mongrel. Five steps into his pursuit, Molly was at his side. "Don't look at me like that, Huck. I'm tryin' to keep warm and a nice little walk is just what I need."

"At least you could have brought our snowshoes. I was in such an all-fire hurry to get Bright, I didn't think about them."

"If that little puppy can make it through the snow, then so can we."

Huck was not having a good morning.

Bright's trace was easy to follow in the snow. One hundred yards later, they came upon the fugitive canine enthusiastically wagging his tail. He was standing in front of a woman, an Indian woman. She was sitting on a snow bank, holding something in her arms.

Huck rather loudly exclaimed, "Not another one!" For there was no doubt about this one—she was dead.

When Bright heard Huck's voice, he looked over and barked twice. Then he looked back at the woman, his tail in motion the whole time.

Molly and Huck walked up to an agitated Bright. Molly patted his head, Huck went to the woman. She was wearing only a deerskin shirt, her russet arms exposed. Her leggings were made of seal fur, and she was barefoot. A rolled-up parka rested in her cradled arms.

Expressing his dismay at the sight before him, Huck muttered, "If this don't beat all."

"What's in the parka?" Molly asked.

"Nothing. It's a parka."

"Huck, I saw something move. If you won't look, I will."

Before Huck could react, Molly had the parka in her hands. She unwrapped the bundle to find a baby of about six months old smiling up at her. Its feet, both of them, were shoved into the fur of a moccasin. The baby's hands were in the other moccasin . . . its body wrapped in a red flannel shirt.

Looking over Molly's shoulder, Huck said, "Yep, another red flannel shirt. I should have known." Then he got serious. "What are we gonna do with that thing?"

"It ain't a 'thing.' He or she is a baby who needs our help. What *we* are going to do is take this little Indian back to our camp, and *you,* Mister Finn, are gonna heat up one of those cans of milk that we liberated from McQuesten's trading post."

"Yes, ma'am! Come on, Bright. We've got our work cut out for us."

Molly took a second to scratch Bright behind the ear and say, "Good boy. You'll get an extra salmon tonight."

Back at camp, Jass stared open-mouth at the discovery, and asked Huck, "What happened?"

"It looks like a squaw gave her life in an effort to save her baby. She must have been caught in the snowstorm and knew she was dying. She took off her parka and wrapped the baby in it, making sure its hands and feet would stay warm. It's kinda sad. She must have died hoping that someone would come along before the baby froze to death."

Huck drew his knife and punctured a hole in the top of the milk can and placed it near the fire to thaw. Molly hugged the bundle to her bosom. Bright danced around, wanting to be a part of things. It was his find after all.

"Reckon we'll be gittin' a late start today," ventured Huck to no one in particular and went to check on the dogs. Jass asked Molly if there was anything that he could do.

"Keep an eye on the milk. When it's melted and a little warm, please hand it over."

While she waited, Molly ascertained that the baby was a boy. A boy in dire need of a new blanket-shirt. He had messed the current one. Jass volunteered to find something suitable. He did—his best shirt. He wasn't wearing it because he wanted it clean for when he first saw Mae. But he offered it up gladly.

Molly was gingerly getting the boy to drink the milk when Huck walked up. "Where's my lead dog? Look at him. Sitting there like he's the proud uncle. Come on, Bright, time to hook you up. You can check on the kid at the end of trail tonight. Until then, you've gotta get us north." As an aside, he said to Molly, "As soon as he's had his fill, we're leaving."

Molly nodded, but said nothing. Her attention was fixated on the baby.

After Molly, Jass, and the baby were snug in the sled, but before giving the command to mush, Huck asked Molly what they were going to do about the kid. "I know we can't leave him. But shouldn't we try to find out if he has any kin in this neck of the woods?"

"If we run into any Indians, we'll describe the woman and inquire if they knew her. That's about all we can do."

Huck was fine with that.

Cluck got Bright's attention. *Mush* started him moving. The other eight dogs followed, and they were off and onto the ice.

Near about noon, Huck noticed smoke up ahead. It was drifting from a camp on the eastern side of the river.

People being such a rarity in that country, Huck would have headed over anyway to get the lay of the land and chew the fat for a few minutes. Maybe even enjoy the warmth and taste of an offered cup of hot coffee. The possibility of discovering the baby's origins was just an added inducement.

Pulling up to the bank, Huck informed Molly and Jass, "I'm gonna reconnoiter and then I'll come back for you. It's time we stopped anyway. The dogs need a breather and we could do with something to eat."

Huck was gone for only a few minutes. He returned with five Indians at his back. "I think I found the kid's kinfolks. And they don't seem none too happy that we have him."

Twenty-Two

Huck stood on the bank of the Yukon, smiling at his friends. "Molly, Jass, now listen. We're going with these Indians because they have asked very nicely by pointing their guns at me and telling me that if we did not, they'd kill us and take our dogs. But first, Molly, you're gonna have to hand over the papoose. They're kinda insistent about that. So hand me the baby."

"There's only five of 'em, Huck. I can take 'em with my .36 and have a bullet to spare."

"You gonna do it with a baby in one arm? And besides, I thought you didn't cotton to killing anymore?"

"I'm just funnin' with you. Here . . . take the little tyke."

As Huck reached for the baby, he whispered, "I'm glad you were only funnin' because they understand English and there are six more of 'em back at their camp over the rise. Stay in the sled because we're leaving for their village right away. They insist on that also. On the way, I'll tell you and Jass what little I know."

Molly rode the runners with Huck. Jass sat in the sled "Well, folks, here's the way it stands. When I walked into their camp, they were friendly enough, even invited me to sit down and have something to eat. I told them about my friends back at the sled and, then just in passing, I asked if they knew of a squaw woman with a baby that might be missing.

"That changed everything. They wanted to know what I knew about her and if I knew where she was. Of course, I told them about our discovery this morning, hoping they would take the baby and then we could be on our way. They grabbed me by the arms and practically dragged me back to the sled. On the way, they told me we would have to talk to their chief, and that they would take us to him as soon as they had charge of the baby. They also demanded to know the exact location of the woman, which I told them. I figured they were hankerin' to give her a decent burial. I tried to tell 'em that we had to be movin' on, but they weren't having any of that. So here we are. Your guess about what's going on is as good as mine."

Molly ventured, "Maybe the woman and baby are important people in their tribe. Perhaps they're taking us to the chief so that he can thank us personally for saving the baby's life."

"Maybe," said a not-too-convinced Huck. "What do you think, Jass?"

"If she was so all-fired important, what was she doing out on the trail alone, without even a kit?"

"I can tell you this much," said a bewildered Huck, "the next frozen body we find, we ain't stopping. No way, no how! And especially if it's wearin' a red flannel shirt."

The dogs of the Indian village ran out and attacked the sled dogs as they came in. Huck jumped off the runners and got into the thick of it. He beat the dogs back one at a time with his fist. He had refused the dog whip offered by Adams when he retrieved the sled back on the Klondike. "I won't use a thing like that on another living thing," he had told old Wes Adams.

The Indians thought it great sport. They encircled the sled, laughing and pointing as Huck did battle. At length, things simmered down. The village dogs went back to their depressions in the snow and curled up to await the bidding of their masters or another team of unfamiliar dogs entering their domain.

Huck had been bitten a few times through his mittens, and once on the leg, but that was of no concern to him. He was angry. He stood in the midst of twenty braves, ten or so women, and myriad children. He turned in a circle, looking each brave in the eye—one at a time. When he came back to where he had started, he said in a deceptively soft voice, "Bring me your goddamn chief." When no one moved, he yelled, *"Now!"*

From behind him, a voice said, "You seek me, White Man?"

Huck turned to see a man of unknown years. Huck's first impression was that he was ancient. He certainly looked it. He was bent with age; his skin brown and weathered from countless summers and innumerable winters. However, when Huck looked into his ageless, clear-blue eyes, he had to reassess his first thoughts.

"My name is Neekaii Laii, Two Dog in your tongue. I am the chief of this band. We are The People of the Caribou. You whites call us Gwich'in. We know your tongue because the missionaries taught it to us many, many winters ago.

"If you are wroth because of the dogs, then I offer you apologies. If there is another reason, we will speak of it. But first we will eat. Mayhap we can satisfy your anger and your hunger at the same time."

212

Huck's rage had abated some. He took a deep breath before saying, "Yes, my friends and I will partake of your food. However, we have many questions that must be answered."

"And they shall be, my friend. You and your companions are the honored guests of The Caribou People. You have done us a great service. However, we will speak of that as we eat. Follow me in your sled. Our dogs will be into your food stock if you leave it here."

Two Dog brought them to his log cabin. Holding the door wide open, and with a smile to match, he bid his guests to enter.

A girl of exceptional beauty, looking to be about sixteen years old, awaited them. "This is my daughter. Her name is Oozrii' Oonjit, or Moon Woman. She is still a maiden; however, this year she will build her fire," said Two Dog by way of an introduction.

The cabin consisted of one large room. There were no windows; light was provided by a fire that burned in a crude stone fireplace in the corner. The middle of the room was taken up by a low table, about two feet high. There were no chairs, but furs covered the floor. "Please sit," entreated Two Dog. "Moon Woman will serve us."

Huck helped Jass get situated and then sat down next to Molly.

Two Dog opened the conversation by addressing Huck. "Will you introduce your friends?"

"This here is Molly and the gent is Jass Holloway. Now I have a question."

"Greetings, Molly, and greetings Jass Holloway. Before I answer your questions, may I know your name?"

"I'm Huck Finn."

"Huck Finn, I will answer your questions if I can," replied Two Dog.

"Why were we brought here against our will?"

"My men had to confirm your story. The woman has been located and we now know that you spoke the truth. If you so desire, you may leave at any time. However, since you are here . . ."

Huck looked to Molly and Jass. They both nodded.

"Alright, Two Dog. As you said, we are here already. It is getting late, so tonight we'll enjoy your hospitality. But we leave in the morning."

"That is good, Huck Finn."

Moon Woman approached with a large wooden platter of roasted meat and placed it on the table. She had previously provided bowls and knives.

"I am sorry I can offer you nothing else; the winter is hard and there is no game. But that will soon change. Please pass the meat to your friends, Huck Finn. We will have spruce tea after we have eaten."

There were chunks of burnt meat and ribs of some type of animal. It wasn't half bad.

As Molly chewed on a rib, she asked Two Dog what he meant by Moon Woman lighting her fire this year.

"When a maiden is ready for marriage, she builds her fire to let the young men know that they may approach her. They bring gifts and try to woo her . . . as you whites would say."

Huck nodded and told Two Dog that it wasn't such a bad way of doing things. "It takes the onus off the man."

When Huck said that, there had been a glint in his eye that Molly did not appreciate.

Then Molly enquired. "May I ask you something?"

"Yes, my child. Please do."

"I noticed your blue eyes. And if you don't mind me saying, they are breathtaking. But how is it that an Indian has blue eyes? And by the way, how is it that you speak English so well?"

"My grandfather was an American trapper. He taught me English on his knee. I had a good start on your language by the time the missionaries arrived."

The meal was satisfying. It was warm in the cabin and the spruce tea had put Huck in a better frame of mind. He was ready to forgive Two Dog for having them brought to the village. "You mind if Jass and I smoke our pipes?"

"You have tobacco?"

The question was asked with such wistfulness, such longing, that Huck had to smile. "Sure, we've got plenty. Care to join us in a pipe?"

Two Dog reached under the table and came out holding a corn cobb pipe.

Huck reminisced. "I used to smoke one of them when I was boy. I sure enjoyed the taste."

Huck handed his pouch over to Two Dog and let him have at it. By the time he got it back, Jass was already puffing away. Huck got busy loading his pipe, trying to catch up, so Molly made small talk. "That meat was pretty good. What was it?"

Two Dog looked surprised. "I thought you knew. It was dog. We are eating our dogs, there is nothing else to eat this winter."

Molly looked to be a little sick. Jass and Huck seemed just fine.

Two Dog continued, "But as I have said, you people have changed all that. In three days, the game will return and there will be no more hunger."

"What do you mean?" asked Huck.

"The boy you found is my grandson. His name is Dagaii Laii: White Dog. His mother, my other daughter, was the woman you found on the trail."

"By the way," asked Molly, "where is her husband, White Dog's father?"

"He was killed last spring while hunting bear. His gun misfired and a bald-face grizzly made short work of him."

Huck brought the conversation back on subject. "What do you mean that we have changed things in your village? All we did was find a baby on the trail."

"It is something white men may not understand. But I will try to explain."

Huck, Molly, and Jass settled in for what they thought would be a good Indian tale.

"When the game became scarce, we did not worry. There was always game. Sometimes we had to travel far outside of our land to find it. But find it we did. Then the days turned into moons and the moons became an entire winter without game. We managed in the summer, but it has been many, many sleeps since we have eaten moose meat. The caribou no longer come to the crossings. We consulted our priest. He told us there was an evil upon the land.

"He said he would pray to the Great Being and ask if we had offended Him in some manner, if we were being punished for our sins. After days of fasting and prayer, our priest came to us and told us he knew the cause of our misfortune and what we must do if we were to survive.

"Yes, we had offended the Great Being by forgetting our ways. We had lapsed in the giving of sacrifice. In the old times when we had a good catch of fish, we always gave a portion back to the river. When we killed a moose, we would leave a portion in the trees as a sign of thanks. But over time, we forgot our ways. A haunch of moose was too valuable to leave for the wolves. It was hard work setting the fish traps and then emptying them. Why should we allow any of our catch back into the streams and rivers? We *had* sinned."

At that point, Moon Woman came in with a vessel of spruce tea and refilled their sipping bowls. Afterwards, Two Dog continued with his narrative.

"The priest informed us that he had been told there was only one way to make amends. We must give sacrifice, but

217

not just any sacrifice. We had been too long negligent in doing what was required of us. Only a sacrifice of monumental import would satisfy the Great Being. Our priest informed us that the offering must be from a member of a chief's family. Only in that manner would the Great Being be appeased. I put forward myself, but was told that only the sacrifice of Dagaii Laii will bring back the game. When his mother heard of this, she ran away, taking her son with her. There is no blame. She was his mother. I am his grandfather. I would gladly die in his stead, but that would do no good. I am the chief of *all* my people. I must do what is right for them.

"Hence, in three days' time—when the moon fills the sky—White Dog, my grandson, will be placed on the fire of the gods so that my people may live."

Molly sat bolt upright. Huck knew she was going to say something and he tried to cut her off, but she ignored his look of disapproval. "Are you telling us that you're gonna throw that little baby on a fire and burn him alive?"

"I did not think white men would understand."

Huck squeezed Molly's arm and whispered in her ear, "Not now. We'll talk about it later." Then he had to contend with Jass because he could see that he was going to throw in his two cents worth. "Jass, we are Two Dog's guests. We must respect his ways and the ways of his people. Do you understand me?"

Jass caught the tone of Huck's voice and he knew that he was speaking more for Two Dog's benefit, so he leaned back. He would wait and talk to Huck in private before starting a ruckus.

Huck turned back to Two Dog and said, "It's not our way, so what you said came as a shock to my friends."

"I understand. But now it is late. Your dogs will need attending to and I am sure that you are tired. My daughter's hut is yours to sleep in. I will take you there."

Molly asked, "Moon Woman's hut?"

"No, my other daughter, White Dog's mother."

"Where is White Dog? Can we see him?"

"He is with the priest. They are being purified for the ceremony. I am sorry, but you cannot see him."

Huck jumped in at that point. Holding out his tobacco pouch, he said, "Take some for later. And then if you would show us where we're gonna sleep, we'd be mighty grateful."

Two Dog took a liberal pinch of tobacco, placed it in his pipe, and then put it back under the table.

"Thank you. Now follow me."

He led them to the edge of the village, to a hut that looked like every other hut—a wooden frame covered with skins. "This is where you will sleep," said Two Dog.

Once the chief had departed and they were alone, Molly started to pace back and forth. When she could no longer hold her tongue, she inquired of Huck, "Well, what are we gonna do about it?"

Huck looked over at Jass and said, "Why don't you start a fire. I'll take care of the dogs. And Molly, you can continue to wear a furrow into the ground."

219

As he was leaving, Molly called after him, "Don't forget to give Bright an extra salmon."

With the dogs taken care of, and Huck, Molly, and Jass sitting in front of the fire warming themselves, Molly opened the conversation. "Huck, you know we gotta do something."

"No, I don't know that, Molly. What about you Jass? Are you as incensed as Molly is?"

"I think Molly's right. What they're planning is barbaric. But I don't know what we can do about it."

Huck sighed. "Molly, we're responsible for getting Jass home. If we poke our noses into this affair, *we* may never get home, never mind him."

Molly said nothing. She knew Huck was leading up to something. But Jass, not knowing Huck as well as she did, said, "I've got a say in this. And if you're worried about me, then don't be. I'll go along with whatever you two say or do."

Huck smiled at his friends. In the firelight, he looked much like that small boy who played on the Mississippi River a long time back and who had once snuck up into a church's choir loft to listen to eulogies about himself when it was believed he had been murdered.

"Alright. We're gonna steal the boy. I just don't know how. Let me sleep on it."

With that out of the way, they bedded down, but not before Molly gave Huck a long kiss and said, "Thank you."

Twenty-Three

In the morning, they cooked their breakfast in the hut's fireplace and, as they ate, Huck laid out his plan, such as it was. "I don't have everything worked out yet, although I have a general sense of what we have to do. There's no reason for Two Dog not to trust us, but just to make sure the old bird has no doubts, we will ingratiate ourselves with him. When we're done eating, I want you, Molly, to dig out the tea we found at McQuesten's, and some of the evaporated potatoes and onions. Take that over to Two Dog and tell him you wished it was more, but that's all we can spare. I'll meet up with you in a spell. Until I get there, keep him busy. Ask about his people. Most importantly, how many braves are in his band. And if he asks when we're leaving, act like a squaw and tell him he'll have to ask me."

"Jass, all the dogs except Bright are out visiting their canine friends. I'd appreciate it if you could walk around and make sure that they're not causing any trouble with the Indians' dogs; if they are, round them up and bring them back here. When they're accounted for, come back and wait for Molly and me."

Molly sipped her coffee and asked, "What are you gonna be doing?"

"I'm gonna find out where they're holding White Dog."

Jass wanted to know how he was going to accomplish that.

"Bright will lead me to him." After a moment's hesitation, he added, "You know, we should give White

Dog a white man's name because if we pull this off, we may be saddled with him for a spell. And don't neither one of you suggest Huck!"

"John has a nice sound to it," said Molly.

"Then John it is. Some of this I'll be making up as I go along, so if I say anything to White Dog that you find off or might disagree with, just follow my lead and trust in 'ol Huck."

"Alright, 'ol Huck. Now go find John," instructed Molly.

At the door of the hut, they split up. Molly went to the sled to fetch the items for Two Dog. Jass hobbled away on his crutches in search of their dogs. And Huck went to where Bright was lying in the snow and knelt down on one knee. "So, you're not interested in exploring? That's good because I have a job for you. I want you to show me where the baby is. He's your find and you should know his scent. Now go find him."

Bright jumped to his feet and wagged his tail. He thought this was a good game. He would show Huck how well he could play it. He raised his snoot into the air, and his nose started a- twitching. After a moment, he took off running, but *out* of the village. Huck thought for sure that Bright had misunderstood him or just didn't understand at all. *Probably has the scent of a beaver or something. I better catch up before he gets into trouble.*

Huck followed the dog's trail in the snow, weaving between the snow-capped pine trees. He did not run, for he remembered what Jass had said about scorching his lungs. His vapor breath preceded him and fell back onto his beard and brows, covering them in the same fine, crystalline-white substance he had been wearing since leaving Dawson.

A mile into his trek, he slowed his progress—up ahead he spied Bright. He was in front of a small shelter whose frame was covered in skins and furs. When he saw Huck, he began barking, wagging his tail, and prancing about. By the time Huck reached the hut, an Indian had pushed aside the skin-flap covering the entrance and poked his head out.

"Wherefore are you here, Hair-Face?" he asked in a not-too-friendly manner.

"I was chasing after my dog and he led me here. My name is Huck Finn. I don't reckon I've met you yet."

"I have no concern for your name. But I know you. You are not welcomed here. You are one of the whites that brought White Dog back. I am Chuu Zraii, priest to The People of the Caribou. I will forgive your intrusion this one time, but leave and do not return. And take your dog with you!" Having issued his orders, Chuu Zraii pulled his head back into the hut and closed the flap.

"Well, Bright, I reckon I owe you an apology. Let's go. There just might be half a salmon waiting for you at the village."

Jass was already back at their hut when Huck returned. After giving Bright his half of salmon, Huck asked about the dogs.

"It seems they made peace with the Indian dogs. Some of them are playing with the other dogs and a few are curled up in the snow close to an Indian dog. It looks like they're keeping each other warm."

"That's good. And as long as you're here, you might as well come over to Two Dog's with me whilst I set my scheme in motion."

"You mind telling me what that scheme is?"

"Not at all, but I'd rather do it only once. When we're back here with Molly, I'll tell you both about it at the same time."

Two Dog welcomed them into his lodge with a big smile. "I thank you for the tea and other things."

"That's alright, Two Dog. You shared your limited food with us. It was the least we could do. But that brings me to something I'd like to talk about. Why don't we sit down and smoke a pipe?"

"That will be good," said Two Dog.

As Huck seated himself at the table, he caught Molly's eye and arched an eyebrow, silently asking, *"Did you find out how many braves?"* She nodded *yes.*

Once their pipes were going, Huck said, "You know, Two Dog, we've been thinking that maybe we can help you out. Our dogs need a rest. So if you don't mind, we figured we'd hold up here for a day."

"You are welcome to stay as long as you wish."

"Thank you. But here's what I wanted to say. We know that in three days' time the evil will be cleansed from the land and the game will return. However, in the meantime, wouldn't it be nice to chow down a nice, big moose steak or perhaps a slab of caribou? Besides, from what I can see, you don't have that many dogs left. And the ones you do have, you'll be needing to pull your sleds."

Two Dog drew on his pipe with a faraway look in his eyes. He was thinking on how good it was to taste tobacco once again. At length, his attention returned to the room. "What you say is true, and any meat other than dog would be good, but I have told you, there is no game to hunt."

"I know you've told me, but I want to ask you . . . is it that there is no game? Or what little there is, your braves scare off while hunting them? I've noticed their guns. Most of them are one-shot muskets. They have to get up pretty close to what they're shooting at. And if they miss, the game is long gone before they can reload."

Two Dog was a little hesitant. "Perhaps . . . but what are you saying?"

"What I'm saying is that Molly and I are fair to middling shots. And we would consider it an honor to hunt up some meat for you. Our rifles can take down game from over a hundred yards away. And we seldom miss. So while our dogs are getting rested, we were thinking of doing a little hunting. But we're gonna need some help."

"Help?"

Two Dog's pipe had gone out and Huck held out his pouch to the chief, "Yes, help. Reload and I'll explain."

While Two Dog attended to his pipe, Molly stood up. "You men do your smoking and talking. I want to look around the village and visit with the people." Looking towards Huck, she added, "I'll see *you* back at the hut." To Jass, she simply nodded.

With Two Dog again enveloped in a cloud of tobacco smoke, Huck finished with his spiel. "We will need a few braves to accompany us and show us the game trails. When we hunt, we mostly get what we go after. But we cannot leave the dead game for even a short while to come back and report the kill. The meat would freeze and there'd be no cutting it up. As you know, a thousand-pound moose ain't easy to move around from place to place unless he's movin' under his own power."

Two Dog bowed his head in a sagely manner, indicating his understanding. "When do you want to leave?"

"Might as well get the show on the road. How about we start out in an hour?"

"The men will be ready."

On the way back to the hut, Jass had one simple and straightforward question: "Hunting?"

Huck winked at his friend and said. "Let's round up Molly, then I'll explain."

As it turned out, they did not have to go looking for her; Molly was outside the hut, playing with Bright as they walked up.

"Howdy, boys. Got everything worked out?"

Huck pulled the skin-flap back so Jass could go inside. "Come on, Molly. Leave Bright be, and I'll tell you what's what. We gotta get our guns because we're going hunting."

Jass stoked the fire to get a blaze going. Huck threw on a few sticks. Molly pulled out their Winchesters and pistols.

As they waited for the room to warm up enough to remove their parkas, Molly said to Huck, "I take it we're going hunting instead of grabbing the boy and hightailin' it outta here."

"Here's the deal. I'll lay out what I've come up with, but I'm gonna ask you both to hold your tongues until I'm finished. If you have any questions afterwards, you can ask 'em then."

Molly was wiping down her Winchester with an oily rag and nodded her head. Jass was putting coffee in the pot and said, "Sure thing, Huck."

In spite of agreeing not to ask any questions, Molly needed one answered before things proceeded. "Did you find John?"

Huck sighed and sat down crossed-legged on a bear-skin in front of the fire. "Bright did. He's in a hut outside the village. The witch-doctor is looking after him, which is good 'cause that means we have only one man to overpower instead of half the tribe. Here's my thinking: If we just take the boy and skedaddle, they'll be right behind us. Our runner marks aren't gonna be hard to follow in the snow. By the way, Molly, how many braves in the village?"

"There are twenty-four men, counting Two Dog, twenty-six women, and thirty-one children. I don't think Two Dog included John in that number."

"Okay, White Dog . . . I mean John . . . is awfully important to the tribe, so we can reckon on most, if not all, of the men coming after us once they know he's gone. What *we* have to think about is what they'll do *if* we get away. They'll still be hungry, so will their witch-doctor tell them to throw Moon Woman onto a fire to appease the gods?"

Huck paused long enough to accept a cup of coffee from Jass. Then went on, "This is the way I figure it. We go out and get enough meat to hold 'em until the thaw, which is three months away. For roughly sixty people, half of 'em kids, three good-sized moose should do it, or five or six caribou. But there's another reason I want to supply them with food. It will be a pretty big deal after all this time of eating nothing but dog. I'm sure they'll throw some sort of shindig to celebrate. While they're whoopin' it up, we'll take John and be on our way. If we're lucky, we might get a few hours head start."

Jass asked, "What do you want me to do while you and Molly are out hunting?"

"Round up our dogs and keep them here even if you have to put them in harness. When it's time to go, I want us to be ready."

They all stood. Molly handed Huck his six-shooter and he strapped it on. She was already wearing hers. Then she tossed him his Winchester saying, "I've got the ammunition sack, so are you ready?"

"Ready as I'll ever be. Jass, you hold down the fort. We'll be back as soon as we've bagged us some game."

Six braves were waiting for them outside of Two Dog's cabin when they walked up. They were not looking any too happy. One of the men knocked on the door. A moment later, it opened and Two Dog came out. Pointing to his braves, he said, "These men will go with you; they speak English. They will take charge of any game you may kill. But I must tell you, they are not too pleased. They believe it an insult that you say you can kill game when they cannot."

Huck turned to the Indians and said. "It is not that we are better hunters. It is that our guns can shoot farther than yours. When we heard of your difficulty, we said we would help. Not to show that we are mighty hunters, but to put good meat on the fires of your lodges; to put good meat in the bellies of your women and your children."

The Indian men said nothing, though their hostile looks faded somewhat.

They left the village headed north with the Indians leading the way. It had stopped snowing; the sky was dark and overcast and there was no wind. After an hour of slogging through the snow, the lead Indian put his hand up, and pointed off to the right. Five hundred yards away, a magnificent specimen of Yukon moose flesh stood with his back to them—enjoying a meal of pine needles from a low-hanging branch of an evergreen tree.

Huck leaned into Molly and whispered, "He's gotta be at least twenty hands at the shoulder. Do you want him?"

"I'll take this one to show the Indians that a white woman can shoot. You can have the next one." Without another word, Molly left the hunting party and shortened the distance between herself and her prey. She kept low to the ground and walked quietly. When she was one hundred fifty yards away, the moose stopped his dining and looked around, sensing something. Molly froze where she was and crouched even lower. The rest of the hunting party were well-hidden behind a snow drift.

Molly knew she was a tad too far away to assure a kill on the first shot, but she had, over the years, brought down more than a few deer from this distance. If she tried to get any closer, she would surely spook the animal, so she opted for a lung shot. Even if he ran, he would not make it very far.

Already on her knees, she brought the rifle to her shoulder and sighted her quarry. She could see that he was getting anxious. Thankfully there was no wind, hence, she did not think he could smell her presence and she just might be able to make the shot from this distance because of that lack of wind. If she waited much longer, he would bolt. And even a few more feet farther away would put him out of rifle distance. Molly exhaled, the vapor settling on the blue metal of the gun, freezing into a thin white ice-cloud. Looking down the barrel of the Winchester with the sight resting just below the beast's left shoulder blade, she slowly squeezed the trigger.

The resulting explosion startled the landscape. Several ptarmigans flew into the air from their hiding place off to the right. A snowshoe rabbit that had escaped Molly's notice scampered into the tree line, whereas the moose stood still for an extended moment before taking off, thrashing his way through the snow. He made only a few strides before falling over on his side. He wasn't yet dead, but he soon would be.

The Indians came out from behind the drift and clamored around Molly, patting her on the back and asking to inspect the rifle. She handed it around and, one by one, the Gwich'in admired its workmanship and held it to their shoulders, sighting down the barrel. Huck walked up and said, "That was a pretty good shot. Now if you're done taking your bows, perhaps we should move on. We don't have that much daylight left."

"What do you mean a '*pretty good*' shot?" asked an incredulous Molly Lee McMasters.

Huck smiled at her and amended his statement. "That was a damn good shot. *Now* can we move on?"

"Of course, Huck. Why didn't you just say so?"

They left two Indians to dress the kill. When done, they would cache what they could not carry and then come back for the rest.

The hunting went about the way Huck and Molly had thought it would. They got two more moose and on the way back to the village, they ran into a small herd of caribou. They brought down three of the animals before they could scatter. By the time darkness descended, they had secured enough fresh meat for The People of the Caribou to keep them fed for a while.

They returned as heroes. They were welcomed and cheered by the men, women, and children who stood around an open fire where two large moose haunches roasted over the flames. It seemed that all the people of the village were there. It was cold, but the fire *and* the thought of the soon-to-be-distributed moose meat kept everyone warm.

Huck pushed through the throng and made his way to their hut without acknowledging any of the accolades. Molly held back and shook a few hands and allowed herself to be slapped on the back in gratitude. When thanked for their efforts, she told the well-wishers that what she and Huck had done had been their pleasure.

Separating upon entering the village had been by design. Molly was to keep the villagers' attention focused on her and the moose meat, while Huck made sure that Jass and the dogs were ready to go.

It was full dark and, even though a wolf moon—what the Gwich'in called a full moon—was only two days away, cloud cover obscured the light from that celestial body. Which to Huck's way of thinking was just dandy. He would trust Bright to find the trail in the darkness and stay on it until they hit the river.

Molly was finally allowed to make her way to the hut where she found Huck loading the last of their kit into the sled. Jass was standing nearby, leaning on his crutches.

"You boys ready to go? I understand Two Dog will be passing out the first of the moose meat himself. They want us to attend the ceremony. I said that I would fetch you fellas and be back soon. I just hope that they'll be too busy with the meat to know or care where we've gone off to."

When the sled was loaded, Huck motioned for Jass to get in. "Molly, you ride the runners with me. I may need you at the hut. That witch-doctor is an ornery old cuss and I don't know what kind of remonstrations he'll put up. Either way, we're gonna have to leave him tied up . . . unless you want to kill him."

"I don't want to kill nobody."

"I know, Molly. Just funnin' with ya. Let's go and get your baby."

Twenty-Four

The closest they could get to the hut was about half mile. As good a lead dog as Bright was, he couldn't maneuver a sled through the trees. And neither could Huck for that matter. They left Jass with the sled; he would keep an eye on it and the dogs. Huck and Molly made their way through the woods in silence, the only sound—the crunching of snow underfoot.

When the dark shadow-outline of the hut, silhouetted against the ambient light, loomed before them, Molly whispered, "How are you gonna play this?"

Huck halted his progress and said, "I hadn't thought about it. I figure we'll just go in and tell Chuu Zraii we'll be taking the boy and see what he says about it."

"Chuu Zraii?"

'I might have forgotten to mention it, but that's the witch-doctor's name. I asked around, it means Dark Water. Or maybe Black Water, I don't rightly recollect. But either way, it seems an appropriate name for the jasper. He ain't exactly the friendliest cuss around."

"That's real interesting, Huck. I only asked what the hell you were talking about. I didn't need a thousand word explanation."

"Feeling a mite anxious?"

"I sure am."

"Then let's do it so that we can get up to Circle City and get warm."

They pulled out their six-shooters and walked up to the entrance of the structure. With a nod to his partner, Huck pushed the flap aside and entered. Molly came in right behind him.

It was a small enclosure; dim light emanated from a dying fire. Chuu Zraii lay asleep on a deer skin; the baby next to him—wrapped in some kind of fur. He was fully awake. He smiled and brought his hands together, as though he was trying to clap, when he saw the intruders. Molly's heart melted at the sight of him. She holstered her gun and started in his direction. But Huck touched her arm, causing her to hesitate. He pointed to the sleeping priest and mouthed: *Him first.*

Molly took one more look at the baby and then drew her gun. "Wake up, you son-of-a-bitch," she said in a rather loud voice. Huck shook his head, thinking the play could have started with a mite more delicacy. However, he was content to let Molly run things.

Chuu Zraii came out of his sleep slowly. When he finally realized what was happening, he started to get to his feet. Huck pushed him back down with one hand. "If I were you, I'd stay where you are. This lady standing next to me, I think, wants to blow your head off for what you're planning on doing to that innocent little baby lying over yonder. So if you're smart, you won't say anything to further antagonize her."

Molly *was* angry, but she took a moment to get it under control before saying, "Huck, do you have the rawhide to tie him up with?"

Huck looked confused. "I thought you brought it."

Molly slowly shook her head in mock despair "Alright, I'll keep him covered while you find something."

Huck picked up a rabbit skin and was about to cut it into strips when Molly said, "Not that. The baby might need it. Throw it over here."

He did so and then slowly looked around the hut until his eyes came to rest on Chuu Zraii's headdress. Among other things, it was adorned with strips of beaded rawhide. Huck pointed to it and sardonically asked, "Do you mind if I use *that*?"

Feigning not to hear his tone of voice, Molly answered innocently, "Use whatever you want, but please hurry it up."

He cut three lengths of rawhide off the headpiece, each about eighteen inches long. After getting the priest to lie on his stomach, Huck tied his hands behind him and then tied his ankles together. Bending his legs back, he pulled the last piece of rawhide through the two pieces that bound his feet and hands, tying them together. Now there was no way the man could move around.

When he was finished, he said, "Get John and let's go."

"Aren't you going to put a gag in his mouth?"

"No need to way out here. Let him yell his fool head off. It will help him pass the time until someone finds him."

With the priest taken care of and the baby in Molly's arms, they were ready to leave. But when Huck pulled back the flap of the hut to let Molly go out first, they got the surprise of their lives. Standing at the door were two teenage boys, one of whom held a skewered piece of roasted moose meat.

Huck moved quickly to the entrance to block their view of the inner hut. With his best Huck Finn smile, he temporized, "Howdy, boys. We have just been visiting with your medicine man. He's a little busy now. Can you come back later?"

The boys looked confused. Of course, they knew who the white people were, but why were they visiting with Chuu Zraii?

Ultimately deciding that it was none of their business, the one with the meat held it out towards Huck. "Two Dog asked that we bring this to Chuu Zraii." Huck was about to accept the offering when the priest yelled out, "They lie! They have come to steal White Dog. Run and tell the people."

It took a tick or two for the boys to comprehend what they had just heard. But that was all, just a tick or two. The one holding the meat dropped it onto the snow, causing a hissing sound as the still-hot moose meat came into contact with the cold snow. But the boys were too far away to hear it because by then they were in the trees, running towards the village like two young antelope.

Huck drew his Colt from its holster, but he did not fire. Molly touched his arm and said, "You're not gonna shoot them, are you?"

"Nope, I drew my gun out of instinct. I'm not even gonna wound 'em. And I'm sure as hell ain't gonna run after 'em. So we better get going."

On the way back to the sled, Molly could not help herself; she just had to say it, "*Let him yell his fool head off. It will help him pass the time until someone finds him.*"

Huck shrugged. "I had a feeling things were going too easy."

"I'm sorry I said that. I was just being a woman. I love you for not shooting those boys."

"Don't worry. I'm sure I'm gonna have to shoot someone before too long."

At the sled, Molly pulled up her parka and placed John to her breast. Then she slid the parka back down. She was going to have him do his travelling next to her body in an effort to ward off frostbite and to keep him warm.

They told Jass what had happened and asked him to pull out one of the Winchesters and be ready to use it.

When Molly was in the sled next to Jass, he covered her with a wolf fur, smiled, and said, "I'm curious, Molly. Do you and Huck always live like this?"

"No, sometimes it gets exciting."

Huck clucked to Bright which got the dogs up on their feet. With the word *mush,* they were on their way.

While they were busy getting John, the sky had cleared. The moon's ghostly light reflected off the snow, turning the landscape into one of stark contrast—a contrast of black and white. A carpet of gentle white snow interspersed with foreboding black shapes that projected long, dark shadows. Most were trees, but one black form, not as tall as a tree, stood in the middle of the trail, pointing a rifle at the fast-approaching sled.

Huck told Jass to hold his fire. And instead of calling for Bright to slow up or halt, he spurred him on with the voice command *"Hike!"* The figure in the trail held his position until the last possible second, then jumped aside. As the dogs passed, he tossed his gun in the air and caught it by the barrel. When Huck was abreast of him, he swung it like a club. Huck easily ducked the intended blow and they were down the trace, safe for the time being. Approaching a bend in the trail, Huck turned to see the dark figure jumping up and down, waving his arms about. He was soon joined by other vague shapes; they too danced about in anger. Huck waved to them as they passed out of sight.

Jass yelled to Huck over the creaking of the wood runners, "Why didn't he shoot?"

"His powder was wet or he had orders not to shoot because he might hit the boy. They need him alive if he's to be a decent sacrifice."

There was no more talking after that. They were about an hour from the river, which gave Huck time to think as he rode the runners. *If they're afraid to shoot at us for fear of hitting the boy, that might give us a slight advantage.*

It was cold. There was no doubt about that. Huck's cheeks were stinging and he could not feel his nose. The ice from his breath had encrusted his beard and mustache to the point where he had to crack the thin layer of ice with his hand before he could open his mouth to speak.

He drove the dogs hard. His hope that they might not be pursued right away had flown out the window when they encountered the man on the trail. At the river, he would give the dogs a breather and feed them. He was long overdue on that count. They were good dogs and they worked hard for their one salmon a day. He had to keep them fed or they would become too weak to pull the sled, which would allow Two Dog to catch up with them. If that happened, the best they could hope for would be to join John on the fire. At least it would be a faster death than what the priest probably had in mind for their demise.

It was at least ten days to Circle City and safe harbor. He believed he could count on Two Dog to chase him and his companions all the way there, but perhaps the residents of that burg might dissuade the old Indian from his intended revenge. That is, if they had not all stampeded down to Dawson in search of gold since Jass' last visit.

At the river's edge, Huck pulled up. "Okay folks, time to stretch your muscles. I gotta feed the dogs and give 'em a break. I figure the Indians are about an hour behind us. It would have taken them time to organize and harness their dogs. Maybe we got an hour and a half, if we're lucky."

Jass walked around on his crutches to get his blood flowing. Molly stood by Huck, holding on tight to the slight bulge in her parka. "We have to feed John. Do we have time to build a fire and melt a little milk?"

"We'll have to make the time. We still have half of that opened can and another full one. If there's any left after he's eaten, let me know. I'll fix up something to hold it. You can keep it next to your body so it won't freeze. We're gonna make a good run after this. There won't be no more fire-building for a spell."

They got the dogs and the baby fed, but had nothing themselves. They would eat later when the dogs were played out and they had to make a longer stop of four or five hours. Stopping then would not be so risky because the Indians would have to rest their dogs also. Huck found an empty skin in their kit that had been stitched together to hold water. He gave it to Molly and she poured the remainder of the milk into it, then placed it under her parka, next to John.

Taking a deep breath, and with Molly, Jass, and the child on the sled, secure under layers of wolf fur, Huck got the dogs on their feet. Before giving the command to move out, he took a moment to reflect on something. *You wanted to come to Alaska for a little adventure, Huck Finn. Well, now you got your wish. Hope you're happy. But if anything happens to Molly, I'll never forgive you.*

Bright was looking back over his shoulder at Huck, wondering what the holdup was. He wanted to run. Huck smiled. *You're right, boy.* "Mush!"

They swung out onto the river. The snow was deep enough to protect the dogs' paws, but not too deep to inhibit their movement. The northern lights were playing havoc in the night sky. Huck stood on the runners, hung on tight to the handlebars, and threw his head back to enjoy the wondrous sight as the miles passed under his sled. *If we weren't in so much trouble, this might be enjoyable.*

Neither Molly nor Jass spoke as the dogs strained in their harnesses. Huck's face was caked with ice. He rubbed his nose and cheeks frequently to bring the feeling back. Frostbite turns the skin black and leaves deep scars. If he lived to see Circle City, he wanted to be his old handsome self. Then he laughed at the thought as the lights over his head turned from green to white, then spun clockwise, exploding into every hue in the rainbow. "Come on, Bright, make them miles," he said aloud, but not loud enough for anyone to hear—as they ran for their lives.

Huck worked the dogs for six hours with only short breaks in between. The sun would not be making much of an appearance that day, but when morning's twilight came, he halted at a place that would give them the high ground and good cover if the Indians showed up.

Jass took the axe and set about collecting firewood. Molly paced back and forth to get warm while holding her little bundle close. Huck unhitched the dogs, and after checking their paws, fed them.

As he was building the fire, Jass offered to do the cooking. "I'm learning to get around pretty good on only one crutch and I think it's about time that I start pulling my fair share of the freight." Molly had John to look after and Huck was exhausted from hours of mushing, hence, Jass received no argument.

As they sat by the fire awaiting the coffee that would bring a little warmth into their bodies, they discussed what they should do next.

"How long do we have to rest the dogs?" asked Molly.

"I'd reckon two or three hours at least," offered Huck. "What do you say, Jass?"

"I would say that's about right. You didn't work 'em too hard. But *you're* gonna need some sleep. Molly and I caught ours while you were mushing. Now it's your turn. I'll keep watch while you catch forty winks."

"I won't deny that I'm beat, but let's get some grub in us first. Then I'll see how I feel."

Jass prepared a half-way decent meal of bacon and slices of fried potato. It was their last potato, but it had been a large one.

Huck handed his empty plate to Jass and yawned. "Reckon I'll curl up in the sled for a spell. If there's any sign of the Indians, don't hesitate to get my ass moving. Okay?" He said this looking at Jass, but it was Molly who responded.

"Don't bother getting too comfortable. The Indians are here."

Huck spun around and looked downriver, and sure enough, seven sleds were coming their way. They were too far in the distance to tell who was driving them, but it was a good bet that Two Dog and his men were riding the runners.

"How did they catch up so fast?" asked Molly.

"Reckon it didn't take them as long to get organized and underway as I thought it would," answered Huck.

Jass went to the sled and retrieved the guns. He didn't own a gun himself, so he asked Molly if it would be alright if he used her Winchester. "Seein' as how you're a little preoccupied with John and all."

"Sure, Jass. But I don't want you shooting at anything until I've had a little talk with Huck. Okay?"

"Sure, Molly. I ain't hankering to get into a war out here in the middle of nowhere."

Molly went over to where Huck was standing, his eyes downriver, his thoughts, she knew not where. She stood next to him for a second or two before she enquired in a scared, small voice, "What are you gonna do?"

He turned his head and looked at her in disbelief. She sounded like a little girl; he couldn't believe it was Molly Lee standing next to him. Then his demeanor softened and he asked gently, in a quiet voice of his own, "What do *you* want me to do?"

"I don't really know, Huck. A few days ago, I would not have hesitated a Yankee moment to defend myself. But things are different now. Maybe it's the baby, but even before we came up here to Alaska, I was regretting being so loose with a gun. Yet, I've killed four men since we've been here. The killing has to stop sometime. So I think that right here, right now, in the middle of this goddamn Yukon Territory, hundreds of miles from civilization, I am going to renounce killing. You can do whatever you wish. I do want to live and I want John to live, but if it means killing another human being to do so, then I will die now. I don't aim to ever raise a gun in anger again, even to save John's life."

Huck smiled a tender smile, a loving smile. He was thinking on how beautiful she looked in the eternal twilight. "Okay, Molly. I'm with you, but what about Jass?"

"I was thinking on giving myself up . . . with John . . . then maybe they'd let you and Jass go. All they really want is the baby, but I'm going with him. I couldn't live with myself if I gave him up."

"Talk about living with yourself! I'm getting angry with you, woman. Do you really think I'd leave you behind? Don't answer that. Just go back to the fire and take Jass with you. If I'm alive in an hour, I *might* forgive you."

In the cold, callous arctic air, Huck stood alone upon an isolated bluff overlooking the frozen Yukon River, deep in the Yukon Territory, awaiting the man who had come to kill him.

Twenty-Five

The seven sleds came down the river in a single line. When they were below the bluff, they fanned out into a semi-circle facing west and there they waited.

Huck sighed, and for the second time that day he asked himself what was he thinking when he said he wanted to go to Alaska. He went to the sled and pulled out two of the wolf furs, then stopped by the fire. "Jass, while I'm down there, I want you to harness the dogs and get ready to leave. If things don't go well, I mean if you hear a shot, take Molly and beat it for Circle City."

"Like hell I will! I couldn't get Molly in that sled short of knocking her unconscious. And *I* sure as hell ain't leaving you." Jass was worked up and angry that Huck would think he'd leave a friend behind.

Huck understood. "Thanks, Jass. It's just that we promised to get you home and I was trying to keep that promise as best I could."

"Don't matter, Huck. Molly and me is stayin'. Right, Molly?"

"Right." She said the word softly and without emphasis because, for her, it was a foregone conclusion that she would never leave Huck behind.

As he made his way down the hill carrying the two furs, he was thinking that he would have to do some fancy talking. *I got three lives hanging in the balance. Four if I count myself. So, Huck Finn, you better put those talking skills you learned from Tom Sawyer to good use in the next few minutes.*

He stepped a few feet out onto the hard ice and stopped. One of the Indians left his sled and started walking towards him. He couldn't see who it was because the hood of the Indian's parka covered half his face. But from his stance and his gait, Huck knew who it was. It was Two Dog.

He stopped ten feet from Huck and spoke through the cold, his breath misting in the air. "I won't ask why you did what you did. White men do not understand our ways. So be it. But now we will take the boy. And you and your friends will come back with us. Chuu Zraii has asked that we not kill you on the trail. He wants to personally mete out your punishment."

"From my short acquaintance of the man, I figured he'd want to do just that. Your grandson is fine; he's with my friends up there on the rise, warm around our fire. And we will go with you peacefully. We could have fired on you when you first arrived. As you know, we are fairly good shots and our rifles can quite easily reach to where your sleds stand. But we do not want to kill. Our only intention was to save your grandson's life."

"Bring the boy to me. Are your dogs ready to travel?"

"Are yours?"

Two Dog smiled. "It seems we have some time on our hands."

"I reckon we do. I brought these furs so that we may sit while we wait. And perhaps you can tell me of your ways that I do not understand."

246

Two Dog gave orders for his men to build a fire on the eastern bank and wait for the dogs to regain their strength for the return trip. He put them at ease by telling them that the white people would come without a fight. There would not be gun play.

On the western bank, Huck handed Two Dog one of the furs which he placed on the snow. Huck did likewise. After they were seated cross-legged, opposite each other, Huck pulled out his pipe and tobacco pouch. "You got your pipe with you, Two Dog?"

Two Dog looked a little embarrassed. "I brought it. The first thing I was going to do once we captured you was take your tobacco."

"I don't blame you. Tobacco's hard to come by in this neck of the woods." Huck filled his pipe and handed the pouch over to Two Dog. When his pipe was filled, Two Dog offered the pouch back. "You might as well keep it. It won't be doing me any good," said Huck in way of refusal.

Two Dog hesitated, but then said, "You keep it . . . for now." Huck nodded and accepted the proffered pouch.

They took a few minutes to enjoy their pipes. Neither speaking. At length, Huck asked a question. "What makes you think that the Great Being wants your grandson as a sacrifice? I know that is what Chuu Zraii told you, but how do you know it to be true?"

Two Dog took the pipe from his mouth and slowly shook his head. "Our priests talk with the Great Being for us. They tell us his commands, his laws, how he wants us to live. It has always been thus."

"I thought you said you learned English from the missionaries. Did you learn nothing else from them?"

"There is no difference between our religions. We both believe in the Great Being. That he can be a most angry god at times and that he will demand sacrifice if we are to be forgiven for our transgressions."

The statement shocked Huck. He was no Sunday-Go-To-Meeting type, but he did know that Christians did not sacrifice anything to their god, let alone babies.

"Where did you get the idea that white men make human sacrifices?"

"From the missionaries, of course."

"Please explain," he implored.

"Did not the Great Being demand the sacrifice of his own son to save us? Did he not demand of Abraham his son's life? If he can offer up his own son to suffer and die in sacrifice, how can I not tender my grandson, if so commanded, in order to save my people?"

Huck was beginning to wish that he had paid more attention to the preacher the few times he had attended Sunday services. Not being a theologian, he thought that maybe he should take a different approach. But first he needed time to figure something out, so he reloaded his pipe and handed over the pouch, this time insisting that Two Dog keep it.

By the time Two Dog had loaded his pipe and got it going, Huck knew what he was going to say. If it didn't work out, he would just have to get used to the idea of slowly roasting over an open fire. An open fire stoked by Chuu Zraii.

"Did not the missionary tell you that the Great Being works in mysterious ways? And did you not tell me that you have no heart for burning White Dog alive, but feel you must do so in order to save your people?" Huck had intentionally used the term "burn alive." When Two Dog heard it, he visibly winced and looked away.

Huck now had the advantage. He had to drive it home or come the morrow, he and the others would die a slow and an exceptionally painful death.

"What I'm saying, Two Dog, is that you can believe that the Great Being sent me and my friends to feed you as easily as you can believe he wants you to offer up your grandson. You now have enough meat to last until the thaw when the bear will awaken from his sleep, when the herds of caribou will return from their winter wanderings, when the moose will come out of hiding to enjoy the sun on his skin. Isn't that why you were going to throw White Dog onto a fire? To bring back the game so that your people would have food? So now that you have meat, what's the point of killing him?"

Two Dog said nothing.

Huck kept trying. "We have shown you the way. Make trade for better guns. The game has not left; it is there for the hunter with the right weapon. Our rifles are now yours regardless of what you do with us. Trade for more like them and your people will not go hungry again."

Still, Two Dog said nothing.

"And your priest. He is like every other preacher I've ever known. Long on tellin' you what God wants you to do, and short on really helping people live day to day. If things are bad, it's because you have displeased the Great Being. If things are good, it's because he, the Holy Priest, has interceded on your behalf. He does not hunt. He does not bring meat into the camp. Yet he takes the choice pieces. Has he told you that is the way the Great Being wants things? I bet he has."

And still, White Dog said nothing.

Huck gave up. He had used all the cards in his deck. He put out his pipe, placed it his pocket, and awaited the directive to round up his people; that it was time to return to the village.

Two Dog also put out his pipe. "It is cold; we must sit by a fire. And I would like to see my grandson. Also I am hungry. Is there food in your camp?"

Huck had not realized it, but his body had tensed up. He let out a deep breath and relaxed a little before saying, "We have bacon and beans, and maybe my woman can rustle up some pan biscuits."

They walked up the bluff together without speaking. At the camp, Huck told Molly to wrap White Dog— deliberately using the boy's Indian name—in a warm fur and hand him to Two Dog. She hesitated a moment, but the look from Huck prompted her into action. When the baby was in Two Dog's arms, Huck asked Molly to fix something to eat for their guest.

Molly and Jass looked at each other, silently asking, *"What's going on?"*

There was no conversation while Molly prepared the food. Whilst she attended to that, Jass got the coffee going. Two Dog played with the baby by chucking him under the chin and talking and cooing to him in his native tongue.

When the food was ready, Two Dog handed White Dog back to Molly and thanked her for allowing him to hold the baby. Now Molly was really confused, and so was Jass. Huck alone had an inkling of what was about to transpire.

Two Dog delved into the meal, all the while saying nothing. When he had sopped up the last of the bacon grease with the last of the biscuits, and his coffee cup was empty, he wiped his mouth with the back of his hand and spoke: "I have never liked Chuu Zraii. The things you have spoken of, Huck Finn, ring true. If I allow you to leave and take White Dog with you, what will become of him?"

It was Molly who answered his question. "He will be raised as a white man, yet he will know of The People of the Caribou, and of his grandfather, the great chief, Two Dog. He will know of his mother who gave her life that he may live. His name will be John and he will be raised as my son."

Two Dog looked at Huck. "Does she speak for you also, Huck Finn?"

"Yes, she does. I will be his father. His name shall be John Finn."

Two Dog nodded. "It is good. You may wonder why I do not take him back with me. I will tell you. I go back now to engage Chuu Zraii in a battle to determine which one of us will lead our people from this point onward. His power over us must come to an end. He had me convinced that I must slay my own grandson. It is not right. I now believe that The Great Being never demanded that of me. Because of you, Huck Finn, my eyes have been opened. My ears have heard your words. However, there are many who have faith in Chuu Zraii's power. In some respects, he has more sway over my people than I do. If I should lose to him and he is victorious over me, then my life is forfeit. And so would be White Dog's."

Huck nodded his understanding and said, "Let's have a pipe on it." Then with a smile, he asked, "By the way, can you spare a small pinch of tobacco?"

Two Dog laughed and pulled out the pouch.

After their pipes had gone out, it was time for the Indian to head for home and for the whites to continue on to Circle City. With one, last, loving look at White Dog, Two Dog bid Molly and Jass farewell. After taking one of the Winchesters from the sled and a sack of .44 bullets, Huck walked down the bluff with the old Indian. At the edge of the river ice, he held out the rifle to Two Dog. "Take this. It shall be the first of your many new guns." Before turning away, he added, "That was an act of real love back there. You have my word that the boy will lack for nothing and that he will grow up to be proud of his Gwich'in heritage."

Two Dog nodded and they shook hands. Huck waited until the old man was halfway across the ice before going back up the rise.

Twenty-Six

Back on the bluff, Huck suggested they pack up and get moving. "We're five days outta Circle City and I'm hankerin' for that nice warm seat around a nice hot stove."

Before agreeing to anything, Molly and Jass wanted to know how Huck had pulled their bacon out of the fire. He explained, "I only pointed out the many deficiencies of his medicine man and Two Dog concurred."

Molly asked incredulously, "'Concurred'?"

"Yeah, I read it in a book once. I've been holding it back, but thought now was as good a time as any to use it. You know how I like to improve my mind."

Molly kissed him on the cheek and then, one-handed, while holding John close to her bosom, helped Jass pack up. Huck thought he had earned himself a cup of coffee, so he poured the last of it and enjoyed its warmth, if not its taste, as his partners loaded the sled.

Circle City was the largest town Huck and Molly had been in since Skagway. There were many buildings scattered about. However, most of them were dark and empty; only a few had a warm, welcoming glow emanating from their windows. Jass pointed out the only saloon that seemed to be open and Huck steered the dogs in that direction.

As they pulled close to the saloon, a few dogs came out to inspect the interlopers, but it was too cold for any aggressive behavior and they soon went back to their beds of snow.

Huck helped Molly and Jass out of the sled, and as they headed for the saloon, he yelled after them, "I'll catch up as soon as I've checked over the dogs."

Jass went up to the bar to rekindle his acquaintance with the bartender, explain about his leg, and procure a bottle. Molly sat herself down at an empty table. When Huck came in he went to the stove and stood over it, picking ice off his face. A few pieces fell onto the stovetop causing a vigorous sizzle and bit of steam to emanate therefrom. When he could feel his nose and cheeks again, he walked over and joined Molly.

She had the baby out from under her parka, holding him in her arms. "We have to get John something to eat. He had the last of the milk this morning. And I think he's ready for something a little more substantial. What do you think, Huck?"

"I think you oughta be in charge of his feeding. If you leave it to me, I'd probably have him knocking down Three Star."

Molly gave a faux disgusted look in his direction and hugged John a little closer. "Don't you worry none, Johnny Boy. I ain't gonna let that nasty old man get anywhere near you."

Jass came up with a bottle tucked under his arm, working his crutches. "I'm sorry. This is all I could handle. Can you get the glasses, Huck?"

"You got the important stuff. That's all that matters. Sit down and I'll handle it." Before going to the bar, he asked Molly what he should order for John.

"I'd say get some mush with a little milk on it. If they don't have that, then see what they do have and come back and tell me what it is before you order. I don't want you getting him a steak . . . or Three Star."

Huck looked at Jass and declared, with a smile, "Things ain't ever gonna be the same."

There was no milk, but there was cornmeal mush. And John took right to it. The three adults had to be content with whiskey until *their* food was ready.

After everyone had eaten, they were sitting at the table discussing the next leg of their trek when Jass put forth, "It's about ninety miles to my cabin. In the summer, I pole down Birch Creek to get to town. The creek comes to within six miles of this burg. My boat is cached up on the creek, a little southeast of here. However, it ain't gonna do us much good with everything frozen. So we'll have to take the sled across the mountains, but don't worry, there's a good trail that passes through to the other side."

Huck asked if there was a place where they could hole up for the night and Jass was more than happy to fill him in on the situation. "There are plenty of empty cabins and not a lock on any one of 'em. It's the way it is up here. Not many men steal in this country, but those who do, seldom have the chance to do so a second time. The miners are pretty strict concerning that matter. We've had more than a few hangings."

"Can we take over one of the cabins without the owner's permission?"

"That's also the way up here. When it's as cold as it is now, you don't even have to ask."

"Alrighty. I'll go find us a cabin. You two stay here. And, Molly, try to stay outta trouble while I'm gone."

"Should be easy enough if you're not here to start any."

As he pushed through the door to go outside, Huck inadvertently bumped into a young man of about twenty years who was coming in. "Why don't you watch where yer going, grandpa?"

"I'm sorry, sonny. My mistake."

"Just watch it in the future."

Huck chuckled to himself and then went about finding lodging for the night.

When he came back into the saloon, he informed his partners that he had found a nice empty cabin complete with a stove and firewood. He had already started a fire to get the place warmed up. "One or two more drinks and we'll call it a night. You okay with that, Jass?"

"I can't wait to hit the hay. It's been a long haul up from Dawson."

Molly was holding John, gently rocking him back and forth. "Come on, baby, time to sleep."

Things were quiet in the saloon, no one was talking. There were maybe twenty-five people sitting at tables, or standing at the bar, enjoying their liquor and the welcoming warmth of human companionship in such an inhospitable environment.

Huck was just about to stand and help Molly to her feet when a voice rang out in the stillness. "Is that a siwash papoose?" It was the young boy that Huck had encountered earlier.

Molly looked at Huck and said, "Let it be."

Huck shrugged. It didn't matter to him one way or another. "Alright, Molly, let's go."

"I asked you a question, grandpa."

Huck glanced at Molly. "Do you mind? I need a little exercise."

"As long as you don't kill him."

"Thanks."

Huck got up and walked over to the bar and faced the inquisitor. "I'm sorry, but would you please repeat your question? I don't think I heard you right."

"You heard me alright, mister. Indians are not allowed in saloons. Don't matter their age. It's the law."

"It is? Who made that law?"

"We did. Us miners."

"Who's gonna enforce it?"

At this point the boy looked around the small room for support. There was none forthcoming, so he did the only thing a young man who had had a little too much to drink could do. "I'm gonna enforce it. You take that siwash outta here right now or you'll have to answer to me."

Huck turned his back to the boy and asked the citizenry of Circle City if anyone else had a problem with the baby being there. There were a few murmurs of "No," and all of the men and the few women who were present shook their heads.

Huck turned back to the boy and declaimed, "Looks like you're the only one that has a problem concerning my son. So why don't you give it a rest and I'll buy you a drink?"

"You're his father? How does a white man end up with a siwash for a kid? That lady over there sure don't look like no squaw."

Huck looked back towards Molly and said, "I tried." Then he hit the boy so hard on the jaw that he flipped him over the bar. To no one in particular, Huck said, "Not bad for a grandpa."

He had learned a long time ago that, in situations such as the one he found himself in at the moment, it was always best to see if the aggrieved had any friends about. "Anyone got anything to say? Anybody want to take up his cause?"

Nobody did.

Huck nodded to the room in general, then he got Molly and Jass moving toward the door. He was the last to leave—just in case.

Huck drove the sled to the cabin, Molly and Jass followed on foot. It was a short walk and when they arrived, Molly went inside. Huck and Jass stayed out to unharness the dogs and feed them.

Once she had warmed herself up by the stove, Molly lay John down on one of the four bunks and changed his makeshift diaper. She was using Jass and Huck's extra shirts. On the trail, when she had rinsed them out in melted snow, they froze solid. She had to break the ice off and then place them near the fire for a while before putting them under her parka, next to her skin, so that they would be warm enough for John at the next changing. It would be a great pleasure to do her laundry, such as it was, in a warm cabin and have it dry without turning to ice.

Shortly after Molly heard the dogs' *thank-you* howl, Huck and Jass came in and went right to the stove. "Before you get too comfortable, Huck, can you melt me a little snow? I've got to clean me some diapers tonight."

Huck was tempted to give out with an exaggerated sigh, but thought better of it. Molly was doing a bang-up job caring for the boy, so he figured he'd be as helpful as possible without funnin' around, which reminded him that there was something he wanted to do for Molly

While Molly rinsed out the shirts and Jass sat on a bunk smoking his pipe, Huck sat by the stove and worked on one of the spare dog harnesses. He wouldn't say what he was doing, but occasionally, he'd look over at Molly as though studying her. She was busy and did not notice. However, Jass did notice and started to say something, but Huck shook his head and put his finger to his mouth, like what he was doing was a secret.

In time, Huck went over to Molly and said, "Try this on."

She looked at what he was holding and asked, "A dog harness?"

"It's a baby harness. Look, these straps you put on your shoulders like you would a pack, but you wear it in front. These other straps are where John's legs go, and this other one goes across his back. This way, you won't have to hold him all the time."

Molly tried it on. It was a good fit. She then put John into the contraption and it worked pretty well. He was held in his little seat facing her, and she had both hands free.

"I thought of it when I saw you loading the sled one-handed because you were holding the baby."

"Thank you, Huck. That was very sweet of you."

"Not at all. This way you can get twice the amount of work done."

She gave him a good-natured swat with a damp shirt, then leaned into him and kissed him lightly on the lips.

When it was time to bed down, Huck stood at the bunk with his arm hugging Molly close, her head resting on his shoulder. They were looking down at John, and Molly observed, "Isn't he the best-behaved baby? You notice he hasn't cried once. Well, just that one time when he was hungry. But all babies do that."

Huck nodded his agreement, gave her a light squeeze, and puffed out his chest. "I don't know much about babies, but I must admit he is about the best-looking kid I ever did meet." Huck Finn had become a proud father at the age of fifty-nine . . . in the middle of the Yukon Territory.

In the morning, as Jass prepared flapjacks and coffee, he said to Huck, "When you go over to the trading post, keep in mind that once we cross the mountain, game is gonna be kinda scarce. We won't be able to count on getting any fresh meat, so better stock up on enough food to last us until we get to my place."

At the trading post, Huck bought two sacks of corn meal for John in addition to everything else they needed. He was pleased to find that tobacco was available. He bought a cheap pouch and had it filled with the precious substance. Jass had also advised him to buy a pair of snow goggles. "They might come in handy on the mountain. If you were to go snow blind, it would take three or four days for you to get right."

After their meal, they sat around the stove and made their plans. Huck was the first to speak. "We have everything we need, so I don't see any reason why we shouldn't take off today. It's nice sitting in a cabin instead of freezing in the snow, but Jass is anxious to get home and we've lost enough time as it is fooling around with those Indians." He became momentarily distracted while he filled his pipe, then he asked, "Do either of you know the date?"

Molly shook her head, but Jass spoke up. "I've been keeping track. It's January 20th. At this rate, we'll make it in plenty of time for the birth."

Huck took charge as was his wont. "Okay, let's hit the trail. Molly, you're in charge of John. I'll harness the dogs, and Jass, seeing how you're moving around so well on those crutches, you can load the sled."

Molly and Jass looked at one another and laughed. At first, Huck didn't understand, but soon, he blushed under his beard and laughed too. "Sorry. It goes back to my lawman days when I had to bark out orders all the time or nothing would ever get done. It's a hard habit to break even all these years down the road."

They started out traveling southwest; when they came to Birch Creek, they swung due west and headed toward the mountains.

Huck Finn mushed his dogs; he had a one-legged man he had to get back to his wife in time for the birth of their child. Molly Lee McMasters hugged a six-month-old baby to her breast. The temperature was fifty-eight degrees below zero and falling fast. In the far distance loomed the mountain they had to cross—shrouded in ominous gray-black snow clouds.

Twenty-Seven

A few miles later, as they were following the winding trail up the mountain, the storm let loose with all its frozen fury. Molly held John closer as she and Jass hunkered down under their furs. Huck had no choice but to stay where he was. He yelled over the wind, encouraging Bright to mush on.

Visibility became a problem. At first, he could not see past Bright; soon however, he could not see his wheel dogs. The blizzard, full of rage, assaulted him head-on, laughing at his misery. At one point, his eyelids froze shut, forcing him to ride the runners blind while breaking the ice from his eyes. When he could see again, he pulled the snow goggles from under his parka and put them on. It was some help, but not much. His visibility was still less than five feet, but at least they kept his eyelids from freezing shut.

The dogs drew the sled higher and higher up the mountain. If there had been a place to make camp, Huck would have pulled them over, but there were no trees—no wood for a fire—only boulders and large snow drifts. Higher still they climbed, higher still. He could not tell when they went through the pass, but two hours into the storm, the ground beneath the sled leveled off for a short while before inclining once again. However, now they were descending.

Once they were off the mountain, Huck would have to find a place to make camp where they could wait out the storm. He had no feeling in his face. The vigorous rubbing of his cheeks did little to bring forth the sought-after prickling feeling of returning blood. He *had* to warm up or else he'd lose skin, maybe even lose his nose. His feet and hands were not faring much better.

Abruptly, the sled came to a full stop. In the middle of a snowstorm, on top of a mountain, his lead dog had halted his progression! Huck yelled over the wind and through the snow for Bright to get moving. He clucked his tongue until it was sore. He yelled *mush* until he was hoarse. Still, the sled did not move.

Shaking his head and cursing the gods, Huck trudged through the knee-deep snow until he came to Bright. He was not hurt, and neither were any of the other dogs. He grabbed Bright's trace and pulled. *Nothing!* Bright had dug in, he would not budge. Huck pleaded and even tried to bribe him with a promise of extra salmon, but Bright stayed immobile.

In frustration, Huck returned to the sled and asked Jass, "What's with Bright? He refuses to move."

"I have no idea. Molly and I were wondering why you had stopped. We seem to be sitting at a rather steep angle. Maybe Bright has lost the trail, and, as any sensible creature would do, he's waiting for the snow to let up so he can find his way back."

"Well, I can't wait. I'm gonna lose fingers and toes if I don't warm up."

Jass started to get out of the sled and Huck asked him what he thought he was doing.

"Look, Huck, I told you from the beginning that you had to trust your lead dog. So that's what we're gonna do. I've had it easy riding the sled, covered in furs. But there ain't room for the three of us in here, so you take my place and I'll hunker down behind the handle bars. It's a fast-moving storm, it can't last much longer."

"Like hell you will! I'm the musher and that's like being the captain of a ship. Okay, we'll listen to Bright, but you stay where you are. And that's an order!" He then grabbed one of the extra furs and wrapped it around himself.

Molly had poked her head out from under a protective covering of wolf fur to take in the exchange between the two men. Huck told her to cover up and that he would see her when the storm had passed. She said nothing, but her eyes begged him to come into the sled and lay down beside her. He knew what she was asking and he shook his head.

Jass tried to stand, but because of his missing leg, he didn't make a very good job of it and fell back down. "That'll teach you to disobey your captain," said Huck as he threw the furs over their heads. He went and huddled down between the handlebars. With his back up against the sled—which afforded scant protection from the wind and snow—he thought about how he could go for a cup of hot coffee and a pipe right about then.

As he was imagining his second cup of coffee, with maybe a shot of whiskey in it, a sudden stillness came over the mountain. The wind died down and the snow went from blowing almost horizontally to falling gently from a clearing sky. Within minutes, it had stopped completely.

Huck was near-frozen to death. He now knew how that man they had found on the trail and John's mother felt shortly before they died. Just before the storm abated, as he was thinking about that second cup of coffee, he was also thinking about how pleasant it would be to lie down in the snow and just catch a little sleep. He was so cold and so very tired.

With an effort, he stood up, took off the goggles, and turned around. Molly and Jass were sitting up, looking toward the dogs. He followed their gaze. The wheel dogs and swing dogs were buried in snow. It had protected them from the wind. They were fine. He would let them rest in their snow igloos until he was ready to move on. Only Bright was standing, half turned around, looking back at Huck. He seemed to be smiling and gave out with one loud bark when their eyes met. Then he faced front and wagged his tail, as if to say, "Look, didn't I do good?"

In a blinding blizzard and disobeying his musher's commands, Bright had stopped not twenty feet from a cliff with a thousand-foot drop-off.

Huck forgot all about his frozen flesh. He looked to his lead dog, and in the quiet stillness that was the aftermath of the storm, his words carried, even though they were said in an awed whisper. "Yes, boy, you did good."

Huck ordered Jass and Molly to not move and to stay calm until he got to them. He didn't know why gravity hadn't yet taken the sled over the precipice, but he did know that if it started to slide, it wouldn't come to a stop for at least one thousand and twenty feet—more or less.

He walked around to the side of the sled, and first, very carefully, helped Molly stand up and step out into the snow. She hugged John closer to herself and, afraid to breathe too deeply, backed slowly away. Next, Huck got Jass up and lifted him clear of the rail. When he was stable on his crutches, Huck gave him his orders: "You stay with Molly.

I need you to look after her and the boy while I get this contraption turned around."

"Might I make a suggestion?"

"Sure."

"It would be a lot safer, especially for the dogs, if there was an anchor for the sled."

"Such as?"

"My weight on one of the runners will help. I promise you, if it starts to go, I'll jump off."

"Okay, Jass. I'm gonna get the dogs standing up and then get Bright to turn 'em and go back up the mountain a ways. But we've gotta do this slow. There's ice under the snow, I've slipped on it a few times already."

With Molly a few yards up-mountain, leaning against a large boulder, and Jass standing on the sled's left runner, Huck gave Bright the command to turn and come to him. When the dog tugged on his harness, the other dogs, one by one, stood and shook the feathery snow off their furry coats. After their rest, they were ready to go to work.

Huck walked down to Bright and quietly spoke to him. "You're doing good, boy. Nice and easy, there's no rush. I know how you wanna run, but now ain't the time."

Inch by inch, the team followed Bright until they had brought the sled all the way around and had it pointed in the right direction. Huck told Jass to stay on the runner. There was no way a man on crutches could make it through snow that deep. Hell, even he was having trouble.

Huck got to Molly and they walked in front of Bright, forging a path in the snow for the dogs to follow. It was all uphill. At length, the ground beneath them leveled off and they knew they were back at the pass. Now all they had to do was find the down-trail under many feet of snow. And they had to do it fast because Huck was in danger of losing flesh. Patches of skin on his face had turned black. They were small blotches, but they were only going to get bigger if he didn't get near a fire soon.

Huck paid no mind to the numbness of his cheeks. His only concern at that moment was finding a way off the mountain before they all froze to death. It was sixty-two below zero—ninety-four degrees below freezing—and still the temperature was falling.

"Are you alright, Molly?"

Looking at the black spots on Huck's face, Molly said, "Don't worry about me. I'm fine and John's fine. And so is Jass. We have to build a fire for you!"

Huck crinkled his eyes in reply. They were about the only part of his face still working. Most of the flesh had frozen.

Huck was thinking he would unharness Bright and let him find the trail, but before he could do anything, Jass exclaimed, "There it is! I recognize that rock." Jass was pointing to a large boulder, fifteen feet in height and about ten feet across. "It's where the trail splits. One path doesn't go anywhere and the other is the pass over the mountain. Bright must have gone the wrong way because that snow drift was blocking the trail."

The drift he was referring to was a buildup of snow against the boulder, about five feet high. Huck kicked at the powdery substance and trampled it down until there was room for the dogs to get through.

"Alright, everyone on board. We're going down to level ground right now and build us a fire!" said Huck in a peremptory tone.

As Molly and Jass were getting situated, Huck went to Bright, scratched him behind the ear, and said, "You're a good boy. You saved our bacon back there. Thanks for not listening to me. I know I've said this before, but this time, I mean it. From now on, I'll listen to you more closely."

Bright wagged his tail in agreement.

Once they were off the mountain and had made camp, Jass and Huck collected wood for the fire. While Jass got it going, Huck rubbed his face with snow. When his cheeks started to burn like they were afire, he knew he would be okay.

At first, Molly held his coffee cup as he sipped from it. His hands (and his feet) still had a ways to go before they thawed out completely. The deep-purple and black-scabbed skin on his face would eventually heal, leaving only minor scars. All things considered, Huck had come through the storm in relatively good shape.

They had not made many miles that day—they still had eighty-five more snow-covered miles to go. They were only days away from journey's end and they were anxious to once again know the pleasure of sleeping in a warm bed with a roof over their heads.

They decided to stay where they were for the night even though it was only mid-afternoon. Huck needed a respite from the rigors of mushing through a blizzard.

The camp was situated next to a small creek of crystal-clear ice. Darkness descended, but the aurora borealis was late in making its appearance. In its stead, one million stars flickered on and off in the crisp, clean air. Molly looked into the creek; the reflection of the stars seemed as though a thousand pins of light were embedded just below the surface, twinkling up at her and her alone. She turned to share the ethereal sight with Huck, but he had fallen asleep sitting up, with a coffee cup in his hand. She and Jass lay down some spruce boughs for his bed and got him situated. As Molly covered him with a blanket, he whispered in her ear, "I saw the stars in the creek. I was just too plumb tuckered out to say anything about them. They *are* a pretty sight." A few seconds later, he was sound asleep.

Jass made up Molly's bed while she held John. Of all of them, John was faring the best. Before she fell off to sleep, the northern lights exploded in a misty green and violet wave over her head, momentarily obliterating the silver stars from the sky.

The next morning, the temperature inched toward seventy below zero as they mushed west. There was no sunset to ride into, only the interminable twilight of the day.

Twenty-Eight

Making headway through the freshly fallen snow was an arduous process. Powdery as it was, it still came up to the dogs' necks, though for the most part they could mush through it without Huck having to stop, lace up his snowshoes, and walk out in front. But on occasion, the drifts became insuperable and he did have to break trail, which slowed their progress considerably.

Because of the extreme cold—seventy below—they were compelled to stop and build a fire every few hours in order to thaw out. Consequently, they made only nine miles that first full day after coming down from the mountain. They still had seventy-six freezing, snow-and-ice-covered miles to go.

In camp that night, Molly and Huck played with John for a few minutes while she had him out from beneath her parka to feed him and change his shirt-diaper. "How's he bearing up with the cold?" asked Huck.

"We're doing a grand job of keeping each other warm."

"I thought babies cried all the time. This little fella hasn't let out with a peep."

"He *is* a wonderful baby, isn't he?"

"Of course he is. He's a Finn!"

"Look at those darling brown eyes."

"All us Finns have darling brown eyes."

Molly ignored Huck's facetiousness and continued on with her inventory.

"And his chubby little cheeks. And his black hair! I know women that would kill for hair like that. Do you think we should keep it long until he can decide for himself how he wants to wear it?"

Huck looked lovingly at the woman sitting next to him and could not help but smile. She had raised her step-daughter alone after her husband was killed. But the girl was already eleven by the time Molly had met and married McMasters. She had never taken care of a baby before and her motherly instincts were showing.

They got an early start in the morning. Even though it was still full dark, the whiteness of the landscape drew in light from the billions of stars floating in the sky above. The reflection off the snow was more than enough to show them the way. Nonetheless, it was slow going. By the time the darkness had turned to twilight, about mid-morning, they had made only three miles. Shortly thereafter, Huck halted the dogs at what seemed to be a rather large lake. He wanted to confer with Jass.

"What do you think? The snow is slowing us down somethin' fearful. If we cut across this lake, we'll shave off miles. We could probably make it in an hour; otherwise, it looks like it'll take us to the end of day to get around to the other side."

"You're in charge. Whatever you say will be fine with me. However, it's not a lake. It's a river that widens out here. I don't know if it has a name, I've been in this neck of the woods only once before, but I know the trail we're on will take us south to where the river narrows, then back north to that point right across the ice . . . over there."

Huck looked to where Jass was pointing, and thought for a moment. "It's a hell of a short cut. I reckon that in the summer you have to follow the trail, unless you happen to be carrying a boat in your kit."

"You're right. Before freeze-up, the trail is the only way. All told, it's about a ten mile go-around."

"Alright then, let's do it, and when we get to the other side, we'll stop and build a fire. By the by, do you think this cold snap is ever gonna end? What do you reckon the temperature is?"

"Spit."

"What?"

"I'm in the sled, you're out there. Spit and I'll tell you how cold it is."

Huck wanted to get going, but his curiosity got the better of him. He let fly a goodly amount of saliva just to see what Jass was talking about. Instantly, he heard a sharp crackle as it froze solid, a foot from his face, and fell onto the snow.

"It's about seventy below," Jass informed an astonished Huck Finn.

"Reckon it is. Get back under those furs. I'm getting us to a fire on the other side."

With Jass re-situated, Huck got Bright and the other dogs moving again. A few minutes later, the birch-wood runners, sliding across the slick, icy surface of an unnamed river deep within the Alaskan interior, was the only sound heard for miles.

They were approaching the halfway point and Huck was searching for a likely place to camp on the far shore. He was looking for a good concentration of trees; they needed wood to build the large fire that would warm their insides once and for all. Huck was tired of being cold all the time, and was thinking that he should have brought some whiskey after all. *That would have helped keep us warm.* But then, smiling a slight, rueful smile, he realized the whiskey would have been long gone by now anyway.

Then it happened.

There was a loud CRACK! The ice Bright had just passed over shattered, plunging the six swing dogs and the two wheel dogs into the frigid water where they splashed about and struggled to be free of their harnesses. Bright immediately stopped where he was. If he had continued on, the sled would have followed the dogs into the river.

There was nothing but open water between Bright and the sled. He was on solid ice, but the weight of the drowning dogs pulled him closer and closer to his death. He dug in with his paws as best he could, but still, he slid ever closer to the hole in the ice.

It took Huck a moment to comprehend what had just happened, but as soon as he realized Bright's predicament, he was off the runners and rushing to Bright's rescue. When he reached his lead dog, he already had his knife in hand. He cut Bright's tug line, freeing him from the other dogs. Then he looked back to see Jass cutting at the gang-line so that the sled would not follow the other dogs into the bitter cold water. With the line severed, the current swept all eight dogs under the ice and out of sight.

Jass lay back down next to Molly and whispered, "Don't move a muscle. The sled is resting on severely cracked ice and we could follow the dogs at any moment."

Huck walked back toward the sled, careful to keep his distance. Bright walked at his heels. The fissures in the ice emanated out from under the center of the sled to a distance of about two to three feet.

"Are you two okay?" he inquired.

Molly answered, "We're fine. Jass tells me we're in a spot of trouble."

"Nothing really. But you've gotta do exactly like I say. You need to get outta the sled. You can't stand on the ice and, because you have John, you can't slide. So I want you to crawl out and then stay on your hands and knees and inch your way over to me—very slowly. If the ice starts to go, don't worry. I'll get ya.

"Jass, as soon as she reaches hard ice, I want you to get the hell outta there too. I don't have to tell you how to do it. Just do it!"

Molly made her way over the top rail and onto the ice. John was secured in the harness Huck had made, so she had full use of her hands. She did as Huck had told her and when she reached him, he pulled her to her feet.

"Okay, Jass, now you!"

"First, I'm gonna throw out a couple of packs. We're gonna need supplies."

"Alright, but if I yell for you to move, you move and get over that damn rail. The damn ice could give way at any time."

Jass tossed the furs and his crutches onto the ice. Then he grabbed the closest pack and that followed. He looked down and saw the two skins holding his gold and started to reach for them, but then pulled his hand back and looked around for something that would help keep them alive. He spotted the rifle. It was half buried under one of the boxes of salmon. He was fighting to free it when Huck hollered at him to move it.

"The cracks are lengthening! Get out now!"

But Jass kept at it until he had the gun in hand and then scurried over the top rail to safety.

Huck saw that Jass had left his gold. With a deep sigh, he raced out to the sled, grabbed the sacks and sent them sliding across the ice; they came to rest at Molly's feet. He could hear the ice cracking and he could feel it giving way. He was about to run back when he noticed one of the sacks of corn mush he had bought in Circle City lying on the floor. He seized hold of it and bounded back to solid ice just as the sled disappeared from view, leaving a trail of bubbles and small pieces of ice floating where it had been only a moment before. As they stood, shivering on the ice, looking on in disbelief at a hole big enough for a large freight sled to slide into, a wooden crate bobbed to the surface.

Jass was on the opposite side of the ice hole. Huck went over and picked the pack and furs up off the ice. Jass was holding the rifle. "Give me that. You have a hard enough time as it is maneuvering around on those crutches without having to fiddle with a long gun too."

As Jass handed over the gun, he said. "I want to know something. I want to know why you risked *your* life to get *my* gold."

Huck joked that he was after the cornmeal for John.

Jass wouldn't be put off. "If you had gone down with the sled, how do you think I'd feel? Do you think I could ever look Molly in the eye again?"

Huck got serious. "You lost a leg getting that gold. You have a wife and two—well, almost two—kids that are going to need it. I'm sorry to say this, but you're not gonna find much work with a missing leg and all. Now, let's collect Molly and John and make camp. We gotta figure out what we're gonna do next."

Jass said nothing, but he felt honored to know a man like Huck Finn.

They made their way off the ice and found a suitable place to set up their camp. The only dry wood available lay directly under the tall pine trees. Their overreaching branches had caught and held much of the snowfall. Even though the snow was not as deep under the trees, they still had a job uncovering enough wood to start a fire and to keep it going for a while.

At first, no one spoke. The great white silence that pervaded the land inhibited speech. Their primary goal was to get warm. They sat in front of the fire, wrapped in the furs Jass had saved, rubbing their hands together trying to get the feeling to return.

277

It took a few moments for the magnitude of their situation to sink in. It was quite a shock seeing the sled and the dogs sink beneath the ice. It was even more of a shock to know that they were seventy miles from their destination, every mile covered in snow of at least two feet deep. It was going to be challenging enough for Huck and Molly to negotiate those seventy miles without snowshoes, but for a one-legged man on crutches, it'd be damn near impossible. Then there was the question of food. They were closer to Circle City, but two things prohibited them from taking off in that direction: They would have to go back over the mountain on foot, an impossibility for Jass; and they *had* to be there when Mae gave birth. If they backtracked, they would never make it in time.

Huck was the first to speak. "I reckon we oughta find out what we have to work with and go from there. But before we do that, I gotta ask you, Jass . . . why did the ice give way at seventy below?"

"It's what's called a black-hole. It's where the current under the river eats away at the ice until it's pretty thin. They're very dangerous and impossible to detect. Even a good lead dog like Bright can run over one and not know it."

Molly had John in her arms, sitting close enough to the fire to keep him warm, but not so close as to make him uncomfortable. "Seventy miles doesn't seem that far. I know the snow will slow us up some; still, we should make it in a week at the most."

Huck admired her tenacity, and although he thought her mistaken about how long it would take to get to Jass' cabin, he had resolved to hold his tongue for the time being. Right now, he just wanted to know what they had in the way of supplies. With a grunt of weariness, he stood and went to the small pile that constituted their provisions. It looked rather pitiful lying there in the snow.

There was the rifle, the sack of corn meal, the two bags of gold, and the pack. *Not much*, he thought, but he said nothing aloud. Opening the pack, on top he found his Colt .45, resting in its holster. Under it lay two pounds of flour, a pound of sugar, and two tin coffee cups. There should have been three. *The other one's probably on the bottom of that damn river.*

Next, he checked the guns. The Winchester held two cartridges and he had another two in his pocket. The Colt was fully loaded with six bullets. But that was all the ammunition they had, ten bullets—ten shots.

He went back to the fire and told Molly and Jass the bad news concerning the food, or lack thereof. "I think there's enough cornmeal for the boy, if we space it out. If things get tight, we can always suck marrow out of the bones from whatever I'm lucky enough to kill and give it to him. He should be able to eat that. Right, Molly?"

"I reckon that'll be okay." She did not sound any too sure about that, having never been in charge of feeding a baby before.

"You know," interjected Jass, "there's still that box of salmon out in the river, the one that floated up."

Huck's dour expression turned to one of hope. "You're right! I'll check on it. I think that was the half-filled one, but there should be enough in there to keep us going for a few days." Huck looked down at Bright, who was curled up next to him. "That is, if you don't mind sharin' your food with us, old boy."

Bright half-heartily wagged his tail, as though saying, "If you insist."

Back on the river, Huck gave out with a heavy sigh. The opening had already started to freeze up. The box of salmon was out of reach, encased in a layer of ice far too thin for anyone to walk on. He went back to the camp where he informed his partners that there would be no eating of salmon in the foreseeable future. At least not for them.

He took a moment to warm himself by the fire, then said, "I have some hunting to do. Jass, Molly, you stay here and keep the fire going. I'm gonna try to get us something to eat."

Huck strapped on his Colt and took the Winchester in hand. He nodded to Jass and smiled at Molly. "I'll be back as soon as I got us some meat."

He started to sigh, but then caught himself. *You've been doin' a lot of sighing lately. Just get to doin' what ya gotta do and stop with the theatrics.*

He turned his back on the camp, faced west, and started tramping through the snow. He did not sigh, although he wanted to.

Bright followed in his tracks—wagging his tail.

Twenty-Nine

The country before him was an expanse—an unbounded expanse—of white. Hoarfrost covered everything in its sheen of fine, delicate ice crystals—trees, rocks, the snow itself. Huck's brows and lashes were caked with the white substance, as was his beard. He had to stop constantly and rub his cheeks and nose to get the feeling back. The rest of his body, to a certain extent, was kept warm by the strenuous effort of making his way through the deep snow.

After a mile, he had come to the conclusion that, as Jass had said, it was not going to be easy to find game in that part of the country. But he kept on until he came upon a squirrel clinging to the side of a pine. He raised his gun and sighted its head. It had to be a head shot or he would lose most of the meat.

After a moment's pause, he lowered the Winchester. *I got only four shots. Best not waste 'em on the scant pickings a squirrel will provide.* He thought it better to save what little ammunition he had for bigger game—if there was any thereabouts.

He was ready to give up and return to camp and the warmth of the fire when he heard the croaking of a male ptarmigan. He looked around and saw nothing. But Bright was fixated on something off to his left. On a rocky slope, not too far away, sat three fat birds, but he needed to get a little closer to ensure that he did not waste a bullet.

At one point, as he crept up on his prey, he tripped in the deep snow and was sure that the resultant and strident swearing that came forth from his mouth would have scared the birds away. However, they were still lounging on the slope after he got back on his feet. When he felt he was close enough, he whispered to Bright to stay put. He did not want the dog chasing after the birds, thinking it was a game. He took three shots and all three hit home, though one was a body-shot that destroyed most of the meat. No matter, Bright had to eat too.

Back at camp, Jass cleaned the birds while Huck warmed himself by the fire. As the ice melted from his face, he could feel the blood returning to his cheeks. It stung, but at the same time, it was a good feeling.

Jass tossed the body-shot bird, less its feathers, to Bright before it froze completely. The dog made short work of what meat there was and then took his sweet time crunching and savoring the bones before swallowing them. He looked as though he thoroughly enjoyed the change in diet.

"Probably just tired of eating salmon," observed Molly.

They ate *their* birds roasted, and when the bones had been picked nearly clean, Jass broke them up and boiled them in a coffee cup. Because of the size of the cup, it took him six go-rounds to get them all boiled. Then Molly stripped the softened meat from the bone fragments and placed it on a small, square piece of leather. When she had finished her task, she folded the leather onto itself and positioned the packet under her arm where her body heat would keep the meat from freezing; it would be ready for John when he started feeling a mite peckish.

Because the men had carried their tobacco on their person and not in the sled, they were able to enjoy a comforting pipe after their meal. They allowed themselves the pleasure of only one pipe before they got down to the business of discussing the next phase of their journey.

After consulting his watch, Huck said, "It's nearing two o'clock and that means the sun will be below the mountains in a few minutes, so we'll have four or five hours of twilight before full dark. I say we get moving and walk for as long as we can make out the trail."

Jass cleared his throat and said what he had to say. "It's gonna be real slow getting through that snow, even for you two. I'm just gonna hold you up. If I fall behind, I don't want you waiting for me. The trail is clearly marked from here to my cabin. So you go on and I'll see you there. I got my matches, and if you leave me with a little of the flour and sugar, I can mix them in melted ice and live off that for a week . . . easy."

Huck looked over at Molly. "Did you hear somethin'?"

"Nope. It must have been the wind."

"I reckon so."

Jass was not amused. "There ain't no wind. There never is when it's this cold. And I won't be put off. I won't let you jeopardize your lives haulin' a cripple seventy miles through some of the worst country in Alaska . . . and when it's one hundred and two degrees *below* freezing!"

Huck threw another thick spruce branch on the fire and waited for the ensuing sparks to die down before speaking.

"Look here, Jass. You gotta know one thing about Huck Finn and Molly Lee McMasters, and that is when we say we're gonna do something and we give our word on it, then we do it or else we die tryin'."

"But . . ."

"Ain't no buts about it. I'll break trail as best I can. Molly will follow me, and you, Jass, you'll bring up the rear. The three of us are gonna make it, or the three of us are gonna die together in this godforsaken country. You understand?"

"But what about the baby? You gonna chance his life?"

Huck looked to Molly. He wanted her to answer that question.

"John has thrown his lot in with us—he had no say in it, but that don't matter none. The four of us are leagued for better or worse. Now do you understand?"

Jass nodded, but said nothing.

"Alright," agreed Huck, "that's good. Now let's get a move on. I'll carry the pack holding the food and furs. By the way, Jass, I put the gold in there too. Molly, you are in charge of the baby. And Jass, after Molly and I have compacted the snow a mite, you should have hardly a problem keeping up."

Jass struggled to his feet, and once steady on his crutches, he looked Huck in the eye and dictated, "I ain't movin' until you hand me that pack. No man is gonna carry my gold for me. Least of all, you, Huck. It weighs thirty-five pounds! If you don't hand it over, then you might as well sit back down, 'cause we ain't goin' nowhere."

Huck gave Molly a side glance and she nodded her answer. Huck shrugged and took off the pack. After handing it over, he said, "*Now* can we get going?"

Jass smiled and said, "Sure enough, Huck. But please, try to keep up with me and Molly."

Huck threw his hands up in mock despair.

With Bright at his side, Huck started for the trail—Molly and Jass followed. They had all thought that it would be slow-going and they were right. After an hour, they had barely made half a mile. They were breathing hard and in danger of cold-scorching their lungs.

Huck kept looking back at Molly and Jass. Compared to them, he had it easy. He had only to lug a nearly empty rifle. Molly carried a twenty-pound baby, and Jass was having a hard time making forward movement because his arms felt like they were about to fall off, so tired were they from supporting his full weight, and the full weight of the gold, on his crutches.

Huck came to the conclusion that they were going about it in the wrong way. Plus, the cold was sapping their strength as much as the physical exertion. At the rate they were going, they'd be frozen stiff within the hour. They had to move down trail faster if they were to keep warm. He needed snowshoes.

He noticed, off to his right, a small copse of pine trees. He had no axe, but he did have his knife, and he figured that he'd be able to make a pair of snowshoes from pine boughs. Turning to his companions, he said, "Let's make our way to the trees and get a fire going. There's been a change of plans."

As they warmed themselves by the fire, Huck explained things. "I'm gonna break off some of the thicker boughs from these trees and see if I can fashion me a rough pair of snowshoes. Jass, I'll need you to cut me two good-sized

285

lengths of canvas from the pack. I'll need them to lace the boughs to my feet. And try to do your cutting in such a way so that we can still use the pack."

"Tell you what, Huck. Let me get the boughs, and while you're cutting them to size, I'll make you the straps."

"I *could* use a little more time by the fire, but I'll cut the straps while you're gone. We've got to move out as soon as possible." It was true that Huck could have used more time by the fire, but Jass could have also; however, he was bound and determined to carry his own weight. Being a man himself, Huck knew what it meant to Jass; he could not, in good conscience, take that striving for self-respect away from him by treating him as a cripple.

Molly was utterly exhausted. She sat by the fire, holding John tight against her breast, gently rocking him back and forth. "How are we ever going to make seventy miles in snow like that?" she wanted to know. There was desperation in her voice that Huck had not heard before and that he did not like.

He had been just about to cut a piece of canvas from the pack, but instead, he went over and sat down next to her. Putting his arm around her, he drew her in close, and in the gentlest voice he could muster, he said, "We'll make it because we have to make it. Too many people are depending on us. There's John. He stayed alive and held on to life as his mother died because he was waiting for us; then the Indians tried to kill him and once again, he counted on us. So there's no way we're gonna let that little fella down. And what about Jass' wife and boy? They don't know it, but they're counting on us also, not to mention the little one not yet born. We gave our word, so you gotta hold on, Molly. This cold will fool you into thinking that everything would be just fine if you could only stop for a while and rest up. I know, because back there on the mountain, I wanted to do just that. But no matter what, we can't stop. We *have* to make those miles. Don't worry; I'll be with you every step of the way. And if you get too worn out from holding John, then give him to me. Alright?" Leaning in close, he gave her a soft kiss on the tip of her very cold nose.

"You're right, Huck. And things *are* looking up. Now we have only sixty-nine and a half miles to go."

"That's my girl."

Jass came back with the boughs and Huck fashioned two snowshoes from them. Each shoe took two crisscrossed boughs tied together. When they were securely lashed to his feet, he tried them out. It was awkward, but they would get the job done.

Huck helped Molly to her feet and waited while she put John back in his harness and got him situated under her parka. "We'll walk until it gets dark. It don't matter if we make one mile or ten. We walk till it gets too dark to see where we're going." So said *Captain* Huck Finn.

The brief rest and the warmth of the fire had reinvigorated their spirits and they set off with a new determination. Jass ignored the pain in his arms. Molly held John close to keep him warm, and Huck thought himself pretty smart to have thought of the snowshoes because they were working out rather well. John was thinking how nice and warm it was snuggled up against Molly and wondered when his next meal of that delicious corn mush would be served . . . or maybe he was only sleeping. And Bright was having the time of his life running through the snow, ahead of Huck and barking back at him to hurry up.

Two hours later and thoroughly fatigued, they stumbled off the trail when they came to a stand of spruce. They quickly made a fire and sat with their backs to it, not speaking. They could not speak. Their facial muscles were frozen; they just would not work. The immediate chore was to rub snow on their faces to get that stinging feeling. Then they would turn around and face the fire, the heat of which would keep their blood circulating.

They had traveled a little over two miles on this, the most recent leg of their journey. And considering the depth of the snow, that wasn't too bad. Now that Huck had his snowshoes, they would eat up trail like nobody's business when they set out in the morning. And they felt good about that. Molly took out a portion of the boiled bird meat she had been carrying and fed it to John. She thought she would save the mush for down trail when it might be the only thing available.

As they started to thaw out, their thoughts turned to food for themselves, but there was only flour and sugar. Jass cut out a chunk of ice from a small creek and melted it in the coffee cups. Then he added flour and sugar to each cup in a two-to-one ratio. After fully mixing the ingredients, he handed a cup to Molly, saying, "If nothing else, it'll warm up your insides." Then he held out a cup to Huck. "When you're done, I'll heat up some for myself."

Huck accepted the cup, but instead of drinking the concoction, he held it so that Bright could get at it. "I'll have mine when you have yours, Jass. Bright saved our lives back there on the mountain, so it's only fair that he gets his share."

"Right you are, Huck."

Seeing as how there were no thick and juicy caribou steaks available for a main course, they finished their meager meal and bedded down for the night, wrapped in their furs.

In the morning, the only one that had anything to eat was John. He consumed his food like a lumberjack. Everyone else had warm water, sans the flour and sugar. That had to be rationed.

They were feeling pretty good, though a bit hungry, as they set out. They now knew that they would make it and were confident of being there in time for the birth of Jass' child. They may well arrive a little the worse for wear, but arrive they would.

Then the wolves showed up.

Thirty

So far it has been an exceptionally harsh winter. The extreme cold has driven the great herds of caribou farther south in search of food. And there never were very many moose in that stretch of Alaska. The wolves that live in the vicinity are hungry and not too particular from whence they get their next meal.

The pack is made up of five adults—two males and three females—and a male pup of one year. It is he who has discovered the prey. He had been playing and wandered a little too far afield when he suddenly sensed something new, a scent he had never encountered before. His instincts told him that he should inform his family right away.

He joyfully runs back to the adults, barking his good news. The alpha male stands from his bed in the snow and raises his muzzle into the air. His nose twitches a few times and he senses the game . . . as the pup had. Unlike the pup, he knows what they are. He has encountered their species before. They go about on only two legs; they are slow moving, but at the same time, they are very dangerous. However, deprivation dictates that he start the hunt. He does not have to bark out his commands. He starts off in the direction of the two-legged prey and his pack obediently follows. They move in unison, intent on their purpose, except for the pup. He dances and prances around the others, letting them know that it was he who had found the prey. It is because of him that their long night of hunger has come to an end.

• • • • •

Huck had one bullet left in his long gun and he was itching to put it to use for two reasons. They were getting mighty hungry. A few times before, he had gone days without eating, and it was funny . . . after a while, the pain ceased. So it wasn't as much about *him* being hungry; he had three other people that he was responsible for. Plus, he thought it foolish to be carrying a rifle with only one cartridge in it. *Best use it up getting something to eat and then leave the gun by the side of the trail.* Besides, he still had his Colt and its six bullets if a gun was needed down trail. If he saw any game, no matter how small, he'd put that last .44 cartridge to good use. Until then, he would tread onward carrying an almost-empty gun.

They walked in silence, each following an inner rhythm that kept them going. Huck lifted one snowshoe-branch and placed it on the two-foot-deep virgin snow in front of him. Then he put his full weight on it, and in the process compressed the snow in one small area. He would then repeat the maneuver with his other foot. It was mechanical—one step after another, bringing him further into an infinity of white. After a mile, he did not have to think about what he was doing. He was only a machine—a snow-compressing machine—nothing more. His entire life consisted of putting one foot in front of the other.

Bright stayed near Huck.

Molly followed Huck's trail. She was careful to step where he had stepped, lest the snow entrap her and cause her to fall down. She could not chance that, not holding John. Her forward movement was slower than Huck's. After a while, she was a good fifty yards behind him.

Jass put one foot down, and using the crutches to lift his full body-weight, he swung his leg forward, being careful not to let the crutches slip on the compacted snow. The only thing that kept him moving forward were thoughts of his family. After five hundred miles, he was so close to home—and to realizing his and Mae's dream—that in spite of the crutches and the agonizing pain in his arms, he couldn't help but smile. But his progress was even slower than Molly's. He was one hundred yards behind her and a good one hundred fifty behind Huck.

They were stretched out in a long line, moving slowly. Lost in their own thoughts, they never noticed the wolves coming up behind them.

• • • • •

The alpha male is the first to crest the rise. He looks down upon his prey. It is foolish of them to be so spread out. If they had been caribou, he would have already been bounding down the slope, leading his pack to the slaughter. But he knows the two-legs can be sly, and they can kill from afar. He will watch them for a time to assess their vulnerabilities, as any leader would.

The other adults come up from behind and join him on the precipice. Though they are hungry, they will await the alpha's decision on when to attack. That is the way of the hunter. There are no verbal commands. Each member of the pack knows its job. The females, who are lighter and faster, will herd the prey toward the bigger, stronger males, who will then take the prey down. It is dangerous work. Last winter, the pack lost two of its number—both males. One bled to death, after having been gored by the antler of an elk as the pack struggled to bring him down. The other had his jaw broken by the hoof of a thrashing moose; as a result, he could not feed himself and, after a few days, went off to die.

The pup will stay out of it. He will watch his family deal with the prey and thus learn the way of the wolf. In his third year, he will join in the hunt.

• • • • •

Molly called out to Huck, "We've been at this for four hours and we've made seven miles best as I can figure. Can we stop for a while? I have to feed the baby and a warm fire won't hurt us none."

Even though she was fifty yards back, Huck heard every word she spoke. The Great Silence hung over them and amplified all sound. Wordlessly, Huck pointed to a strand of pines off to the left and headed in that direction. Molly and Jass veered off trail and followed in his tracks. As ever, it was slow going. It took a good fifteen minutes for them to reach the trees.

Once they had a fire going and had thawed out a bit, Huck put forth that he was going out to hunt something up. "We can't live on flour and sugar for very long and still keep the fire of life burning within us. We have to feed that fire with meat if we're gonna cover these last miles."

He had no complaints from his fellow sojourners. Jass was heating up water for John's corn mush while Molly changed the baby's shirt-diaper. "I sure wish we had our pot back. These small cups don't hold enough water for me to do a decent job cleaning these shirts."

Huck looked over to Jass. "You think *we* have it tough?"

Jass laughed out loud. "Something tells me Mae will have me washing diapers in the very near future."

Huck chuckled and picked up his Winchester. "Wish me luck." He made ten steps out of camp, following the tracks they had made on their way in, when Bright let out with a low growl and bared his teeth. Huck looked around to see what was bothering the dog. Glancing over his right shoulder, he saw the wolves above them, up on the rise.

• • • • •

The alpha wonders why the two-legs have now bunched together. No matter, they will watch, they will be ready, and when the time is right, they will feed on the meat from their bones.

It is time to move closer to the two-legs, though it is not yet time for the attack. They must be cautious. He remembers—from long ago—the sticks the two-legs use to kill. His mother was killed by one. The sticks bark loudly and blood spouts from a wolf-brother or a wolf-sister, then they are no more. He will keep his family safe. They will not strike until the two-legs are struggling in the snow or separated from one another, making themselves easy for the kill.

No matter the wolves' hunger, they will wait . . . it is their way.

The two-legs have their ways and the wolves have theirs. Before very long, they will tear at the flesh of the two-legs; their warm blood will drip from the wolves' jaws—before very long, their hunger will have fled their wolf-bodies and they will lie in the snow with full bellies.

• • • • •

Huck went back to the fire, bringing Bright with him, and sat down on his heels. With one hand, he held onto his

Winchester, the stock resting in the snow, the barrel pointing to the sky. With the other, he held onto Bright's collar. He did not want the dog to start anything that he could not finish. He did not say anything. He was thinking. Jass stopped stirring the mush and Molly looked up from what she was doing. They looked at each other, then back at Huck.

Molly asked, "Did you change your mind about hunting?"

Slowly, Huck came out of his reverie and looked at Molly and then at Jass. Turning back to Molly, he said, "Get John fed and get ready to move out." To Jass, he said, "Hurry up with that mush. We gotta be going."

"What's the matter, Huck?" asked Jass.

"We have company. There are four or five wolves up there, back on the rise, that seem to have an extraordinary interest in us. Don't worry, we'll be all right. We just have to keep moving, but from now on, we stay together. If they don't follow us, we'll be fine."

Both Molly and Jass looked up to the rise and saw nothing. "I don't see any wolves," said Molly.

"Me either," interjected Jass.

Huck hurriedly stood up and turned to where they were looking. They were right, the wolves were gone. He was about to sigh in relief when Bright growled again and he saw a dark speck moving in the snow, then another, and another. The wolves had come down off the rise and were coming their way.

"Feed John," ordered Huck. "It may be a while before we can stop again." He did not have to explain. Molly and Jass had also seen the wolves.

• • • • •

They move to within a hundred yards of the two-legs and spread out in a half circle. If they had been a larger family, they would have completely surrounded their prey. Now is the time to observe their weaknesses and look for opportunities to mount an attack.

The pup knows his place, but being young, he wants to show off some. He's behind the adults, running back and forth, when all of a sudden he darts past the line the adults have set. He'll show them what a great hunter he is. As he runs past one of the females, she turns and nips him on his right haunch. He yelps, and with a painful whine, runs back to where he should have been. It was his mother who had put an end to his foolishness. The alpha male observes the interplay between mother and pup and remembers back to when he was a pup and his mother had kept him in line in a similar manner. But that was before she was killed by the two-legs.

• • • • •

When they were ready to set out, Huck apprised Jass and Molly of his plans and on how he was going to handle things. "We stay together. Wolves usually don't attack people. They're probably just curious. Probably never seen a human before. But just in case they're a little more than just curious, we'll stay together. Jass, I'm gonna need you to move a mite faster, so I'll take the pack for now. If the wolves don't follow our trail, then you can have it back."

Jass decided not to argue the point and handed over the pack. He knew Huck was right.

Before they had stopped to rest themselves and to feed John, they were making a good pace of about a mile and a half an hour. Huck did not think they could increase their speed, but that was alright. They would make their way until just before full dark, then stop for the night. If the wolves stayed behind, then everything was all right. If the wolves *did* follow, they would have to build a bigger fire than usual and keep it blazing all night. If the wolves attacked, Huck would kill them with his six-shooter. He had seen no more than five, so he knew he had enough ammunition, but he would have to make every shot count.

With his improvised snowshoes tied to his moccasins, Huck broke trail with Bright beside him. Molly and Jass did their best to keep up. After a hundred yards or so, Huck turned to see what the wolves were up to, but there was no sign of them. They had either gone about their business or they were well-hidden and lurking in the snow. He looked down at a smiling Bright, wagging his tale. He seemed unconcerned. The wolves must not have followed them.

• • • • •

The two-legs leave their den and move farther away from where the wolves watch and wait. The alpha male notices that one of them has trouble walking. Is he wounded? It does not matter. He is the one they will take down first. They'll separate him from the others; the females will attend to that. They'll drive him to the males who will make short work of him.

But what is it that the lead two-leg carries? It is one of the sticks that kill. The alpha was about to flick his ears forward, commanding the pack to follow; instead—for his family's safety—his ears flatten. They will stay where they are . . . for now.

Are they worth stalking? It is the only meat they have seen in days and his family must be fed. He decides that they will track the two-legs and make the kill, but they will let the two-legs think they have given up the hunt. They must use caution, the two-legs travel with a four-leg that looks like a wolf, but is not. Perhaps he has the same senses as a wolf? As hunters do, they will hide their presence from the four-leg until they have assessed his capabilities.

When the two-legs have gone up and over a hill and are out of sight, the alpha flicks his ears forward. As one, the wolves rise from the snow to stalk their prey. The pup, wagging his tail, thinks this is the best game ever.

• • • • •

As they fought their way through the snow and tried to ignore the cold, they did not see any indication of the wolves. However, they took no chances. They did not dawdle and they kept close together. Huck frequently looked at Bright to see if there was sign of the wolves' return. Bright seemed unconcerned.

By the time full darkness began its advance from the east, they had covered a good six miles. Therefore, they decided to halt their trek for the day while it was still light enough to find firewood. This night, Huck wanted to lay in a goodly supply. He still had the jitters.

They were hungry and tired, nearly frozen—and only fifty-seven miles from their goal.

Thirty-One

Jass was lying on his fur, facing the fire. Molly was sitting on hers—half turned from the flames, holding John. Huck sat cross-legged, with Bright curled up in the snow beside him. Other than the small circle of light from the fire, they were surrounded by blackness. The hairs on the back of Huck's neck were doing their little dance. He had a feeling they were being watched.

They had set up camp two hours earlier. John ate his mush and then fell asleep in Molly's arms. The adults dined on flour and sugar, as did Bright. Huck figured he would have to hunt up some game the next day if they were going to make the last fifty or so miles to Jass' cabin; it had been two days since they had last eaten anything substantial. However, at the moment, he was more concerned with what was lurking out there in the darkness. If it were only him being anxious, he might have doubted himself, but Bright was also uneasy.

Molly saw the apprehension in Huck's face and asked him what was wrong.

"Nothing. I think we oughta turn in. If the weather holds, we should be able to make miles tomorrow. And along the way, I'll get us some meat."

Frowning, Molly stood up and came around the fire to where Huck was sitting. "Here, hold on to John for me." Huck reached out and obediently accepted the baby from Molly's grasp.

"Now that I have him, what do you want me to do?"

As she lifted her fur from the snow and placed it next to Huck's, she explained, "Act like a father."

Huck wasn't quite sure how a father should act when holding a baby, but that was the point. Molly wanted to get his mind off whatever was bothering him, if only for a few minutes. As she positioned herself next to him, she thought that he *would* make a good father. She liked the picture of the big, tough man holding the little, delicate baby as tenderly as he could. As though he might break John if he were not careful.

With Molly close and her face reflecting the firelight, Huck saw for the first time that she too was suffering from frostbite. There were a few black scabs on her face that he had not noticed before. However, to his way of thinking, they did not take away from her beauty one little bit. The fact that she had suffered in silence only made her all the more beautiful in his eyes.

Molly looked over to Jass and saw that he was asleep. She whispered to Huck that it was time they did likewise. Huck handed the baby over and then threw a few sticks onto the fire. "In this cold, we're gonna have to keep it going all night."

Molly wrapped herself in her fur and hugged John close. She was about to lie down when Bright jumped to his feet and growled into the darkness beyond the firelight. Huck grabbed his collar and held him from running off. He and Molly looked in the direction in which Bright was straining and beheld a pair of yellow eyes floating in a sea of blackness.

• • • • •

The wolves stalk their prey for many miles, always staying out of sight. The time is never right for an attack. The two-legs remain bunched together and their leader still has his killing stick. When they stop their migration for the day, the alpha male waits for dark and then creeps up close to observe. His family is adept at night-hunting and if the two-legs let down their guard, the pack will strike and they will feast this night. But after being in position for only a short while, the alpha has been detected by his scent. The four-leg stands and looks right at him. Now that he has been found out, the attack will have to wait until the morrow when the two-legs are not on alert and once again take to the snow. He goes back to where his family awaits and is met by the energetic pup. The rest of the pack are content to lie in the snow. They know from their leader's demeanor that the time is not yet ripe for the killing to begin. They also know that two-legs cannot travel in the night as a wolf can . . . they will be where they can be found come the twilight.

• • • • •

"Damn! The wolves are back!" shouted Huck. The commotion woke up Jass, and as soon as he understood what the hullabaloo was all about, he picked up the Winchester and made his way over to Molly. Huck was already on his feet with his Colt in hand.

"Jass, you stay with Molly. Bright and me are gonna take a look around."

"Don't worry, Huck. No wolf is gonna get anywhere near Molly or the baby."

Huck nodded, called Bright to his side, and walked away from the fire and out of camp. He walked into a freezing, black night—on alert but unafraid, knowing that Bright would know of the presence of any wolves long before he did. He went to the place he had seen the yellow eyes and let Bright sniff at the snow. When he had the scent, he wanted to run off after it, but Huck restrained him with his voice, "No, boy. We're gonna walk around the camp and make sure none of them wolves are close by. If you smell one, let out with a bark."

Bright did not pick up any other scents as they circled the camp, so Huck went back to the fire. After he had warmed up some, he said, "Jass, you and I will take turns keeping the fire blazing. Molly, your job is to look after John and you can't do that if you stay up half the night throwing wood on a fire." His intention was to nullify the arguments he knew she was about to put forth for her helping to keep the fire going. At the moment, he did not feel like quarrelling with her.

If Huck had known the wolves were a mile away, sleeping in their snow-beds and dreaming of full stomachs come the morrow, perhaps he could have caught some sleep himself. Instead, he alternated with Jass keeping watch and keeping a large fire going. Molly had to force herself into a little sleep. For John's sake, she would have to be at the top of her game if the wolves attacked.

The cold snap finally ended on that night. The temperature went from seventy below to fifty-eight below zero, allowing a slight wind to come in from the north. The wind brought with it all the moisture that had been accumulating in the Arctic Circle for the past month, but which had been unable to move south because of the extreme cold. The vapor, when it came in contact with the relatively warmer clime south of the Arctic Circle, formed minute ice crystals that floated effortlessly in the air. It is a phenomenon known as ice fog. And as Huck stood watch through the night, the gray mist imperceptibly settled on the countryside; it was not until morning's twilight that he became aware of it. Although the ice fog would have been hard to miss in the daylight—he could not see more than three feet into the mist, in any direction.

• • • • •

The alpha male awakens and perceives the fog. He now knows with certainty that the kill is nigh. With a soft guttural command, he assembles his family. They are somber and they are hungry. The only one that is enjoying himself is the pup.

• • • • •

The fog worried Huck. If he could not see the wolves coming, they were in big trouble. He'd have to depend on Bright to warn him of their approach. There was no doubt in his mind that they were coming—they had been on their trail for two days now. Today will bring the showdown.

Jass prepared John's corn mush. There was little left, perhaps enough for two more meals. The thought was unspoken: Everyone was hoping that John would be around to eat what was left, and that someone would be around to feed it to him.

They were as hungry as the wolves, but they took no time to mix their flour and sugar. Their only thought was to put miles between themselves and their adversaries—if that was possible.

It was hard going with no visibility. But Huck had discerned in the last few days that the snow on the trail lay about three inches lower than on the rest of the terrain. To his eyes, the trail was clearly marked; he kept to it without difficulty.

It was a gray world in which they traveled.

• • • • •

The fog does not deter the wolves. They easily follow the scent of the two-legs.

• • • • •

They were way out in the open. Huck had on his "snowshoes" and was in the process of taking another step when the hair along Bright's back stood up and his upper lip curled, exposing his teeth. Huck stopped what he was doing and rapidly removed the snowshoes. He could not see more than a few feet out, but he knew that they were in trouble.

"They're here," was all he said to his companions.

• • • • •

The two-legs are just ahead. The three females fan out to attack on the left—to drive the two-legs to the rear, where the males await. The pup, in happy anticipation, watches and learns the way of the hunter.

• • • • •

"Here, Molly, take the pistol! Jass! Get back-to-back with Molly and get ready with one of your crutches. You may have to use it as a club."

Bright was itching to fly into the grayness and have at the interlopers, but Huck ordered him to stay put. So far, the dog had done as he had been told. Just then, a wolf shot out of the fog and snapped its jaws an inch from Huck's arm. Bright did not wait for permission. He was off the mark and had his jaws clamped on the wolf's neck before Huck could react. The wolf was bigger and stronger than Bright and easily shook him off. Then it started to melt back into the icy mist, but before it was completely swallowed up by the frozen vapor, another wolf attacked. It snarled and snapped at Molly, but did not go in for the kill.

Molly couldn't get off a shot because she was afraid of hitting Huck or Bright. Huck went to her side, handed her the rifle, and took the Colt. But before he could use it, the wolves were gone.

"Why didn't they finish us off?" stammered Molly.

"They're trying to drive us back a ways. The rest of the pack must be back there. But we're gonna fool 'em. We ain't movin'," answered Huck. "You okay, Jass?"

"Yup."

• • • • •

The alpha sees that the two-legs are not as easily stampeded as the caribou are. No matter. They will try once more. If they cannot be driven to the males, the males will go to them and kill them where they stand. The females know what they have to do and set out to do it. The pup runs back and forth in the deep snow, wishing that he could join in on the hunt.

• • • • •

The females came in for another try, but this time Huck got off a shot with his Colt and hit one of them in the chest. All three broke off the attack and retreated. Huck figured he could press the advantage. He commanded Bright to stay with Molly and Jass and protect them. He then disappeared into the fog.

• • • • •

The wounded female makes it back to where the males are waiting before she keels over. As the female's bloods seeps onto the surrounding snow, the other two females and the male look to the alpha, awaiting his decision. The pup has stopped his excited rushing about. The dying wolf is his mother.

• • • • •

With his attention focused on the deep crimson trail of blood, Huck unexpectedly stumbled upon the wolves. They all turned in his direction with teeth bared, but did not attack. The dying wolf lay at their feet, panting as her life slowly ebbed away.

Huck pointed his pistol at Yellow Eyes, but did not fire.

• • • • •

The pup runs out from the protection of his family, yipping and barking. He runs right for the two-leg and circles him twice. Then he heads back to the safety of the pack and peers out from behind the alpha to assess the damage he has inflicted on his prey.

• • • • •

When the pup first ran out, Huck swung his arm down and aimed the gun at the young wolf. Then he smiled and lowered it completely, its barrel directed to the ground. He looked the leader in the eye for a long minute and then turned away. The pack had attacked because they were hungry. They now had food in the form of the wolf Huck had killed. The wolves would bother them no more.

• • • • •

When the two-leg had not killed the pup, the alpha wolf had decided he would let him live. Besides, the two-leg still had his killing stick and he did not want any more of his family to die. They needed meat and now they had it. It is the way of the wolf.

• • • • •

Huck could not swear to it and he was positive he *must* be mistaken, but it sure looked like old Yellow Eyes had nodded at him just before he turned to leave.

Thirty-Two

It was hard-going in the fog. Huck had to follow the wolf's blood stains to find his way back to where he had left Molly and Jass.

"Are you two alright?"

Molly assured him that they were.

"Then let's get moving. We'll do some miles and then make camp. Maybe I can rustle us up a little meat."

Jass asked about the wolves.

"I think I made a deal with them."

"You did what?" exclaimed Molly.

"I'll tell you about it along the way."

They covered six miles and then made camp under a clump of pine trees. After thawing out a bit, Huck called to Bright and together they went in search of game. Food was sorely needed. It was hard fighting their way through the snow on empty stomachs. And they couldn't survive on only flour and sugar for very long. Besides, those two commodities were about used up.

Thankfully, the ice fog was gradually dissipating. Huck would be able to spot any game that might be in the vicinity. By the time he and Bright had gone about a mile, they had not seen a sign of even a bird or a rabbit. Not even old tracks in the snow.

With no one else to talk to, Huck started a conversation with Bright. "Are you as hungry as I am, boy?"

In response, Bright enthusiastically wagged his bushy tail.

"That's what I thought. Let's find us somethin' to eat."

After more minutes of slogging through the snow, they came to a small hill. Huck figured he'd climb it to get the lay of the land. *Maybe I can spot some game from up there.*

He was in luck. Just as he reached the top, a snowshoe rabbit darted out from behind a rock, heading for low ground. Huck took his stance and took his time. He had only the one bullet, and it had to count. His six-shooter would do him little good firing at a fast-moving rabbit fifty yards away.

It was a good, clean head shot. He tossed the now useless gun into the snow and took off downhill to retrieve the kill, with Bright right behind him. It was a big rabbit, big enough to go around. It looked as though they would finally have a little solid food, and just in time as far as Huck was concerned.

Back at the camp, Huck was careful not to waste any part of his kill. The entrails and blood went to Bright, as did the skin. When the carcass was on a stick and roasting over the fire, Molly sat down next to him, holding John, who was quietly tugging and playing with the fur border on the hood of her parka after having enjoyed his meal of corn mush.

"You hungry, Huck?"

"Sure am. How about you?"

"Of course I am. But I want to speak to you about something."

"Such as?"

"How long do you figure before we get to Jass' cabin?"

"Well, I've been keeping track of the miles since we left Circle City. I figure we have about fifty miles to go. So that should take us about five days . . . if we can do ten miles a day."

He looked over to Jass and asked, "You reckon that's right?"

"That's about right."

Molly took a deep breath and said what she had to say.

"We've got one feeding of mush left and a few cups of sugar and flour. What I want to know is, what is John gonna eat for the five days it's gonna take us to get Jass' cabin?"

Huck had been in the process of adding sticks to the fire, but stopped and slowly looked up to face Molly. "Damn! I hadn't thought of that!"

"That's alright, Huck. You're a man and, as you've said, I'm in charge of looking after John. You have your mind on looking out for the rest of us. But now you've got to think on it. With only your Colt, do you think you can hunt up enough game for all of us in the next five days?"

"Even if I had the Winchester, I doubt if I could. There just doesn't seem to be any around."

"So this is what I'm getting at," stated Molly. "I think we should save the meat for John. We can hold out if worse comes to worse and we find no other game, but the baby can't. That's a big rabbit, big enough to last John for a few days. Along with what else we have, the flour and sugar and what's left of the mush, he should be okay. He's gotta eat, even if we don't."

"You're right, Molly," agreed Huck.

Jass threw in his two cents by saying that he subscribed to the same way of thinking.

Huck had one question. "How's the little fella gonna chew the meat?"

"I'll chew it for him," explained Molly.

They were all extremely hungry and the smell of the roasting rabbit was kind of hard to take. But they had made their decision, so they settled in and thought about the moose steaks waiting for them at Jass' cabin. At least, for today, John and Bright had been well-fed.

Huck cut the cooked rabbit into strips and gave them to Molly. She, in turn, wrapped them in her piece of leather and placed it under her parka next to her skin.

"No use sitting around. We've got miles to cover and a few hours of daylight left; we best be getting to it," said Huck. He received no argument from his companions, so they set out once again onto the frozen trail.

Even though the temperature had risen to a balmy fifty below zero, the snow had not gone anywhere. It was still one agonizing step at a time for Huck to make the trail passable. And still one agonizing step at a time for an exhausted Molly holding a twenty-pound baby, and for a one-legged Jass carrying thirty-five pounds of gold on his back. Huck noticed that they were both slowing up and he was determined to do something about it. But he would wait until they made camp that night. *No use quarreling out in the bitter cold when you can do it by a nice warm fire.*

They made five more miles before stopping; only another forty-five miles to go before they could sit by a hot stove and eat moose steaks to their heart's contentment.

After John had been fed, Huck laid down the law. "Jass, I'm taking the pack tomorrow. And, Molly, I'll be carrying John." With a smile, he lightheartedly added, "But you can still attend to the diapers."

Molly rolled her eyes in an exaggerated manner while Huck continued declaring his dictates.

"Now, before either one of you say anything, listen to me. We were lucky that we ended up doing ten miles today, what with the wolves and everything else. But on the last few miles, you two were flagging a bit, and I don't blame you. You're weak from hunger *and* you're carrying extra weight. Me, I'm just strolling down the lane. Hell, I don't even have to carry a gun no more. So, this is the way it's gonna be. I'll break trail and do the haulin' and you two keep up. Because come hell or high water, we're gonna be sleeping in Jass' cabin five days from now or I'll know the reason why."

What he said made sense, so no one disagreed with him. Besides, they were too worn out to put up much of a fight. They went off to sleep hungry that night, as they knew they would for at least the next four nights.

By the time darkness gave way to twilight, John had been fed the last of his mush and was securely strapped to Huck's chest, content under a voluminous parka.

When the time came for him to strap on his homemade snowshoes, Huck was sorely tempted to leave them behind. It was tedious work crunching snow one step at a time, but then he thought of Jass. He and Molly could probably make it alright, but there was no way that Jass could get along unless a way had been trampled for him. Huck slipped on the pack holding the gold and started walking westward with Bright at his side. He was now carrying an extra fifty-five pounds—thirty-five in gold and twenty in baby.

Of the three of them, Huck was the strongest and it was a good thing he had taken the others' burdens. They were getting weak from lack of food. It was all that Molly could do to lift one foot in front of the other. And in Jass' case, one crutch in front of the other. If they had been carrying extra weight, they would not have been able to move forward at all.

Huck was a hard taskmaster. When Molly occasionally ceased her endless trudging and swayed back and forth, appearing for all the world as though she couldn't take another step if her life depended on it, or Jass paused in his forward struggle and leaned on his crutches, looking down into the snow, lost in thought, Huck would urge them on with words. Sometimes with kind words and other times with words that were a mite derisive. But in the end, he got the job done. They made close to ten miles that day before they had to stop and make camp.

Again, no one ate except John. He seemed to relish his rabbit. Molly felt a bit guilty as she chewed it for him because, try as she might, she could not keep some of the meat-juice from sliding down her throat. It was not filling, but it tasted oh-so good.

They didn't know if it would help with their hunger, but for themselves, they made a spruce tea. If nothing else, it was warm.

In the morning, Molly fed John warm sugar-water with a little flour mixed in. She was saving the rabbit for his dinners. All in all, he was being a good boy, though he had cried a few times when he was hungry. So far there had always been something on hand for him to eat, but Molly wasn't sure how long that would last and asked Huck to keep an eye out for game. Any game, no matter how small.

When they stopped at noon, Huck noticed for the first time Molly's deep-sunken eyes and her fallen-in cheeks. And Jass wasn't looking much better. It had been four days since they had eaten any solid food and two since they had had anything at all. At least Molly's frostbite had not gotten any worse.

While Jass built a fire and Molly held John and masticated his dinner, Huck took Bright through the trees a little ways to the east in an effort to locate game. At that point, even a squirrel would have been welcomed. However, they came up empty.

They went back to the camp and Huck laid out his fur and sat down next to Molly. "There's nothing out there. It hasn't snowed in days. If there had been any tracks, I would have seen them. But there's nothing!"

Molly handed him a cup of spruce tea with a little sugar in it. "Here, this will warm you up some. Then when you're rested, we should hit the trail. I don't know if you've noticed, but it looks like it might snow."

Huck accepted the cup and looked to the north before taking a sip. Sure enough, the sky was fast filling with dark snow clouds.

Jass sat across the fire from Molly and Huck, holding John, cooing at him and chucking him under the chin, causing the baby to squeal with delight. Without looking up, he offered, "There's an old, abandoned cabin around here somewhere. A while back, I was traveling with an old fur trapper and he showed it to me. It's about a half mile off trail, to the south. If my memory serves me right, it's three or four miles from here. The turn-off is marked by a double pine. I mean it has a single trunk that splits into two trees, forming sort of a big 'V' . . . you can't miss it."

Huck stood up and said, "Hand me John. I'd like to find that cabin before the snow hits."

After a short interval, they headed back out and they all were thinking the same thing: They had to find that cabin. The wind was picking up and the temperature was falling. To be caught out in a blizzard in their weakened condition would—perhaps—portend their demise.

The black clouds rolled in three hours later. They had made only two miles and Huck was in an anxious state of mind. He had not come that far only to freeze to death forty miles from his objective. If that cabin existed, he was going to find it!

Molly was ten feet to his rear and he retraced his steps until he stood before her. "I want you to take John. Bright and me are going on to find the cabin. We'll move faster if you and Jass wait here. I figure we've less than an hour before all hell breaks loose. If I don't find the pine, I'll be back before the full force of the storm hits and we'll make us a snow igloo."

After Molly had John secured under her parka, Huck looked over her shoulder to Jass who had come up while they were transferring the baby. "Jass, are you sure about that pine?"

"Unless it got hit by lightning or someone cut it down, it'll be there. I seem to remember the view of that mountain over yonder," he said earnestly as he pointed towards a mountain range to the southeast.

"Alright. You and Molly wait here. You might want to scout out a place to hole up just in case I can't locate the damn tree."

The wind blew in from the north at a frightful velocity and the first snow swirls embraced them—man and dog— as they made their way down trail. After a mile, the snowfall picked up and it was hard to see through the white, frozen water as it fell on him and all around him. Right about then, Huck was wishing he hadn't lost his snow goggles somewhere along the way. He was ready to give up and turn back when Bright barked once.

"What is it, boy?"

Bright barked again and looked west. All Huck could see was a wall of white.

"Come on, boy. Let's go back."

Instead of obeying his master, the dog broke and ran in the direction he had been looking.

"Damn you!" But Huck was not about to leave Bright out in the storm alone. With one of his mighty sighs, Huck Finn trudged after his dog.

He had gone only a few feet when he came upon the wayward canine contently sitting in the snow with his tail swishing back and forth about a mile a minute. He was facing a double pine.

Huck reached down and rubbed the top of Bright's head and wearily said, "I *really* gotta start listening to you. Let's make sure the cabin is where it's supposed to be and then we'll go and get the others before it gets so thick out here that we can't find our way back."

He thought he must have miscalculated his steps. He was sure he had walked half a mile, yet he saw no cabin. The heavy snowfall inhibited his forward movement, but if he did not find it, they all might perish, so he pressed on. When he was sure he had gone a full mile, he gave up. He could not see more than a few feet anyway; it was hopeless. He would return to the others and they would have to wait out the storm as best they could. Although it would be rough going without protection from the elements or the warmth of a fire, and there was no way to build a fire in this wind and snow.

On the return trip, he noticed a rather large mound of wind-blown snow about ten feet in height that he had missed before. *That's odd*. He approached it and started digging, using his large black mittens as miniature shovels. Bright, thinking what Huck was doing looked like fun, joined in. Together, they dug a tunnel through the snow and came to a log wall. They had found the cabin! After digging around and locating the door, he and Bright went off to fetch the others.

Somehow, they all made it to the shelter before the brunt of the storm hit. It was a dank, dark cabin. The tin chimney had collapsed long ago. Nonetheless, Huck got it back to a workable approximation of a chimney. And they were in luck. Someone had left a supply of firewood, so as the arctic storm spent its rage and fury outside, they sat in the dim light of a small fire and thought thoughts of thick steaks and roasted potatoes, of yellow corn, crisp on the cobb, of blueberry pie and freshly whipped cream.

The three of them were feeble from hunger and almost delirious from deprivation. However, for the time being, they were safe and they were warm.

They had thirty-eight miles to go.

Thirty-Three

They sat huddled by the small fire and listened to the wailing of the wind and the staccato drumbeat of ice pellets hitting against the roof, and were thankful for having found shelter. Still, there was one small problem. The place was overrun with mice. They could not sleep. Every time they lay down and closed their eyes, the mice would emerge from their hiding places and run over and around their recumbent forms. At one point, Huck grew so frustrated that he drew his Colt and was about to blast away at the hateful rodents until Molly put a restraining hand on his arm.

"You're not gonna make too much of a difference. All you're gonna do is use up the last of your ammunition."

Huck slipped the Colt back into its leather home and smiled a slight, sheepish smile. "Reckon you're right," was all he had to say as he leaned his back against the wall of the cabin and folded his arms across his chest. There was no more conversation that night. They were waiting out the storm and that was all there was to it. There was nothing to eat, nothing to say, and nothing to do until they could once again hit the trail.

The snowstorm had passed to the southeast by the time twilight broke. It had been a hard and fast-moving storm, but it had not substantially added to the depth of the snow cover. Although the temperature again hovered around seventy below.

Huck opened the door of the cabin and a chill went through his body. Not from the bitter cold, but from the

319

realization of what lay before them. Because of the food situation, or lack thereof, they would have to travel faster than they had previously. It had been six days since they had eaten anything substantial. Even if they made ten miles every day, they still would not make it to Jass' homestead before they keeled over, faint from hunger. They *had* to find some game. The fires within their bodies were down to embers. It was an agony to put one foot in front of the other. They'd been traveling on pure willpower for the past two days. Huck knew that just their will to survive would not sustain them very much longer. If they did not eat, they would end up sitting down in the snow and waiting for—perhaps praying for—sweet Death to come and take them to a better land . . . a land of warmth, a land of milk and honey where no one ever grew cold or hungry. They were going to die if they did not eat.

Huck carried John under his parka, strapped to his chest. The pack with the gold in it was on his back. Molly and Jass followed, wrapped in their wolf furs. Huck's fur was in the pack. Bright ran ahead sniffing the snow as though he was looking to scare up some game. *Good boy*, thought Huck.

He had decided to forego the snowshoes. Using them consumed too much time and energy. He would plow through the snow on his own two feet and Molly and Jass would just have to keep up the best they could. They both had assured him that they could do it. He was determined to get them to Jass' cabin if he had to carry them there one at a time. The date was February 1. In ten days, Huck Finn would turn sixty years old and he planned on celebrating the event in a warm cabin with a glass of good whiskey in hand.

They staggered down trail, fighting their way west—ever westward. After a few hours, they had to stop and build a fire. The biting cold was getting to them. They would have been able to handle the cold better if they had not been in such of state of weakness. Around the fire, they held their council of war.

In a barely audible voice, Molly addressed Huck. "This isn't getting us anywhere. We're too faint and feeble to make meaningful miles. Besides, John's food is running out. It'll be gone by tomorrow."

Huck was rubbing his nose, trying to get the feeling back, so it took him a moment before he responded. "You're right. I've been pondering on it too, and I think I've got an idea. But it might be risky."

Jass, who sat across the fire from Huck, nodded and said, "Let's hear it."

Molly gave a half smile and whispered, "I have faith in you, Huck. Whatever you say, I'll go along with—I think."

Huck held his bare hands, palms outward, to the fire and kept them there as he spoke. "I'm going out to get us some meat and I ain't coming back until I got some. In the meantime, I want you two to build a more permanent camp. I have only five bullets, so I won't be coming back with much. I certainly don't expect to get a moose. But whatever I do get will be enough to keep you two and John going for a little while. It won't be enough to last thirty-five miles of fighting our way through snow. But if you sit still and don't expend too much energy, then you'll be good for a few days."

Molly was holding John, preparing to chew some rabbit meat for him. She stopped what she was doing and her eyes flickered with suspicion. "You better explain yourself, Mister Finn. What do you mean by 'enough to keep *you two* going'?"

"I would like to know that also," interjected Jass.

"Alright. I'll lay it out and I don't want no arguments. Okay?"

Jass nodded his head, but Molly only put forth with, "We'll see."

Fearful to look straight at Molly, Huck addressed his pitch to Jass. "This is the way I see it. If we keep going like we're going, it's gonna take us two weeks to get to the cabin. We'll be outta whatever meat I get today and the ammunition will be long gone. This morning, we barely made a mile. It was mighty slow going."

Before he continued, he looked over at Molly to see how she was taking what he was saying. She stared back at him impassively and said not a word. He had to admit that she had a good poker-face.

Taking a deep breath, he went on.

"I'll leave you with enough meat to last a few days—if you husband it carefully. Then me and Bright will take off for Jass' and get some real food and bring it back. With full stomachs, the thirty-five miles will be easy. Jass, you once told me that you had a small sled at your place. If I get there in two days or less, eat something, and rest up for a few hours, then start back with Bright pulling the sled, I'll be gone three days, four at the most. Then with the sled, we'll make it back to your cabin in no time at all. We'll be done with this damn trek in five days instead of the twelve or fourteen it'll take us otherwise. And to be truthful, I don't think we can last that long.

"Furthermore, Jass, it will be better all-around if I let your wife know what to expect when you get there. I mean about your leg and all. In her condition, we don't want to shock her too much."

"Sounds like the only option we have. I know I've been slowing you up, and we're so close. But I'll go along with whatever Molly says."

Huck had to take charge. "I'm not putting this up for a vote. I told you what I'm gonna do and I'm gonna do it! That's all there is to it. Of course, I'd rather not have to fight with anyone on the subject . . . *Molly*!"

She had been chewing John's rabbit meat. She stopped and spit it into her hand, took a small portion between thumb and forefinger, and held it to the baby's mouth. He smiled and happily accepted it. While he was busy getting the soft food down his gullet, Molly looked at Huck and said, "I noticed that you're talking like you're not going to be taking any meat with you. How do you figure on lasting another three or four days? That will make it almost ten since you last ate anything."

"If I come back from hunting with a mountain lion, then of course, I'll take a supply with me. But if I come back with only a damn squirrel, then I ain't taking anything." Softening his voice, he said, "Tell you what. Let's see what Bright and me come up with before we start a war over it. Alright?"

Molly agreed. Huck gave her a quick kiss on the cheek, then he and Bright went out to hunt.

After they were gone, Molly handed the baby to Jass to look after while she hollowed out a good portion of a six-foot-high snow drift that sat a few feet from the fire, turning it into a temporary shelter. Using Jass' knife, she cut a few pine boughs and placed them on the snow inside the refuge. Then she threw her and Jass' wolf furs over the boughs and they moved into their new abode. It was close quarters, but it would afford some protection from the wind and from the elements if it snowed again. In one respect they were lucky. Earlier in the season, the snow had melted a little and then refroze, making it hard-packed. All things considered, it would do very nicely for a few days. Molly thought it quite cozy.

Huck was having some luck of his own. Not a mile away, he came across four ptarmigans sitting on a branch of a tree. He got three of them with four shots and had just picked them up out of the snow when a weasel darted past him. With a quick draw, he dispatched him to weasel heaven. That left the Colt empty.

Back at camp, Jass cleaned the birds and dressed the weasel. Huck had a good fire going and they cooked all the game at once. They split one bird three ways and put the rest of the meat away. Bright ate better than anyone. Huck fed him the entrails and bones of two of the birds and put away the rest of the waste for Bright to eat along the trail.

Within a few hours, they all felt reinvigorated, and both Molly and Jass said they believed they could make the trek with Huck.

"You feel that way now, but there's not enough meat to sustain you on the trail. A good half of it will be going to John. By tomorrow night, you'll be weak from hunger all over again. No, it's better this way. Now that I know you won't starve, I believe my plan is still the best way to go about things. And you stay right here so I know where to find you when I come back!"

So that was it. Huck Finn had spoken.

The next morning, as he said goodbye, he gave Molly a tight hug and tenderly kissed her on her cracked and weather-beaten lips. Jass had told him the trail would be easy to follow, and that it led right up to his cabin. Huck had refused to take any of the meat. The only thing he carried was the pack on his back holding his wolf fur and bones for Bright. The gold, he left behind.

He started out strong. He was kicking snow out of his way and moving down trail at a brisk pace. Bright was having fun running ahead and then waiting for Huck to catch up. Then he'd run down trail again . . . and again wait for the slow human to catch up.

It was good to once more be moving at a fast rate. Not since they had lost the sled had he covered as many miles in so short a time. For the briefest moment, he resented Jass for holding them up with his slow struggle on the crutches. But then, he guiltily banished that thought from his mind. *Jass hasn't made one complaint this whole damn time. If I was him, I probably would have lain down in the snow and died a long time ago.*

, After four hours, he had covered almost nine miles and it was time to stop. He had to build a fire. The cold was oppressive. He could not feel his toes and his face was caked with frost. He would rest and warm up for an hour, then continue on.

As he sat in front of the fire and the ice melted from his beard, he took out his pouch and filled his pipe with the last few shreds of tobacco contained therein. It wasn't much, but he'd get a few puffs. If nothing else, the warm smoke would thaw out his insides a bit.

Bright was sniffing at the pack lying in the snow next to Huck. "No, boy. Those bones are for later. And though I hadn't planned on it, you might have to share some of them with me."

It was funny; he was feeling drained, but how could that be? He had eaten the night before. Granted, not much, but he figured it was enough to last him the two days it would take to get to the cabin. Except, here he was feeling almost as weak as he had before. No matter, as soon as the numbness left his toes and he could feel his nose again, he would press on.

When all his parts had thawed sufficiently to continue his journey, he called to Bright. "Time to hit the trail, boy. I reckon we got twenty-five miles to go, more or less, before we can taste those steaks we were promised. So let's get a move on."

The warmth of the fire had revived him somewhat, and for the next few hours he marched on. However, in time, he started to flag. Each step cost him. He finally had to admit it to himself that he was weak from hunger. It gnawed at his stomach and played with his mind. But there was nothing he could do about it. He had to make Jass' cabin and he was determined to do just that.

As darkness gently replaced the endless twilight, he looked for a suitable place to bed down for the night, and found it under the large overhanging branches of an old hemlock tree. With his fire going, he doled out Bright's allotment of bones for the day and watched with quiet yearning as the dog devoured them. Although the weakness in his soul and the emptiness of his stomach urged him to take a bone and gnaw on it, he knew there wasn't enough meat on any of them that would make much of a difference to his condition. With a slight shrug, he wrapped himself in his wolf fur and lay down in the snow, hoping sleep would give him a brief respite from the hunger that stalked him.

In the morning, or what passed for morning in that neck of the woods, he set out with Bright for what he hoped would be the last leg of their journey—the twenty-one miles to Jass' cabin.

Since they had left Dawson, the sun had been gradually coming up a little earlier each day and staying in the sky a little longer before sinking behind the western mountains. Huck had been on the trail for only two hours when the light from the elusive orb came rushing over the mountain and rebounded off the expanse of white before him. The resulting glare burned his eyes, and again he regretted losing his snow goggles.

An old-timer in Dawson had warned him about snow blindness and what to do if he found himself out on the trail without goggles. He lowered his eyelids and squinted to reduce the light-glare coming in and looked around for a birch tree. He was in luck; there were a few to the north, just off the trail.

He pulled a piece of bark from one of the trees and cut it into a strip of about three inches wide and eight inches long. Then he wrapped it around his head, covering his eyes. With his fingers, he marked where the bark shielded his eyes and cut two narrow slits into it. At each end, he cut a small hole and fixed a ribbon of canvas to each. He now had snow goggles. He tied the bark to his head, covering his eyes, and started back down trail. The makeshift goggles worked well enough. Had he temporarily lost his sight, he would most likely have died from cold or hunger, probably both and, by extension, so would have Molly, Jass, and John.

Half-blind, with parts of his body frozen solid, he struggled through knee-deep snow in the relentless cold, one weary step at a time. Although taunted by his hunger, and with his vitality and strength rapidly ebbing away, he battled on with determination.

He had only eighteen miles to go.

In what seemed like days, but in reality was only hours, he came to a little valley. A series of small, pine-covered hills bordered the south. The northern boundary was made up of an outcropping of rock running its length; ahead of him stretched a vastness of virgin, white snow for as far as he could see. It was hard to tell, but he estimated the breadth of the plain to be about ten miles.

The twilight had returned by then, so he took off his snow goggles, gently folded them, and put them away in one of his pockets. *I might have need of them again.*

He sat on his heels and got eye-level with Bright. While rubbing the dog's neck, in a voice barely above a hoarse whisper, he said, "Here we are, boy, almost home. If you're as sore and tired as me, then you'll want to stay here a while and rest up. But we can't. There are others depending on us. We'll have to stop and make a fire soon to thaw out, but let's try to make a few more miles first."

Huck got to his feet and, summoning every last bit of fortitude he had left in him, took his first step into the valley.

Thirty-Four

He was Huck Finn, the celebrated lawman. In his day, back when the frontier was still wild, he had tracked men through fiery deserts, up impassable mountain trails, and into places no sane man would venture. He'd been shot at and wounded; his blood had marked his back trail. Once, in the Sonora Desert, he went without water for an agonizing four days and had almost died of thirst. But he had always traced his man and brought him back to face justice—or if the *hombre* put up a fight—buried him where he had found him. However, he was younger in those days. Time had not taken as much a toll on him as it does on some men. But all men slow down with age and, yes, even Huck Finn.

He walked the valley as in a dream. He would halt his forward movement every ten steps. And standing knee-deep in the snow, swaying back and forth like a sapling in the wind, he would wait for his life-force to return. He had set that measure for himself. Ten steps at a time. No more and certainly no less.

Bright, frustrated with the slow pace, ran up ahead and then back to urge his master on. Huck smiled at the dog and thought, *Good boy. Keep me going, don't let me stand still for too long. So much depends on me—and on you, old friend.*

He lost track of time and before he knew it, it was dark, though his situation was not entirely dire. There was sufficient light from the stars and the borealis to allow him to find wood enough for a small fire. He had to attend to his feet. They were like blocks of ice and almost as white as the snow that he crouched in. Another few hours and they would have started to turn black. After vigorously rubbing them with snow for an hour, the feeling started to come back. As the painful tingling moved from his ankles to his toes, he moved his feet nearer to the fire. Then he had to deal with his blackened and scarred face.

Will I ever feel warm again?

With blood once again flowing to all parts of his body, he took a moment to raise his gaunt eyes to the heavens to take in the wonder of God in the form of the aurora borealis. He was not a religious man. He hadn't had much truck with God over the years, but on that night, he said his first prayer in many a year. He prayed that he might live to get to Jass' cabin. He had no concern for himself. He *had* to live for Molly and John. If not for thoughts of them, he would have lain down in the snow a long time ago and fallen off to his blessed, eternal sleep.

When Bright had finished his last ration of bird and weasel bones, Huck stood up . . . and on pure willpower, he plodded on—he trudged on—to the west . . . always to the west.

A short while later, the air was filled with the diamond dust of ice fog reflecting the starlight. What a spectacular sight it was! If he hadn't been so close to death, he might have marveled at it—thousands and thousands of miniscule points of light, glittering and floating in the air.

As the fog descended and grew thicker, it blotted out the starlight and covered him in frost dust. Without the stars to guide him, Huck was in danger of veering off course. But he could not stop or he'd freeze to death. He would have to depend on Bright to keep to the trail.

Hours later, as twilight neared, the fog started to lift and he saw that they had kept on track through the night, more or less. The boundless valley stretched out before him, forever without end. He saw no cabin, no sign that anyone lived within a thousand miles. There was no place he could rest his weary body . . . or his weary soul. He had walked all night; it was time to build another fire. His feet were frozen again, his face, numb. He had to stop if he was to go on.

He could not dally . . . he could not afford to. He would build his fire, warm up, and be back on the trail as the sun hauled itself up from the other side of the world.

When he had partially thawed out, he wistfully looked at the comforting fire one last time, then called Bright to his side. His world consisted of an unbroken expanse of snow and silence. Not a breath of wind stirred; not a bird called to its mate. As far as he was concerned, not another human being existed on the entire planet. Into this white and silent world, Huck Finn and his trusty dog Bright set forth once again.

As he hit the trail, he saw three suns in the sky, witnessing the extraordinary phenomenon known as *sun dogs*. His first thought was that he was seeing things. He rubbed his eyes and still he beheld three suns—what he assumed was the actual sun and two mock suns on either side of it. He figured he was seeing a mirage because he had eaten but once in the last eight or nine days. Whatever it was—hallucination or reality—he could not dwell on it. He had a cabin to find.

His feet were heavy. He had dispensed with trying for ten steps. It might as well have been ten thousand. The sun was to his back, casting his shadow ahead of him. He told himself that all he had to do was walk to the shadow's edge and then he could rest. But he had no rest coming. He never reached the end of the shadow; it always moved when he moved. After a few steps, he would stop, wanting nothing more in the world than to lay down in the soft snow and go to sleep, but then he would try again, and again the shadow would move. He knew it was only a game he was playing with himself, but it was all he had to keep him going.

He did his best not to fall to his knees. He was sure if he went down he'd never get up again.

He had no idea how many miles he had covered since leaving Molly and Jass. But he did know that he wasn't going to cover many more. He wasn't even sure how many days he'd been gone from them. He was as played out as a man could be and still be alive. He was starved, frozen, and so tired that it took all his will not to lie down in the snow and just give up.

On his next step, he stumbled and fell headlong into the waiting and beguiling arms of The White Death.

• • • • •

"You reckon Huck will be back today?" asked Molly.

Jass was in the act of breaking up sticks for the fire, but stopped what he was doing before offering an answer. "It's been two and a half days, so if he was right about the length of time it would take him to get to the cabin, then he should be there by now or he's very close to it. And he'll have to rest up for a spell, so I don't figure we'll see him until late tomorrow at the earliest. By the way, how's the meat holding out?"

They had been eating once a day, and that was only two skimpy portions—one for each of them—of the remaining meat. The bulk of their supply had been put aside for the baby.

"You know, I was thinking that maybe we should hold off on eating anymore and save what's left for John. I mean, if Huck's delayed for any reason, I don't think the little fella will understand why he's not being fed."

"That's a good idea."

Molly nodded and hugged the baby a little tighter. "I just wish Huck would get back."

"Don't worry about him. From what I've seen, if any man can make it, it's Huck."

"I'm not *worried* about him. I just miss the big galoot."

• • • • •

He was flowing down the Mississippi in a small skiff he had "found," enjoying the sun on his face. Summertime was the best time in the world. The weather was warm and the breezes gentle. He knew of a watermelon patch about a mile down river. Perhaps he should pull in and liberate a few. He could take one to his friend, Tom, and they could sit out behind his Aunt Polly's house and eat watermelon and smoke their corncob pipes. He couldn't think of a better way to spend a lazy summer day.

Then out of nowhere, the Widow Douglas was bending over him and washing his face with a damp cloth. Next, it would be his ears. She was always cleaning his face and his ears. Then she would tell him to go and wash his hands and put on his shoes. Well, not this time. He did not appreciate being disturbed while enjoying his idyllic interlude on the river. He went to push her hand away . . . and . . . regained consciousness.

He was not on the river, but lying in snow with a dog licking his face. Huck blinked his eyes a few times trying to get his bearings. It had been so pleasant being back on the Mississippi. All he had to do was stay where he was and let the cold carry him back to the sun-filled banks of the mighty, muddy Mississippi River of his boyhood days. Instead, he said, "Thanks, Bright. Reckon you've got better sense than me. We've got to keep moving or people will die, people that we care about."

He tried to push himself up into a standing position, but he had no strength left. For the life of him, he could not right himself. Bright's smiling and happy face was only a few inches from his. Looking into the dog's gray eyes, he croaked in his hoarse and cracked voice, "Reckon it's up to you to break trail. You lead and I'll follow as best I can."

Bright understood and took off down trail, leading the way for his master. Huck crawled on his hands and knees. He was determined to go as far as his inner strength would take him. He barely made half a mile before collapsing. As the misty blackness gently descended and again carried him away, his last conscious thought was of Molly and how he had let her down.

• • • • •

Molly was nervous. What if it took Huck longer to get to the cabin than he had thought it would? If he wasn't back tomorrow, he'd be back the next day. There was nothing to fret about. If she was sure of anything in this world, it was of the fact that Huck Finn would return and take them all to warmth and sustenance.

So then why was she worried?

• • • • •

He existed in a black void. There was nothing. No light, no river, no snow . . . no Molly. *So this is what death is like. Besides that recurring sharp pain in my chest, it ain't so bad.*

"Mister. *Mister!* Are you alive?"

Huck opened his eyes to see a young boy standing over him, poking him in the chest with a stick.

"I thought you was dead. You sure looked dead."

In a whisper, Huck said, "You can stop poking me with that damn branch. I'm alive . . . for now."

"Sorry, mister."

"That's alright. Can you help me sit up?"

When he was in a sitting position, he appraised his savior. The boy was covered in layers of clothing, wore a red hat with ear flaps; he was kind of thin, and looked to be ten or eleven years old.

"Your name wouldn't be Jack, would it?"

The boy smiled and said, "It sure would be. How did you know?"

"I'm a friend of your father's. But let me ask you, how did you find me?"

"Your dog led me to you. I was outside getting wood for our fire when he ran up and barked at me. Then he ran off down the trail. I always wanted a dog, so I thought I'd try to catch him and bring him home. But he led me to you instead. What's your dog's name?"

"His name is Bright. Where's your cabin?"

Jack raised his arm and pointed off to the side. "It's right there in those trees. Can't you see the smoke rising from the chimney?"

"I reckon I must have missed it."

His short time resting in the black void had replenished some of Huck's energy, but he still required Jack's help to get to his feet and to the cabin.

Jack pushed open the door and Bright rushed in, followed by Huck. A woman stood at the stove and she jumped a mite when they entered.

"Don't worry, Mom. This man's a friend of pa's."

Huck was quite a sight. Black scabs from frostbite dotted his face. And in other places, the flesh was purple where the skin was just beginning to die. His brows and beard were covered in a fine white frost.

His dog sniffed around the cabin like he owned the place.

It took everything he had in him, but Huck managed to say in a rasping voice, "Hello, Missus Holloway. My name is Huck Finn and I bring word from your husband."

Then he fainted.

Thirty-five miles away, Molly relaxed for the first time that day.

Thirty-Five

He opened his eyes to see rough-hewn logs supporting a roof. He was in a bed, but where?

"Good morning, Mister Finn."

Huck turned his head in the direction of the voice, and beheld an attractive woman holding a coffee cup in her hands.

"Where am I?" he asked.

"Don't you remember? I'm Missus Holloway and you are in our cabin. Here, take this coffee and then we'll get some food into you. You look like you could use some. We've already fed your dog."

"Is this your bed?"

"Yes, it is."

"I'm sorry for putting you out."

"Don't be. I bunked with Jack last night. Now do as I say and take this. The coffee's getting cold."

As he took hold of the cup, it all came flooding back into his memory: the trail, Molly, Jass, John. He had to get back to them!

"How long have I been out?"

"About twelve hours."

"What day is it?"

"The 5th day of February. But please, drink your coffee. Because I have a question for you."

Huck sipped at the hot brew; it tasted mighty fine.

Mae Holloway waited for Huck to take a few sips before she ventured to ask about Jass. She was a bit fearful of what she might learn. But eventually she found the courage to ask, "You said you had word from my husband. May I ask what it is?"

"Yes, ma'am, you may. Jass is fine and will be here soon. I'll tell you all about it, but first, can Jack go out and get the sled ready? Your husband said I could have use of it and I'm gonna have to leave right quick." He did not want the boy in the room when he told her about Jass losing his leg.

Mae had divined what Huck was up to and turned to Jack who had been listening intently to the conversation. "Jack, please go out and dig the sled out of the snow. And get the harness ready. You can bring the dog with you if you want."

Jack put on his coat and said, "Come on, Bright, let's go." Boy and dog went out the door, letting in a blast of frigid air.

Mae rose from her chair and held out her hand. "Give me the cup and I'll fill it with some soup. By the looks of you, that is about all I think you'll be able to keep down at present. How long has it been since you last ate?"

Huck handed over the cup and said, "It's been a few days. But let me ask you, how did I get into this bed?"

"Jack and I put you in it."

Huck nodded at her extended belly and asked, "You lifted me in *your* condition?"

"I don't know what you weighed before, but right now you're nothing more than skin and bones. And pregnant women aren't as delicate as you men seem to think we are. Now, what about my husband?"

As Huck drank his soup, he told Mae the whole story. He told her about the gold, of Jass losing his leg, of their journey to get him home, and about Jass and Molly waiting for him thirty-five miles up trail. But most importantly, he made sure she knew of her husband's fortitude and good spirits. "You should have seen the look in his eyes as he spoke of your future home and the life you'll have growing apples on the Oregon coast."

When he had told her all there was to tell, Mae stood without saying a word, went over to the stove, and made herself busy. With her back to the room and in a muffled voice, she whispered, "I thank you for what you have done for us." Then she became quiet. But Huck could see her shoulders shake and hear her soft crying.

A while later, when she had control of her emotions, she asked Huck what he would need for the trip back.

"Just food, ma'am. If you can pack up a few days' supply, then I'll be on my way. I've been gone far too long as it is. They'll be thinking something happened to me."

Jack came in just then. "All set, Mister Finn. If you want, I can harness up Bright for you."

"Thanks, Jack. While you're doing that, I think I'll enjoy another cup of your mother's wonderful soup."

Huck sat at the table sipping soup while Mae filled his pack with moose steaks, bread, and a jar of canned blueberries. There was also corn mush for John, and a small frying pan for cooking the steaks. She even put in some scraps for Bright. Before lacing it up, she asked, "Do you want to take the coffee pot and some coffee?"

"Yes, ma'am. I'm sure Jass and Molly would appreciate a cup of good, hot coffee right about now."

Once she had everything packed and ready to go, Mae sat down at the table. She watched the big man delicately sip his soup and smiled. "I can't thank you enough for what you and your lady friend have done for Jass and me. And I can't wait to meet her."

"I'm sure you two will hit it off. But I've got to ask you one question because it will be the first thing out of Jass' mouth when I see him." His face would have shown him blushing if his skin had not been so weather-beaten.

"Yes, Mister Finn?"

"Well, ah . . . I mean . . ."

"I think I know what you want to ask. You want to know when the baby is due?"

"Yes, ma'am. You kinda look like you're a little bit overripe."

"I am. The little fella is kicking up quite a storm. But I figure I've got a few more days. So you tell Jass not to worry. He'll be here in plenty of time."

"That's good. I figure with the sled, it'll take me twenty-four hours to get to them and then the same to make it back here."

Huck finished his soup and stood up. "Reckon I best go see how Jack and Bright are making out."

Mae accompanied Huck to the door. She put out her right hand and, with wet eyes, she said, "God speed, Mister Finn."

As he was shaking her hand, she cried out and doubled over in pain. It was so bad that she fell to her knees. Huck laid her down on her back. "What is it? The baby?" he asked in a panicky voice.

"I'm afraid it is," she gasped.

"Don't move. I'll be right back."

He opened the door and called to Jack. "Unharness Bright and then come in here, pronto!"

• • • • •

"He should have been here by now. It's been a full three days!"

"Listen, Molly. Huck said it might take him two and a half days to get to the cabin and then he would have to rest up. So let's say three days total. That means he's just now leaving to get back here. He'll be here by this time tomorrow or my name ain't Jass Holloway."

Jass was as worried about Huck as Molly was, but he didn't want her to know it. He offered to hold John for a while so she could move around and dispel some of her nervous energy. "We're gonna be needing more fire wood, so why don't you go and scare some up while I'm holding John. The exercise will do you good and help keep you warm."

Molly *was* worried. But not for John's sake, he had enough food to last for a few more days. And not for herself or Jass was she worried. But Huck was out there somewhere in a vast, frozen land all by himself—without her there to look after him.

• • • • •

Huck lifted Mae off the floor and carried her to the bed. As he put her down, he said, "Don't worry. I've been through this before. I know what to do."

Mae smiled up at him through clenched teeth. "I've been through this before too. And if you know what to do, that's more than I can say for most men. You must be a father."

"No, ma'am. Just an ex-marshal."

There were a few times back in his lawman days when he had assisted a midwife with a birth. And there was that one time out on the trail when he came across a lone woman in the back of a covered wagon, deep in labor. Being the only one around, it was up to him to help with the delivery. In the end, she gave birth to a beautiful little girl and he was named an honorary uncle.

Jack burst through the door with Bright right behind him. "Whatcha need, Mister Finn?"

"Your mother's gonna have her baby now and us men have to do our part. I want you to stoke the fire and get it good and hot. Then boil me a kettle of water and make sure it's got a real fast boil going before you take it off the stove."

"Yes, sir."

"Missus Holloway, do you have a clean sheet that I can rip into strips? I mean one you won't mind giving up."

Now that the pain had subsided, Mae thought she should try to put Huck at his ease. Because in spite of his declaration to the contrary, she could see that he was a bit apprehensive.

"I think you better call me Mae. It'll save time. And you'll find sheets in the chest at the foot of the bed. Please don't use the one with the lace border. That was a wedding present from my mother."

Jack announced that the water was fully boiled and then some. Huck told him to place the kettle on the kitchen table. "And then come over here."

When the boy was standing next to the bed, Huck said, "This is gonna take a while, and most of the men I know would rather wait outside until it's over. But seeing as how it's seventy below out there, you better stay inside. Your mother might do a little yellin' but that's normal, so don't go getting upset."

"Mister Finn, the thermometer says it's only fifty-two below. Can I go out and play with Bright for a while? If you need me, I'll be just outside, and if I get cold, I'll come in. I promise."

Huck looked at Mae and she nodded.

"Alright. But stay close. I don't want to have to go looking for you if I need you."

"Yes, sir!" And he was gone.

Huck smiled at Mae and said, "I reckon he is like most men."

Mae smiled back. "Yes, like most men, but not like you, Mister Finn."

"Call me Huck. And I only do what I have to do. If there was a doctor here or even another woman, I'd be out playing with Jack and Bright right about now."

"Somehow, I don't believe that, Mister Finn . . . I mean, Huck."

The pains started coming at closer intervals until they were only minutes apart. When the latest pain had receded, Mae told Huck about Jack's birth and how he had to be turned around before he could come out. "I only wanted you to know in case it happens again."

There was fear in her voice and Huck, wanting to put her at ease, said, "I've gone through that about twenty times. Don't you worry, I know what to do."

It was a lie. But a lie he thought he might be forgiven for.

A short while later, the Holloway household had grown by one. A little girl with a full head of blonde hair. There had been no problem. That head with the blonde hair had popped out just like it was supposed to.

After he had wrapped the baby in a portion of the torn sheet and placed her in her mother's arms, he cleaned up the afterbirth and called Jack in to meet his new sister. "Your mother is going to have to stay in bed for a while. So you take care of her. I'll be back in two days with your father. And Bright and I are gonna want to get a good report on you."

"Yes, sir."

He tousled the boy's hair and smiled at his mother. Then he grabbed his pack and was gone.

Outside, he quickly hitched Bright to the sled and threw in the pack. It was late in the day, which meant he would have to mush throughout the night. He would travel until Bright showed signs of weariness. Then they would stop so that the dog could rest and he could warm up. *I'll be with Molly by this time tomorrow.*

He called *mush* and pedaled behind the sled for a few feet before jumping on the runners. They headed east as the aurora borealis started its nightly show. Huck was feeling pretty damn good about himself and smiled, even though the cold air was burning his cheeks.

It's not every day that you help bring a new life into the world, he thought as the green-violet light in the sky undulated north to south and then back again.

● ● ● ● ●

Huck Finn might have been feeling pretty dang good about himself, but there was at least one person who seemed to think differently.

"That sonavabitch! Where is he? I bet he found the only goddamn saloon in this godforsaken country and he's in there right now, sitting by a nice hot stove, with a dancehall girl on his lap!"

Molly wasn't really angry at Huck. And she certainly didn't think he was in a saloon. It was just her way of dealing with the fact that he was almost a full day late in getting back. She didn't want Jass to know how really worried she was.

But she didn't fool anybody. Jass was worried too.

Molly was in quite a quandary. If it had been just her, she would have set out a day earlier in search of Huck. For all she knew, he might be lying somewhere on the trail, hurt and half frozen to death. But she had John to think of and, to a lesser extent, Jass. It was the morning of the 6th. If he wasn't there by nightfall, then she and Jass would have to figure something out. John had meat for only one more day. Things were getting serious.

When it grew full dark, Molly and Jass sat by the fire— neither of them said anything. It was time to make a decision, but they didn't know what to do. At length, Molly said, "If he's not back here by morning, then we set out. And I mean at the crack of dawn, or twilight, or whatever passes for morning around here. We've wasted enough time."

Jass agreed with her. It would be much better to die trying to get home than just sitting there waiting for Death to show up.

So that was it. They would, for better or worse, shove off in the morning. They said their goodnights and turned in.

Soon thereafter, they were awakened by somebody bellowing in the night, "Ahoy there! Anyone to home?"

Even though the voice was raspy and coarse, Molly recognized it. *Huck!* She was about to hand John to Jass to look after while she ran out to meet him, but before she could do so, Huck walked into the light of the dying fire wearing a big smile.

"Howdy, folks. Anyone up for some grub?"

347

Molly handed the baby over to Jass and ran to Huck. She hugged him so tightly that he had to ask her to lighten up a mite so that he could breathe. When Molly relinquished her hold, he went over to Jass and shook his hand. On the way in, he had been wondering on how to break the news to Jass about the birth of his daughter. Should he tell him right out or get some food into him first so that he'd have the strength to deal with the information? Then he realized that Jass was going to ask him right off how Mae was, no matter what.

"Jass, you're the proud father of a new baby girl. I was there when she came a-knocking, so don't worry, Mae was not alone. Both mother and daughter are doing good and are just fine. You'll be seeing 'em soon enough. And Jack is in fine health too. A little rambunctious, but still a good boy."

When the hoopla of Huck's return had died down, he asked Jass to build up the fire. Then, after giving Molly a proper kiss and saying hello to John by stroking his hair, he went back out into the darkness to unharness Bright and get his pack.

That night they ate well, and the next morning, with Jass, John, and the gold in the sled—with Molly riding the runners and Huck trotting alongside—they hit the trail.

Jass almost broke down and cried at the sight of his little family. It was a shock for Mae to see Jass with only one leg, but he put her at ease by telling her how well he was going to get around as soon as he got himself a peg leg.

Jass and Mae talked it over and decided to name the baby Molly. When they told Molly, her eyes got a little misty.

No one could go anywhere until the ice in Birch Creek busted up, which was about a month away. So while they waited for spring to come around, Huck and Molly took things easy and let their flesh heal from the ravages of frostbite.

On the 11th day of February, 1897, Huck Finn celebrated his 60th birthday with a glass of Jass' good whiskey. It wasn't Three Star, but it did the trick.

Jass and Mae talked about and planned for their new life in Oregon. Jack practically wore Bright out playing with him, but Bright seemed to like Jack as much as Jack liked him. And every day, John and Little Molly grew by leaps and bounds.

Epilogue

Nowadays, Huck sits in his rocker on the porch of a little log cabin on Molly's ranch in Montana and sips whiskey with Bright by his side. He and Molly got married shortly after their return to the states and John is almost two years old.

Mae and Jass have their orchard, and Jass has a new wooden leg that he got down in San Francisco. The foot has a hinge, and when he puts on his boots and walks the streets, no one can tell that he's missing a leg. Jack works the orchard with his father when he's not in school and now has a dog of his own. Little Molly is a year old and starting to walk.

George Carmack, as the man who discovered the Klondike gold, made a big splash when he returned to the States; he was in all the papers. He bought himself a spread outside of Seattle and is currently living the life of a country squire.

Tom gave up being the marshal of Redemption a while back. Then Mary sold the hotel and restaurant and they got hitched. They presently live in California near Mary's daughter.

Molly is always trying to get Huck up on a horse to ride the range with her, and sometimes he does. But more often than not, Huck is content to sit and sip his whiskey. His favorite time of day is when the western sky turns a deep and vivid orange, and around the edges of the cottony white clouds are hints of purple.

He and Molly are very happy and look forward to a long life together.

But Huck Finn's greatest adventure still lies ahead—he has a son to raise.

Thank you for reading **Resolution: Huck Finn's Greatest Adventure.**

If you enjoyed the story, please leave a review.

If you would like to share your thoughts on the book, visit http://andrewjoyce76.com and please click the "Contact" button.

You can read all about how Huck and Molly first met in *Redemption: The Further Adventures of Huck Finn and Tom Sawyer* And you can learn how Molly became *Molly Lee*, in her own book. They are both available for sale online.

For a short excerpt from **Yellow Hair**, my next novel, please turn the page.

Thank you again,

Andrew Joyce

An Excerpt from the Novel, *YELLOW HAIR*

As the warriors came over the hill, they saw in the distance the white cotton covers of the two unburned wagons. The girl pointed and exclaimed, "Look, horse canoes!" Her name was Fighting Woman and she was the only female member of the war party.

The war party consisted of eighty braves of the Mdewakanton Dakota, their war chief, Big Eagle, and his daughter, Fighting Woman. Big Eagle wore leggings, no shirt. In his hair, he wore a single feather of the eagle, denoting bravery.

The warriors wore moccasins and breechclouts or leggings, nothing more. All wore coup feathers in their hair or carried them on their coup sticks. Fighting Woman wore leggings and a deerskin shirt. Her raven-colored braid fell to the middle of her back. She was a good-looking woman with high cheekbones and a strong chin. She stood almost six feet tall. Her most outstanding attribute—the one that set her apart from all the other women of her tribe—were her blue eyes, accounted for by the fact that her maternal great-grandmother had married a French fur trapper. At eighteen winters, she could ride and shoot as well as any man in her village.

The Indians drew near and saw that there were more wagons than just the two they had seen from the bluff. But all the others had been put to the torch. Riding slowly past the still-smoldering remains, they observed that a few of the wagons had been incinerated completely—their wheels eerily standing upright, alone, attached by their metal axles. Between the wheels lay human bones and gleaming white skulls of those that were fully cremated. However, the majority of the wagons had not been fully consumed by fire. Only their cotton covers were gone, revealing the terrible sight of partially incinerated men, women and children lying on their backs staring skyward, toward their heaven. Some, with their lips burned away, smiled macabre smiles. Their white teeth reflecting the bright sunlight stood in sharp contrast to the blackened bodies and charred wagons.

The nearby livestock gave an unnatural feel to the location. The peaceful, pastoral background of oxen contently grazing, surrounded by the abhorrent sight of half-burned bodies, made some of the Indians want to flee this place of death. They were already uneasy because they were south of their homeland. They believed that a south wind brought sickness. That the south was a land of death, and that when you died, your spirit went south. Nevertheless, they were soldiers; they followed their war chief through the horrifying tableau.

Fighting Woman asked her father, "Do you think it might have been the Pawnee that did this terrible thing?"

"I don't think so. If it were the Pawnee, why would they go to the trouble of putting the bodies in the horse canoes? Nothing has been taken." He pointed to a partially burned wagon with sacks of flour lying beneath it. "Look there. Those bags are filled with food. And the animals . . . they would not still be here if a war party of Indians had done this."

They gradually made their way to the two unburned wagons and came upon Jacob. He was unconscious but alive. Fighting Woman slipped her pony and ran to him. She knelt down and looked at the dying *Wasichu*, this White-Man, with the yellow hair. In an instant, she decided that Zi Hin—Yellow Hair—would not die; she would see to it!

Big Eagle ordered two of his braves to look into the unburned wagons and see if there were bodies within. In one, they found the body of Hamilton Richards, in the other, nothing but food stock.

The braves talked of rounding up the animals and herding them back to their village. One brave suggested that anything of value found in the wagons should also be taken. Big Eagle allowed the talk until the braves had quieted down. Then he said, "The animals, we will take to our village, but touch nothing from the horse canoes. This is a place of death. We do not know what killed these people." He had lived forty-five winters; most of his braves, only half that. He was their war chief—they would defer to his wishes.

At length, Big Eagle told his braves to mount their ponies; it was time to move on. Fighting Woman stood and looked down at Jacob for a long moment. She then walked over to her father, sitting his horse with the sun to his back. Looking up to him, she shielded her eyes and declaimed, "We cannot leave him here alone. Yellow Hair must not die."

"If it is the wish of *Wakan Tan'ka* that he dies, he will die. If it is the wish of *Wakan Tan'ka* that he lives, then he will live."

"No, he *will not* die! I will not allow it!" cried Fighting Woman.

Her father, the great war chief Big Eagle, looked down at his daughter and sighed; how he loved her. Before he spoke, he thought back to the day she had come into his life. At first, he had been disappointed that it was not a male child he had sired, but when he looked at her for the first time, he was glad that he had fathered a girl child. He nicknamed her Suni. The name in itself meant nothing; it was a term of affection, a name that would be between father and daughter only. That was how it had been for eighteen winters. She would allow no one but her father to call her Suni.

Big Eagle gently said, "He cannot travel, and even if he could, we do not have a pony for him."

Fighting Woman responded, "I will stay with him, and when he is well enough, he will ride my pony and I will walk."

Once again, her father sighed. He knew his daughter only too well. If she had made up her mind to stay with the *Wasichu,* there was little he could do about it. Of course, he could have two—no, it would probably take four—of his braves to hold her, while a fifth tied her hands and feet. She could then be flung over her pony and brought back to their village like a freshly killed deer. However, Big Eagle said only, "Suni, if you were a man, you would obey your war chief. But follow when you can." He had no fear for her safety; he knew she could take care of herself as well as any one of his braves.

Fighting Woman stood for a moment watching her father, the war party, and the animals as they headed northeast, back to her village. She then went through Jacob's wagon looking for blankets. Having found what she was looking for, she covered him with two blankets, thus taking the first step in saving Jacob Ariesen's life.

For five days and nights, she stayed with him. He could not eat, but Fighting Woman forced him to drink as much water as possible. The medicine man of her village had once told her that water is the mother of all life. At night, she slept next to him to keep him warm She touched nothing from what she called "the horse canoe of death," the wagon that held the body of Hamilton Richards. She drank water and secured food only from the Ariesen family wagon.

On the sixth day, she awoke with a start. Her patient was up on one arm and looking down at her. He said nothing when her eyes opened; he just continued staring at her. Her first impulse was to back away in embarrassment. After a moment, Jacob said, "Are you real? I have been dreaming of you." When she did not answer, he asked, "Do you speak English?"

Fighting Woman stood up and vigorously brushed the dirt from her shirt and leggings before answering. "I speak your tongue; my people have traded with the Americans and English for many winters now."

"I am an American . . . a hungry American."

"Yes, you are an American . . . *Isantanka* in my tongue. I will feed you, but first you must bathe. Remove your leggings and shirt. I will find you new ones in your horse canoe."

Disoriented and confused, he scrutinized the beautiful Indian girl standing over him with the captivating blue eyes who was telling him to take off his clothes before she would feed him. He shook his head as if to clear it. At length, he said, "Who *are* you?"

"My name is Kićizapi Winohinća, daughter to Tan'ka Wanmdi of the Mdewakanton Dakota. But you may call me Suni."

"Well, Suni, can you tell me what has happened? The last thing I remember is going to sleep. I remember getting sick . . . wait . . . I had Mountain Fever! I should be dead!"

Fighting Woman drew herself up to her full five-foot, eleven-inch height before saying, "You are not dead because I would not let you die. Now take off your coverings and bathe; you smell like a dead buffalo. If you want to eat, you must bathe."

Jacob did not understand, but when the girl had gone to the back of the wagon, he disrobed and quickly wrapped himself in a blanket in an effort at modesty. The girl soon returned and handed Jacob a pair of pants and a shirt. "While you bathe, I will start a fire, then you shall eat. We must be on our way; my father may worry of me."

Once again, Jacob shook his head in confusion. "Your father?"

Fighting Woman simply said, "We will talk while you eat." She abruptly turned her back on him and walked away. Jacob mentally shrugged, walked over to the water barrel on his wagon, and first drank his fill, then used the cup to pour water onto himself.

Once he had made himself as presentable as possible, he dressed and walked to the other side of the wagon where Fighting Woman was frying bacon over a fire of buffalo chips. He sat on his heels and smelled the bacon. "Smells good, I feel like I haven't eaten in days."

"You have not eaten in five sleeps that I know of," said Fighting Woman.

While Jacob waited for the bacon to cook, he looked out over the plain at the half-burned wagons, and the horror of what had happened to his family and the others came flooding back into his consciousness. He suddenly remembered Hamilton Richards and asked Fighting Woman, "Was there another White-Man here when you arrived at this place?"

"Yes."

"Well, did he say anything before he left?"

"No."

"He said nothing at all, he just left?"

"He did not leave. Can you not smell him over there?" said Fighting Woman, pointing to the wagon in which lay the body of Hamilton Richards.

No need to go over and look inside because, as the girl has said, I can smell him from here.

Fighting Woman placed the frying pan between them and said, "Eat."

Jacob picked up a piece of bacon, and as he chewed it, he asked, "Can we talk now?"

"Yes, we may talk, but first tell me of what has happened here."

About the Author

Andrew Joyce left high school at seventeen to hitchhike throughout the US, Canada, and Mexico. He wouldn't return from his journey until decades later when he decided to become a writer. Joyce has written four books, including a two-volume collection of one hundred and forty short stories comprised of his hitching adventures called *BEDTIME STORIES FOR GROWN-UPS* (as yet unpublished), and his latest novel, *RESOLUTION*. He now lives aboard a boat in Fort Lauderdale, Florida, with his dog, Danny, where he is busy working on his next book, *YELLOW HAIR*.

Books by Andrew Joyce:

REDEMPTION: The Further Adventures of Huck Finn and Tom Sawyer

MOLLY LEE

RESOLUTION: Huck Finn's Greatest Adventure